The Apocalypse of Marlon Brando

Death and Retribution in the Philippine Jungle

Michael Coenen

Ex Nihilo Media
St. Paul, MN

Copyright © 2019 by Michael Coenen

All rights reserved. No part of this book may be reproduced in any form or by any electronic or mechanical means, including storage and retrieval systems, without permission in writing from the publisher, except by a reviewer, who may quote brief passages in a review. Scanning, uploading, and electronic distribution of this book or the facilitation of such without the permission of the publisher is prohibited. Please purchase only authorized electric editions, and do not participate in or encourage electronic piracy of copyrighted materials. Your support of the author's rights is appreciated.

Published and printed in the United States of America

FIRST EDITION

ISBN: 9781097638383

Ex Nihilo Media
364 Warwick Street
St. Paul, MN 55105

If we are not our brother's keeper, at least let us not be his executioner.

-Marlon Brando

The Apocalypse of Marlon Brando

Death and Retribution
in the Philippine Jungle

PREFACE

The diverse group of covert operatives were ingesting the rich, spirited essence from a particular line of red grapes grown in the Bordeaux region of France, along with the slightly pungent meat of Southeast Asian swine. Having feasted upon the wine and still-bloodied flesh until full, they smeared both dark red substances on their bodies and then danced wildly as if trying to shake themselves free from their earth-bound carcasses.

With his skin red and mind maddened, Colonel Walter E. Kurtz radioed I-Core for a full-scale air strike, claiming several large columns of North Vietnamese army regulars and Vietcong were pushing equipment and munitions down the foliage-dense Ho Chi Minh Trail a few miles to their north. Walter had no knowledge of any such enemy activity. He simply wanted the jungle destroyed. When the earth-shaking rumblings of the B52s became audible, Walter, the handful of American soldiers under his command, as well as a few montagnard tribesmen from the Cambodian highlands and lowlands, all of whom were both physically and spiritually intoxicated, went into a frenzy of exaltation, falling to their knees as if the sounds were those of God walking through the heavens. Soon thereafter, the thunderous bursts of gasoline exploding onto the earth and consuming the jungle filled their ears, bringing even greater enthusiasm from these guzzlers of godly libations. The winds were blowing from the northwest, sending the smell of gasoline and burning jungle their way, eventually overwhelming their nostrils and lungs. As far as they were concerned it was the hot breath of God, puffing and snorting as he scalded and burned the otherwise plush and opulent jungle into a barren wasteland of scorched earth and dead ash.

Satisfied that his labors for the day were complete, Walter sat down next to a fire and drank from a leftover bottle of cognac. A light rain began to fall, only serving to further excite the celebrants. Soon the drizzle turned into a steady downpour, creating large puddles in the already moist jungle mud. The rains would eventually douse all the fires in the camp, sending the U.S. soldiers and the montagnards running for cover while Walter stayed out in the rainstorm. The drunk colonel sat in the mud and watched the smoke billow up from the fires, which had turned into smudge pots. The rain, its intensity now very powerful, eventually washed the blood and wine off his body, dispersing the crimson stain onto the watery earth and into the ground.

The celestial baptism was sweeping over the bulwark of fire executed by the napalm, smothering the rolling walls of flames, saving the jungle from extinction in the fiery hell, as well as the Vietnamese who withstood the inferno as long as they could, fighting this obstacle the same way they have every other adversary that has come their way over the past one-thousand years—with unrelenting effort and determination.

Thunder shook the basecamp all night long, and lightning shot through the sky, casting momentary illuminations of the saturated jungle. Walter woke to the sounds of a steady rain hitting the top of his hut. He was hungover from wine and cognac, but it was a feeling he had grown used to. In an attempt to shake off the usual physical and psychological letdown from a previous night's spiritual and liquor-induced intoxication, Walter turned on his field radio and dialed up the Armed Forces Radio Network to get the latest reports on the war. Between updates was an array of jazz and orchestral music. Baseball scores would come after a couple musical numbers, and then finally reports from Saigon and Danang. In some ways, very little had changed since the days when Walter laid on the Persian rug in his parent's house as a child, listening to music, baseball games, and updates from the World War II battlefield. That little world still existed. Not where he was now, but back home, enveloping the lives of other young American children, where names like Miller, DiMaggio, and MacArthur had been replaced with those of Sinatra, Mantle, and Westmoreland.

Walter currently inhabited a world that was much different than the one he knew as a child. It was a place that made his mind twist with frustration, confusion, and despair, things that were only tightening their grip on him, pulling Walter down into an underworld of guiltless iniquity.

After listening to a four-hour tapestry of jazz music, sports scores, Hollywood gossip, as well as updates on American and Vietnamese death tolls, Walter could stand the radio, nor his basecamp, any longer. It was obvious to him that neither air strikes nor operating from a single position were contributing much, if anything, to winning the war. Walter would decide to take his covert unit out on a major offensive to actively hunt and kill the North Vietnamese in the deep, dimly lit places of the jungle, those yet untouched by American firepower.

The amalgamation of Americans, South Vietnamese, and montaganards would take with them only those things they deemed necessary to kill their enemy. The radio, sleeping cots, even cooking utensils were left behind, while rifles, ammunition, spears, and various religious talismans went with them. That night, like a pack of wolves, or perhaps demons, they made their way even deeper into the jungle. Walter lead his men to the places that so easily concealed their enemy, the low, overgrown areas that the napalm and its ensuing explosion of flames seemingly could not even illuminate, much less destroy, the places where the snakes slithered to, rats scurried, and leeches, mosquitoes, and flies lie in-wait to steal the blood from those who pass through.

They walked through the night, carrying lit torches to guide their way, defeating the whole purpose of traveling in the dark. But they were not concerned with being seen. They were predator not prey, hunters and killers, and everything in their path was expected to tremble, quake, and ultimately submit at the mere sight of them. Walter believed that they were soldiers of God, sent to this quasi purgatory to judge the living, but the genus and qualities of his deity were in constant flux. The colonel talked often of the righteousness of their deeds, yet it was no longer the smell of the dead that sickened them, but rather the foul odor of the living. They would leave an occasional cross burning in the ground to mark their trail of death and to let the North Vietnamese know whose wrath they have evoked, conjuring up images not of a first-century Galilean suffering servant, but rather Caesar's preferred method of capital punishment and political intimidation.

The perpetrators of this carnage were nearly unrecognizable as human beings with their faces and bodies colored red from wine and wild boar blood. They instead looked more like individual tiles of a Byzantine mosaic, emerging from the darkness to form an image of a wrathful deity whose divine will they believed themselves to be carrying out. When finished, Walter and his men would scatter back into the darkness, dissolving the unintentionally formed icon, one made of flesh and blood as opposed to colored glass, but their collective madness remained very much intact.

PROLOGUE

Captain Willard tossed the blood-soaked machete onto the ground of the stone temple. The sound was startlingly loud, reverberating off the many stone walls as well as Buddhist and Hindu effigies in what was once a Khmer temple, and most recently, the base of operations for Colonel Walter E. Kurtz.

Having completed his mission of killing Colonel Kurtz in what turned out to be an uncontested assassination, Captain Willard's adrenaline began to recede, slowly bringing him back to the reality of his surroundings. There he stood, elevated about twenty feet off the jungle floor, where at least a couple hundred of Colonel Kurtz's montagnard followers had ceased their sacrificial quartering of a large water buffalo in order to pay heed to what had just transpired atop the ancient Khmer temple.

Captain Willard was not sure what would happen next. His initial assumption was that they would attack him for killing the man whom they appeared to be following, and perhaps even worshipping in a god-like manner. Willard stood there. The silence was deafening and the tension palpable. Hundreds of faces were looking up at him. Willard had no idea as to their specific ethnicity, but they were mostly Stieng tribesmen. The Americans, following the lead of the French, refer to them and all other indigenous peoples of Vietnam and Cambodia as montagard or mountain people, having been driven up to the highlands hundreds of years ago by many different conquering and colonizing peoples, including southerly migrating Chinese, as well as those emigrating from the Indian sub-continent. The Stieng were different from many of their indigenous brethren of Southeast Asia, beginning with the fact that they do not live in the highlands, but rather the low, swampy area along the southernmost border between Cambodia and South Vietnam. Their skin is darker than the other indigenous peoples of Southeast Asia, and they wear their hair longer. But what really distinguished them was that they regularly cover themselves with a kind of red and black war paint, made from a combination of soot, water, blood, and the extractions from various fruits and plants. They smear or streak these colorful concoctions on their faces, arms, legs and bear torsos. It is part celebration, as well as an indication that they are at war. The Stieng are a fierce, serious people, who live as if their very survival is on the line every minute of each day, because it is, and has been for hundreds of years now.

    For his part, Captain Willard was wearing green and black camouflage paint on his face. He is at war too. And like the Stieng, the captain believed his very survival was on the line, never more so than at that very moment. He had been in Kurtz's camp for only a few days, both as a prisoner and as a free man. But in that time, he came to consider the Stieng to be unpredictable, dangerous, ruthless, brutal, and even savage. If they all suddenly leapt up and began to devour him with their bare hands he would be none too surprised. In fact, he kind of expected it. And there would be no way he could stop them. His M-16 rifle was back in the boat. And Lance, his only remaining crew-member, was so high on a mixture of LSD, marijuana, the rice alcohol given him by the Stieng, as well as the personal freedom he found out in the Cambodian jungle, that he would be of no help, not to mention that Lance had integrated with the Stieng to the point he now considered himself one of them.

    Captain Willard looked over at Lance. The young surfer from California was seemingly out of his mind. Covered with the blood/ash/mud combination, he was gazing upward as if entranced and perhaps even mesmerized by the fact that a light rain had begun to fall from the black sky, illuminated only slightly by the various ceremonial fires lit around the camp. Being the soldier that he is, one trained not only to kill but to survive, Captain Willard considered for a moment how he might live through this situation, that is, how he would get to the boat and begin making his way up river, back to Nha Trang.

There was very little sound emanating from the jungle. No birds. No animals. Nothing, which only added to the surreal, eerie and ominous nature of the moment. Then suddenly, in the blink of an eye the excruciating tautness permeating what had been the basecamp of the now deceased Colonel Walter E. Kurtz was relaxed. In unison, the hundred-or-so Stieng went down on either one or both knees, many bowing their heads in the direction of Captain Willard. In the ensuing first few seconds, the expression on the face of Captain Willard changed very little. He was still in survival mode, unsure as to the meaning of the knee bending and head bowing gesture. Willard knew it was better than the alternative scenario he imagined of being rushed and ripped to pieces by an angry mob of Kurtz's montagnard followers, but he was still uncertain as to what would transpire next.

Captain Willard glanced again over at Lance, who remained oblivious as to the seriousness and potential dangers of the situation. He was still looking up at the night sky, giving the impression he was peering into a world other than the one he was currently living in. Feelings of contempt permeated the thoughts of the captain, who had observed the lack of discipline and immaturity of Lance and the other young draftees aboard the PBR throughout the two-week mission. The other two were dead, and Captain Willard could not understand why Lance, easily the dumbest of the draftees, was still alive. Within the first hour of the first day he grew tired of the school-boy antics of the three teenagers, kids who were just putting their time in so they could go home. Captain Willard, on the other hand, was a professional soldier, an assassin to be more specific. He did not understand why he had been burdened with having to bring them along in the first place, playing the role of referee and even babysitter the entire trip down the river. On several different occasions, he considered killing any one of the draftees, believing that nobody would know, much less care, as long as his mission of killing Colonel Kurtz was carried out. Now, with the other two draftees and the captain of the boat dead, and in the midst of a couple hundred Stieng whose loyalties lie with the man he just killed, Captain Willard was glad to have at least one member of his crew still alive, even though he did not seem capable of offering any sort of assistance, physical or strategic.

Throwing caution to the wind, Captain Willard walked over to Lance, grabbed him by the wrist and began leading him back to the boat, much like a father would a child. For their part, the Stieng, again in unison, rose to their feet and backed up, allowing the two Americans a comfortable space in which to pass through as if royalty, perhaps gods, or simply out of fear. They starred hard at the two strangers, trying to decipher what and who they were. Captain Willard tried hard not to make eye-contact, lest the montagnards discern his trepidation.

Once back inside the boat, the incessant squawks of *"PBR Street gang, this is Almighty. Do you copy?"* coming through the boat's radio from the command center in Nha Trang were silenced as Captain Willard shut off the radio. Even before donning the camouflage paint and picking up the machete he would use to kill Kurtz, Willard acknowledged to himself that he was not in the United States Army anymore, and was no longer following orders, but rather doing Colonel Kurtz a favor by killing him. Like Colonel Kurtz, and perhaps because of him, Captain Willard has come to understand the hypocrisy of the American involvement in Vietnam, and perhaps even the hypocrisy of the entire American enterprise for that matter.

Having seen the boat's captain, a man they called Chief, do it many times, Captain Willard proceeded to start the boat's engine and slowly pull away from what was Colonel Kurtz's Cambodian outpost, one littered with decapitated heads and numerous corpses—the carnage and outward manifestations of his apparent madness.

"The horror, the horror", were the final words of Colonel Walter E. Kurtz just before he expired on the damp, dirty floor of the Khmer temple, which served as a kind of headquarters-bungalow for the renegade colonel. These words were still reverberating in the mind of Captain Willard, becoming more pronounced as he looked around the dimly-lit camp while the PBR exited the murky river channel that served as both entrance to, and exit from, the colonel's compound. Even though Colonel Kurtz was able to enlighten and convince him of certain things, there was still a lot Captain Willard did not understand about the colonel and

what he was doing or trying to accomplish so deep in the Cambodian jungle. Captain Willard was not able to untangle all that he had seen, heard, and experienced while in Kurtz's camp, and was not sure if he ever would.

A million thoughts were racing through Captain Willard's mind, including the things said to him during his meeting with certain military officials back in Nha Trang just a couple weeks earlier.

"And quite obviously, he has gone insane," pointed out General Corman in an attempt to sell the mission to Captain Willard, words that resonated with him, perhaps more now that he has heard and seen the colonel for himself. Everything Willard saw in the Kurtz compound, and most of what Colonel Kurtz said to him, told Captain Willard that the colonel had in fact gone insane. But yet, there was a lot of evidence indicating to him that there was much more going on here than a man losing his mind during the middle of a war.

As he looked back at the Kurtz compound, Willard could see that many of the Stieng had moved to the riverbank to get a better look at the departing boat, while still others were going so far as to wade into the water as if trying to beckon the boat and its two crew members back. They seemed like children to Captain Willard, now abandoned, lost and alone. And in effect they were. Their god-man had been killed. And the man who killed him, and who by default as per their unwritten primordial code of divine-king succession had now become their new god-man, appeared to be forsaking them. In contrast, Captain Willard looked back at them with disinterest. It was Colonel Kurtz whom he was interested in, even though he was dead, a man who had risen through the ranks of what was perhaps the greatest military in what was arguably the most powerful empire the world had ever seen. And yet he gave it all up to live out in the jungle with a people whom by the standards of his culture would be considered 'primitive savages'.

In this raw, vulnerable moment, Captain Willard was torn. Part of him could relate to Colonel Kurtz, while the other part of him wanted to simply dismiss the colonel as some kind of confused old man who succumbed to the pressure, and had 'gone native' as it is called back in the Western world, which is simply a non-clinical way of saying someone has gone insane, when in reality they have abandoned certain Western sensibilities in favor of their primordial instincts.

During his 'captivity' in the Kurtz compound, Captain Willard would go from being intrigued, to embarrassed for the man, back to being intrigued, the cycle repeating itself over and over again. And for a brief moment, Captain Willard was unsure if he was going to carry out his mission and kill Colonel Kurtz. He was not enamored enough, though, nor did he buy into what Colonel Kurtz was saying to the point that he ever considered joining the colonel like Captain Colby apparently did before him, a man sent on a similar mission prior to Captain Willard. Instead, Willard carried out his mission, which was to kill Colonel Kurtz. But it was more complicated than that. Captain Willard killed Colonel Kurtz, not because he was some kind of threat to the American mission in Vietnam, but rather as a kind of mercy killing. As he saw it, Colonel Kurtz was like a crippled or wounded animal who needed to be put out of his misery.

Colonel Kurtz was a man who stared too deep into himself, and for too long, eventually recoiling violently at what he saw, causing the army officer to charge hard in the opposite direction and run too far away to ever be brought back into the fold. With mighty abandon, Walter Kurtz fled the Western, Judeo-Christian religious, political, and philosophical tradition holding his mind and body captive. And while somewhat fearful of the unknown, what he knew for certain was that he could never return to that cage of conformance even if he wanted to. Colonel Kurtz was not completely comfortable walking out of his restrictive, albeit comfortable, societal pen, nor with the freedom of the open space that stood in front of him, either. The cage would have been tolerable had he not seen what existed outside of it. But once he did, he could never go back and live within its confines ever again.

* * *

Captain Willard listened to the distant sounds of thunder as he and Lance continued to make their way out of the Kurtz compound by following a narrow channel which would take them to the river's main vein. He looked back and could see the orange glow of the many ceremonial fires still burning amidst the ancient

Khmer ruins and the subsequent smoke billowing upwards. The night, the jungle, as well as what was the Kurtz compound were still deathly silent. Willard could no longer see the montagnards, but he could feel their stare, perhaps a few hundred of them, wondering where the mysterious man who killed their father was going. Captain Willard did not care, however. They were not his problem. They were a backward people from the other side of the world, living in a manner his own ancestors had not lived for thousands of years. They followed and worshipped a man whom the United States army determined to be insane. Captain Willard did not believe Colonel Kurtz was insane, nor did he believe him to be a god either, despite the fact that the U.S. military, as well as hundreds of indigenous people living deep in the Cambodian jungle, had both taken firm, albeit antithetical, positions on this matter.

Captain Willard did not have any idea what he was going to do, or where he was going to go. Colonel Kurtz, the river, and the jungle had all got to him, to the point that he no longer considered himself a soldier in the United States Army, an entity that has given him an identity and a purpose for the past decade or so. He thought about turning the radio back on, but knew he would only hear the urgent inquiries from headquarters in Nha Trang, wondering if he had carried out his mission. But Captain Willard was not yet ready to deal with the realities and politics of the American military machine, and so the radio would stay off. He knew they did not have enough fuel to get them all the way back to Nha Trang anyway, or any other South Vietnamese outpost for that matter. They were deep inside Cambodia, low on fuel, food and ammunition. And without the help of Nha Trang, they would probably remain there.

Because Cambodia was officially neutral and off-limits to U.S. military operations, the very word *Cambodia* possessed a kind of ominous ring for many Americans, whether they were military or civilian, including Captain Willard. It may have been a place restricted to the Americans and the North Vietnamese, but ironically it was where the war was being won and lost. It was a land already bloated with thousands of years of its own history that it had not yet digested, only to have America's Cold War paranoia and subsequent policy of 'containment' shoved down its gullet.

Cambodia is a country thick with jungle foliage, as well as a vast array of different peoples and ethnic groups, many whom have fought, warred, and conspired against one another for thousands of years, but has for the most part remained unsullied by the Western world.

"That's Cambodia, captain!" announced Chief to Captain Willard about a week prior upon coming to realize where the captain's mission was going to take him and his boat. *"And now he's crossed into Cambodia, with his montagnard army,"* said Colonel Lucas back in Nha Trang when they were trying to sell the mission to Captain Willard.

For all intents and purposes, Cambodia was just as much at war as was Vietnam. But whereas the Vietnam War was being fought on television sets all across the United States and reported on by every major and most minor news outlets across America, the war in Cambodia was a shadow war, fought covertly and secretly, hidden away from the camera's eye. Most of the rural peasantry out in the jungle and rice paddies, as well as the educated middle-class living in the capital city of Phnom Penh, wanted the prime minister, Prince Sihanouk, deposed. Many considered him more of a king than an elected official. He did not distance himself far enough from the old ways of the monarchy in the opinion of many Cambodians, nor did he embrace it enough for still others. Sihanouk did not do enough in the way of opposing the French when they were the colonial overlords of what they called Indochina, nor did he show enough support for the Japanese when they showed up in Cambodia during their takeover of East Asia during World War II. He was not nationalistic enough for the Cambodians, not anti-Western enough, not anti-communist enough, not anti-Thai, anti-Laotian, and anti-Vietnamese enough. Yet, in what has been one of the world's colonial, as well as communist battlegrounds, Prince Sihanouk somehow managed to keep Cambodia free of the atrocities and annihilation befalling many other East Asian countries before and during the Cold War. There were many nationalist, ideological and political groups plotting his overthrow, amassing themselves throughout the Cambodian countryside and jungle, waiting to move on the prime minister. The Americans were there, too, mainly their napalm and other chemical exfoliates, used to devour its jungle vegetation.

Erstwhile, the many and varied indigenous peoples were in the highlands and lowlands, scratching and clawing just to survive, doing the things their ancestors did for thousands of years, and were still common-place in their cultures, but a savage and primitive abhorrence to all who have come to this part of Southeast Asia throughout the centuries to conquer and exploit the Cambodian countryside, marginalizing and even slaughtering those who already lived there.

Captain Willard saw Cambodia as a dark and evil place, its deception, blood lust and savagery concealed from the world behind a façade of ancient mystique and physical beauty. Whereas the sins and transgressions of Vietnamese society were very visible and transparent to the world, Cambodia was not what it appeared to be. Its top layer is gorgeous, a veritable tropical paradise. There were no American or Vietnamese soldiers walking its city streets. There was very little in the way of bomb craters or any other kind of overt destruction. This could have been said about Vietnam before the coming of the French, Japanese, and now the Americans. Vietnam is like an old prostitute, standing on a street corner under a flashing neon light. She is past her prime, wearing too much make-up in an attempt to hide her advanced age, but to no avail. Her well-tread exterior shines brightly in its polluted streets, overflowing with the trappings and perils of Western capitalism. But if Vietnam is an overt and unapologetic whore, then Cambodia is a reluctant one, still able to conceal its true self to the world, but whose thin veneer of ancient validity, overt beauty, and false innocence are quickly wearing away.

As Captain Willard continued to carefully navigate the small river boat away from Kurtz's compound he could feel, smell, even taste Cambodia's rich history. He may have been ignorant as to its details, but he felt it wrapping itself around him, permeating and filling his every pore, much like the intense humidity.

"We're almost out of fuel," announced Lance, showing signs of life. Captain Willard gave him a steely stare and then returned his attention to what was in front of him.

"How are we going to make it back?" Lance asked. He received no answer so he asked again. "How are we going to make it back? We don't have enough fuel."

"I don't know," replied the captain in a manner indicating he was not all that concerned. Lance looked at him as if he were crazy, scared to ask him any more questions.

Lance's inquiry did force the captain to consider his next move, however. Willard's adrenaline was beginning to subside. He had killed Colonel Kurtz, and the potential danger of the Stieng appeared to be over. It was very dark out and there would not be light for another eight hours. Captain Willard surmised that they had enough fuel for only a few more miles, certainly not enough to get them back up river.

"Let's call headquarters and let them know where we are."

Lance was sounding more and more like the eighteen-year old surfer kid from Los Angeles than he did the psychedelic gone-native jungle tripper he evolved into while going down river. "Why won't you fucken answer me?"

Captain Willard looked over at Lance. The green and black camouflage paint was still on both their faces, but now smeared and smudged.

"We're not calling headquarters," he said in a matter-of-fact sort of way.

"Why not?" Lance shot back.

Captain Willard hesitated. He had his reasons, but he really did not want to have to explain them to Lance, someone he considered a bit of a half-wit.

"Why not?" again asked Lance upon receiving no response the first time.

"Why? You want to know why?" screamed Captain Willard as if Lance should already know the answer. "If we call headquarters, they will more than likely just drop a bomb on our ass. We're not supposed to be here, Lance. I was told back in Nha Trang that this mission does not exist, and so neither do we, making it very easy for I-core to just kill us."

Captain Willard believed it possible that I-core would in fact simply have them killed once they learned of their location, but what he really thought would happen is that the army would send a rescue helicopter to come and airlift them out of the river and back to Nha Trang, and Captain Willard really did not want that. He figured that I-core would want to debrief him on Colonel Kurtz's Cambodian operation, which would in effect guarantee that I-core would try to assist them in their return to Nha Trang. But the reason he told Lance that I-core would have them killed is because he did not know what he wanted to do yet. Things have changed for him, as they usually do after he kills or assassinates someone. Captain Willard was not sure if he even wanted to go back. He knows there is nothing there for him. The captain is more concerned about the now-deceased Colonel Kurtz, and is having a certain amount of regret about killing him. In fact, he is now beginning to wonder if staying in the Kurtz compound would have been the best course of action, at least in the interim.

It was nighttime. They were low on food, fuel, and ammunition. And they were down to two men. The crew had been ambushed on its way down the river. More than likely they would be hit again. Proceeding up river seemed the worst of their options.

"I'm going to pull over for the night," announced the captain as he veered the slow-moving boat off to the right side of the river bank.

Lance wanted to radio headquarters, but was afraid to bring up the idea again, considering how upset the captain got when he did so earlier. Lance was nervous that Captain Willard would simply shoot him. He saw how he so callously shot an injured Vietnamese woman on their way down river when Chief wanted to take her to an ARVIN. Captain Willard would have none of it, shooting the woman with as much ease and indifference as taking his next breath. The men were scared of him. He was violent, yet always with a kind of Zen-like repose. But now that his mission was over, Lance did not find him any less intimidating.

"Okay," said Lance, standing up and looking toward the riverbank, anticipating having to leap onto the muddy shoreline in order to position the boat. Once the boat was located in some tall reeds in order to both secure and camouflage it, Lance began scrounging around the small vessel for food while Captain Willard looked for booze. The captain was more successful than was the private in his quest. Captain Willard proceeded to take a couple swigs from a whiskey bottle he had stashed away deep down in the boat's hull before they entered the Kurtz compound. He could immediately feel it take the edge off, making his receding adrenaline subside even more.

"I'm hungry," complained Lance. "I'm hungry," he said again after getting no response.

"Look down below for some MREs," yelled an annoyed Captain Willard. He wanted to settle in and read some of Colonel Kurtz' documents, and not have to have to deal with any more adolescent nonsense. Captain Willard needed very little in the way of creature comports. He actually felt better when hungry and tired and unsure of his physical safety.

"I don't think there's any left."

Captain Willard closed the makeshift curtain he installed early in the mission to give himself some privacy from the antics of the draftees. Lance noticed this and knew it meant that he wanted to be left alone. He stopped talking to the captain, but did not stop talking altogether. Lance began ransacking the boat in an attempt to find something to eat while at the same time complaining out loud that he was not finding anything. Captain Willard appeared from the other side of his curtain to give Lance the same steely stare he gave Colonel Kurtz before hacking him to death with a machete. The captain waited for Lance to notice him before speaking.

"This part of the jungle is full of montagnards and VC," he said in a very calm, yet authoritative manner. "You keep yelling like that and someone will find us before the sun comes up. Now if you want to live to see morning I suggest you shut the fuck up and go to sleep. Do you understand me?"

Lance understood the captain's words to be a threat as much as it was a warning. He looked to see if the captain was holding his pistol. There was no gun in his hand, but Lance took his captain's words no less serious. Without saying anything he went off to the other side of the boat to lie down. Captain Willard went back behind the curtain to have a closer look into the heart, mind, and soul of the man whom he killed no more than an hour earlier.

* * *

When looking through Colonel Kurtz's writings, Captain Willard felt as if he was reviewing official military documents. They were meticulously typed, some of them on official U.S. Army stationary, until Kurtz apparently ran out and then began using plain white paper. Colonel Kurtz talked at length about his frustration with the American war effort in Vietnam, and how the United States did not have the stomach for the kind of war being fought there. Kurtz distinguished the war in Vietnam as one different from World War I, Korea, and World War II, mainly because of all the video and still-pictures appearing on America's television screens, and in its newspapers and magazines. He talked at length about how during the previous twentieth-century wars, much of the battlefield butchery and slaughter never made it into print, much less on televised evening news broadcasts. Kurtz argued that this made America's military and political leaders squeamish, paralyzing them from carrying out the things necessary in order to win a war, much of it now deemed too horrific for public consumption via television news, newspapers, and magazines, lest it turn the American people against the war in Vietnam.

There were pages upon pages of this kind of stuff. Much of it went on and on with Colonel Kurtz veering off course and rambling on about everything from his childhood, to the idiosyncrasies of the montagnards. Captain Willard was not searching for tidbits of intelligence pertaining to the North Vietnamese, or anything that would help with the war effort, per se. What he was looking for was any kind of hint, clue, or advice, perhaps, as to what he should do next. Captain Willard could not see himself back in the fold of the United States Army, nor simply as an American civilian. He tried that a couple of times now. Neither went well. In both instances, he craved the freedom and danger he had left behind. Captain Willard did not know if it was just the war, or the combination of war and jungle that he missed. He felt comfortable in the jungle and could not imagine being in a war in an urban or city setting. He loved the palm trees and others kinds of green fauna and foliage, none of which he could name. It was beautiful yet at the same time foreboding. Both war and the jungle gave him an incredible adrenaline rush. Willard needed an element of danger in his life. He believed that without the army he would have been living a life of crime, and perhaps even be in jail now. Willard was not all that patriotic. He only pretended to be for the consumption of the commanding officers who could send him on the dangerous missions he so desperately needed.

Captain Willard had the kind of qualities the military looked for in a soldier; he was unflappable and remorseless. Willard was assigned to Military Assistance Command, Vietnam – Studies and Observations Group, or MACV-SOG, soon after finishing Airborne Ranger school, where he was immediately utilized as an assassin, killing six people and promoted to captain before getting called in by General Corman and his crew in Nha Trang during the summer of 1969.

"I watched a snail...," began the nasally audio taped voice of Colonel Kurtz, speaking from his Cambodian outpost, *"...crawling along the edge of a straight razor, and surviving."*

Captain Willard did not quite understand what the mysterious man was trying to say, or why a United States Army general and his assistants were playing it for him. Willard wanted them to get to the point. He did not like abstractions, or when people tried to put things in philosophic terms. Willard liked things laid out and explained in a very straight-forward manner. He wanted his world to be clear-cut, and his military training only reinforced this.

"This is my dream. This is my nightmare."

With fidgety fingers, Colonel Lucas shut off the tape player. He, as well as General Corman and the CIA agent, identified only as "Jerry", wore looks of disgust on their faces as if Walter Kurtz had just burned an American flag on the steps of Capital Hill. Captain Willard looked around for clues on how he was supposed to react to these words, because he did not understand what he had just heard. General Corman would first wax poetically for a couple minutes, none of which Captain Willard understood either, mainly because his mind was exhausted from too much booze and lack of sleep, eventually concluding with the tell-tale words.

"And very obviously, he has gone insane."

Again, Captain Willard looked around the room. Everyone was stone-faced. He sensed that they were waiting for his reaction, for him to agree with General Corman's assessment.

"Yes, sir. Very much so, sir. Obviously insane," replied Willard.

The irony was that Captain Willard had been questioning his own sanity, back in the states in-between missions, and the last few weeks spent drunk and out of his mind in a Saigon hotel room. His wife seemed like an alien to him. He could no longer relate to her, nor to civilian life. Initially, Willard could not wait to get back home to his wife after his first tour of duty in Vietnam. But he was happy only until he finished having sex with her his first night back. He no more than caught his breath when he realized that he could not stay there. Willard felt like a caged animal in their bed and immediately got up and drank a half bottle of whiskey before passing out on the couch. For the next several weeks he laid around hungover all day while staying out getting drunk all night. He rarely even talked to his wife and eventually she filed for divorce. Willard could not have cared less. He would have done it himself, but in reality, he no longer believed in its sanctity, nor its legal bind.

"Terminate the colonel's command!" announced Colonel Lucas.

"Terminate the colonel?" replied Captain Willard, which was more of a confirmation of what he had just heard than it was a question.

They wanted him to kill an American, and an officer. Captain Willard could not believe his ears. But after the initial shock he settled into assassin mode and proceeded to carry out his task, "with extreme prejudice," as the CIA operative advised him.

* * *

Captain Willard was lost in a kind of malaise in the hours after the death of Colonel Kurtz. The past, present and even the future all seemed to blur together. He could not get the words of Colonel Kurtz out of his head. For days he had in effect been forced to listen to the colonel speak about everything from his childhood, to his admiration for the Vietnamese, to his frustrations with the American war effort. After a while Captain Willard began to actually enjoy listening to the colonel speak on such a full range of issues. He was not given much food to eat and he never really slept all that well, putting him in a kind of hazy, meditative state, which the captain found conducive to listening to long monologues.

Captain Willard dutifully played the role of brainwashed, ignorant errand boy to that of Kurtz's enlightened sage. Willard knew that the estranged colonel was trying to justify, perhaps to both of them, what he was doing there in the Cambodian jungle, and that he was preparing his would-be assassin to in effect set the record straight for all who were judging him.

Colonel Kurtz did in fact open up Willard's eyes to a lot of things he had never thought about before, and now the captain saw the heads and other signs of brutality strewn along the riverbank, intended to intimidate and horrify all who encroached upon the Kurtz compound, in a different light. Coming back through, Willard would not see these things as a sign of the horrors to come in Colonel Kurtz's compound, but rather a symptom of the maladies that lie back up river, in the direction of the American enterprise in South Vietnam, and beyond.

The following morning, Captain Willard slowly maneuvered the PBR away from the reed bed holding it up against the shore. As the two men approached the spot where they were ambushed on their way down river, the place where Clean was killed, Willard sped the boat up while Lance stood at the ready behind the big sixty-caliber machine gun. This time nothing would happen. Captain Willard slowed the boat's engine. Memories of the three lost members of his crew began to run through Willard's mind. He shuddered at the sight of Chief impaled with a spear, in the moment it happened, as well as now when thinking about it. Willard could not believe that in such a high-tech war, he would actually see a man killed by a spear. But then again, he used a machete to kill Colonel Kurtz. Willard always thought he would simply shoot the colonel, not quarter him with cold steel.

In addition to certain memories of their two-week trip down river en route to the Kurtz compound, Willard and Lance revisited many of the bizarre and horrible sights, as well as a few they did not notice the first time through. Some of them were simply the remnants of mechanical or operational mishaps, while others the end result of various small-scale skirmishes that had not yet been cleaned up, nor the dead bodies removed, and probably never will be considering the fact they are so deep in the Cambodian jungle, a place off-limits to all combatants, living or dead, in what the Americans were referring to as the Vietnam War. There were downed helicopters, American and Vietnamese corpses, and even a large cargo plane that was three-quarters submerged in the river. These kinds of things were common-place in any war zone, and no one in the crew was too shocked to see them. There were, however, certain sights and scenes not so common or reminiscent of a conventional war. For example, initially, on their way down the river and the closer they got to the Kurtz compound, Captain Willard and his crew saw signs of ritualistic slaughter and bodily desecration in the form of hundreds of human heads stuck on pikes, strewn about the river's edge, as well as whole bodies, dead, bloodied and hanging from tree branches by ropes or vines. On the way into the Kurtz compound, the sight of the heads and bodies made Captain Willard understand that he was sent to assassinate a madman more than hearing Kurtz's voice on audio tape ever could. However, having listened to the colonel talk for hours on-end in person, and now heading back in the direction from whence he came, Willard felt as if these same heads and bodies were portending a madness coming from up river as well.

INTRODUCTION

Marlon Brando was undoubtedly handsome, but he was also an amazing actor, and that is what he really prided himself on. Being good at his craft—his art—was important to Marlon. He did not want to merely be good at it. Marlon wanted to be great. He wanted to be the best.

Marlon Brando was arrogant and haughty as a young stage actor. He knew he was good-looking with amazing charisma and stage presence. These are things you either have or you do not. They cannot be learned or even faked. Marlon pretended that these things were not important to him, and that being good at his art was his only obsession. But in reality, he was well aware how much his looks and charisma contributed to his believability as an actor, as well as his personal magnetism. These were the things that made people want to watch him, to look at him, to hear him speak. Marlon even convinced himself that his physical beauty and roguish bohemian attitude and demeanor were a burden rather than an asset, which only seemed to make these traits more appealing to his fans.

Marlon Brando did not want to be physically attractive, but he was. He did not want to be charismatic, but he was. Marlon did not want people to be drawn to him because of some animal magnetic charm that he emanated, but they were. And his apparent loathing of these traits made him more attractive, more charismatic, and gave him even more animal magnetic charm.

On the Big Screen Marlon Brando played characters with an edge and with attitude, but they were also always handsome and charming. Many, especially his roles as American servicemen, espoused what could be referred to as 'good ol' American values, because they were always young, handsome, brave, and the purveyor of good over evil. Audie Murphy he was not, but Marlon Brando played the part of GI Joe more than once, albeit with a certain devil-may-care style and flair not typical of 1950s and 60s war movies.

Marlon Brando was always his own worst critic, and one of the worst critics of the motion picture industry itself. In time, he came to consider all the roles he played to be shallow, unimaginative, unoriginal caricatures, that is, propaganda personalities that only served to perpetuate white racism and a shallow American nationalism.

By the 1970s Marlon was still a big name in the movie business, but was no longer Hollywood's golden boy, thanks in part to a string of failed roles over the past ten years. Worse yet, his personal life and public persona had suffered greatly in that time as well. Failed marriages and his inability to be taken serious as a human rights activist left Marlon with much regret, self-loathing, as well as an intense disdain for American popular culture.

In the summer of 1975 movie director Francis Ford Coppola contacted Marlon Brando regarding his latest project, *Apocalypse Now*, telling Marlon it was going to win a Nobel Prize and perhaps even bring an end to armed conflict around the world, as well as solidify him as the greatest actor of all time. Marlon was intrigued. The lengthy process of filming the movie, as well as the freedom afforded him out in the Philippine jungle, would give Marlon the time and space to evaluate his life and legacy, coming to determine that both have been miserable failures. At the behest of his director, Marlon uses the occasion of playing Colonel Walter E. Kurtz as an opportunity to perish his off-screen persona as an eccentric weirdo, as well as kill his professional image as Hollywood's failed demi-god. Or so he hoped. But the jungle and the long process of filming the epic feature would have other ideas, as both would lead Marlon into the deep, dark recesses of his mind, a place teaming with the ghosts, skeletons and demons of his many past lives and movie roles.

CHAPTER 1

The palm trees were becoming visible as the Boeing 727 continued its descent to the Manila airport. It is a sight that Marlon has seen many times now over the years—the tropics, the jungle, a world different from the one he came from. Marlon loves the sight of blue ocean as it gives way to sandy beaches and then to the palm trees. Ah, the jungle! It reminds him of various movie sets he has worked on throughout his career, as well as his newly adopted home of Tahiti. Marlon feels at home in the jungle, even though he sees it as a place harboring many of Western civilization's deepest, darkest, most vile indiscretions and dirty secrets. But he also sees it as a place where the truth can be found, no matter how hard it is for the Western world to look at or acknowledge it. Ah, the jungle!

Marlon is not quite sure which world he belonged to anymore, the Western world or the jungle. That is, the world where Marlon was born and raised, one that has been at the world's apex for the past four-hundred years, or the world that has been conquered, colonized, and exploited by the Western world. In the Western world he was a king, of sorts, but a reluctant king. So reluctant in fact that he purposefully became a parody of himself, a court jester who no longer cared about being taken seriously as an actor in an attempt to become a different kind of king, not of stage and screen, but of the oppressed and exploited. Marlon has been trying to merge the two for the past decade or so, attempting to make movies with a message, ones intended to enlighten white middle America to the fact they and their kind have committed evils and atrocities against the dark-skinned peoples of the world, the likes of which they could not ever even fathom. Marlon wanted to be the one to break the news to them, this former heartthrob and Hollywood pretty boy, an actor who was once considered the would-be savior of the motion picture industry, a moniker that was short-lived. But Marlon did not care. He would rather be the messenger of what Western civilization has wrought upon the world, and not some kind of demi-god who took a turn propping up Hollywood. He tried to do this by way of the very silver screen that glamorized the conquest of the Asians, Arabs, Indians and Africans by the white Europeans. But Marlon's efforts, and the message therein, never grew legs. People just saw an aging actor with a knack for choosing bad projects, a man with too many ex-wives and children to support to turn down a role of any kind, no matter how bad.

By the time he was in his early fifties Marlon Brando's attempt to bring meaning and depth to Hollywood had resulted in almost two decades of disastrous movies and failed roles for the man who once seemed to have the Midas Touch in regard to both scripts and acting ability. Undeterred, Marlon was going to try again, having been contacted by his old friend, Francis Ford Coppola, regarding a new and exciting project. Francis convinced Marlon to participate by articulating the project's objective of enlightening and educating the world to the injustices and hypocrisies of the Western world, as well as the fact it would mean a multi-million-dollar payday for him. And therein lies the contradiction, the enigma that is Marlon Brando.

Marlon did not know exactly what the project was all about. All he knew for sure was that he had been contacted by Francis Coppola, a man whom he had great love and respect for, having worked with him on the critically acclaimed *The Godfather* movie, to play a role in a movie about the Vietnam War. Coppola, admittedly, was short on details, but had given Marlon some research tools to help him prepare for his role. Over the years, Marlon has developed a knack for not doing what was expected or recommended by his directors in preparation for a role. And this would be no different. Francis had sent Marlon a book to read, a novella that was almost one-hundred years old about Western Europe's colonization and exploitation of central Africa in the nineteenth century. Marlon never read the book. It must have got lost somewhere in transit, or at least this was what he would tell Francis when he arrived on the movie set.

* * *

In the meantime, with his plane still in descent, Marlon would enjoy the feeling he got whenever he saw palm trees. It was one of freedom, liberation, a sensation of shedding his old skin and becoming somebody else, the person whom he wanted to be and not the Hollywood creation he has been for the past quarter of a century.

Marlon's elation dissolved quickly once having landed in Manila. It was loud, smoggy, hot, and chaotic. And to top it off he walked around virtually unnoticed, which was a kind of double-edged sword for Marlon. He wanted people to know who he is, to recognize him as some kind of superstar. But when he was singled out as a celebrity, Marlon resented it and wished he could just walk around anonymously. For all his talk about equal rights and his apparent dislike of white privilege, Marlon, perhaps unwittingly, expected to be treated like a superstar, a celebrity, perhaps even a king when he landed in Manila. Not necessarily by the Filipino people themselves, but certainly by the cast and crew of the movie.

Marlon was transported to his hotel in Pagsanjan where he had arranged a reception for himself. It would in effect be his grand entrance, even though he did not want to make one. Again, the contradiction—the enigma—that is Marlon Brando.

When he was younger, Marlon was known for his dramatic party entrances, resembling very much his 1953 role as Johnny Strabler in *The Wild One*, a young, rebellious, sexy, dangerous man, the envy of men and the object of desire for women. Marlon's entrance in Pagsanjan would be much different. Not of someone young and dangerous, but of a man looking even older than his fifty-three years of age, accentuated by his gray and thinning hair, bloated stomach, and cane used to help steady his legs that are no longer able to support his expanding girth. Nonetheless, despite his failing body, Marlon was no doubt the center of attention at the party. The presence that he has on-film has always translated well off-screen, and still does. Although many were taken aback by Marlon's physical appearance, including his director, he was indeed the hub on which everything spun. Marlon spotted Francis across the room, but pretended as if he did not. He wanted the now famous director—famous in Marlon's opinion because he himself put *The Godfather* movie on the map—to come over to him instead of slogging all the way across the room to greet Francis. The reason for this was two-fold. First, Marlon did not want everyone to see how crippled up he was, which would have been made painfully evident with a long, drawn out trudge across the room while leaning on a cane. Secondly, Marlon did not want it to appear that he was merely the second most important person in the room.

Marlon and Francis developed a very good friendship and rapport during the filming of *The Godfather* a few years earlier. Both men genuinely liked and respected one another. Plus, the fact that the movie was a critical as well as box-office success in effect sealed their relationship. They had already gone into battle together, fighting all the things one does when making a major motion picture—the other actors, the production crew, the people and politics of the movie's locale, the critics, the movie-going public—and emerged victorious. Marlon had not made a commercially successful movie in well over a decade prior to *The Godfather*, nor one that pleased his critics. Brando's role as Vito Corleone put him back on the front page of the newspapers and magazines. No longer was he a leading man, but that was okay with Marlon. He was fine letting some of the younger guys circle the sun for a while.

Francis was more than comfortable walking across the room to greet such a legendary actor and biggest star on the set of his new movie. Even though this was Marlon's party, it was Francis' movie and his movie set, and he felt obliged to greet Marlon, as well as all the other actors, writers, and whomever else would be on his studio's payroll.

When they finally came together, both men—two gargantuan forces of nature—exchanged pleasantries, including kisses on the cheek, which was something they began doing on the set of *The Godfather*.

"What do you think of the script so far?" asked Francis over the loud chatter of the party. Upon asking the question, he realized it was a mistake to talk business with Marlon unless on the set, and even then it was not always a good idea.

"What?" asked Marlon.

"The script. Do you like the script?"

"I can't hear you."

Francis was actually relieved that Marlon did not hear him, and decided not repeat himself, knowing that Marlon probably had not read the script anyway, what there was of it. A wave of uncertainty and even fear washed over Francis. Marlon is such a wild card. He can literally make or break a movie. It was a gamble to bring him on board in the first place. Marlon was fat. He did not look the part he would be playing. Francis wanted Marlon to play the Kurtz character as depicted in Joseph Conrad's *Heart of Darkness*, a late nineteenth-century novella that illuminated the horrors of the African ivory trade in the Congo at the hands of the Dutch. Kurtz in Conrad's book was emaciated, ground down and eaten away by the guilt he accumulated at the hands of the atrocities he had inflicted upon the Congolese people. Marlon did not look like a man who has spent the last couple years living in the jungle, melting down to nothing more than skin and bone while losing his sanity, like Conrad's Kurtz. Francis started to have flashbacks about how ill-prepared Marlon was when he showed up on the set for any given shoot throughout the making of *The Godfather*. He rarely, if ever, had even read his lines much less memorized them. And he would always want to discuss and debate in great detail every word that was going to be uttered by his character, always wanting things changed or rewritten altogether.

"Good to see you again, Marlon. Welcome to the Philippines." Francis would worry about all that tomorrow.

"Good to see you, too, Francis," said Marlon, appearing tired and in pain, then used his cane to lower himself onto a chair. Marlon was not feeling well. He was a bit out of sorts, physically and mentally. He knew people were at best surprised at his physical appearance, and at worst horrified. Marlon always took his looks for granted when he was younger. He could always eat whatever he wanted, drink, smoke, never exercise, and still his features were youthful and beautiful, his physique lean and muscular. Marlon's physical appearance never concerned him back in the day. He was always the most handsome man in the room.

Now, Marlon thinks a lot about his looks, only because he does not have them anymore, and it bothers him. He sees the irony. In his youth, Marlon had very little respect for other actors who were too focused or reliant on how good-looking they were. Now, as a man of fifty who looks more like sixty, he understands how easy it is for someone who is young and attractive to be so nonchalant and even passively haughty about how they look. Marlon now longs for those days when people used to make an issue about how good-looking he was. People now find him more interesting than they do attractive. And in an ironic twist of fate, Marlon would rather be considered beautiful than interesting, whereas when he was younger, he hated the fact that people would rather look at him than listen to what he had to say.

Marlon was edgy this evening and many people at the party sensed it, including Francis Coppola, and even Marlon himself. He was tired and his knees hurt. Marlon was not on his game. There was a lot of tension and negative energy in the room. Marlon felt as if everybody was judging him and his appearance. He would quietly leave very early in the evening, telling only his director and a few other people. As Marlon walked out of the reception room, limping, cane in-hand, and a two-hundred-pound weight gain since making *On the Water Front* twenty years earlier, the star actor believed he could sense the stares, pity, and even disdain directed toward him from many who were in attendance. Marlon felt like a tired, broken down old man, and was painfully aware that he looked like one too.

CHAPTER 2

Marlon's time on the set of *Apocalypse Now* would be different than any other he has ever experienced before, and in more ways than one. To begin with, more times than not Marlon has been cast as the lead actor, and so his presence was needed throughout the filming, from beginning to end. In *Apocalypse Now*, Marlon's character does not appear until about three-fourths of the way through the film. And that was actually a good thing in this instance because it would take Marlon a while to grasp both the storyline and his character. He and Francis would spend a lot of time together, trying to flesh out the Kurtz character, as well as charting the course of the movie, especially how it would end. The fact of the matter is that Francis and a host of writers whom he has been working with have been unable to come up with a satisfactory conclusion to the film. All kinds of grandiose possibilities have been posed, including simply using the ending employed by Conrad in his novella. But Coppola's movie is only loosely based on Conrad's book. It is about the 1960s and the Vietnam War, not the 1860s African ivory trade. And so the idea of using Conrad's ending was quickly dismissed in favor of something more contemporary. The only problem is that neither Francis Coppola, nor his team of writers, knows what that is yet.

At their first official meeting regarding the script and the Kurtz character in Manila, Marlon sat there with a blank face, staring at Francis, waiting for his director to enlighten him in regard to who this Kurtz fellow is, why he is in Cambodia, and what it is exactly that he is doing there. But the truth, however, is that Francis himself does not know the answers to these questions. Not yet, anyway.

"He's an army colonel who's gone mad. He's completely out of his mind."

Francis gave this description with a grand accompaniment of hand gestures, while Marlon sat stone-faced.

"How could he be an army colonel and be completely mad and out of his mind?"

"You tell me, Marlon. Aren't most of these guys insane?"

"Let me rephrase that. How is it that he can still function, that is, conduct troops and lead men, if he's insane?"

"He's kind of a mad genius. He's lucid. But the war, the military and all its bureaucratic red tape, have frustrated him to the point he has thrown aside all convention, and he is going to fight the war the way he thinks it should be fought, and not handcuffed by the politicians in Washington."

"Is this Kurtz a good guy, or is he a bad guy?"

"That's going to depend on your own perspective, Marlon."

"Well, do you consider Kurtz to be a good guy?"

"No. I see Kurtz as the embodiment of all that is wrong, not just with the Vietnam War and America, but with Western imperialism. So, taking all that into consideration, no, I don't consider Kurtz a good guy, much less some kind of hero."

There was a long pause as Marlon thought about what Francis had said.

"Is he an archetype?" asked Marlon.

"Well, I don't know. I suppose he is kind of an archetype, a symbol of Western imperialism run amok. But I want this Kurtz to be a real life, unique individual, and not just some symbol or archetype. He is unique in and of himself, Marlon."

There was a pause as Francis studied Marlon's face.

"Joseph Conrad's Kurtz is of course an archetype or proto-type, or at least, at a bare minimum, an influence for the Kurtz we are developing here," added Francis, who then went back to studying Marlon's reaction. Marlon said nothing. "Conrad's Kurtz is a complex character. He is very clear in what he is doing. He believes in his cause, which is making a profit by harvesting and selling ivory and making his country more powerful in the process. He doesn't care about issues of morality. Conrad's Kurtz sees the world very much as Darwin describes it—as survival of the fittest—and that his kind, the Western Europeans, at this time in history, are the most powerful race of people on earth, and that the world is theirs for the taking. And he is going to take, or pick, the various fruits of the world, so to speak. And he doesn't care how many people he has to kill and butcher in the process. He doesn't care how much of the world's natural resources he has to pillage to get what he wants. He just doesn't care. But it takes a toll on him, nonetheless. It affects him. It kills him from the inside out."

Francis paused, hoping to get some kind of reaction from Marlon. Again Marlon was a blank slate. This was not like him, and Francis was starting to understand why.

"What was your take on Kurtz, Marlon?"

Marlon looked at Francis with a coy grin on his face.

"You didn't read the book, did you Marlon?"

"What book?"

"What book, Marlon?"

There was a long, awkward pause.

"Joseph Conrad's *Heart of Darkness*, Marlon. I sent you a copy months ago, and asked you to read it to prepare for the role. Your character is based on the Kurtz character. But your Kurtz—our Kurtz—is an American fighting the Vietnam War, and not a Belgian looting Africa of its ivory."

Again Francis sized up his star actor. Marlin grinned.

"Do you think this is a role you might be interested in, Marlon?"

"I don't know. I should probably read the book."

"Yes, Marlon. Perhaps you should read the book."

* * *

Marlon was extremely frustrated with the lack of organization and progress on the set upon his arrival. Very little of the script had even been written, and only a few scenes had actually been shot. Francis and his crew seemed to be making up the dialogue and plot as they went along, and the director had no idea how the movie was going to end. In regard to his own role, all Marlon knew for sure was that his character was somewhat based on a certain anti-hero from a book written at the turn of the century, one that he had heard of but never read. Marlon was expecting to walk onto a set that was much more organized, disciplined, and certainly much further along in both the writing and shooting processes. But instead, he found a movie set already way over budget, full of egomaniacs, and seemingly lost in terms of its direction. Marlon was under the impression that Francis was going to make a film with a profound anti-war and anti-imperialism message, but was convinced that he was simply creating some kind of weird, psychedelic film reminiscent of something Stanley Kubrick or even Federico Fellini would do.

Marlon never liked the hippy psychedelic drug scene of the late 1960s and early '70s. Marlon was a man of the 1950s. He himself is in fact an archetype. Marlon was the consummate leather-jacket-wearing, motorcycle-riding, epitome of the 1950s-era counter-culture, which was not a message of 'turn on, tune in, drop out', but rather one of aggressively challenging and fighting the established order when it came to injustice. But then again, Marlon is not necessarily happy with the 1950s-era image that he conveyed in movies like *The Men*, *The Wild One*, *On the Waterfront*, and *A Streetcar Named Desire*. These roles have been a kind of double-edged sword for Marlon. He not only used them to showcase his talent, he made these characters into real life human beings. More specifically, he formed them in the image of Marlon Brando, or perhaps Marlon Brando formed himself in their image. Whatever the case, they were a means for Marlon to vent his anger and frustration, each a gaping window into his tormented soul. His characters were brilliant, and so was he. But looking back now, Marlon is embarrassed and even a bit regretful, yet at the same time proud of these characters and the way he played them. Like him, these characters are American icons. They are timeless and eternal, yet stuck in time, just like Marlon.

Marlon respected what the hippies represented in the '60s and '70s, or at least what they were fighting for, but he did not see enough passion in their efforts. During the late 1960s he always thought that if the anti-war protest had a few Terry Malloys and Johnny Strablers, the Vietnam War would have ended much sooner than it did. On the other hand, it is not lost on Marlon that it was this very kind of aggression that led to the Vietnam War and other American imperialist activities around the world in the first place. Throughout the late '60s he felt like some kind of dinosaur.

His kind had grown obsolete. The 'hoods' had become part of the established order. They were in their thirties and forties during the late 1960s. The world condition was partly their doing. And so maybe it was the over-inflated masculinity of American society, which many of Marlon's characters exemplified, that was to blame. This concerned Marlon, but did not endear him to the hippies of the 1960s Flower Power generation. He believed that their kind of passivity only enabled fascist dictators like Hitler and Mussolini, as well as Nixon and Kissinger, whom Marlon in fact considered to be fascist dictators, perhaps even war criminals. A little more bravado and urgency from the anti-war protesters might have staved off some of the atrocities committed against the Vietnamese and Cambodian people. But on the other hand, Marlon also conceded that perhaps it was the Johnny Strablers and Terry Malloys of this world who were responsible for the Vietnam War, its inception as well as the brutality and barbarism that ensued. They once served a purpose for the American people, especially its youth. But by the time American soldiers were fighting the Vietnamese in the steamy jungles and hot, sun baked rice paddies of Southeast Asia, these types had become fossils of a time and place that no longer existed, and so had Marlon.

* * *

Marlon would not be staying in the kind of luxury trailer he was accustomed to when on a movie set. The movie was already over budget and such indulgences were not being granted, not even to a man of Marlon's stature.

"A hotel? You want me to stay in a fucking hotel?"

Marlon was not happy when he received the news. He was thinking very seriously about pulling the plug and going home. There was no real script, the set was in chaos, the budget had been blown, and the director—a man whom Marlon loved and admired—did not seem to fully comprehend the dire situation his film was in. Marlon had the utmost respect and confidence in Francis Coppola, but this was far from what he had promised him. Francis told Marlon that his movie was going to change the world, and perhaps even win a Nobel Prize. Although skeptical about such a claim, it was a project that piqued Marlon's curiosity. If

Francis thinks it is capable of winning a Nobel Prize, there must be something special about it. But what Marlon found waiting for him in the Philippines was a recipe for failure, and Marlon's career could not afford another critic-panned, box-office disaster. He had finally made a bit of a comeback with *The Godfather* after two decades of living off the laurels of his work from the early 1950s, and did not want to follow it up with some big grandiose fiasco.

Marlon believes that the course of his career has been a perfect reflection of who he is. When he was younger the first impression that people got of Marlon was somebody who is brutally handsome, aggressive, and tough, with the courage to throw fists with anybody as well as bed down the best-looking woman in the room. This is who Stanley, Johnny and Terry are. And this is who Marlon used to be. But when people got to know Marlon a little better they realized that there was much more to this image. There was a certain inner struggle, a battle, a war that was raging deep within Marlon Brando. He did not like the shallow, almost superficial image of himself that shown so brightly and brilliantly on the movie screen. People who knew Marlon Brando were very aware, sometimes painfully so, that there was a lot Marlon kept hidden about himself, becoming altogether obvious whenever he would let certain bits and pieces of himself out. Marlon could be kind and caring, passionate and compassionate. He could also be the polar opposite of these things. In fact, Marlon could be downright weird, bizarre, almost psychotic in his behavior. And it was this side, or perhaps better stated, these *sides*, of his personality that he was allowed to showcase in many of his movies from the late 1950s until the early 1970s. There he was, on full display to the world in all his lewd, odd, peculiar, creepy glory. And the people who knew him were well aware that these roles were not much of a stretch for Marlon. When his friends saw him in *Nightcomers* and *Last Tango in Paris*, they were none too surprised. Everybody who knew Marlon understood that he could be sexually deviant, downright mean, and even a little uncomfortable to be around because his personality could change so drastically from one minute to the next, oftentimes into something quite frightening. In these roles, Marlon was allowed to rape, manipulate and mentally torture people who could not otherwise defend themselves. These roles were a release for him, as well as confining. This was a side of Marlon that began to grow and mutate as a result of all the praise he received as a young actor. All the accolades he received for his looks and his theatre performances, and then his early big screen roles, created and sustained that monster who believed it was his right to fuck any woman he wanted, and that all men would be best served to fear and envy him. Marlon was not to be blamed completely for these delusions which fostered unwitting notions of godliness within his tormented mind. People did not have to succumb to his every need and desire, but they usually did. And each time, it fed the hungry Dionysian beast that lived inside him. The world made him a god, even to the point that he himself believed it. But it was these very god-like traits that made him all too human. Love, adoration and lenience were heaped upon him. Marlon could get away with anything. But when you are young, beautiful, and at the top of your acting game, all that people see are your youth, beauty, as well as your stage-presence and well-honed skills as an actor.

Terry, Johnny, and Stanley are still young, and they are still beautiful. They have become sainted, perhaps even deified. On the other hand, Marlon is no longer young, no longer pleasing to the eye, and it has been a long time since he has been considered Hollywood's golden god. But Marlon is still revered and oftentimes treated like a god, and has come to expect, even demand, this kind of courtesy. Marlon both loves and loathes this about himself.

* * *

Despite his protest, Marlon was eventually settled into a houseboat situated on the Pagsanjan River. Every day he would have a two-man crew commandeer the boat to the movie set a few miles up-river. It was to Marlon's boat where Francis had his copy of *Heart of Darkness* delivered. By the time of its arrival Marlon had already forgotten that Francis was going to send it, and was initially confused as to why the book had been sent to him in the first place. The book was left to lie around the houseboat a couple days before Marlon even picked it up. Marlon's first attempt found him thumbing through it in an uninterested fashion. It was much thinner than he anticipated. He was hoping he would be reading a script at this point, and not a book that the impending script would be loosely based on. He was more interested in the notes and comments that Francis wrote on the various pages than he was the actual text itself.

After many starts and stops, Marlon eventually found himself being pulled into Conrad's book. The way that the Marlowe character describes the native Congolese at first surprised, and then infuriated Marlon. He kept reminding himself that the book had been written over seventy years ago, and even though its anti-colonial message was well ahead of its time, it was still steeped in racist depictions of black people. Marlon found the first part of the novella hard to read and somewhat dull. But eventually the anticipation of reaching Kurtz demonstrated by the book's protagonist, Marlowe, as he journeyed down the river en route to the Belgian outpost, infected Marlon as well. It did not take Marlon long before he grew curious about this Kurtz. He wanted to jump ahead and get to the Kurtz character but refrained, choosing instead to experience the journey and eventual arrival along with the Marlowe character in Conrad's book. Just like Marlowe, Marlon too was not sure whom he would find when he got there. But what he did know is that he would have to do more than just get to know this mysterious man for the sake of the movie. He would have to become Kurtz. Marlon had a feeling that Kurtz would not be a likable person, but also that there was a probably a reason for this, and that he had a story to tell.

Marlon began to proceed quickly with the book because he wanted to hear what Kurtz had to say for himself. Marlon was used to other people in effect speaking for him, or basing their opinion of him on rumors and hearsay, which focus primarily on his eccentricities. Marlon read as Marlowe explained how he was fascinated with Mr. Kurtz's theory that native peoples, no matter which continent the white man has made contact with them, see the Europeans as gods or deities, their physical features, as well as their technological and engineering skills. Marlon was in his houseboat proceeding down the Pagsanjan River, pondering this passage while at the same time anticipating his entrance onto the movie set compound of the Kurtz character that he would be portraying in *Apocalypse Now*, one filled with indigenous montagnards played by the local Ifugao people of the Philippines.

The irony was not lost on Marlon how now, almost a hundred years since Conrad's book, the peoples and nations who had been colonized by the West no longer consider the white Europeans to be gods, but rather devils. This had been true in Vietnam, and Marlon wanted Francis' movie to somehow drive that point home to the American public. He was tired of people in America always asking why the United States lost the war in Vietnam, and why the Vietnamese people fought so fervently, first the French, and then the Americans. Marlon hated all the Cold War perspectives and diatribes on the Vietnam War that he would hear at parties and social gatherings, as well as in the news and media coverage, both during and since the war ended. He believed the truth about what had happened in Vietnam was loud and clear, but simply that nobody wanted to hear it. America's war in Vietnam was a grand and ostentatious act of imperialism, and an attempt to take over Southeast Asia piece by piece, he believed. The domino theory, indeed, but in reverse. The Vietnamese people, so sick of French imperialism, so tired of the 'white devils' and their hypocrisy and lies, fought the Americans tooth and nail, and were willing to do so until the last man, woman and child in order to keep them from taking over their country. They did not want the Americans in their country, nor the American way of life. Marlon wanted so desperately to be the one to somehow break the news to the American people that the Vietnamese were unimpressed with American culture and wanted no part of it. That they would rather live in the same manner their ancestors have for the last several hundred, or perhaps even thousands of years than enter into the dysfunctional world of the Americans, one which was being offered to them in mythological and even salvific terms.

   Marlon believes that he himself is a part of that American myth and landscape. Even though many of his characters in effect spoke out against it, Marlon feels that the point has always been missed, and that he too—his characters and what they are presumed to represent, as well as his own celebrity—have been pressed upon the non-white, non-Western peoples of the world, those who have been conquered and colonized in the name of Western-style progress. Marlon has seen what Western-style progress did to him, his friends and his family, and understands why people would not want it for themselves. Everybody he knows has some kind of mental or psychological disorder. And they all do things destructive to their bodies and minds in order to medicate their pain. Marlon sees Western civilization as cold, lonely, brutal, and organized so that only the "strong" are able to access political power, which he has come to understand as those in a state of derangement and even devolvement from the rest of the human race. Marlon believes that those who attain positions of power, and subsequently make war against other peoples and nations, do so because they are either so completely devoid of the emotion of fear, or they are so completely controlled by it. Marlon knew he fell into the latter category. Fear has driven much of what he has done in his life—fear of his mother, fear of his father, fear of failure, fear of rejection, fear of the media, fear of his fan base, fear of himself. Fear is what caused his catapult in Hollywood, and fear is responsible for his decade and a half fall from grace. It is fear that caused him to fornicate, to get married, and it is fear that is responsible for his failure as a father. It is fear that caused him to act weird and sometimes even a bit psychotic. And as it turned out, Marlon's greatest fears have in fact come to pass. He lost his youth, his looks, and his skills as an actor. And like the Western Europeans in the eyes of the colonized peoples of the world, Marlon has lost his god-like aura. Some fans and critics even consider him to have been a fraud all along, that he really never was all that talented, or even good-looking for that matter, that it was all a clever ruse, an allusion, a con that a lot of people bought into.

CHAPTER 3

"What do you think, Marlon?"

"Well, I haven't been given a script yet, so I can't really comment."

"No, about the book. *Heart of Darkness*? Kurtz? What did you think?"

There was a long pause.

"I haven't finished the book yet."

Marlon's comment was met with a look of disbelief on his director's face.

"Marlon, it's a novella. It's barely a hundred pages. Have you at least started it?"

"Yes, I'm just to the point in which Marlowe enters Kurtz's camp. It is a very good read thus far. I am trying to absorb it slowly. Each paragraph, each sentence conjures up a million questions that I have."

Francis knew all too well what this meant for him.

"Well, just read the rest of the book and then we will talk about Kurtz."

Marlon smiled at Francis. Francis recognized the smile. He knew Marlon wanted to begin dialoging right now about Kurtz.

"Not today, Marlon. I've got a thousand and one things to deal with before noon. Read the rest of the book and we will talk all you want," he said while hurrying away. Francis had neither the time nor the inclination to deal with Marlon's inquisitive nature on this day, but knew he and the star actor would have their time together, and lots of it, before Marlon would even begin to think about getting into his role.

Marlon wanted to be on the houseboat, moving down the river, preferably around dusk, when he finally met Kurtz from Conrad's book, perhaps soon upon leaving the movie set and heading back toward the place on the river where his houseboat is parked every evening. But before Marlon would come face to face with Kurtz, he first encountered yet another character from *Heart of Darkness*, someone who is trying to prepare the Marlowe character, and the reader for that matter, for their meeting with the mysterious Mr. Kurtz. The unnamed man is Russian, and he too is in the Congo to extract ivory and whatever else he could in order to get rich. He is seemingly in awe of Kurtz and was not shy in conveying his admiration for the man, as well as divulging Kurtz's flaws. The Russian told Marlowe that Kurtz tried to kill him the other day, to Marlowe's horror. Yet the man still held Kurtz in high esteem. Then the Russian, as a way of conceding that the decapitated heads and dead bodies Marlowe was seeing in Kurtz's camp were instigated by a man who had perhaps gone insane, told Marlowe that Mr. Kurtz himself acknowledges that there is something "not quite right" there in his compound.

"He hates all this," confessed the Russian while looking around the camp, a place teaming with the sights and smells of death. There were skulls detached from their bodies and placed on pikes strewn about. The reader is led to believe that they are a testament to both Kurtz's genius and to his insanity. The Russian tries to explain to Marlowe that these two things are really one and the same, that the fine line between genius and madness is in reality so thin that perhaps the two are identical. He hints to Marlowe that Kurtz is beyond comprehension to people of the Western world, that his methods and way of thinking are at the same time primitive and yet advanced, and that this is something the Western mindset cannot understand. Marlowe ignores this assertion and immediately begins to believe the heads are evidence that there is something wrong with Kurtz, that he is not quite right, and certainly not the great visionary man the Russian is trying to make him out to be, but rather that he is altogether insane.

Marlon is not so quick to take sides in this discussion. He refuses to hastily make Kurtz out to be some kind of monster, or some kind of hero figure, either. Marlon is still willing to suspend judgment even though he believes he has been hired to play Kurtz as a villain. But Marlon wants to hear from Kurtz himself first. He wants to know how Kurtz got to this kind of mental state, where he grew up, what his parents were like, etc. These are topics not explored by Conrad in his book, nor by Francis when working out the twentieth-century version of Kurtz, but things that Marlon will no doubt want to ask his director about later.

Marlon placed the book on his lap and then watched the sun set behind the palm trees. Ah, the jungle! It has been his escape, his refuge from the world. It was during the filming of *Mutiny on the Bounty* in the early 1960s when Marlon fell in love with the tropical islands of Tahiti. The native peoples were seemingly so naïve from Marlon's perspective, but it was a quality that afforded them a freedom of mind and body that the Hollywood movie star envied, having lost that part of himself a long time ago. He thought it ironic how the Westerners believed that the native Tahitians were so backward and even uncivilized, when in fact they were so very advanced in the way they treated one another and the environment, and how they were not controlled by material possessions or personal status. Nonetheless, in came the Westerners with all their physical and psychological baggage, and who were willing to pass these things along like some kind of addictive and destructive drug to anyone who wanted to partake, while at the same time admiring the simplicity of the Tahitians and their culture. Marlon liked Tahiti so much that in 1966 he purchased the Tahitian island of Tetiaroa. There he would escape from his problems, and subsequently create new ones for himself. Like Kurtz, Marlon would have his own "skulls" and "skeletons" littered throughout his jungle getaway, only they were not quite so visible as those of Mr. Kurtz. Marlon's were in the form of broken relationships—parents, wives, lovers, friends, children—as well as all the shame and regret that goes along with it. Marlon's skulls and skeletons, like Kurtz's, pressed in on him in his jungle abode as well, making him wonder if the jungle was where he could escape the mistakes of his past, or if it was the place they most often confronted him.

"He hates all this." Marlon thought about this assessment made by the Russian in reference to Kurtz. Marlon hates all this too. He hates his mess of a life. Marlon tried to escape himself and his past in the jungles of Tahiti, but in many ways the jungle only served to magnify his problems. It showed him how far he had fallen, how deep he had allowed himself to be sucked into the follies and trappings of Western civilization, and just how dead he and most other Hollywood stars were with their failed relationships, drug and alcohol abuse, as well as perverse sexual addictions. Like Kurtz, the jungle spoke to Marlon the many things he never knew about himself, things that continue to echo and resonate, sometimes loudly, deep within his mind.

* * *

"I finished reading about this Kurtz fellow," announced Marlon to his director.

"Really? What did you think?"

"It was revelatory. I was amazed. I was enlightened. I never read anything like it before."

"That good?"

"It was of course brief, but very dense."

"Uh, huh."

There was a pause as Marlon looked at Francis in an attempt to convey his seriousness about Conrad's book, as well as glean whether or not his director really wanted to hear what he had to say about it. Francis, realizing that Marlon had been very moved by *Heart of Darkness*, wanted to accommodate his star actor despite the fact he was pressed for time with other on-set commitments.

"What did you find most interesting about Kurtz?"

"I don't know if I can really answer that question, Francis," began Marlon, very slowly, which irritated his director who was already pressed for time. "There were so many poignant moments, despite the fact that it's a short book, and the time that Kurtz actually appears in the book is brief."

"Yes, very brief, Marlon."

"It's really the observations made by the Marlowe character that are so extraordinary, and so telling. And I'm assuming, Francis, that Martin Sheen's character is based on Marlowe. Am I right?"

"Uh, yeah, right, Marlon. Marty's character is based on Marlowe.

Marlon looked suspiciously at Francis, who seemed distracted, wondering if he really wanted to hear his opinion and have a meaningful conversation about Conrad's work.

"Marlowe's analysis is extraordinary. His use of metaphor is...is incredible."

"What specifically?"

Marlon paused as he tried to muster up an example.

"When Marlowe sees Kurtz for the first time, he describes him as 'emaciated, nothing but bones'."

There was an uncomfortable moment as the reality of Marlon's excessive weight collided with Marlon's description of the actual physical condition of the character he was commissioned to play.

"Yet when Kurtz...and by the way, Kurtz is a terrible name for this character, for our Kurtz, not necessarily Conrad's Kurtz…"

"What?" said Francis with his heading shaking from side to side, confused by Marlon's sudden detour.

"Nothing. Anyway, when Kurtz begins to talk, when he opens his 'frail mouth' as it's described by Marlowe, Kurtz, albeit frail looking, appears poised to 'swallow and devour', or something like that."

"Yeah, I liked that, too, Marlon."

Marlon waited to see if Francis would elaborate, if he had come up with the same interpretation of what Conrad was getting at with this description of Kurtz as he did.

"What does this tell you about Kurtz, Marlon?"

"Well, at least here, I see Kurtz as a kind of metaphor, a symbolic figure. He represents the West, the white Western Europeans and the Americans. They are a dying empire. The time of the European white man's domination of the world is almost over, and Kurtz, as I said, is a kind of metaphor for this."

"Yes, I agree. This is exactly the point that Conrad, through the Marlowe character, is trying to make. And the way he does it is quite brilliant, because he also gets the point across that the white man, although a mere shell of his former self, is still feared, still obeyed, still treated like some kind of god."

"Yes, and that the white man is still dangerous, still reaching for more. Let me see if I can find what Marlowe says…here it is. Marlowe says, 'he opened his mouth as if wanting to swallow all the air, all the earth, all the men before him'."

"That's how I want you to play Kurtz, Marlon. We're not going to go for the whole 'dying and emaciated' thing," said Francis somewhat uneasily, as it was the first time the issue of Marlon's weight had come up, albeit indirectly. Marlon nodded his head in agreement, perhaps conceding that his weight would not allow for that. "I don't want Kurtz to be sickly, but rather a kind of big, strong, gung-ho military man. You know the type, Marlon, the kind of guy who sports a flat-top and puts Marine Corp bumper stickers on his car, the consummate alpha-male, the kind of guy who still walks around with his military boots on years after he's retired."

"But...but..." Marlon was trying to interrupt.

Francis did not stop talking but rather spoke louder in an attempt to assert himself.

"Yet, Kurtz, this big gung-ho career military man, is dramatically changed as a result of his experience in the jungles of Vietnam and Cambodia. He's still a military man, but the jungle, the Eastern world, the world of Buddhism and Taoism, and all kinds of other non-Western religions and philosophies and ideas, has affected him. I'm not sure how yet. But it's kind of like the big jock becoming a hippy, type of thing."

"Like Kris Kristofferson."

"Yes, like Kris Kristofferson! Exactly, Marlon! He's always had the classical features of an athletic—the muscular build, the rugged good looks. And to see him sitting around with the hippies, playing peace and love songs, and all that stuff...I don't know...he always seemed a little out of place to me, but yet he was fully integrated in the scene. I mean, he still is that jock-type, but he has been enlightened somehow, and sees beyond that narrow stereo-typical world of the jock."

"I agree. He has always seemed an unlikely hippy to me as well..."

"But he's not a hippy. And that's the point!"

"Yes, I know that. What I was going to say, Francis, is that he seems to fit right in, even though he knows he's a jock, and everybody else knows he's a jock, too, and not a hippy."

"Right. And this is how I see you playing Kurtz. He is the kind of guy who would normally look and feel very comfortable in an officer's club. But now, even though he might still look the part, he would no longer feel so comfortable there. And it's not that he would feel *uncomfortable*, but rather that he has seen and experienced a world far beyond the narrow patriotic and dutiful confines of the American military."

"Yes, I agree. But...but...with Conrad's Kurtz, it's not some religious or philosophical insight that causes him to go to this different level or place than everybody else. Here, I marked it with my pen," added Marlon while squinting hard to find what he had written on the page. "Marlowe says that the 'wilderness' drew Kurtz to its 'pitiless breast by the awakening of forgotten and brutal instincts'."

"Yes! Yes!" responded Francis in agreement, and in acknowledgment that he remembered and liked that passage.

"And what comes after that? Something about the bounds of what is *permitted*, or what is *allowed*, or something like that."

"Marlowe then says, in regard to 'the awakening of forgotten and brutal instincts', that this 'beguiled his soul beyond the bounds of permitted aspirations'."

"Yes, that's it, Marlon! *Permitted aspirations*."

"So how I understand this is that Kurtz has in effect thrown off the shackles of civilized society—of Western civilization—and is hearkening back to the ways of his primeval ancestors, those who relied on instinct and adhered to the so-called Law of the Jungle. This 'bounds of permitted aspirations', as I understand it, Francis, is a reference to what is allowed, or what is socially acceptable, according to the standards of Western civilization. It's what is considered normal or proper, morally and ethically speaking, even during times of war, and Kurtz has apparently gone 'beyond' that, according to Conrad."

"Yes, I agree with your assessment, Marlon. And I'll take it even a step further. I would say that Kurtz has not only gone 'beyond' what is permitted, but he has *transcended* it. He has transcended what I would call the timid-line morality of the Western world. Oh, that's good! I've got to write that down—timid-line morality."

"And that's how I see Leighly," said Marlon coyly, which was followed by a pause.

"Leighly? I'm not following you."

"That's what we should call this Kurtz character...we should call him Leighly, or something like that. All these American military guys have smooth sounding names that roll off the tongue. His ethnicity should be English. And his name should be something like 'Leighly.' Kurtz sounds too Germanic. I just think it would be more appropriate."

"I see your point, Marlon, but I want to keep the story somewhat consistent with Conrad's book. We're already changing the time period and the geographic location, and much of the storyline. I would like to keep the name of Kurtz, simply because I don't want to completely stray from Conrad's book. I want to keep the name because I would like this to be a *Heart of Darkness* for the twentieth century, a Kurtz for the twentieth century. Without the name my movie will be neither of these."

Marlon looked down at the ground in disappointment upon hearing his director's explanation.

"Alright," he said begrudgingly. "It's not that big of a deal, I suppose."

"Marlon, America in the twentieth century is such a melting pot, at least for people of European descent. Hell, most people in the United States can't distinguish between a German last name and an English last name, or an Italian last name from a Spanish or French last name. It doesn't matter anymore—last names. Let's get back to Kurtz going beyond the 'bounds of permitted aspirations'."

"Yes, the 'bounds of permitted aspirations'. I understand this to mean that Kurtz has freed himself from the constraints of Western society, this 'timid-line morality' that you called it. But he is no hippy. He has freed himself of all moral and ethical standards and expectations. A little later in the book Conrad writes, and this really helped clarify it for me, he writes, 'there is nothing above or below him'."

Francis took a moment to think about the brief passage Marlon quoted before responding.

"Nothing above or below him. Nothing above or below him. Hmm." Francis was trying to get the gist of the point Conrad was attempting to make, and what Marlon was alluding to.

Marlon waited for a while, watching Francis closely in expectation of his take on these words.

"I don't recall that phrase, Marlon, but I'm guessing that Conrad is referring to the notion that Kurtz fears neither God nor the Devil, neither Heaven nor Hell. I think it's a religious or metaphysical thing. Would you agree with that, Marlon, or am I just way off base here?"

"No, I agree, but I think that Conrad is going deeper than that…"

"And…sorry, Marlon. Just let me say one more thing. And the reason why he no longer fears these things is because he no longer believes in the existence of God, or the Devil for that matter. In other words, he has freed himself of the Western Christian mindset, of its moral and ethical restrictions, as well as any presumed afterlife rewards or punishments."

"Yes, but it goes even deeper than that…"

"How so?" responded Francis quickly.

"It's not that Kurtz simply no longer believes, because a lot of people stop believing. Rather, he was able to rid himself of the ingrained fear of God, which is something imbedded in the mindset of many people of Western European descent—the children of Christendom—to the point that even if they are not practicing Christians, there is still this innate fear of God, which usually rears its head whenever a person is in severe crisis. In times of war, or when someone is facing a serious disease, or the possibility of the death of a loved one, they will seek out God, they will become fearful of God's punishment and want to appease him somehow."

"Yes, yes, I know exactly what you mean, Marlon. My Catholic-instilled fear of God has reared its head out here for me. I've never prayed as much as I have on the set of this damn movie. And it's because I'm afraid."

"Afraid of what?"

"Of failure, Marlon!"

"Yes, exactly," said Marlon while trying to locate his previous train of thought. "Yes, so not only has Kurtz freed himself of his cultural, and perhaps even hereditary fear of God, but also the ethics and morality often associated with that fear. And it is because of this that Kurtz is able to go 'beyond the bounds of what is permitted', or the 'timid-line morality' of Western society, as you put it, Francis. It's because he no longer adheres to any boundaries, or timid-lines, anymore."

"Yes, Marlon. That's great. But how does this happen? I know it's because his belief in God, and subsequently his fear of God, are completely gone, erased from his mindset and psyche. But how does this happen? How does he free himself from the timid-line morality of his Western mindset? And by the way, I'm going to start using the term 'timid-line morality' from now on instead of 'the bounds of what is permitted' because I want this conversation to evolve into one about our Kurtz, as opposed to Conrad's Kurtz. You see what I'm saying, Marlon?"

There was a pause as Marlon thought for a moment.

"Yes, I see what you're saying, Francis. But to answer your question, I don't remember if Conrad really explains how or why Kurtz got to that place, other than the fact he was so far away from the Western world, literally and figuratively."

"Right, Marlon. And so maybe a lot of it had to do with the fact he had been living in the Congolese jungle for so long."

"As well as living amongst the native Congolese."

"Right, Marlon. Good point. I think this is an important connection that we need to make with our Kurtz, because I want the Kurtz you're going to be playing to do the same thing. With that said, what our Kurtz comes to learn, to respect and eventually to emulate, is that the North Vietnamese, the montagnards, and the jungle itself for that matter, do not feel the need for superficial outward manifestations of what amounts to a false civility."

"Superficial outward manifestations of…what did you say?"

"Superficial outward manifestations of false civility."

"I don't think I know what that means, Francis."

"Yes you do, Marlon. This is something I've heard you talk about in the past."

"It is?"

"Yes, Marlon. You've probably phrased it differently than I did, but you've made this point as well. And I'm sure there's many ways of saying it, I suppose, but the point I'm trying to make here is that the North Vietnamese, the montagnards, and the jungle— none of them are restricted or limited in their actions by certain moral or ethical codes pressed upon them by some ancient religious system."

"What about Buddhism and Confucianism?"

"Ah ha! Good point, Marlon. But I would make the argument that when fighting the Americans, not only did the North Vietnamese refuse to pay heed to these or any other sort of moral or ethical code, but they did not pretend to either. And it's because they couldn't afford to. Let me explain," said Francis quickly upon noticing Marlon's confusion.

"Okay."

"They—the North Vietnamese—like the jungle, were locked in a life and death struggle, and so they fought the war as ruthlessly as they possibly could. And, Marlon…and this is important…they did so with *no judgment* upon themselves."

"The law of the jungle."

"Yes. Or Darwin's survival of the fittest. There's no morals, ethics, judgment, or guilt in the jungle, nor in the way in which the North Vietnamese fought the war. Kurtz comes to see this, and to understand, not just the brilliance of it, but its effectiveness."

"Hmm," said Marlon, interested and intrigued by what his director was saying. "And, so, getting back to Darwin…does Kurtz, then, sort of *devolve*? Because, if I understand you correctly, Francis, Kurtz is hearkening back to his primordial instincts."

"That's an interesting take, Marlon. But let me propose an alternative perspective. Considering the fact that he's fighting a jungle war in which he is perhaps only seconds away from death at the hands of man or beast, could it be that instead of devolving, Kurtz has perhaps *evolved*?"

Without realizing it, Francis upset Marlon by so quickly and abruptly dismissing his question regarding the possible devolution of Kurtz in favor of his own theory of Kurtz's evolution.

"You see what I'm saying, Marlon?" asked Francis after getting no response from his star actor. "Kurtz is evolving or changing out of necessity. If he doesn't, he won't survive."

"Yes, I get it, Francis. But do you see what *I'm* saying, or *trying* to say?" said Marlon with more than a hint of sarcasm in his voice.

"Yes. Yes, I do, Marlon. I know what you're saying. And what I'm saying actually speaks to what you're saying about Kurtz's devolvement."

Francis stopped to gauge his star actor. Deadpan.

"What I'm saying, Marlon, or perhaps what I'm asking, is why is it that when we human beings utilize our primordial instincts, we are acting like animals, or we've become savages, or that we're somehow devolving in some sort of way? Why is that?"

Marlon grinned slightly and looked away.

"According to anthropologists, or whoever the fuck studies this stuff, Marlon, our ability to fight and survive against man and beast is considered a part of our *evolutionary* process, it's what brought us to the pinnacle of the animal kingdom. But now, if human beings resort to their primordial instincts in order to survive, even in times of war, it is not only an indication of our devolvement, but of our insanity."

"Are we going to take that angle, Francis?" asked Marlon. "Are we going to portray Kurtz as insane? Because I don't want to play the role of somebody who's gone insane."

"Does it hit too close to home?" joked Francis.

"Ha! Well, kind of. But I just don't want to play somebody who's supposed to be crazy, and I don't think portraying Kurtz as such would be good for the success of the movie."

"Why not?"

"You're asking me *why not*?"

"Yes. Why not?"

"Because if my character—if Kurtz—is crazy, then everything that I say in the movie—everything that Kurtz says—will be dismissed as utter nonsense. And subsequently, the movie will have no real profound message, no matter how good my dialogue, but rather just the ramblings of a crazy person."

"I see what you're saying, Marlon, and that's a really good point. But this is not a simple yes or no question. And therein lies the tension, Marlon. I think that this is the very question that Conrad wants us to wrestle with. Is Kurtz really insane, or are all the rest of us the crazy ones for thinking that it is normal for human beings to live by certain societal constraints?"

"Okay, I get that. But, is our Kurtz...oh, hell, this is so confusing. We should just change the name."

"No, Marlon. We can't change the name."

"So, is Leighly..."

Marlon stopped and looked at Francis to get his reaction. Francis smiled back as coyly as Marlon was smiling at him. "Okay, so, does our Kurtz—the Vietnam War, twentieth-century Kurtz—does he go insane?"

"I don't know if he's insane, Marlon. That's going to depend on a person's perspective."

"Okay, let me phrase this differently. Is the movie going to pose the question of Kurtz's sanity? And if so, will it attempt to answer this question? That is, will the movie take a position on this issue, or leave it open to interpretation?"

"I don't know yet, Marlon. I just don't know."

Francis looked at his watch and realized he was late for a briefing with Martin Sheen. They would be shooting more footage of the patrol boat making its way down river later today.

"Marlon, I'm sorry, but I am late for my meeting with Marty. We will pick back up on this later. This is all good stuff, though. Good stuff! I will talk to you tomorrow some time, Marlon." He then rushed off. Marlon watched him for a moment, then turned his attention back to his copy of *Heart of Darkness*.

CHAPTER 4

Marlon's contract stipulated he is to receive two-million dollars, and that the actor remain on the set for four weeks. Marlon considered himself to be on the clock even though he has not shot a scene yet. Every day he would make the trek up the river on his houseboat to the film site and hang out at the recently constructed Kurtz compound. There Marlon would spend his time playing with the local Ifugao children who were on the set as extras, as well as reading old *Time* and *Newsweek* articles about the Vietnam War and various books supplied by Francis, such as *The Golden Bough*, *From Ritual to Romance*, and some works by T.S. Eliot.

"So, Marlon, I want you to read through some of these books I've put out here, in addition to the Conrad book," said Francis.

Marlon picked them up in obligatory fashion and scanned their pages, looking for pictures.

"*The Golden Bough!*" he announced while holding the book out a fair distance from his face, straining to discern the title. "And this one...*From Ritual to Romance!*"

Francis could sense Marlon's initial disinterest, and felt he better try to sell them to his lead actor, lest this be the first and last time he touches them.

"*The Golden Bough*, Marlon, was published around the time that Conrad's *Heart of Darkness* came out."

Marlon still looked uninterested, but politely listened to his director.

"It was extremely controversial, even more so than Conrad's book."

"Then why aren't we making a movie about this book?"

"Well, that would be hard, and in more ways than one. It wasn't a novel, for one thing."

"Why do you have it here on the set in the first place, Francis? Or, maybe I don't want to know."

"No, you're going to want to know, Marlon. It's here so you have something to read when you're taking a shit."

The two men laughed.

"Or maybe to wipe my ass with."

The two men laughed again, but with more enthusiasm.

"No, actually, Marlon, it's because I see Kurtz as a man, and we touched upon this earlier, who has shifted his thinking from one paradigm to another. Do you know what I mean, Marlon?"

Marlon nodded his head as an indication he understood the point his director was attempting to make. Francis was skeptical, but decided to continue.

"And we mentioned how he does this, to a certain extent, by watching and experiencing the North Vietnamese, the montagnards, as well as the jungle, but he also finds things *Western* that actually supports this new line of thinking. He is not the first Westerner to in effect slip the bonds of Western rationalism."

"Or to go mad."

"Right, Marlon. And you've been a victim of this too."

"Of what?"

"Whenever somebody starts interpreting things, or expressing themselves a little differently than the so-called normal, conventional way, they are sometimes considered mad or insane. Am I right, Marlon?"

"Yes," said Marlon after taking a few seconds to think. "It usually depends on how far off the rails a person has gone, but I know what you mean, Francis. And you're right. I've been called mad or insane by people—critics and fans alike—for my supposedly bizarre behavior, as well as for my political and social views because they don't always jibe with that of the mainstream."

"There are of course even more extreme examples, such as Timothy Leary, and a whole host of '60s-era avant-garde folks, who were considered crazy or mad because they perceived things differently than what was, or is, considered normal."

"The Merry Pranksters! Charles Manson!"

"Yes, Charles Manson is a great example. He had a worldview and an historical perspective that literally scared the hell out of white, middle-America. And he was considered to be quite mad."

"Still is."

"Yes. He still is, for that matter, as he sits in his Los Angeles prison cell."

"Francis, I don't condone the killing," said Marlon with his eyes closed as a means of conveying his regret over the murders carried out by the followers of Charles Manson, as well as to help himself find the right words, "but Manson, if you listen to him, made some really good points, about race, and about how big corporations are polluting the environment. Things like that."

Marlon looked over at his director with the hope that he was not too scandalized by what he just said.

Francis waited for a moment before responding.

"I know what you're saying, Marlon. Manson was a skinny little, greasy dirtball, and uneducated in the traditional sense, but was extremely articulate. And he poked and prodded white, middle-class America about its hypocrisy."

"And his words resonated with America's young people to a certain extent," interjected Marlon.

"Actually, Marlon, Charles Manson's words resonated quite a bit with young people in America during the late '60s. And I don't condone the killing either, of course, but some of the points that he made were spot-on, and yet were so very grating to many white Americans."

"They were grating primarily to the *older* generation of white Americans, and because they were so spot-on."

"Yes. As I said, his words resonated with young people, many of whom used the whole Charles Manson episode as an opportunity to rebel against their parents and that generation. Manson made some good points. He was just a terrible messenger."

"Nobody wanted to be preached at by a long-haired, dirt-ball hippy," added Marlon.

"No. They certainly didn't," said Francis while chuckling.

Both men became quiet as they pondered what they could add to their conversation about the bizarre chapter that Charles Manson was to Vietnam War-era America.

"I would like to include some kind of reference to Charles Manson in the movie," said Francis. Marlon looked up at him curiously. "I don't know…perhaps one of the Americans gets word of what happened from an American newspaper sent to them, or over the radio, and maybe we make a subtle comparison between Manson and Kurtz, how they are both misunderstood. I don't know. I'll need to formulate that some more. Anyway…where were we before we got sidetracked talking about Charles Manson?"

"Wait a minute, Francis. I know this Kurtz fellow I'm going to be playing has certain issues and problems, but I don't want to be portraying someone who's going to be compared to Charles Manson…"

"Marlon, I don't know what we're going to do yet in regard to Manson, probably nothing!" interrupted Francis with voice raised.

"I hate that little creep, Francis! A lot of people do. And if you compare the Kurtz character to Charles Manson, then most people are going to automatically reject him and everything he says right from the beginning, and subsequently tune out everything your movie is trying to say."

"Yes, Marlon. I get that."

"Francis, I told you just the other day that Kurtz cannot be portrayed as insane, much less weird and creepy like Charles Manson…"

"I have no intention of portraying Kurtz as any of these things, Marlon! For Christ sake!"

"Let me finish, Francis!"

"By all means," answered Francis, gesturing with his right hand for Marlon to continue.

"Kurtz must be intriguing and a bit of a mystery, not some over-the-top weirdo."

Marlon paused to make sure his director was in agreement.

"Yes, Marlon. I didn't really mean that I wanted to compare Kurtz and Manson, per se. But rather simply raise the idea that Kurtz, his ideas—his reasoning—and his methods, are misunderstood."

"I think we should just leave Manson out of the equation."

"Okay, Marlon. We don't have to talk about Charles Manson in the movie. We're just throwing out ideas here, that's all."

"Francis, as I mentioned earlier, I've played a lot of crazies and weirdos in the last ten to fifteen years. I don't want to play one here. Plus, that kind of portrayal of Kurtz won't work. Trust me. He's got to be low-key, a kind of shadowy, mysterious figure, yet smart and insightful. Not crazy."

"Okay. Gotcha, Marlon. Let's move on."

"We can move on, Francis, but I just want to be clear about this," said Marlon after a brief pause.

"Okay. Fine. Now what were we talking about?"

Marlon did not answer, but rather starred at his director.

"Yes. I get it, Marlon!"

"Okay. Good." replied Marlon, seemingly satisfied with the response.

"Now, what were we talking about?"

"Some books you brought."

"Oh yes. I want Kurtz to have a little collection of reading material at his compound. And I don't know how we will introduce or highlight it, but I want Kurtz to have a small library of interesting, eclectic books that he has been reading, things that have contributed to his mindset change, and I am considering *The Golden Bough* and *From Ritual to Romance* as a couple of them."

"How about Conrad's book?" asked Marlon in jest.

"*Heart of Darkness*?"

"Yeah. That would be funny."

"That *would* be funny, Marlon. But then we would probably have to change the name to...uh, what was that other name you suggested?"

"Leighly."

"Then we would have to change Kurtz's name to Leighly, because we really couldn't have the twentieth-century Kurtz reading a book about the nineteenth-century Kurtz, could we?"

"Why not, Francis?" asked Marlon. "I mean...it would make for an interesting, perhaps poignant, moment in the movie."

"In what sort of way? Because it would have nothing to do with the actual storyline of the movie. Rather, it would be a kind of cryptic, almost subliminal social or historical message or statement of some kind. And I don't even know what that message would even be, to be perfectly honest with you, Marlon. Plus, I don't think anybody would even make the connection."

"Somebody would."

"Well, of course somebody would, but for the most part it would go unnoticed, so I don't think it would even be worth exploring."

"There are a lot of things in movies, some subtle, some not-so-subtle, that moviegoers often miss, Francis. And that doesn't mean they're not worth doing."

"That's true, Marlon. Hell, even when I watch my own movies, after literally hundreds of hours of filming and editing, there are things I see that I never noticed before."

"I do that too. No matter how many times I've watched *Streetcar* or *Waterfront*, I always see new things."

"So what are we saying here, Marlon?"

"That we apparently have limited brain capacity."

"Yes. Well, that's obvious. But I'm wondering what, if anything, are we saying about the idea of putting *Heart of Darkness* in the book collection of Kurtz? Is it something worth exploring?"

"I was really just kidding about the whole thing, Francis."

"Yes. I know you were. But it's actually an intriguing idea."

"In what way?"

"In a lot of ways."

"Such as?"

"Well, in a kind of alternate reality sort of way."

"This whole movie seems to be an alternate reality, at least from what I can tell, Francis."

"I'll take that as a compliment, Marlon, because I do consider this an attempt to offer up an alternative perspective from the more traditional commentary about the Vietnam War. And I assume this is something you can appreciate, Marlon."

"It is something I can appreciate. I've tried this kind of thing myself in various films over the years, as you know, and it always falls flat. But nothing on the scale of what you're trying to do here, Francis."

"Yeah, my movie is probably going to be weird enough for people without inserting some bizarre, confusing psychoanalytical moment that metaphorically speaks to the idea or notion of Kurtz coming face-to-face with himself in some kind of cyclical historical loop."

Francis paused and looked over at Marlon who was getting fidgety and apparently wearied by yet another diversion to their conversation.

"Okay…well, we'll worry about that later, Marlon," said the director, who was surprised that Marlon was not a little more interested in the idea of including Conrad's book in the Kurtz collection of reading material, considering the fact that he himself came up with the concept.

"There's a lot of things that you're apparently going to worry about later, Francis."

"I know. Most of them I'll never even remember. That's why I need to start writing things down, Marlon. I've been saying that for twenty years now. But I never actually do it."

"Maybe you should write down that you need to start writing things down, Francis."

"Ha. I knew that was coming, Marlon. Very clever."

"Sorry, Francis. That was stupid."

"No. It wasn't stupid as much as it was predictable."

"When I was younger I never wanted to be predictable."

"How about now that you're older?"

Marlon thought for a moment before answering.

"Being predictable is as bad, and as embarrassing and pathetic, as I always thought it would be."

Francis laughed, but not Marlon.

"Okay. Let's get back on track here, Marlon."

"Alright."

"So…*The Golden Bough.*"

"Right."

"Well, Marlon, the author, James Frazer…make that *Sir* James Frazer…"

"Big deal!" interrupted Marlon while rolling his eyes.

"What?"

"The whole *Sir* thing."

"What about it?"

"The British are so fucking pretentious."

"You just noticed that?"

"No. I just don't understand the whole getting 'knighted' thing."

"Are you jealous, Marlon?"

"Of course not."

"Non-Brits can get knighted, too, Marlon."

"Yes. I know."

"Do you want to be knighted?"

"Hell no!"

"I think you do. Laurence Olivier was knighted."

"I know that, Francis. But he was British."

"Right. I'm just pointing him out because he was a great actor, and one of the people you were compared to when you were younger, at least in terms of your acting skills. Maybe after this movie you will be knighted."

"I'd turn it down."

"Oh, the hell you would, Marlon."

"The hell I wouldn't! I've refused Oscars without batting an eye," said Marlon with his voice raised. "Can we please get back to the fucking book…*The Golden Bough*, or whatever the fuck it's called?"

"Sure, Marlon. No problem." Francis paused for a moment in order to let some of the tension subside. "So back in the late 1800s, Frazer was as revolutionary and as controversial as was Marx..."

"Groucho?" said Marlon jokingly. He had a knack for becoming silly right on the heels of throwing a temper tantrum.

"Ha ha. Yes, Marlon, Groucho Marx." They both laughed. "No! Karl Marx, Marlon. Karl fucking Marx. So, back in the day, James Frazer was as revolutionary of thought as was Karl Marx, as well as Sigmund Freud and Charles Darwin for that matter."

"I've heard of him, but I have no idea what he did or wrote about."

"Well, Sir James wrote a book, a very controversial book. It was a comparative study of various religions—all the world's religions—including Christianity, and all on the same level. In other words, it does not put Christianity in an ascendant place or position. It talks about how most, if not all, ancient religions, big and small, including Christianity, were fertility cults, centered on the worship and subsequent death or sacrifice of a sacred godking."

"Like Christ."

"Yes, Marlon. Like Christ!" said Francis in a matter-of-fact sort of way. "Frazer's study points out that most early, primitive, agrarian societies understood their religion, their world, and time itself, from the perspective of the growing season or seasonal cycles of birth, life, death...birth, life, death...birth, life, death, and so on. And that time is cyclical, not linear. It keeps repeating itself, over and over again."

"Okay, I get that. But what do you mean by *linear*?" asked Marlon.

"Linear, Marlon, in regard to history, means that time is in effect moving from point A to point B. It's not cyclical. Does that make sense?"

"Not really."

"Linear means that there's a starting point to time, and of human history, and there will be an end-point sometime in the future. You see what I'm saying?"

"Kind of," replied Marlon sheepishly.

"The Christian perspective is linear. Christians do not think the world will go on forever. The focus isn't on the seasonal cycles. Creation was point A. And the Last Judgement—the End Times, the Rapture, the Apocalypse, whatever you want to call it, basically the end of the world—will be point B. Now do you see what I'm saying, Marlon?" asked Francis impatiently.

"Yes. I get it."

"And Frazer points out that there was a common denominator among so many of these early societies, most of which never had any contact whatsoever with one another. He says that many of them adhered to the same idea or concept of the dying and subsequently rising or resurrected god."

"What? There have been other resurrected gods?"

"Well, yes. It's not something exclusive to Christianity, Marlon."

"Yes, Francis. I know that. I said that facetiously, for fuck sake!"

"I know you did, Marlon..."

"Then why did you look and sound as if I said something stupid?"

"I didn't, Marlon. I didn't," said Francis with as much conviction as he could muster, lest he make his star actor even more upset. "Anyway, in many societies throughout history, the god, when he got old, was in effect sacrificed as an offering for the health of the crops or the harvest, so basically for the well-being of the people and the community as a whole. And in some cultures, that same god would rise or come back to life along with that year's new crops, while in other cultures the old god would be replaced by a new, young god."

"A younger model, so to speak? Like when I replaced Olivier?"

"Well, yes, you could say that, Marlon. Good analogy. But the point of having the book as a part of Kurtz's library is to convey the message that Kurtz has come to a point in which he has in fact slipped the bonds of Western rationalism, including its dominant religion of Christianity, along with its prevailing perspective of time and history."

"Ah!"

"Do you like that idea, Marlon?"

"Very much. There's a lot we can work with there."

"I'm not trying to resurrect the Manson conversation, Marlon, but…"

"Ha! Very clever, Francis," said Marlon after noticing that his director had paused for dramatic effect.

"Yes. That was a good segue, wasn't it. But just to put a bookend on the Charles Manson stuff, he too can be considered as having slipped the bonds of Western rationalism."

"Yes, but you just ruined what you were saying about slipping the bonds of Western rationalism and coming to see beyond the Christian paradigm, or illusion, by bringing that fucken little weirdo up again."

"My reason for bringing Manson back up, Marlon, is to make the point that what Kurtz is doing—what we're calling slipping the bonds of Western rationalism—will often take the shape or form of something very strange to our Western and even our modern sensibilities, and will ultimately be something that makes people very uncomfortable, like Manson did. It's not going to be pretty. Whatever it is that Kurtz is doing, and how he's doing it, and why he's doing it, is going to be difficult for people to accept, as well as comprehend."

"Well, I'm good at making people feel uncomfortable, Francis, so you've got the right man for the job."

"I have little doubt of that, Marlon."

"That I'm the right man for the job?"

"No. That you make people uncomfortable. Ha! You walked right into that one, Marlon."

"On purpose, though, Francis. I walked into that on purpose. In case you didn't know, I will often lob softballs like that to people."

"Yes. I know that about you, Marlon."

"But a lot of people don't realize I'm doing it. They think I'm unwittingly walking right into these things, like I'm some kind of idiot. In fact, I don't think you knew that that's what I was doing right there."

"I actually did, Marlon, but I can see your efforts being misinterpreted in that way. Why do it, then, if people are going to misunderstand you, and have a laugh at your expense like that, especially if it bothers you?"

"I guess I'm a glutton for punishment." Marlon chuckled softly at what was intended to be a joke, but then quickly went into the real explanation for why he sometimes willingly opens himself up to ridicule. "No. In reality it's part of my acting style. A good actor makes it easy for the other actors to ad lib, to feel comfortable and act natural. And humor, especially self-deprecating humor, can create opportunities for conversation and dialogue for the other actors. I do this to help loosen the other actors up."

"Because many of them feel intimidated by you, is that it? And they tense up around you?"

"Yes, Francis. That's right."

"You do it so the dialogue and conversations sound more natural and less contrived than just following a script, am I right?"

"Precisely."

"Well, speaking of less contrived and not following a script, and to circle back to the Frazer book…" Francis paused in order to give Marlon time to track the impending shift in the conversation. "Kurtz, out in the Cambodian jungle, comes to believe that Christianity is no more true or real than any other ancient religion or belief system, and that the Western world used the assumed, and perhaps *scripted* and *contrived*, validity of its religion to justify the conquest and colonization of the rest of the world."

Francis stopped and smiled coyly, assuming Marlon noticed and would acknowledge how he cleverly worked the words *scripted* and *contrived* into his sentence, but to no avail.

"And of course, Francis, you're referring to the English, Spanish, and French colonial
powers, who all believed that Christ was an imperial god, a god of warfare and conquest, and that this god was exclusively on their side."

"Uh, yes, Marlon, and the United States to a certain extent as well, despite the fact that it is much more secular than those earlier empires, and certainly was so by the time of the Vietnam War, although not completely secular by any means."

"No. Not at all."

"The Western European Christian-colonial paradigm had been disintegrating long before the American involvement in Vietnam, and wasn't so clearly defined or easily articulated anymore at that point. Hell, even Conrad's Kurtz could no longer glean any practical, much less spiritual or even philosophical, meaning from it anymore. And neither can our Kurtz. In regard to Conrad's Kurtz, the ground shifted underneath him while out in the Congolese jungle to the point that he eventually lost his political, cultural, spiritual, and even racial footing. He becomes cavernous, hollowed out."

"Yes. Conrad's Kurtz seems very hollow."

"Well, I definitely think that that was Conrad's point. The jungle…but it wasn't just the jungle. The jungle, the Congolese people and culture, as well as his exploitation of these things completely guts Kurtz of everything he knows and believes, creating a vacuum. But it's only things nihilistic, as well as sickness and disease, that rush in and fill the void."

"Yes. But we're not going to portray Kurtz as sickly, am I right, Francis?"

"No. Not physically, but perhaps in certain other aspects, like his psyche. But even in that regard I don't think *sickly* is the right word here. Our Kurtz is going to be less defeated and deflated, less withdrawn than Conrad's Kurtz. So no, I don't want our Kurtz to be sick and dying. I don't want the first three-quarters of the movie to be a lead-up to nothing more than a sickly, bed-ridden man on the cusp of death. We've got to have something more waiting for the viewer at the end of the river than that."

"I agree."

"I would like your portrayal to be of a man who is more awake, less defeated than Conrad's Kurtz. But he's still lost, perhaps hovering between where he came from and where he is now."

"Maybe Kurtz should be portrayed as someone who's desperately trying to hold onto, maybe resuscitate, or perhaps even relocate a past that no longer exists, and maybe never did exist."

"A lost paradise theme?"

"Yes."

"Like Milton?"

"Sure."

"That's a good, Marlon. Because the Vietnam War-era is definitely the point in which the American mythological landscape was called into question, and even dismantled to a certain extent in the opinion of many. Lost, if you will."

"Yes. And Kurtz tries to find all that he once knew and loved, but having to do so in the confusion of war while immersed in the strangeness of the jungle, which only serves to lead him further astray from his Western grounding. And maybe this is where the whole cyclical as opposed to linear thing can come in, Francis."

"How so?"

Marlon paused. He was trying to figure out how he was going to express such a complex concept. The actor was taking too long for Francis. The director wanted so desperately to answer his question himself, but refrained.

"Well," began Marlon, hesitantly. "Kurtz can be understood as a kind of microcosm of the United States…"

"How do you mean?" interrupted Francis.

"I was about to tell you Francis."

"Sorry."

"Kurtz can be understood as a kind of microcosm of the United States, and I know you don't want Kurtz to be an archetype, but I think this analogy or comparison will help me get my point across."

"Go ahead, Marlon," replied Francis upon realizing the Oscar winning actor was in effect asking his permission to continue.

"Okay, so whatever I say about Kurtz, the same could be said about the United Sates, but at a much larger level, mind you."

"Kind of like a micro and micro thing, right?"

"You could say that, I guess," said Marlon after a brief pause. He did not like it when people tried to neatly categorize his ideas.

"Let's hear it, Marlon."

The director was getting impatient with his lead actor's seeming inability to articulate his idea, one that may or may not be worth exploring, anyway.

"Okay. So Instead of his religious and political beliefs remaining constant and simply progressing in the same shape and form until the end of time, much like those of the Western world itself, the waves of cyclical or circular change keep coming at him and are in effect rasping away his old, long-standing beliefs."

"That's good, but be more specific, Marlon."

"Okay. I'll try." Marlon cleared his throat. He was nervous. "The god of the Western European world, the god that subdued the Americas, and the one whose ghost the Americans tried to cast over Southeast Asia, was the god of the two-thousand year-old Western European empire—the god of the later Roman Empire, as well as the Spanish, French, and England empires."

Marlon stopped to assess Francis' reaction.

"Okay. You always tend to begin at the macro level, but I think I know where you're going with this. Say more."

"Well, as we've talked about, Kurtz comes to understand that time and history are cyclical, as many eastern religions and philosophies teach, and not linear as Western thought steeped in Christianity teaches. That all things run their course, whether it's a god, a religion, a political system, or an empire. Everything naturally gives way to something new, and that this is a process constantly repeating itself, over and over again. And during the late 1960s, during the Vietnam War, this change, or evolution—whatever you want to call it—of the Western empire and the American mythical landscape was changing very suddenly and abruptly."

"I like this, Marlon. But can you circle this discussion back around to *The Golden Bough?*" asked the impatient director.

Marlon was taken aback by Francis' sudden and seemingly mammoth interruption.

"I suppose I could, Francis, but there was more I was going to say. Why do you ask me to comment on things and then interrupt me and basically tell me I'm not talking about anything that interests you? Why do you do that, Francis? It's very frustrating."

"I'm sure it is, Marlon. But as you've told me many times in the past, you do tend to have a hard time getting to the point, and I'm just trying to help you focus, that's all."

Marlon looked away. He was agitated.

"Where I would like this conversation to go is how *The Golden Bough* relates to you and your role, or place, in Hollywood's pantheon of great actors, because I believe the idea of the dying and reviving god, or new god, could be a great jumping-on point for you, Marlon."

"Jumping-on point?"

"Yes, Marlon," began Francis, frustrated with his lead actor's inability to quickly and seamlessly comprehend what he was implying. "This angle is a great way for you to transition into Kurtz."

"So now you want me to read Frazer's book?"

"Well, Frazer's thesis is actually much more interesting than the book itself. There is some good stuff here, but he just goes on and on with the different examples of the dying and rising god thing. Don't get me wrong, it's interesting, but Sir Frazer really hammers his point home with a lot of volume. But to answer your question, no, I don't expect you to read Frazer's book."

"How many pages is it?"

"Oh, about four-, maybe five-hundred pages," answered Francis as both men looked over at the book that Marlon had long since set off to the side.

"Okay, maybe I won't read it. But I admit I find Frazer's thesis interesting, from what you've told me about it, anyway."

"Yes, I definitely think it has opened up another perspective, or slant, to this story that we can explore, Marlon."

Marlon agreed, but was hoping that Francis would elaborate further.

"How so?"

"Well, two things, Marlon. First, at the macro-level, Kurtz comes to understand the things we've been talking about regarding dying and rising gods and empires, and so forth. And second, at the micro-level, Kurtz comes to understand a few things about himself as well. Kurtz is a kind of celebrity in the world of the American military. He comes from a family with a very rich military pedigree, and so big things are expected from him. As a student of history, and especially military history, Kurtz understands the concept that important, powerful figures sometimes die for the health and welfare of the rest of the clan or tribe, or in this case, the nation-state. Yet Kurtz is a man who is not at ease with the notion of individual celebrity, at least not his own. He is not comfortable with the reverence he was given as the son of a prestigious military man, nor with his own supposed greatness, afforded him by certain titles and medals pinned to his uniform."

"I would think, Francis, that Kurtz eventually comes to the realization that the world in which he comes from—the military culture—is a fake world, a mythological world, one propped up by illusion. I can see Kurtz as a man who is trying to shed his old skin, trying, perhaps unwittingly, to die a symbolic death, and maybe even a literal death."

"And when you say 'symbolic', Marlon, do you mean a death that will help sustain the future of the tribe, or one that will simply destroy the fake image of Kurtz created by the world of military mythology?"

"A little bit of both, I think. But more so the second thing you mentioned. Kurtz comes to hate the image of himself as the brave, strong, hero-figure. He sees the hypocrisy of it."

"Okay. So is Kurtz looking for a real or a symbolic death?"

"I think he wants a symbolic death. He no longer wants to be the man he is, one produced by the United States Army and the Western world. But a literal death would not be completely unwelcome, either, I don't think. There needs to be more character development before this determination can be made. But Kurtz is definitely in a lot of pain. He has seen and comes to understand things about himself and the Western world that have forever changed him and his perception of his country, and there is no going back for him in that regard…"

"That is very good, Marlon. I like it."

"Thanks," said Marlon after a brief pause, which further stalled his momentum, making Francis regret interrupting him.

"I think that Kurtz is carrying around a lot of baggage, much like we all have once we get to a certain age," coaxed the director.

"Yes. I can relate to that," answered Marlon begrudgingly. "I never liked my public persona, nor who I really am, either, I guess. My image, which I suppose is an extension of who I was, and who I am now, is in part a Hollywood creation, and part of my own doing, too, unfortunately."

"I've always had the sense that you've never been comfortable with your public image."

"I don't like a whole lot of things about myself, not just my image. You know that, Francis."

"But you have always seemed like a man who is…well, I was going to say happy, but happy isn't the right word."

"No. Probably not."

"How would you describe yourself, Marlon?"

"I was hoping to hear how you would describe me, Francis."

"Now, or when you were younger?"

"Both."

"Both?"

"Yes, both. The whole picture."

Francis hesitated. He really did not want to psycho-analyze his temperamental star actor.

"Well, as I said, I don't see you as happy, Marlon, when you were young, or now. I think, especially when you were younger, that you were a confidant man, at least overtly. You were, and perhaps still are, arrogant to a certain extent. But who can blame you, Marlon. You are one of the greatest actors who has ever lived. People accuse me of being arrogant. A lot of people are arrogant, but have accomplished far, far less than you have."

"So, you're using the word *arrogant* to describe me?"

"Well, kind of, but of course that's not the whole picture, Marlon. It's just one word. I haven't got to all the other wonderful words I was going to use yet."

"But apparently, that's the first adjective that came to mind, once you dismissed *happy* as a way of describing me."

"Well, yes, I guess so. Damn it, Marlon. Why did you make me do this?"

"I didn't make you do anything, Francis."

"But you encouraged it. I'm just going to give it to you straight, Marlon. You are arrogant! But you have every reason to be arrogant. You are Marlon fucking Brando, for Christ sake!"

Marlon looked away as if slightly annoyed with Francis' analysis.

"What? What is it, Marlon? Don't be insulted because I said you are arrogant, and have a right to be so."

"No, I'm not insulted. It's just that you touched on something that's always bothered me."

"What's that?"

"When you said 'you're Marlon *fucking* Brando'."

"Yeah?"

"This is what has enabled me to fail and to be a failure for the last twenty-plus years, this free pass, of sorts. It's because of those movies I did in the early fifties, and the image that developed around me."

"How so?"

"Well, you can compare it to what Frazer is talking about, I guess. I was young, good-looking, the king of Hollywood, a god almost. But eventually I was replaced by other, younger actors, at least physically, but not necessarily in spirit."

"Right. Go on."

"That young, good-looking Marlon Brando of the 1950's is still alive in spirit, roaming around, haunting Hollywood, haunting me and my family, haunting every future role I play, haunting every societal cause I try to take up. It's a Marlon Brando I can never live up to, nor can I live him down. Do you understand me, Francis? He's a curse."

"But he saved Hollywood."

Marlon smiled regretfully.

"Yes, but for a brief moment. There have been many others who have come along since then and 'saved Hollywood'."

"The reason why I said that, Marlon, is because this is exactly what the other book I have here, *From Ritual to Romance*, talks about."

Marlon shook his head, indicating he did not understand.

"By who?"

"It's written by Jessie Weston, an English folklorist, around 1920."

"Never heard of him."

"Anyway, *From Ritual to Romance*, Marlon, centers on the hero-type, a savior of sorts, who is going to rescue or save the people, the land, whatever the case may be. You, Marlon, have been this kind of savior archetype, just as you have been the dying and rising god as explained by Sir James Frazer in *The Golden Bough*."

"Yes, I was the hero and even a kind of savior. Saviors and messiahs are always young and attractive. And they almost always burn out quickly, and not fade away as I have done, and am still in the process of doing. And I guess that this does in fact kind of tie-in with the whole dying and rising god idea. I was the new, young Hollywood god, replacing the likes of Bogart and others. But I never died or went away. Instead, for the past twenty years people have expected me to do something that would equal or maybe even surpass those earlier roles, to save Hollywood again, never really letting me relinquish my throne, so to speak. But with every year that passed, and with every film that flopped, it has been harder and harder to live up to people's expectations of me, and my own expectations of myself as well. I have always wanted to start over, to be somebody other than those fucken roles I played in the '50s and early '60s. But the fans, and the whole Hollywood industry for that matter, have never let me move beyond the Marlon Brando of the 1950's. And the Marlon Brando of the late 1960's and 1970's just can't compete with that Marlon Brando and those classic roles. That Marlon Brando is dead."

CHAPTER 5

"What was Kurtz's childhood like?"

"His childhood, Marlon? I don't even know how I'm going to finish my movie, much less be able to tell you about the man's childhood. Why do you want to know about his childhood?"

"I want to know how he got to this place, this mental state he's in."

"I don't even think we have Kurtz's mental state all worked out yet. Maybe we should figure out exactly what his mental state is first."

"I could better figure it out if I knew what came before all this."

"I don't know, Marlon. We could try to work a few things out. How much do you think you'll need to know? I only have you for four weeks, Marlon. It could take us four weeks just to figure out his childhood, much less his pre-pubescence, his pubescence, his adulthood and so forth."

"I just need to know a little bit about what he's carrying around with him."

"Okay. I can understand that. But I don't have any ideas, Marlon. Maybe you could get us started?"

"Sure," said Marlon with not much enthusiasm, and then paused before speaking again. "I see him growing up in a very restrictive setting, somewhere in the Midwest. His childhood is a typical, very American story."

Marlon paused again. Francis hated it when Marlon paused. Marlon talked too slow for Francis, who in-turn talked very quickly, which irritated Marlon, who subsequently envied Francis' ability to explain things so quickly and articulately. Marlon tried not to pause, but needed to on occasion in order to clarify his thought processes, even though Francis would sometimes use the opportunity to jump in.

"I can see his father being a very strict military man, Marlon. His family is a military family, going way back. His father fights in World War II. His grandfather fights in World War I. What do you think his mother is like?"

"His *father*..." began Marlon, accentuating the word *father* as a means of letting Francis know he wanted to speak more about him before moving on to Kurtz's mother. "...his *father* is a stern man. And because he is a career military man, his father has probably been gone from...what's Kurtz's name?"

"What?"

"Kurtz's first name. What is it?"

"It's Walter."

"Walter? Really?"

"Yes. Walter."

"Why, Walter?"

"It just fits. I don't have a better explanation than that, Marlon. He just seems like he'd be a Walter."

Marlon rolled his eyes and sighed.

"Okay, so, *Walter* did not get to see his father very often when he was a child, and he is raised primarily by his mother, who probably has an affinity for alcohol." Marlon paused for a moment to ponder what he had just said. "Yes, she's an alcoholic. She drinks in order to fill the void caused by her husband's absence," confirmed Marlon to himself.

"Why does his mother need to be an alcoholic?"

"Because alcoholism was very common among women in America in the 1930s, '40s, and '50s. I think a lot of people do not realize this. Especially among women whose husbands were domineering, which I believe that Walter's father would have been. As well as with women whose husbands would have spent a lot of time away from home, either because of military duty or for business, which again would have been the case with Walter's father."

The more Francis heard Marlon describe Kurtz's childhood the more he came to realize that he was describing his own young life as the son of an overbearing yet often absent father, and an alcoholic mother.

"Okay. I see," said Francis with a hint of empathy in his voice.

"This is good, Marlon. Please continue."

"And because of this, Walter would have needed a place of refuge to get away from things once in a while. Someplace outdoors, perhaps along a river or a lake or something, a place teaming with flowers and plants—his own little Garden of Eden."

"Does Walter…and that's good, by the way, Marlon."

"Thank you."

"Does Walter revere or revile his father? Does he love him or hate him? What does his father represent for him, Marlon?"

"Well, of course Walter would have some issues with his father, as all boys do growing up. But Walter, and again, as all boys do, wants his father's approval. He is very much in awe of his father, his uniform, the war stories he tells, his father's self-assuredness. Young Walter believed his was a world where goodness would always prevail, that all things were…uh, oh hell, I can't think of the word…"

Marlon looked at Francis, hoping his director could help him.

"It's a word used in religious circles and conversations. It's another way of saying that things are willed by God."

"Uh, I'm not sure, Marlon. Oh, uh, providence…divine providence!"

"Yes, that's it."

"I knew my Catholic upbringing would come in handy someday."

Marlon laughed.

"Walter came to believe that all things were providentially ordained. And he thinks this because his father spoke in these kinds of religious terms, but in a very politicized sort of way."

"So, Kurtz's religion and his patriotism are somewhat intertwined, is that what you're saying?"

"Yes, Francis. They are. And this is not something new or unique."

"No. Of course not. The blurring of lines between religion and government goes back to the ancient world, and it still happens in the United States, even though there's supposed to be a separation between church and state."

"Right."

"Yes. I can see that, Marlon. But I want to get back to the riverbank for a moment," said Francis upon noticing that his star actor was losing steam.

"Sure."

"So, would you say that the riverbank kind of symbolized, or encapsulated, much of what young Walter believed in?"

There was a pause in the conversation while Marlon thought for a moment.

"In terms of what, Francis? I'm not…"

"Okay. Let me phrase that differently, Marlon. And sorry for interrupting," apologized Francis after seeing Marlon look away.

"Yet again!"

"Sorry, Marlon."

"That's okay. I'm getting used to it." Marlon paused and looked around, seemingly distracted. Francis was afraid to say anything out of fear it would be construed as him interrupting his lead actor again. "What I was going to say, Francis, is that I'm not sure what you're talking about when you say 'what young Walter believed in'. I don't think we've discussed what young Walter actually did believe in."

"No, you're right, Marlon. We haven't," replied Francis, who was getting irritated by Marlon's slow delivery and need for detail. "I was speaking more in terms of young Walter's personal perception and understanding of the world, perhaps even his own little mythological take on things—of the world, of history, and of America for that matter—because we all have skewed, even fanciful, ideas about these things when we are young."

"Even as adults we have and maintain certain myths and fantasies about ourselves and our world."

"Oh, absolutely, Marlon. I couldn't agree with you more."

Francis was then quick to stop talking in order to cede the floor to Marlon, hoping he would say more about Walter Kurtz and the things that had shaped his mindset as a child.

"What is it that the young Walter Kurtz believes, Marlon?"

The star actor simply shrugged his shoulders and looked away.

"Maybe I'm not explaining this well enough, Marlon. I'm talking about how he perceives his country, his world, and the events that are unfolding in his young life. I'm not really looking for detail here, but rather his general perceptions of the world as a young boy living during the mid-1940s. Does that make sense, Marlon?"

"Well, yes…"

"So, does his spot down by the river kind of represent all that is good and right in his world, at least as young Walter understands these things?"

"Yes. Yes, it does…"

"Sorry, Marlon, but I just wanted to add that young Walter can in effect shape his own reality down by the river, basically because he has the space and the freedom to do so."

"Just like we all do, Francis. Just like Walter still does when he's a renegade colonel in the United States Army operating inside Cambodia."

"Yes. Good point. Please continue, Marlon."

"Well, barring any further interruptions, I will try and answer your question, Francis. Yes, the spot down by the river does come to represent something much bigger, because even though he loved his mother and father, things were never quite right at home. His father made him and his mother nervous, simply because they were not comfortable with his aggressive way of doing things. And for some reason, he was not aware that he needed to treat them differently than he did the soldiers under his command. So, between his over-bearing father, and his alcoholic mother, young Walter needed that place where he could sort everything out and make it right, if that makes sense, Francis."

"Yes, it certainly does."

"And yes, I believe his place, or spot, down by the river would have represented all that was good and right in the world, or at least the way in which he wanted the world to be."

"I like the river idea here. And maybe we could incorporate it into the movie somehow. What do you think?"

"Sure," said Marlon in noncommittal fashion.

"It could be a kind of river symbolism thing…"

Marlon shook his head as if he did not understand.

"One where the river of his childhood—his little getaway—represents purity. And then as an adult fighting a war in Cambodia, the river—maybe the Mekong—represents lies and corruption…"

"That's kind of what Conrad does with the Thames and the

Congo River in his book."

"He does?" asked the director, surprised by Marlon's knowledge of this.

"Yes. Didn't you read the book, Francis?" replied Marlon with a hint of tongue-in-cheek haughtiness in his voice.

"Ha, ha, Marlon."

"And he's received a certain amount of criticism for it, too."

"I thought you just recently heard about Conrad's book, Marlon? How would you know about this?"

"I said I only recently read Conrad's book. I certainly heard of it, and of Conrad, and the controversies surrounding the book."

"Why didn't you say anything about it until now?"

"You didn't ask me."

Francis shook and vigorously scratched his head in a clear attempt to show his frustration.

"Okay, Marlon. So before I try to make some kind of comparison between a river in the Western world with one in the Far East, please tell me how Joseph Conrad has been criticized for doing that," said the director, who thought he was about to insert a new idea into the conversation, only to be unexpectedly diverted.

"Well," began Marlon, looking unsure of himself. "Conrad has been accused of trying to make the case that the Thames, and England for that matter, represents or symbolizes civilization and progress, while the Congo and the Congo River represent things backward, wild and savage."

"That's interesting. I didn't know that. Was Conrad criticized for that back in the day, when he was alive, or is that something more recent?"

"It's something more recent."

"Because that's a fear I have with making this movie. I'm afraid I'll fuck something up, and it will be seen by future generations as being backwards, allowing the movie—all this time, money and effort—to be completely dismissed."

"Do you want this movie to live—to be relevant—forever, Francis?"

"I'd like it to be relevant for many decades to come, just like Conrad's book."

Francis reflected for a moment before circling back around to the idea he was previously going to introduce.

"My compare and contrast of the two rivers will be different than Conrad's, though, Marlon."

"How so?"

"There will be that initial, seemingly stark contrast between the two, because that's how Walter himself understands it to a certain extent. But then later, as an adult in Cambodia fighting a war, maybe then he comes to realize that the river as a child, and all it represented to him back then, was really just a lie, a fairytale or myth that he had been lead to believe, only he didn't know this as a kid because he was too young and innocent."

"Sure. I can see that. I've got another idea, Francis."

"Okay, I wasn't done explaining mine, but let's hear it."

"It's something that just came to me. If I wait too long I'll forget it."

"Okay. Go ahead, Marlon."

"I can also see Walter, as a kid, lying on a rug on the living room floor the morning after the Japanese attack on Pearl Harbor…"

"That's probably more detail than we need, Marlon."

"Just hear me out," argued Marlon, annoyed by the interruption. "He and his mother are listening to President Roosevelt trying to calm the nation. And by the way, the real reason that Roosevelt addressed the nation the way he did was not necessarily simply because of what the Japanese did."

"No?"

"Well, yes, it was obviously because of the attack on Pearl Harbor, Francis, but it was also intended to stem the tide of the American propaganda machine that quickly began churning out all kinds of imagery of America's new enemy—the Japanese—ones intended to stimulate urgency, fear, and hatred for them."

"I remember that, Marlon. You're right. The Japanese were depicted as snakes slithering up out of the Pacific and into homes across America, poised to rape and murder its mothers and daughters. They were portrayed as vicious, bloodthirsty sub-humans, driven by a primordial desire to quench their instinctual lust for killing and even sexual gratification. It was unbelievable stuff, yet everybody bought into it. Thinking back now, it was actually a bit disturbing."

"Yeah, I remember that, too. So anyway, as I was saying…"

"Yes. As you were saying."

"Walter would sit or lie on the living room rug every evening after dinner, listening to the radio reports covering the war in Europe and the South Pacific. He hears the stories of how the Japanese, as well as the Germans, were ingesting those around them, devouring all who were weak and unable to defend themselves."

"Does Walter feel scared? You would think so. I know I was afraid of the war, and of the Germans and Japanese."

"He's afraid, of course. But he still felt safe, nonetheless. The attentive love of his mother was like a security blanket for Walter."

"I thought his mother was a drunk, Marlon."

"Well, yes, but she's more attentive when Walter's father is away on military duty. In an ironic twist, it makes her less scared and lonely when he's not around. She actually drinks less."

"Okay, I can see that," said Francis while slowly nodding his head.

Marlon studied his director's face for a moment, gauging the validity of his interest in what he was saying. Convinced Francis was engaged, he continued.

"So, despite the fact that this was a time of war, Walter still reveled in these carefree days of his youth. He possessed a kind of naïve notion, or something, that allowed him to believe things would always be like this, that he would forever sit on the rug after dinner, comforted by the soothing voices coming from the radio and the presence of his mother."

"You mentioned that his father is gone on military duty. Does that mean he's gone off to fight in the war? Because to me that would make sense."

"Yes, Walter's father is sent to the South Pacific."

"What does he do there?"

"He is there to coordinate and lead Allied clandestine units in the liberation of the Pacific islands from the Japanese."

"Does he survive and come back home?"

"Yes, he survives. I think it's important for our story that Walter's dad survives."

"Why is that, Marlon?"

"Well, it gives Walter something to live up to. What I mean is that Walter has to follow in his father's footsteps. If his father died it might have turned Walter away from the military."

"Not necessarily, Marlon. He might feel all the more that he has to follow in his father's footsteps and join the military."

"Well, perhaps, but I can see his father surviving and coming home a war hero, and that's the image that Walter has to live up to."

"What is his return home like?"

"I would imagine that it is long-awaited and joyful, very celebratory like most World War II homecomings, or at least the ones portrayed in *Life* magazine. His father looks perfect in his army uniform, his medals gleaming in the sun. It's just like a scene in one of those post-World War II propaganda pieces put out by Hollywood by the dozens after the war."

"Just like the ones you were in, right?"

"Right, Francis," said Marlon, rolling his eyes. Marlon always despised the assertion that he acted in a lot of World War II movies that celebrated war and were overtly patriotic in nature. Francis knew this and was simply teasing his star actor.

"In September of 1945, Walter's father, Major Edward Kurtz, returned home…"

"Major Edward Kurtz. Nice, Marlon. You have the month, and everything."

"Yes. I need these kind of details, Francis, in order to better understand my character. You know that."

"Yes. I know. Sorry to interrupt."

Marlon rolled his eyes.

"In September of 1945, Major Edward Kurtz returned home from the Pacific. Walter and his mother met him on the Fort McCoy airport runway that warm late summer afternoon. When he first stepped out of the plane he looked like a mythological figure. The heat rising up from the hot tarmac and the airplane engines are creating that blurry effect you see out in the desert or up ahead on a tar road on a hot day. Walter watched his father slowly emerge from that blurry mirage. He looked like some kind of god to his young eyes in his handsome army uniform with his medals gleaming in the sun. It didn't look real to Walter, but rather like some scene out of a movie. It was a very surreal experience for him."

"That's good, Marlon. It would make a hell of a movie scene. You've got to stop coming up with all these great ideas."

"Why?"

"Because I want to put them all in the movie, and we just don't have room for them."

"Okay. I'll stop."

"I'm just kidding, of course. So, tell me this, Marlon…how does his father's return affect Walter?"

"Well, Walter is of course in awe of his father. The war, and seeing him on the tarmac that day seems to have made his father even more awe-inspiring in the eyes of young Walter."

"What about Walter's mother? What have the war years done to her?"

"His mother has become frail. The war years have taken a toll on her."

"Even though she's happier and doesn't drink as much?"

"Yeah, but she still drinks and it's still hard on her. She's a better mother, and she's happier than she was, but she's still not happy. Walter's father doesn't even notice that she is looking infirm. He's too full of enthusiasm about America's victory. He could not be bothered to ask his wife how she is. He's the kind of guy who cannot see beyond himself and his own interests. He thinks his wife is weak, anyway. He'd much rather talk about America's victory in war than coddle his wife. And he only pays attention to Walter, for that matter, if he's willing to engage him in his patriotic rhetoric."

"And I would assume that Walter is eating this stuff up."

"Walter is feeding off of his father's talk of patriotism and bravery. He begins thinking about himself one day coming home a war hero, talking proudly of America and its brave men, just like his father was doing."

"Does his father say anything in particular to the boy? Does he try to offer up any sort of lesson for Walter, or is Walter too young to grasp anything of this magnitude?"

"Edward has a talk with Walter, later on, after all the hubbub has died down."

"Okay. Where does Edward take his son to have this talk?"

"Huh?"

Marlon lost his train of thought.

"Where does this talk take place? I'm trying to envision it."
Marlon paused.

"Probably down by the river."

"Perfect, Marlon."

"He's not the kind of guy who would talk about important or relevant things in front of his wife. I can imagine him being very sexist, and doesn't believe his wife, or any woman for that matter, would understand."

"Tell me the story of this talk, Marlon. Paint me a picture."

Marlon again paused, pondering what he was going to say about Walter's conversation with his father. Then he began.

"The sun shone bright. It was a late September afternoon. The sun's rays are glittering off the river like diamonds. Seagulls are flying overhead, hovering in place against the strong upper-air currents. Flies are buzzing around, attracted by the smell of dead fish and humid heat encapsulated in the mud and thick grass growing along the river."

"Nice, Marlon."

"Thank you. Do you mind if I proceed, Francis?" asked Marlin, irritated by the interruption.

"By all means."

"They sat in silence upon their arrival, both soaking in nature's majesty while Walter's father pondered what great words of wisdom he wanted to convey to his son about the war. Walter watched as his father gazed off into the distance. His father's eyes sparkled with self-righteousness as he seemed to be looking beyond the water, as if envisioning some sacred text he was about to read from. He talks in abstract terms, about good and evil, and about truth. He talks about lies, and how much he hates lies."

"Does he say anything specific to him?"

"Nothing that I can speak to right now. Walter doesn't understand a whole lot that his father is saying to him. But it sticks with him, nonetheless, if that makes any sense. His father does tell him one thing, though."

"What's that?" asked Francis after a bit of a pause by Marlon.

"He tells Walter that the truth, no matter how deep you bury it, will always sift its way to the surface."

"*The truth, no matter how deep you bury it…*"

"Right, Francis, *will always sift its way to the surface*," said

Marlon, finishing his director's sentence after he paused.

"That's good, Marlon! Where did you get that?"

"What do you mean?"

"What philosopher, or book? The 'truth will always sift its way to the surface' thing? I like it."

"I really don't know where I got that from. I think it just came to me now. I guess it's just something I've learned from experience."

"That's pretty good, Marlon. I'm impressed."

"Well, as good as that might be, what Walter remembers most about this talk is how the self-righteous gleam in his father's eyes disappears after he says this, and how it is replaced by a look of despair. And I think this *look* on his father's face stays with Walter, haunting him even into his adult life. He never forgets it."

"Whoa, Marlon! Now that's not something you just came up with. That sounds like it could almost be a personal experience, or something. Is there a story behind that?" asked Francis somewhat hesitantly, not wanting to sound too much like he was prying.

"No. I can't say that there is," said Marlon after a substantial pause.

"Okay," replied Francis, sounding disappointed that Marlon did not elaborate. "Well, that's really good, though, Marlon. That was a fascinating twist at the end. Great story, and great insight into Kurtz. It's so good I'm tempted to try and stick this into the movie, too, maybe as a flash-back or something. Christ, I've got too much footage the way it is, and we haven't even shot anything with you in it yet. I have no idea how I am going to keep this thing under three hours. You know what you could do, though, Marlon?"

"What?" said Marlon reluctantly while looking in the other direction.

"You could help me with the ending. I'm having trouble with how this thing is going to end."

"Okay. But I need to continue developing the person of Walter Kurtz first. We'll see what happens when I get to that point."

"Alright, Marlon. Keep working on this. I really like it, and maybe in the end it will shed some light on how to end this damn thing so we can all go home. I've got to go, Marlon. I will see you tomorrow."

Francis sped off as Marlon watched him, surprised at the suddenness of his director's exit.

CHAPTER 6

Marlon paced around the houseboat, thumbing through Francis' copy of *Heart of Darkness*, as well as studying the palm trees, the sky, the sunset and ultimately the darkness. He was trying to envisage, understand, and comprehend the man whom he would soon be expected to portray, to create, to bring to life. Marlon was trying to demystify and demythologize Conrad's Kurtz, but yet at the same time keep his mystique and mythological qualities. Marlon was looking for little bits and pieces of Kurtz in all that surrounded him physically, as well as all that which filled him emotionally and spiritually, with the hopes of eventually illuminating Kurtz without despoiling Conrad's masterful chiaroscuro portrait of the man. He knew that there would be, or at least should be, a lot of himself in the Kurtz character, and that his director was steering him in that direction. This frightened Marlon. He never felt comfortable exposing too much of himself, neither off- nor on-screen.

Marlon was frustrated that very little of his dialogue as Colonel Kurtz had been written yet, and that Francis was actually leaning on him to come up with material. Normally Marlon would have welcomed this opportunity. Twenty-five years ago, he would have relished the freedom to build such a momentous character from the ground up. Marlon could have ranted and dialoged for days on end, or at least that is how he understands his past-self now.

Marlon's youth follows him around, haunts, goads, chastises, criticizes, makes his current-self feel fat, old, and insecure. He thought about how twenty-five years ago he more than likely would have been playing the role of Captain Willard, perhaps even one of the young draftees on the boat if the role was big enough, with his shirt off and his devil-may-care attitude on full display. And off-set he would not have been staying in a houseboat by himself out in the middle of nowhere, but rather in a nearby town or city, drinking, carousing, and chasing women. Or at least that is how he understands his past-self now. Marlon does not necessarily long for his younger days, but rather he wishes the young Marlon Brando would simply go away and let him age and get old without constantly hovering over him like some flashing neon movie marque.

There was so much that Marlon wanted to do with his role as Walter Kurtz, which only served to contribute to his annoyance and frustration with the slow pace of the filming, as well as the writing processes. But in reality, Marlon was actually very much okay with the lack of progress on the part of Francis and his team of writers, particularly in regard to the script. The fact is that Marlon did not trust anyone other than himself with writing the story of Walter Kurtz, especially the Kurtz dialogue. Marlon was intending to take control of this aspect of the movie, but just did not feel he knew his character well enough yet to do so. His director apparently did not have the time or inclination to flesh out Walter Kurtz's history, much less his mindset and psyche, despite the fact that the entire movie was premised on the mindset and psyche of this one particular character, one with gigantic shoes to fill considering the fact he is based on one of Western civilization's most recognizable literary personalities.

A steady rain began falling. Marlon was bored and restless. He had no television, and his small radio offered only local Philippine and American Armed Forces programming, neither of which interested him. He tried to come up with storyline ideas in his head, but his thoughts were too scrambled. Marlon tried to write some of his thoughts down on paper, but his handwriting has always been illegible and feared he would not be able to later comprehend anything he wrote down anyway.

"Do you have a typewriter, Rafael?" asked Marlon of his Filipino houseboy while simulating the punching of keys with his two index fingers.

Rafael looked befuddled at first, and then suddenly seemed to understand Marlon's request.

"Oh yes, a typewriter," said Rafael in choppy English. He then walked off. Marlon assumed Rafael was going to another room or a storage area on the boat. But when Rafael did not return after thirty minutes, Marlon went looking for him, coming to realize that the Filipino houseboy was no longer on the boat. As it turned out, Rafael had walked to a nearby village to get Marlon an old 1950's era Olympia typewriter.

"You didn't have to do that, Rafael," said the humbled American actor.

"No problem, sir," replied the houseboy, who then bowed and walked off, but not before strategically placing the typewriter on a desk near a window overlooking the river and handing Marlon a large stack of typing paper.

Marlon thanked Rafael and then proceeded to stare at the typewriter as if confused. It is what he wanted, but now that it was there he was not quite sure what to do with it. He was expecting something more modern, and electric, not such a big, heavy, clunky monstrosity the likes his mother used to own. It had been years since Marlon typed anything. He was never any good at it in the first place. He began to reconsider the idea of using pen and paper, but did not want to offend the man who made such an effort to ascertain the heavy contraption. Marlon paced around the room, stopping periodically to study the big metal typewriter. He felt intimidated by it for some reason. Even though nobody was around to see, he still felt self-conscious about the prospect of loading the paper and attempting to write cohesive thoughts and ideas by way of such a large mechanical instrument.

Clunk…clunk…clunk…

Marlon began typing.

```
Marlon Brando
```

Marlon typed his name just to see what it would look like. He liked the look of typed words on paper. Marlon loved looking through and reading movie scripts. He did not understand the need for such complicated formatting, however, preferring them in the format of fiction-style prose.

Clunk…clunk…clunk…

Marlon typed some more.

```
Walter Kurtz
```

Marlon was thinking of a title for what he was about to write. Ultimately, he simply typed the name of his character, Walter Kurtz, at the top of the page. Marlon would do this several times before getting into a flow or rhthymn, starting and stopping, crumpling up at least twenty sheets of paper before finding a groove. Initially Marlon began writing in his own voice, that is, from the perspective of Marlon Brando. The more times that this approach failed or proved inadequate, the more Marlon came to realize that he was doing it all wrong, that he should be writing from the perspective of the man he would be playing. Marlon began writing from the standpoint of Walter Kurtz, the first major step in the process of the two figures melding together into one.

* * *

```
Even though I shuddered to think of
American boys dying in the squalid jungles
of Southeast Asia, I knew it was time for
America to stand up and do what was right in
South Vietnam. I understood what my personal
duties were, and was not about to let my
country down in what was quite possibly its
greatest moment of need.
   I was a top army specialist with field
experience in everything from logistics to
hand-to-hand combat, but was also a very
indispensable man at Fort Wayne. I had to
call in many old favors, wrangling for about
a year before receiving an envelope marked
'TOP SECRET' in 1964, containing my orders
for Vietnam.
   In the days leading up to my departure for
Southeast Asia, I tried hard to espouse to
my family the same confidence and certainty
that my father did before leaving for war in
the Pacific during World War II. I would
```

leave with much sadness, knowing that I would deeply miss my wife and two young children, but with no regret or vacillation. This was a task I had been preparing myself for all my life, and was more than ready and willing to carry the cross of duty until my mission was complete.

In my mind, as I understood things, I was going to Vietnam as a crusader of light, staving off the encroaching darkness threatening to eclipse and extinguish the good and virtuous spark of humanity. I went to Vietnam believing I was defending all the things I once held dear--my country, freedom and democracy, my faith in God, etc. I knew I might never experience any of these things again, conceding that death would be an acceptable price in order to help preserve them for my children. That in order to help save these treasures, I would have to leave the safety and familiarity of my home and country and enter into a world that was different, and much more dangerous, than the one I knew.

I initially did not go to Vietnam as a soldier, however, but rather as part of a fact-finding mission to determine why U.S. military policy in Vietnam had failed so miserably, despite the fact that by 1964 the U.S. had already spent millions of dollars, as well as had thousands of advisors and strategists on the ground in Vietnam. My report more than ruffled a few feathers within both the military establishment and the U.S. government, and was immediately restricted. Neither the Joint Chiefs of Staff, nor the Johnson Administration, would take any action in response to my inquiry.

To say I was frustrated is an understatement. I knew then and there that President Johnson had no real interest in winning the war, at least not in the short-term. Out of frustration I requested entrance into the elite 5th Special Forces Group, but was denied because at age thirty-eight I was considered too old for its intense training program. When I threatened to quit the military altogether I was finally accepted. I returned to Vietnam in 1966 as a member of the Special Forces.

* * *

Marlon looked over his work. He was reasonably satisfied with what he had come up with. His intention was not necessarily for his words and ideas to become part of the script, but rather to bring the character—the person—of Walter Kurtz to life. Marlon laughed out loud, causing his houseboy, Rafael, to look in on him to see if Mr. Brando had a visitor whose entrance somehow eluded him. Marlon was laughing because he knew if the last passage was part of the movie script, it would offer the perfect spot for him to give one of his per usual finger-wagging monologues intended to educate and perhaps even shame other, seemingly ignorant, characters in the movie regarding some social or political issue, but were always really intended for the consumption of the audience. These were often nothing more than thinly-veiled lectures, attempts to teach and/or admonish, which were often charged by critics with cheapening the movie, as well as Brando's acting performance.

Marlon used to welcome these opportunities to speak out about the many social or political causes that he cared very deeply about. But these scenes in such movies as *Sayonara* and *The Ugly American* have not held up very well over time, and Marlon understands this. In less than twenty years, these attempts to enlighten have become old, passé, and out of touch with the cynicism and mistrust of the '60s and '70s hippy and anti-establishment generation. Marlon made it a point to avoid a similar rant in what was a very obvious place for one in his make-shift script, even though his own mindset was that of someone from the post-World War II generation, which usually responded well to lectures and a good scolding.

Marlon did not believe in the effectiveness of subtlety, in his acting, nor in the message he wanted a movie to convey. With both he wanted to jar the viewer out of their complacency. But times and people have changed since the 1950s, not just in America, but around the world. The legitimacy of old institutions and systems of power and authority have been called into question, even becoming harbingers of mistrust in the minds of many, especially young people. The reexamination of the status quo in America has rendered many of Marlon's movie roles, as well as his acting methods and techniques, obsolete, perhaps even offensive. His characters were almost always loud and arrogant, and so was Marlon. That loudness and arrogance often translated into an image of power and authority, both on and off screen for Marlon. But this was no longer the case in the mid-1970s. The political and social footing had shifted underneath Marlon's aging and unsteady feet, and he was still unsure how to navigate it.

CHAPTER 7

Two weeks after receiving my orders, I was helicoptered into the dense green jungle of eastern Cambodia, and base-camp Tigerden, which would be my headquarters and home in-between forays into the jungle. It lay deep in the thick foliage for reasons of concealment. No flag flew above this bastard-child, as the country that birthed it would not allow its colors to fly overhead.

The men whom I would be commanding had already been there for a couple weeks. I was immediately greeted by my radioman. We exchanged titles over the loud sounds of helicopter blades slapping the air with such force it nearly laid the nearby vegetation flat as it ascended back into the sky. I watched the Huey fly away with some trepidation, realizing I may never leave this place.

The rest of Green Tiger was waiting for me in the makeshift strategy and command center, a hut made of bamboo and thatch. They rose to their feet and saluted me as I entered. Wanting to keep the meeting informal, I immediately invited everyone to be at ease. They sat at picnic tables, the kind you would see in a park somewhere in

Midwestern America. There were several detailed maps of eastern Cambodia on the walls. In addition to the radioman, I had four Green Beret special operative soldiers, and one regular army sergeant. Sergeant Wilke was a grizzled, yet deceptively refined veteran of the Korean War who has been in Southeast Asia since the mid-1950s. He is an expert in the field of guerrilla warfare, and well-versed in several Southeast Asian languages, including certain dialects spoken by the many montagnard tribes living in Cambodia and Vietnam. In the early 1960s Wilke played a major role in a U.S. funded program to arm and train these indigenous peoples to fight the Vietminh, but has since been discontinued, at least officially. Rounding out the crew were two South Vietnamese who would act as interpreters and advisors regarding Vietnamese habit and custom.

 The four Green Berets were newly indoctrinated with no real battle experience, but were heavily trained, disciplined, highly motivated, and very deadly, nonetheless. The first one I met was Henderson, an African-American from Alabama whose impoverished childhood in the segregated deep south had already given him a permanent 'thousand-yard stare' usually worn by veterans of the bush, like Wilke. Strapinski was a blond-haired, blue-eyed all-American type from Oklahoma. His nickname was 'killer' because his Green Beret drill instructor said it was, and vowed to come over to Vietnam and kick his ass if he did not live up to that name. Edwards was from Houston, Texas. Strapinski might have been nicknamed 'killer', but Edwards looked as if he was born to be one. You could see it in his eyes. They were gray and cold, a pair of unnerving windows to a soul that looked as if it was unable to harbor sympathy or remorse. Finally, there was LeBetre. He was half-French, half-American Indian. His father was a French soldier who fought in World War II, moving to America at the war's conclusion because he could not stand the thought of living in the same country with people who sided with the Nazis, marrying a native woman in his newly adopted homeland. LeBetre's physical traits leaned heavily towards that of his mother, while French elitism, inherited from his father, shone brightly through his brown exterior and Green Beret conditioning.

Wilke, who was older with much more combat experience, was suspicious of me at first. He heard of me, and thought I had simply positioned myself for a short stint in the combat zone with the hopes of a quick catapult to the rank of full bird colonel. His line of thinking changed somewhat, however, when he found out that I had already served in Korea. For my part, I would make certain concessions to the career grunt, showing my reverence by letting Wilke know I would be relying heavily on his expertise.

Sergeant Wilke was a legend in the world of covert operations, living almost exclusively in the jungles of Vietnam and Cambodia since the end of the Korean conflict, preferring it to the comforts of Western civilization. He is both loved and revered in an almost god-like manner by many of the montagnard peoples living there. Wilke lobbied hard on their behalf for continued American assistance after the Central Intelligence Agency pulled the plug on the program on the heels of the Kennedy assassination, leaving the montagnard peoples to die at the hands of revenge-minded Vietnamese. Wilke was successful in ascertaining the resumption of food, medicine, as well as weapon shipments to the various montagnard tribes who bravely fought the Vietminh on behalf of the Americans. Wilke even went to Capital Hill to plead the case of the montagnard people, where legend has it he still had jungle mud on his boots and Vietminh blood on his shirt.

  I was intrigued by Wilke and spent a lot of time studying him as we tried to pass the initial long, hot, seemingly endless moments of inactivity, and was fascinated by Wilke's animal-like mannerisms and instincts. He walked in and out of the jungle as quiet as a ghost and seemed to have eyes in the back of his head, catching me staring at him from behind on several occasions. Sudden sounds emanating from the jungle could not catch Wilke unprepared for fight-or-flight no matter how quickly they erupted. Years of constantly living only seconds away from death by way of man, nature, and beast, has sharpened his senses like that of fine cutlery, putting him in perfect harmony with the jungle.

  For the first couple of weeks after my arrival, we did not do much except sit and clean the moisture from our weapons, study maps, and get acclimated to our jungle surroundings. That is, everybody except for Wilke. Instead, Wilke prodded and probed the outskirts of the basecamp, moving out a little further each day, trying to get what he called a "whiff" of the enemy. I assumed that Wilke was speaking metaphorically, but he was not. When the wind blew from a certain direction he claimed to be able to smell the Vietcong, contending that their fecal matter and urine have a distinct odor because of their primarily rice and fish diet. He warned the men that theirs does too, and to think about that the next time they felt the need to piss or take a shit when upwind of the enemy.

Wilke gave one more admonition, this time one of action and not words, intended to put an end to the growing nonchalant atmosphere stemming from a subsiding sense of fear among the men. The four Green Beret soldiers were sitting around a small fire, talking and laughing, trying to shrug off the monotony of another day. Unbeknownst to them, up above in a fir tree was Wilke. He had been up there for a while, becoming more and more disgusted by their playground banter and silly antics. He had with him a small gibbon monkey that he caught earlier with a snare, kept alive for precisely this moment. Wilke took out his knife and cut the monkey's stomach open, sending a large stream of blood down to the ground, first running along the leaves and branches before slowly dripping onto the four men.

"Is it raining?" asked Strapinski who then looked up just in time to have a couple beads of blood land on his face

"What the fuck?" yelled Edwards. Then without warning, bullets began to tear through their fire, sending flames and sparks in all directions as well as the four Green Beret soldiers in an attempt to flee the once placid spot that had suddenly erupted into pandemonium. Scrounging for weapons so they could defend themselves, only LeBetre and Edwards were able to find their rifles. They frantically sprayed the treetops with machine gun fire, but not before Wilke was able to make his way back to the ground, yelling for the two shooters to hold their fire. They, along with

Henderson and Strapinski, who had not yet found their rifles, stopped in their tracks, and the mass panic was over as fast as it started. With everyone's complete and undivided attention, Wilke threw the now dead monkey on the ground in front of them and pointed to it.

"That's you right now—-all of you—-if Charlie wanted it that way! This ain't a fucken game, boys. Get your shit together or you will all find yourselves in body bags, and damn fucken quick. Lose focus again out here, and believe me, you stupid son-of-a-bitches, Charlie will rip out your fucking guts. Do you understand!"

With his audience shook up beyond measure, Wilke walked away, leaving them to work out the details of what they had just seen and heard. He accomplished what he set out to do, which was to scare the living hell out of the men, and now considered the Green Berets one step closer in their preparation to do battle with the Vietcong.

* * *

With a pair of reading-glasses down on the tip of his nose, Marlon, head tilted up slightly, carefully read through his latest installment of the prequel story of Walter Kurtz. He chuckled to himself, realizing that unlike the previous entry, this time he had in fact inserted a very 1950s-eque monologue intended to educate and admonish, one coming from the mouth of Sergeant Wilke. Marlon could not help himself. Old habits die hard for him, and many never died at all, no matter how much effort he put into killing them off. Marlon could vividly envision the scene of Wilke reproaching the young soldiers, seeing it in his mind's eye as something emblematic of his early films set in the 1950s. Marlon wished a stern lecture would be enough to persuade or move people. He once believed this were true, but not anymore. On cue, Marlon could always give a convincing, condemning, and forceful speech or diatribe about pretty much anything, whether he believed it himself or not. And in time he grew to hate the fact that he could simply turn this skill or talent on and off so quickly and with such masterful precision. Marlon came to consider himself a great liar as opposed to a good actor. But now, as a man in his mid-50s with only one successful movie role in the past decade, and many failed attempts at making an impact in regard to various social justice issues, Marlon would settle for being a convincing liar. It has been over ten years since Marlon began to suspect that his skills of persuasion were eroding, but only recently has he come to understand that his audience is not the same anymore either, and that many of them have never even heard of Stanley Kowalski and Terry Malloy, nor would they blindly follow them or any other character that Marlon was playing.

CHAPTER 8

Marlon always dreamed of writing a screenplay, but knew he would never be taken seriously as a writer, especially considering the fact that many of his movies have been screen adaptations of novels, the current movie set included. But Francis Coppola's movie is little more than a respectful nod to the Conrad book. Ninety-nine percent of the story-line needs to be filled in. Marlon has always wanted to generate characters, plots, and sub-plots. He has contributed dialogue to a lot of his movies, mostly his own characters, but it is not the same as plot and character development. Marlon knew that the characters and plot twists he was formulating were not going to make it into the movie, but rather were simply a means to the development of the Kurtz character.

    Marlon read the pages of work he had come up with thus far, correcting the spelling and grammar with a pen, and even re-typing several of them, fearing his writing skills would be judged negatively by his director should he see them. Marlon marveled at how he managed to put certain elements of himself in all the characters he came up with, whether they be from previous movie-roles, or perhaps aspects of his own many and varied personality traits. Part of Marlon was the fearful small town boy, Strapinski, because as a young man growing up in Nebraska he could not live up to his father's expectations, which made him nervous and unsure of himself. Another part of Marlon was the fearless, cold-blooded killer that he perceived Edwards to be. This was Marlon when he was in his twenties, at the height of his acting powers in *Streetcar*, *Waterfront*, and *Wild One*. Edwards was who Marlon trained himself to be, at least when the camera was rolling, and whom he wished to spend the rest of his life as, despite that fact that Edwards is despicable. But Edwards cannot be hurt or wounded, at least not emotionally. He is pure brute through and through. Edwards is never vulnerable. And if he is, he does not even realize it, anyway. Marlon knows he can never be like Edwards, just like he can never be like those young, fearless characters he played during his most formidable acting years. Not anymore, anyway.

Whereas Strapinski and Edwards represented the parallel opposites of Marlon's youth, it was Wilke whom Marlon hoped to have become at this point in his life and career. Wilke is Marlon Brando transcended, as well as the transcended version of all the unevolved, one-dimensional U.S. military officers from the World War II era, whose image of American righteousness and bravery were transposed onto movie screens during and immediately after the war. Wilke is the Christ who upturned the moneychanger's tables in the temple, and Gautama Buddha who loosed himself of this world in order to see into the next. He is part Tarzan, and part Nietzsche's Ubermensch. Wilke is everything that Marlon so desperately wants himself to be, and all the things that the United States military establishment fears Walter Kurtz has in fact become.

* * *

Startled and a bit unnerved by Wilke's demonstration, I found it hard to sleep that night. At two o'clock in the morning, my adrenaline still peaked, I stepped out of my shelter to get some air. Unlike during Wilke's earlier rampage, the jungle now seemed to be comfortable and at peace with itself, just the slightest amount of insect and animal sounds to keep the quiet from completely pervading. Without the wind blowing through its leaves or the moonlight illuminating its shape, as was the case on this dark and still evening, the plant life has no voice in the night. It can only sit quietly and wait for the light of day to make it whole again. In the daylight, the jungle is a beautiful garden, a panoramic spectrum of endless colors and life forms, flaunting all of nature's artistic and imaginative power. But hidden in the darkness, its external comeliness is shrouded in a nocturnal dinge illuminating the jungle's true colors, exposing it to be the den of thieves it really is.

I stood gazing out into the black night. I could see neither the jungle nor Wilke, who was walking out of the darkness and into my line of vision. Not until the stealth-like sergeant was about five feet away did I finally sense his presence.

"It's going to rain. I can feel it", said Wilke. His words ran up and down my spine. The suddenness of Wilke's presence startled me and sent my pulse racing even more than it already was. It happened so quickly, however, that I was not given time to lose my composer, for which I was grateful.

Wilke spent a lot of time perusing and studying the jungle. The montagnards had taught him their ancient methods of becoming one with the natural world, its ebb and flow, its shifting tides, and understanding one's role therein. Wilke believes that he has been able to survive for so long out in the jungle, mentally as well as physically, because he understands himself to be merely one of literally millions of living organisms that not only live in the jungle, but constitute or make up the jungle.

No more had Wilke entered his quarters before the sky opened up, dousing the unseen jungle, and me, with nourishing water from the heavens, followed by flashes of lightning which momentarily cut their way through the darkness and for a split second cast a light on nature's Jezebel.

Even though there was an obvious mutual respect between me and Wilke, it was also becoming apparent that we had very different ways of interpreting Green Tiger's mission, and subsequently, contrasting ideas on how to conduct operations. Blame for this could be cast on the fact that up until now we had been living in two completely different worlds. Wilke learned a long time ago that the things he was taught as a young soldier at Basic Training have little if any relevance out in the bush. He has seen countless failed attempts made by man to destroy as well as carve up the jungle into geographically distinct sections, naming and henceforth attempting to place it under man's authority and dominion. But first-hand experience has taught Wilke that the jungle bows down before no man, much less obliges man's sense of duty to divide and conquer all that surrounds him. This sort of reasoning I could not yet comprehend, nor fathom. I initially believed that every situation and circumstance, including the things of nature, can be mastered by man, that God-inspired American ingenuity and know-how can triumph over any and all things. On the other hand, Wilke's many years of living under the green vegetative dome of the jungle—-nature's holy city, a living cathedral complete with timbered pillars and flowered votives—-has taught him that insurrection is futile, and that the jungle excommunicates all subversives by devouring them, first their mind and then their body.

The jungle does not consist solely of the various forms of lush plant life that covers its floor and ceiling. It is not merely the wild cats, monkeys, or snakes that prowl the greenery. Nor is it the bloodthirsty flies and mosquitoes that hover in its humid air, or the leeches that reside in its muddy waters, or the suffocating heat. And the jungle is certainly not the Americans and North Vietnamese who brave these elements in an attempt to kill one another. But brought together in an amalgamation of dissimilar living things competing with one another to stay alive, they become the jungle. Without these things the jungle would cease to exist, much in the same manner that the French needed Tonkin, Annam, and Cochinchina in order to be an empire. The jungle kingdom blinds its subjects of this reality, diverting their attention by keeping its diverse emporium embroiled in constant warfare. The various parts are too busy fighting and killing one another to realize they are doing so only for the sole benefit of their king, an amorphous lord whose altar is nothing more than a slaughter bench abundantly steeped with the flesh and blood of all who enter.

CHAPTER 9

"How old is our Kurtz?" asked Marlon.

"He's late-thirties or early-forties. He's no kid."

"I think our Kurtz would have fought in Korea."

"Yeah, I can see that, Marlon. He would have been about eighteen or nineteen at the time."

"And probably quite hungry for war, considering the political climate of the time—the whole Cold War thing. Plus, his family history would have expected it. His own sense of duty, and patriotism, would have wanted it…to go off to war, that is."

"What does he take away from Korea, Marlon?"

"What he takes away from Korea is that war is not as glamorous as it is in the movies, or in the way his father described it."

"Really? Say more."

"He grew up watching all the World War II movies of the late-forties, those American propaganda pieces, the kind of movies that I avoided making, even though a lot of people believe I did in fact make movies like that. I don't fucken know why, though."

Francis laughed, knowing that this was a very sensitive issue for Marlon.

"Even *The Men* was not like that."

"*The Men*, Marlon?"

"That was the first movie in which I wore a military uniform, my first movie, in fact."

"Oh, yes, yes."

"It was the story of a young man who becomes paralyzed from the waist down during World War II."

"Yes. Right. I remember."

"It does not have a miraculous or even a happy ending, necessarily. He stays paralyzed, and he really never even finds peace with his situation. The old World War II movies, so many of them, had a kind of fairy tale quality, a kind of sick, sappy, over-played patriotism, and a line dividing good and evil which is too clearly drawn."

"Do you think that you've been improperly lumped in with that genre of movie, the pro-American stuff that was coming out of Hollywood in the fifties with very little, if any, checks and balances on it?"

"Yes, I do think I've been improperly lumped into that category. In fact, I think that some of the movies I made *were* the checks and balances, as you put it, to all the other stuff coming out of Hollywood. But then things changed so quickly and so abruptly in the sixties, and the movies I made, the characters I played, got tossed in with everything else from that period."

"A lot of your characters, and movies you were in, had a very counter-cultural message to them." Francis waited for Marlon to concur before continuing, eventually doing so with a nod of his head. "But you're right, Marlon, because you weren't a hippy, or even a beatnik, in those early movies, but rather a hood or a thug, those roles—those characters—never made the cross-over into the sixties. And then in the sixties, you played characters who were over thirty, and so the youth—the hippies and the peaceniks—didn't identify with you then, either, despite the fact that your movies were in effect saying the same things the hippies at Woodstock and on college campuses were all trying to say."

"Yes, that pretty much sums it up."

"Are you bitter about the turn your legacy has taken? I mean, you are, and always will be considered one of the greatest actors ever. But you have to admit, Marlon, that the critics, and even the movie-going public, have not been very kind to you in recent years."

"Well, part of the problem is that I have never really been comfortable just being an actor. I have made comments in the past about how all actors are frauds. I always wanted to do more with acting than simply make interesting movies and to act well. I wanted to use it as a platform to enlighten people, to bring awareness to the ills of society, and ultimately as a means of eradicating the world's problems. This, of course, has not happened."

"Why do you think that is?"

"There's a lot of reasons why," said Marlon after a long pause. "I don't know if *anybody* can do this, much less an actor through the medium of Hollywood movies. But I certainly wish I could have done things differently."

"What would you have done differently?"

"Well, I would have tried a lot harder to not be constantly led around by my dick."

Francis burst out laughing. He did not expect this kind of answer.

"It's true, as ridiculous as it sounds. I wish I could have been more disciplined and more focused on what I really wanted to accomplish. Constantly chasing women leads to erratic behavior, and to unwanted consequences, and to people not respecting and even not trusting you."

"Do you think people haven't respected you as an artist, and perhaps as a person, because of your womanizing?"

"Oh, absolutely. A lot of people don't trust me. They think I'm a con-man, and a fraud, and that I'm just looking to get laid."

"But you yourself said you were a fraud. You can hardly blame people for thinking that about you when you yourself have said it."

"No, I don't blame them. But it's not because I said it that people think I'm a fraud, but rather because of my erratic behavior and bad choices. And then once I had a long list of failed relationships, and my kids had been affected so negatively by my actions, then people remembered that I once called myself a fraud, making it easy for people to think of me as a fraud, or even a freak and an oddball. And therein lies a lot of my regret. Not just for the failed relationships and the ways in which my kids have been affected by my celebrity and my bad or even weird behavior, but also for the fact that whenever I try to take up a particular social cause, my intentions are never taken seriously. Whether it's with civil rights for blacks, or the cause of the American Indian, my involvement, instead of helping to legitimize it, has only served to help keep it on the fringes, something that only the liberal whack-jobs have an interest in."

"What do you blame that on?"

"What do I blame that on?"

"Yes. What? Who? Why did things turn out the way they did?"

"Things turned out the way they did because of Marlon Brando."

"Marlon Brando the person, or Marlon Brando the actor?"

"That's a good point, Francis, but I've come to learn that there is no distinguishing the two. All my roles are extensions of myself, sometimes evolutions and sometimes even devolutions of myself. Marlon Brando the person and Marlon Brando the actor are one and the same."

"Will Kurtz be an extension of Marlon Brando?"

"Kurtz will be Marlon Brando, and vice-versa."

"Should Kurtz die in the movie, Marlon?"

"I think that Marlon Brando should die in the movie."

CHAPTER 10

Marlon's houseboy, Rafael, scurried in the direction of the star actor he was hired to serve upon hearing his distinct nasal voice wafting through the air of the otherwise quiet evening on the houseboat parked along the banks of the Pagsanjan River. As he entered into the area that Marlon was using as a makeshift office to write and research his role, he immediately came to realize that Mr. Brando was not speaking to, or beckoning him. Marlon was not talking to Rafael, or anyone else for that matter, but rather to himself. He was thinking, and mumbling, out loud, which is something Marlon has done for many years now as a way of organizing and clarifying his thoughts. Rafael watched and listened for a few moments, only because Marlon had his back to the door and was unaware that he was there.

"I will never understand why so many American Indians are willing to serve the American government as soldiers, fighting in its wars, some of which are being waged for the very same reasons that their own people and civilizations were pillaged and destroyed one-hundred years ago. Many have come to identify themselves completely with the United States and, perhaps unwittingly, have assumed the same imperialistic mindset as the very American system that reduced their ancestors to mere 'savages', as they are called. I don't understand why every man and woman, young and old, with Indian blood coursing through their veins, aren't resisting this. But unfortunately, many have fallen prey to the powers of assimilation, and soon they will no longer exist outside of the American system—the purveyor of lies, gluttony, and destruction—a system void of humanity and one

without hope."

These words caused Marlon to think about his five-year old daughter, Cheyenne, whom the American actor had with his Tahitian wife, Tarita Teriipaia. He has been worried for some time now about what will happen when the forces of Western civilization finally catch up with his daughter. Marlon knew they were coming for Cheyenne, and the rest of the Tahitian people for that matter, just like they have come for everybody else in the world's remote tropical, paradisiacal islands and cultures. Marlon shuddered to think of the challenges to come. He was contemplating retiring after this movie and living the rest of his life quietly in Tahiti with his family. But in reality, being there for any period of time has been a challenge for Marlon. He gets bored and restless very quickly. In the past, while living in Los Angeles, whenever Marlon would get into a fight with one of his wives, or simply became discontent, there was always a nearby bar, restaurant, lover's house, or perhaps even a distant movie-set he could soon escape to. Tahiti, on the other hand, provided miles of sandy beaches and exquisite tropical fauna, which ironically proved not enough space for Marlon, who has come to realize that at fifty years of age he is way too entrenched in things Western to ever free himself completely. Marlon has a sense of dread and foreboding that instead of living the rest of his life in Tahiti, he will spend his remaining years dying in Los Angeles, and so will his children.

* * *

After three months in the Cambodian jungle, Green Tiger had become a cohesive, fine-tuned group of soldiers, and an efficient killing machine. And kill we did, amassing an impressive enemy death toll. Edwards took great delight in the act of killing, and was also the most reckless at it, bringing instruction from me and disdain from Wilke. Strapinski, the self-proclaimed killer, displayed hesitation and was neither quick nor efficient about it. Wilke feared for the young Oklahoman's future. Henderson was solid, exhibiting no real weaknesses or emotion. LeBetre was good too, and so was I. But of course, Wilke was the best, the perfect jungle assassin, a consummate man-hunter. All the men were in awe of his abilities, especially LeBetre who watched and studied Wilke in an attempt to emulate his unique brand of jungle savvy.

Even though LeBetre looked like his Indian mother, he considered himself French and made every effort to let people know this by constantly referencing his French heritage, while all but ignoring his Indian ancestry. Just as the white man's wars forced his maternal predecessors from their lives among nature's elements, those same wars, not yet having ceased, put LeBetre back into the wilderness, albeit in a different time and place. The longer LeBetre was in the jungle the more he began to unwittingly emulate his forefathers who inhabited the deep woods of North America hundreds of years earlier, even though he still walked on the soil of the colonial world with the Euro-centric arrogance of his French sires.

* * *

"I remember when I was making some of my films in which I tried to put a human face on the so-called 'other', those who were not white and were not American, and how I was told by my directors that it would be hard, if not impossible, to garner respect for Asians, blacks, Indians, and so forth. They told me it would be easier and more realistic to merely try and garner sympathy for them, and that the best way to do this is to show their starving, emaciated, fly-ridden children. But I found that this only increased people's perceptions that all non-Western countries are backward and in need of Americanization, with absolutely nothing to offer the world. They said that if you make a movie showing a brown-skinned man getting hurt or killed by a white American, people

will automatically think the man did something to deserve it. He was a communist, or his savagery was standing in the way of Western-style progress. But show a white man getting hurt or killed by a man with brown skin, and the American public will conjure up sympathy for the white man and bloodlust for the brown-skinned man, no matter what the circumstances. Most American viewers will want vengeance against the brown-skinned man in this instance, and will not adopt a positive opinion of your movie unless it has been carried out. I have left this task to John Wayne and some of the others. I myself refuse to promulgate this kind of shallow nationalism disguised as justice."

* * *

One morning during this period of increasing volatility with the nearby Vietnamese and Cambodian population, Strapinski was late in coming back from monitoring a narrow pathway to the east of Tigerden, where he was watching to see how much Vietcong activity it had been receiving. After an hour, Wilke enlisted the help of LeBetre and they headed to the spot where Strapinski had been posted. The young Green Beret from Oklahoma was still there, but somebody else had found him first. He had been stripped of his uniform, his back pressed against a tree and held there by a large strand of barbed-wire wrapped several times around both him and the tree. There was even a small piece of wire placed in his mouth. The tortuous apparatus was designed to force whomever was ensnared in it to remain standing at an extreme upright position, or be cut to ribbons by the weight of their own body as it went limp from exhaustion. It was apparent that Strapinski's legs had failed him hours earlier as his big frame pressed hard into the barbs, tearing his flesh, the tiny rivers of blood still flowing from the cuts. Unknown to those who found him, Strapinski's tibial artery had been slashed. Having already lost much of his blood, Wilke and LeBetre frantically tried to untangle Strapinski from the wire, cutting their own hands and arms in the process. Once freed, Wilke threw Strapinski over his shoulder and ran with him back to basecamp. From there a helicopter flew the horribly sliced body to a field hospital where Strapinski would be pronounced dead.

The men were fervent with anger and talk of revenge over the torturous death suffered by their comrade. Though shaken from having a man killed under my command, I urged restraint, finding an ally in Wilke amidst Edwards' and LeBetre's pleas for immediate retribution. Wilke did not believe in reprisals fueled by emotion. He tried to never react to his enemy, preferring instead to be the one dictating the action. Yet at the same time, he was extremely concerned that Green Tiger was no longer invisible to its enemy.

* * *

"There were thousands of flag-draped body bags coming back to the United States. There was a lot of false fanfare that would accompany these returns. False, because everybody knew these were lives wasted, but nobody dared to say it out loud. A life lost in war can never be in vain, or so we are supposed to believe. It has to be for the Glorious Cause. Our precious sons, and brothers, and grandsons cannot have died for nothing. They died for the sake of freedom...for democracy...and not for the interests of greedy, old politicians, who are nothing more than puppets on a string for the big corporations. There were literally thousands of Strapinskis in Vietnam—blond-haired boys from farms across America, who were scared and even unprepared for such butchery, despite being *trained to kill, boys who died fighting a jungle war on the other side of the world which served as nothing more than a marketplace and showcase for the wares of Bell Helicopter, Monsanto, Boeing and Dow Chemical. It was a fucking lie!"*

* * *

Marlon liked to speak, and sometimes mumble, his beliefs and perspectives out loud to himself. It helped him clarify his thoughts, and also served as practice should he find himself in a conversation about a certain subject on a talk show, or during a social gathering, or perhaps when in need of dialogue for a movie role. Marlon always found himself to be more clear-headed, more articulate when he was talking to himself. Talk shows and social gatherings he found too nerve-wracking and fraught with distractions to keep his mind focused, and subsequently he never comes off sounding as informed as he actually is on any given subject. But alone, talking to himself, Marlon is confident and clear of thought.

"What about the innocent Vietnamese, especially women and children, who got caught up in the middle of the cluster-fuck known to the American people as the Vietnam War?

'Well, what about them? Who cares. They were communists. They got what they deserved', is what people like to say to me when I ask this question.

Innocent people, especially women and children, don't deserve to be blown to pieces, burned, mutilated, and raped. They weren't Marxists or Leninists. Most had never even heard of these men, nor the names of the two architects of the holocaust unleashed against them in Nixon and Kissinger. Nobody cried for the Vietnamese people, at least not anybody in the United States. They were too busy crying for the blond-haired, blue-eyed farm boys like Strapinski, whose loved-ones were told their sons died protecting freedom and democracy, Christianity and capitalism, from the spread of world communist domination, emanating from Moscow and Beijing. But I don't think it was really that complicated. No. They were just poor fucking peasants sent to kill other poor fucking peasants on the far reaches of the kingdom, a place and people not yet brought under the sway of the modern day Rome, an empire still relying on ritualistic blood-letting as a means of resolving territorial and political conflicts."

* * *

Wilke's fears were confirmed in the days that followed as the local Vietcong began to harass the outpost, becoming more and more daring with each foray.

On one such occasion, which would ultimately become a defining moment for Green Tiger, some Vietcong, who managed to sneak through the clamors, snatched Quac, one of the South Vietnamese soldiers, while he was pulling night watch on the northern perimeter. Both the darkness and the jungle foliage would become the unwitting abettor to the heinous act that followed. It was there that the Vietcong tortured and mutilated the Vietnamese man for the crime of siding with the foreign invaders. They burned his skin, as well as shoved bamboo sticks up his fingernails and into his eyes in slow, meticulous fashion. Carried out only about fifty-yards away from Tigerden, the objective of the Vietcong torturers was to coax from Quac blood curdling screams as a terror-message to Green Tiger. Their plan worked as the rest of us woke to the cries of one of our own dying in the night. The men pleaded with me and Wilke to let them go out into the jungle and save Quac. We both denied permission on the grounds that it was an obvious set-up for an ambush. The horrifying shrieks and shrills went on for hours until everyone, including the fearless sergeant, seemed visibly shaken.

Over and over the pleas of, "help me, please help me," dug into the nerves of everyone in Green Tiger who could only sit and hope that Quac would die soon and be relieved of his pain. He begged for help, first in English, then, when nobody came, he asked for help in Vietnamese with the hopes that the other South Vietnamese soldier would provide assistance, but still none would be forthcoming.

The tension of the situation was bringing out some deep-seated animosities between certain individuals within Green Tiger. In every instance Edwards was the instigator, getting into numerous shouting matches with both Henderson and LeBetre.

Making official the decision that we would do nothing, I ordered everyone back to their shelters, to separate them if nothing else. Wilke volunteered to keep watch. The screams continued, echoing off the trees, making it difficult to determine exactly where they were coming from. Eventually Wilke had had enough. He crawled outside the perimeter, slipping past the Vietcong, worming his way through the mud and thick foliage until he found Quac. Like Strapinski, Quac was still alive, but just barely. He was only able to scream by sheer adrenaline and the fact the Vietcong had not mutilated his tongue like they did his other extremities. Quac had no mortal wounds, and under different circumstances he may have been saved. But with the situation being what it was, there was no way out for Quac, nor would there be for Wilke if he tried to carry him back. With no other choice but to perform a mercy killing, Wilke took out his knife and thrust it across Quac's throat, putting him out of his misery. As Wilke scrambled to make it back, the rest of us breathed a sigh of relief as the night had again become quiet, unbeknownst to us as to why, however. Back in the relative safety of Tigerden, Wilke's only regret was that he did not dispose of Quac's body so that the men would not have to see what the Vietcong did to him.

The following morning, with the darkness and the Vietcong now gone, Wilke, LeBetre, and the other South Vietnamese soldier, formed a search party to find Quac, whom everyone in Green Tiger believed to most likely be dead. Pretending he did not know the exact location, Wilke allowed the quest to go on for a while, finally becoming impatient and 'stumbled' upon the body himself. Even though it was obvious to everyone, LeBetre pointed out that Quac's throat had been cut. Wilke did not have the heart to tell the men that it was in fact he who did this, unsure how he would explain to them why it was okay for one of them to go out and kill Quac, but not to save him. He understood the concept that the circumstances of war sometimes requires a soldier to sacrifice one man in order to save two, but did not expect any of these young men to, at least not in this situation. As far as Wilke was concerned, there was no such thing as a 'friend' or 'buddy' out in the bush, only the living and the dead. When he initially heard Quac screaming from outside the perimeter of basecamp, Wilke already considered him to be dead, and did not believe it made any sense to risk the lives of the living to retrieve one of the dead.

* * *

"Spirit and matter. Body and soul. The living and the dead. Good and evil. The West believes that reality is a kind of duality of polar opposites, which are completely separate, competing and warring with one another in a kind of zero-sum game. There is no blending or blurring of the two. And maybe it's true. Hell, I don't know. Perhaps the Far East has it right, though. Maybe what the West considers to be polar opposite natures are really just

different aspects, different sides, different angles of the same thing. Good and evil, love and hate, heaven and hell all flow in and out of one another, without separateness, without borders, synchronized, not warring, keeping the universe in balance, incessantly merging and blending. Without dark, we would not know light. Without death, we would not know life. Without evil, we would not know good. Without hate, we would not know love. In the West, one man's good is another man's evil. One man's living is another man's dead. How can we know if someone is alive or if they are dead? I mean, if they are really alive! They might be breathing, but that does not mean they are living. My father was never alive. My mother was never alive, either. Or at least I never saw them alive. I have spent most of my life not alive, but dead. I have not been alive since I was a little kid growing up in Nebraska. But that little boy is dead. He died out of necessity before this world could tear him to pieces. Nobody mourned for him but me. I still mourn for him."

CHAPTER 11

"Do you think Walter has seen any of your movies?"

"Ha! That's funny, Francis."

"No, seriously, Marlon. Is Walter Kurtz the kind of guy who would have gone to see a Marlon Brando movie?"

"Some of the early ones, maybe, like *Streetcar*, *Waterfront*, and *The Men*, because it's about the military. He wouldn't have liked them, though, certainly not *Streetcar* or *Waterfront*. My roles were too radical, too non-conformist for Walter, who grew up on his father's patriotic, conformist rhetoric, as well as all those propaganda pieces that came out of Hollywood after the war."

"What about *Zapata*?"

"Ha! Walter would've thought it was unpatriotic to go see such a movie, especially with the anti-communist mood in the country at the time. I myself am surprised Hollywood allowed such a movie to be made in the first place."

"Yeah, looking back, I am too. How did that do at the box office?"

"Actually, better than you might think, all things considered. It was right on the heels of *Streetcar*. It was advertised more as a Western than it was a struggle between social classes, so the message was missed, which happened with all my films that actually tried to say something relevant."

"Yeah, that did seem to happen with your films. We'll continue to explore that later, but I want to get back to Walter and Korea."

"Sure."

"So, Marlon, you said earlier that Walter comes home from Korea a bit disenchanted."

"Yeah, somewhat."

"Why is that?"

"Well, it's not quite the star-spangled homecoming he expected, but his fervor is not dashed too much. He still buys into the ideal of the American empire."

"Manifest Destiny dressed up as the spread of freedom and democracy."

"Precisely, Francis. Walter is a disciple of this ideal."

"An apostle, perhaps even."

"Yes, you could say that."

"Because an apostle is in effect one who is sent. And Walter, in Korea and then in Vietnam, is sent to further the spread of the American ideal."

"I suppose you could say that, Francis. And Walter went into both with a certain naiveté, I guess you could say."

"Well, yes, he's certainly bought into all the hype, all the propaganda. But in Vietnam, something happens. Something changes him. What changes him? What happens to Walter Kurtz in Vietnam, Marlon?"

"What changes him, or what happens, is that the Darwinian world of jungle warfare..."

"The what, Marlon?" quickly interrupted Francis.

"What?" asked Marlon, confused by the suddenness of Francis' interjection.

"What did you say? The Darwinian what?"

"The Darwinian world of jungle warfare."

"Where the hell did you get that from?"

"I'm pretty sure it just came to me now. I don't recall hearing it ever before."

"That's an interesting way of putting it, Marlon. That's another one we might have to use in the movie, in the narration or something. Please continue."

Marlon, annoyed by the interruption, sighed.

"Well, you were asking about what happened to Kurtz in Vietnam."

"Right."

"And I'm trying to tell you that what I think happened is that the jungle pulls Walter's mind and body deep inside a place void of the order and reason he took for granted back inside the confines of Western civilization."

"The jungle does this? How does the jungle do this? I like this idea, but I want you to explain it a bit more."

"The jungle transforms and changes him."

"Not the Vietnamese? Because he's fighting the Vietnamese."

"Yes, I know that, Francis, but the Vietnamese are *part* of the jungle, as are the heat and the bugs, the booby traps, all that shit."

"Okay, I can understand that, but how do all these things pull Walter's mind and body deep inside a place void of…what did you call it…order and reason?"

"Yes, order and reason. That's because the jungle is void of order and reason…as order and reason are understood in the Western world."

"Say more."

"The jungle isn't governed by the same laws, rules, mores, religion, political system, etc., as the United States and Western Europe. It's a different world, a place that Walter doesn't understand, at least not at first. All that he knows has little or no relevance in the jungle. His worldview, his religion, his military training…the jungle defies all these things. Walter becomes disenchanted with the world he comes from because the jungle peels away Walter's long-held convictions for God and country, and then a kind of transformation begins to occur."

"What kind of transformation?"

Marlon paused for a moment.

"Well, it depends."

"On what?"

"On one's own perspective, because it's kind of subjective."

"Okay. So how would *you*—Marlon Brando—how would *you* understand it?"

"Well, I would say Walter experiences a kind of freedom or liberation."

"Freedom from what?"

"Freedom from…oh, hell, I don't know the exact specifics…church and state, maybe.

I don't know." Marlon then grumbled something that Francis could not understand. He was upset that he could not think of a better, more articulate, response.

"What, Marlon? Could you repeat that last part?"

"I said, I don't know," replied Marlon tersely.

"No. After that."

"I don't remember, Francis."

"You mentioned church and state, and then you said something else, but I didn't catch it."

"I don't fucken remember, Francis!"

"Okay. Sorry, Marlon," said Francis, who then sat quietly, waiting for Marlon's suddenly dour mood to pass.

"What I wanted to say, Francis, is that Kurtz frees himself, he finds freedom from the ecclesial and ideological cages constructed by his Western forebears," said Marlon loudly and clearly, confident that what he said sounded intelligent.

"Now that I heard, Marlon. That's good! I like it. But who are his forebears?"

"Uh, well, his father, government and religious leaders…uh, anyone, past and present, who contributed to the system that produced Walter and the way he thinks, the things he believes in."

Marlon paused, giving Francis the opportunity to interject.

"So, you're talking about traditional Western religious, philosophical, and political thought and values, right?"

"Yes, I guess so."

"Okay. I get that."

"And, if you recall, Francis, because we talked about it earlier, turning one's back on the so-called Truth, as it's understood by the Western tradition, can mean either one of two things for Walter, or anyone else whose words or actions run counter to the West's perceived monopoly on Truth." Marlon looked at his director with a sly grin on his face. "Do you remember?"

"Well, kind of. We've already talked about so many different things, Marlon. Maybe you could refresh my memory?"

"You called it the 'slipping the bonds of Western rationalism', Francis."

"Yes, I remember that, Marlon, but I can't figure out where you're going with this. Just tell me."

Francis encouraged his star actor to proceed, and to do so quickly, because he knows Marlon has a propensity to lose his train of thought if distracted for too long.

"Okay. Well, first, if you look at it from the Western perspective, Walter would be considered mad or insane, as we talked about earlier. And second, taken from a non-Western perspective, Walter would perhaps be considered enlightened."

"How about if we narrow it down a bit, Marlon? How about if we say Eastern perspective instead of just non-Wester perspective? After all, Kurtz is in East Asia, the world of Buddhism, Confucianism, Taoism, and even Hinduism."

"Okay. Taken from an Eastern perspective, Walter would perhaps be considered enlightened."

"Why *enlightened*? And who would say this?"

Marlon looked annoyed by his director's inquisition.

"I'm just playing devil's advocate, Marlon, because not everybody would say that he was enlightened. They might say that Kurtz slipped the bonds of Western rationalism, or the Western way of thinking, something like that, but your assertion that people would think of him as *enlightened* might not be completely accurate."

"He's enlightened because he sees through all the bullshit, the propaganda, the lies."

"Okay. But who would see him in this light? Or are you just giving a generalized assessment?"

"I guess I'm giving a general assessment that he's become enlightened."

"But isn't this to assume that the Western perspective is false, and the Eastern perspective is the truth?"

"Well, yes. My assessment is a bit subjective."

"I'm not saying that you're wrong, Marlon."

"Right. I know. But just let me correct your interpretation of what I'm saying. I'm not necessarily implying that Kurtz has found the truth in any Eastern religion or philosophy, or whatever. All I'm saying is that he no longer buys into the ascendancy of traditional Western religion and philosophy. That's all, Francis."

"Okay, I get it," said Francis after a brief pause. "That's good, Marlon. So, and I know you didn't say this specifically, but does Kurtz, once he sheds the philosophical and historical trappings of Western civilization, then assume the mindset or thought processes of the Eastern world, like Buddhism and Taoism?"

"No. I don't think that's the route we should take, Francis. I would say that the answer can be found in Conrad's book."

"How so?"

"Kurtz in Conrad's book does not necessarily become African, or Congolese, in his thinking or mindset. No. He slips the bonds of Western rationalism by becoming acclimated to the rhythms of the jungle. He becomes absorbed into the jungle, not to any religion or culture, per se."

"Okay, that's really helpful, Marlon. It's not necessarily Eastern, but rather something simply primal or primordial."

"That's why I said non-Western in the first place, and not Eastern. But I think both of those assessments are wrong. I think what you just said—primal or primordial—is more appropriate here."

There was a pause as Francis looked out into the vast, lush, green Filipino forest, very pleased with what he just heard.

"Brilliant, Marlon, that is brilliant! My mind is racing."

"Well, I don't know how brilliant it is. Kurtz's story is similar in a lot of ways to my own. I'm really just telling my own story."

* * *

"They've always criticized me and my acting, my technique, my work ethic. That is, until the money starts rolling in at the box-office, and then I'm fucking brilliant...the greatest actor ever! I've never understood why these directors...these writers, and so forth...think they know so much about acting. They should all be required to do some stage acting just to get an idea of what an actor puts into creating a good performance. We're not all fucking robots. There's no one single formula or programming that works for all of us. We are all different, and we all have our own methods that we use to prepare ourselves for a part. I don't expect any of these fuckers to understand, but they always think they've got all the answers, that they know it all. And worse yet, their unfounded and unwarranted criticisms of us—of me—inevitably makes its way into the press and comes to define who we are in the public eye."

Marlon paused for a moment, looking around and behind himself to see if Rafael was close by, perhaps listening to his rant. Marlon got up from his chair and walked around. He looked out the window of the houseboat, and then returned to his chair, the typewriter, and the story of Walter Kurtz.

* * *

The high brass at I-Core were initially upset by some of our so-called "unauthorized" activities, mostly those that took us into South Vietnamese territory. Apparently, there was even some talk of relieving me of my command, as well as rumors of insubordination charges. However, once the press began raving about recent American successes, I-Core, desperate for any sort of good news, came up with a different plan for me––a promotion to full-bird colonel.

In the autumn of 1967, I was called back to Danang to receive my silver eagle as well as present a six-month report and assessment of Green Tiger's mission. I lifted off from Tigerden in the afternoon and was scheduled to be in Danang for dinner. After a year in the bush, eating the army's Meals Ready to Eat and sleeping on a cot always wet from the intense humidity, I was looking forward to some of the luxuries of civilization. Once in my Danang hotel room, I immediately showered which was a welcome change from bathing in muddy swamps and rivers, then put on my dress uniform in preparation for a dining engagement with General Kautzbaum, a three-star overseer of this and other clandestine missions in Vietnam.

An elegant French restaurant overlooking the China Sea, the *La Coursiere* was built in 1920s colonial Indo-China and still maintained a very Gallic ambiance, carrying an array of French dishes on the menu along with certain Vietnamese delicacies. Inside, I tucked my hat underneath my arm, and was then escorted by a Vietnamese waiter over to General Kautzbaum's table. The general and his party of officers were already seated in the back, enjoying their before-dinner drinks and appetizers. All were in uniform, yet the mood was relaxed and jovial. The waiter announced me to the table in extremely choppy English, prompting the general to greet me in the same way I was introduced.

"How the hell are you, Cull-oh-nel Cuts," he said, which was received with an eruption of laughter by his cronies. "I'm sorry, colonel. Please, sit down. I'm still trying to understand what these fucken gooks are saying," said Kautzbaum, unconcerned that the waiter, and butt of both his joke and insult, was still standing there. The general straightened himself up long enough to request another round of drinks from the very tolerant Vietnamese *garcon*, then handed the floor over to me so I could "pick your poison," as Kautzbaum put it. I politely asked for a bourbon and water.

"I apologize for that, Kurtz, but the boys have all been working too damn hard, and need a few laughs," explained the general in his own defense.

"No need, general. Word out in the bush is that a little comic relief is just what Dr. Ho recommends for battle fatigue," I replied, bringing renewed laughter and the acceptance of the group of officers.

The rest of the evening was spent eating French and Vietnamese cuisine, drinking *saké* and beer, and conversing in the low light and soft music of the restaurant, with everyone eventually taking up bar stools.

My itinerary had me scheduled to give a briefing regarding the Cambodian mission at 0800 hours the following morning, but I would spend the evening listening to the opinions and analysis of men who never came out from behind their desks, except to go to an officer's club. The more drinks that were downed by this group of officers the more the topic of the war was brought up. Having been out in the bush for several months now, I had not been privy to the recent news reports, or even official military and government statements pertaining to the war in Vietnam. I was surprised to hear that American troop levels had reached the half-million mark, and that the North was actually resisting peace negotiations. Many of the other officers in attendance told me that escalation has yet to make a difference. Some talked of an anti-war movement in America that bordered on social revolution, while others denied anything of the sort. Looking for the median of opinion, I asked everybody I talked to as to their take on America's involvement thus far, getting a full range of views. On one end of the spectrum, many claimed that victory was close at hand. On the other, some contended that America would eventually win, but still had a long, hard row to hoe. Once the general caught wind of the subject matter, however, there was little doubt he would have the final word.

"These gooks are hanging on by the skin of their yellow teeth. The war will be over within a year. Don't believe any of that commie pinko crap you hear on television. You guys are worse than a bunch of old, nervous women. For Christ sake!" he scolded.

The next morning I was choppered over to I-Core where I again met General Kautzbaum who was not all that different when sober, as well as two men in suits, representing the Central Intelligence Agency. Showing no signs of a hangover, even though he must have had one, the general continued his informal banter as if he was still back in the bar.

"Holy shit! You know what, colonel? I talked to your father the other day, and I forgot to mention it to you last night. How 'bout that shit? Chalk one up to old Jack Daniels. Anyway, he wanted to know if you've been earning your keep over here in the fucken Nam. I told him that earning one's pay over here isn't the problem. It's getting out alive so you can spend it, that's the hard part."

Finding great humor in what he'd just said, the general slapped the top of his desk in a needless attempt to aggrandize the fact he found himself funny, making a loud thundering sound that startled everyone in the room. "Fine man, your father. Fine man," he added as his laughing jig wound down.

Meanwhile, Agent Bladent, a well-scrubbed, middle-aged, extremely serious man who worked for the C.I.A., quickly put an end to Kautzbaum's silliness, abruptly and almost painfully steering the meeting back on course.

"In every sector that you've been in, enemy activity has dropped considerably, and even completely in some instances. The program is working, and we are planning to continue it into the next year."

"But if we get that liberal fucken Humphrey in the White House, we could lose our funding. Hell, that bastard will try to end the war whether we've won it yet or not," noted the general.

"He won't end the war!" interjected Bladent suddenly. "What Humphrey will do is gradually pull the plug, a slow reduction of troops, which is even worse because it gives the impression that we lost when in fact we weren't even trying to win."

Bladent's spiel was delivered crisply, in a monotone drone, making it sound rehearsed, his facial expressions never changing.

At this point the general got up from his chair, throwing his right hand up in the air in disgust before once again putting all speculation to rest.

"We won't have to worry about Humphrey pissin' the war down his leg because that crazy fucken cold-warrior, Nixon, is gonna win that damn election, and then we'll be able to fight this war to win it. He'll wipe the fuckers off the map right quick. Nixon ain't gonna mess around in this piss-ant country year after year like that fucken pole-cat Johnson has. Let's see, he'll be sworn-in sometime during January…" The General began counting on his fingers, half serious, half grandstanding, as to how long it would take Nixon to end the war. "…in a little over three months, by the end of April he'll have the war won and over with."

Bladent, who was not happy that his careful analysis was so quickly dismissed in favor of the general's own boozy sounding blather, rolled his eyes and looked away. The general noticed his discontent.

"Alright, colonel, let's see what you got," said General Kautzbaum while reaching out his hand in anticipation of receiving the envelop I was holding containing my classified report detailing Green Tiger's operations for the past few months. Leaving the technical data to the report, I thought I would use the opportunity to voice some of my personal concerns, conveying to the general my worries that the men might drift into a void of lawlessness as a result of being so far removed from the civilized world. In order to counter-balance the excesses of war, I asked if a priest or minister could be flown in on occasion to speak to the men and to conduct services.

Leaning back in his chair behind a large oaken desk, the general nodded disinterestedly in agreement while I talked. During a momentary pause, he quickly stood up.

"The priest thing can be worked out. I know just the man. He loves the combat zone!"

My report was handed over to Agent Bladent for further review. General Kautzbaum, it appeared, had no interest and would probably never read it. In return, I received I-Core's classified report of new data and information regarding enemy activity in Cambodia. The conversation then took another unexpected turn as the second C.I.A. agent spoke up and asked about Wilke.

"So, how's that crazy bastard Wilke doing, anyway?"

I was surprised to hear him speak so candidly, especially after listening to the robotic Bladent.

"He's fine, a very dedicated and competent soldier," I responded cautiously, only to have Agent Anderson, the man who posed the question, laugh at my choice of words.

"*Competent*? My fucken ass! Wilke's the best God-damn covert operations soldier this country has ever produced, at least in this century. He may be a little, shall we say, *unorthodox*, but that's what makes him so brilliant. We've thrown him into every situation imaginable, and he keeps coming out alive. You can't kill Wilke. Wilke will never die!"

Bladent rolled his eyes at his cohort's bold statement, while Kautzbaum grinned.

"Yep, he's a born jungle guerrilla, that Wilke. And I mean gue-rilla as in member of an irregular army force, not go-rilla as in eatin' bananas and swingin' from vines," chimed in the general to only a small amount of laughter. He was more used to bigger crowds of subordinate officers who had little choice but to laugh at his jokes.

I would spend the next couple of days in Danang before rejoining Green Tiger. While there, I received my promotion to colonel in non-spectacular fashion. General Kautzbaum simply handed me my silver eagle, saluted me, shook my hand, and then whisked me out the door. I was also able to call my wife and talk to the kids for the first time in over half a year. Most of my R&R was spent getting caught up on the news coverage of the war, losing myself in the plethora of American newspapers and television newscasts made available in the South Vietnamese hotels and bars that cater to American servicemen.

On my last evening in Danang, much like I did the ones previous, I sat at the hotel bar before dinner, sipping a beer and watching a delayed broadcast of an American news telecast. The lead story was of course the war in Vietnam, showing film footage of towns and villages in the North that had been leveled by American bombing. There were scenes of refugees fleeing the carnage, many of them children who had been burned from the explosions. I began drinking my beer a little faster as I watched and listened to stories of a growing American death toll, stalled peace negotiations, and anti-war protests in the streets of America. But the thing that really caught my attention, in the newspapers and on television, was how the focus or catch-phrase of American policy seemed to have suddenly shifted from 'hearts and minds' to 'bodycount', realizing that perhaps Green Tiger was a pawn in this new strategy. These revelations prompted me to sit in the bar even longer, drinking far more beer than I planned in order to wash away my doubts that were pressing in on me.

Various officer-types streamed in and out all night, some staying for one or two drinks before heading into the dining area, while many sat there late into the evening as I did. I kept mostly to himself, however, pondering my family, career, and the war while the jukebox in the corner played everything from Frank Sinatra to the Doors.

* * *

"The dichotomy, the distinction between Frank Sinatra and Jim Morrison explains a lot about how the times had changed, people had changed, American culture and even the American mindset had changed. Sinatra represents a time when men were men. They said and did what they wanted, and they didn't give a damn what anybody thought of them. They were generally clear in what they believed in. And I must admit I am torn about this. It's nice to have certainty, and to be man enough to raise fists and defend the things you believe in. That's the generation I was raised into. My father, the monster that he was, was like that, and so was I to a certain extent when I was younger. I believed in standing up, and speaking out for what you believed in. The problem was that I didn't always believe in the things most everybody else believed in. You could say I was more like Jim Morrison in that regard, but with a Frank Sinatra exterior. Both men make a certain amount of sense to me. I feel like I'm caught in the middle between the two. I'm no psychedelic hippy, but I'm not like my father, either. Frank Sinatra's generation fought Hitler and the Germans in France. Jim Morrison's generation fought Ho Chi Minh and the North Vietnamese in the jungles of Southeast Asia. Frank Sinatra drank Jack Daniel's whiskey. Jim Morrison smoked pot and took LSD. I can't really relate to either one. But in an ironic twist of fate, the *older I get the less I identify with the World War II generation crooner—the Chairman of the Board, ol' Blue Eyes—who is fading away, like I am, and the better I understand the young Californian poet—the Lizard King, Mr. Mojo Rising—who died a sudden and mysterious death in Paris, the likes of which I often assumed, perhaps even fantasized, would be my fate when I was younger."*

CHAPTER 12

"You know, Marlon, most Americans had never even heard of a place called Vietnam when stories about the small Asian country began to appear on their evening news in the late 1950s and early 1960s. Hell, I never heard of Vietnam."

"Me neither, to be quite honest with you. But the French had."

"Well, yes, they most definitely had. As Vietnam was becoming commonplace in the American lexicon, it was a word the French had long since grown tired of, and were simply trying to forget."

"To be quite honest, Francis, I don't fully understand what happened in Vietnam before the Americans arrived on the scene."

"Well, I don't think anybody really does, Marlon, including me, despite the fact that in preparation for this movie I studied the history of Vietnam, going back a few hundred years."

"So have I, Francis. But I still don't really understand it. It's much more complicated and nuanced than what the World War II generation experienced. I've always felt myself caught in the middle between the two generations."

"Well, I think a lot of us who have experienced both wars feel the same way. I'll tell you what I know, or what I think I know."

"Alright," said Marlon, sounding disinterested.

"America's involvement really started in 1954 when the Vietnamese, who had been living under French rule since the late 1800s, attacked the French army garrison in the valley of Dien Bien Phu."

Marlon grimaced in anticipation of having to listen to a long, drawn-out explanation about the history of pre-Vietnam War era Vietnam.

"Just relax, Marlon. I'll make this brief and as painless as possible," said Francis upon noticing his star actor's sudden listlessness. "So anyway, at Dien Bien Phu…"

"Where's Dien Bien Phu?"

"It's in the north somewhere."

"North of what?"

"North Vietnam, Marlon. It's in North Vietnam," said Francis Coppola in a manner a bit too condescending for Marlon Brando's taste.

"Okay, Francis. I get it," said the suddenly perturbed star actor.

"So, at Dien Bien Phu, the Vietnamese rained a barrage of canon fire down on the French sentry, and eventually defeated the French. And when they did this, Marlon…when they did this…it showed the Vietnamese, and the French for that matter, that the French Indo-China empire was only an illusion, and that it was always just an illusion, one that was quickly disintegrating into the mud of Dien Bien Phu, pulled under by the weight of French pride and an emerging Vietnamese nationalism. And by 1965, Vietnam had become the centerpiece of American Cold War diplomacy…"

"Just like that?"

"Yes. It was very soon after the French left that the US got involved."

"Why?"

"I was about to tell you, Marlon."

"Sorry."

"The Soviet Union and the People's Republic of China were both supplying monetary and military assistance to the communists of North Vietnam in support of their insurgency into democratic South Vietnam, spreading fear within the United States government, who then spread fear to the American public, that Vietnam would fall the way of the communists, like China did, and like Cuba did."

"The domino theory."

"Exactly, Marlon."

"When did the U.S. get involved militarily?"

"In 1965 U.S. Marines waded ashore the coastal South Vietnamese city of Danang."

"When does Walter go to Vietnam?"

"Well, I'm not exactly sure, Marlon. A couple years after that, I suppose. That's not that important, necessarily..."

"But I think it is, Francis," interrupted Marlon.

Francis stared at Marlon as if irritated.

"What I would like to know, Francis, is what Walter is thinking about when all this stuff was going on. These historical facts are fine. We certainly need to consider them, but I want to know about Walter Kurtz the man."

"Well, then you come up with the details, Marlon," said the director a bit tersely.

"It's your movie."

"But it's your role, and you've always wanted to be the one to develop your characters, Marlon. I don't think you'd like it if I developed your character for you."

"Okay. Fair enough, Francis. I have come up with some things. I've even written some stuff, too. I don't have it here, though. It's back at my boat."

"Wait, Marlon, wait...you've been writing stuff...for this movie?"

"Kind of," said Marlon in non-committal fashion.

Francis stared at Marlon, trying to read him.

"Either you have or you haven't, Marlon. That's great if you did, Marlon. But please share it with me."

"It's not very good."

"I'll take something that's not very good over a lot of nothing, which is all I got at the moment, Marlon—a whole lot of nothing. Can you go get it, or maybe bring it here tomorrow?"

Marlon looked dour. He regretted confessing that he had developed some written material.

"I don't want it circulating around here, Francis. The writers will be resentful, and of course critical of it, and that will spill out into other areas. I never should have mentioned it."

"Are you fucking kidding me, Marlon?"

"You don't even know if it's any good, Francis."

"No I don't, Marlon," said the director with a very loud voice.

"And it probably isn't any good. Most scripts aren't any good, at least not initially. But they can be tweaked, changed, altered—all these things—to make them better. The problem, Marlon, is usually getting started. But yes, I agree, I can see a potential problem with a Marlon Brando-penned script floating around the movie set, so maybe you can just quietly slip me some of what you've come up with. How much have you written so far?"

"Not a lot. A few pages of stuff. But most of it is about the early days—the days leading up to where we are in the movie, or where we're eventually going to be, or whatever. I don't really know where we are in the movie, Francis."

"I know, Marlon, I know. And that's why I need all the help I can get out here. We're *way* behind schedule. And yes, Marlon, we are already way over-budget, too. All the rumors are true. And to be honest with you, Marlon, I feel like we're either on the cusp of complete and utter failure, or we're going to produce something really fucking great, something that will change the world. But I'm going to need your help, Marlon. I need more than just your name on the marquee, or a great acting performance. I need your input."

"Fine. I'm willing to do that, Francis. But how I can best help you is to give a good performance as Walter Kurtz, and that's going to require that I know exactly who Walter Kurtz is, and that means formulating what got him to this point."

"Then by all means, Marlon, please do that. I love the fact that you are working on this stuff back at the houseboat. All I'm saying, Marlon, is that I don't have the time to do it myself, and I don't trust the writers. I trust you, though, Marlon. I trust *you*!"

Upon hearing these words from his director, Marlon wore a proud and perhaps even satisfied look on his face.

"Okay, Marlon, so what do you have so far? I think we were talking about what Walter Kurtz thought of America's impending involvement in Vietnam, and the French defeat at Dien Bien Phu."

"Well, first of all, Francis, I don't see Walter as a warmonger. I don't think Walter likes the idea of America going to war in Vietnam. He will go to war and defend his country, and he will fight tenaciously, but he doesn't like war. And he certainly doesn't like the idea of American boys dying in the jungles of Southeast Asia, but he does come to believe that America's sovereignty is at stake here. He buys into the domino theory, and so Walter understands what his personal duties are, and he was not about to let his country down. Do you concur, Francis, that Kurtz is not a warmonger, but rather a dutiful man?"

"Yes, I can go along with that. So, uh, what about Walter's position or rank in the military, Marlon? What do you think it should be?"

"I'm thinking that Walter is a man of very high rank, perhaps a major or even a lieutenant-colonel by the time of the Vietnam War."

"Why such a high rank? Someone of that high a rank would never end up in the Cambodian jungle. Plus, he would have to be in his fifties to be a lieutenant-colonel, wouldn't he, Marlon?"

"Well, actually, Francis, I see Kurtz as a kind of military superstar, if you will. It's partly because his father was so influential and well known, but also because Walter Kurtz is a very accomplished military man, a good leader, and a good administrator. He's a rising star in the army. He's being groomed for general, maybe even Joint Chief of Staff, or something to that effect."

"So how does he end up in Cambodia, if he's so important?"

"Kurtz is in Cambodia because he's disgruntled with the way the war has been fought up until that point, up until about 1967 or '68."

"It's fought too brutally? Or not brutally enough?"

"Actually, not brutally enough. Kurtz thinks that the U.S. government, and perhaps even the military itself, are not doing what they need to do to win the war, and win it quickly. So, he lobbies for a command post out in the battlefield—out in the jungle—where he's going to conduct the war the way he sees fit."

"And they give it to him?" asked Francis, wanting to hear Marlon's reasoning.

"Well, yes, eventually. But not before he goes so far as to say that he will quit the army if they don't give it to him."

"So, he threatens the top army brass, saying he'll quit if he isn't given a position of command out in the jungle?"

"Yes, that's what I'm saying."

"Okay, so why would the army big-wigs care if Walter Kurtz quits the army, Marlon?"

"Well, it's because of the fact that he is such a high-profile person in the army. It would be bad publicity for the army, within the various military circles, and even outside of it to a certain extent. Plus, Kurtz could have gone public with his beef against the army and the way it was conducting the war."

Marlon paused to gather his thoughts before continuing.

"Much of the American public had already turned against the war effort for one reason or another, and to have a lieutenant-colonel speaking out about how the last several years, and countless lives, had been wasted in Vietnam because the U.S. was not doing what it needed to do, or what it could be doing to win the war, would have sent the country's hawks and doves over the edge."

"So, they give him a command in Cambodia?"

Marlon sighed and took a deep breath. He felt like he was being cross-examined.

"Well, I'm thinking that he goes through some kind of special forces training first, Francis. He wants to do it right, to get trained properly, and to earn this assignment. And this stems from the fact that he understands full-well that he has benefitted professionally because of who his father is. And so, as I said, he wants to make sure that he earns this…this…*command* out in Cambodia, so he applies for entrance into the army's Special Forces unit, just like some kid out of high school."

"And, again, they let him do this, Marlon?"

"No, not at first. The big-wigs don't understand what he is doing. They deny him, saying he's too old. *That's* when he threatens to quit, and *then* they give it to him."

"Please forgive all my questions, Marlon. I just think that what you have is good, and I want to crack your ideas as wide open as we can while we're in the moment. You know how fleeting these moments of inspiration are, Marlon. They come and go very quickly."

"Yes. I understand," grumbled Marlon, who was simply tired more than he was annoyed. "What was your last question, Francis?" asked Marlon with his eyes closed.

"I don't think I asked one. But I would like to know what Kurtz's age is."

"Uh, late-thirties or maybe even in his forties."

"Okay, so he's older, but not too old. He completes the training and requests a command in Vietnam, or Cambodia, which is granted to Kurtz because they don't really think he is that out of his mind yet. They just think he is very duty-driven at this point."

"Yes," replied Marlon, trying to wind down the conversation. "Do you like it, Francis? Does this fit in with your vision of Walter

Kurtz?"

"Yes, Marlon. It's a piece of the puzzle that is Walter Kurtz. There's a lot more to this mysterious man that we'll need to know in order to finish this movie, but that's a great start. I like it."

"I would like to talk a little about his home and family life, Francis."

"His what, Marlon?" replied Francis, not able to hide the fact he did not care to explore this aspect of Walter Kurtz.

"Is Walter a family man at this point in his career, Francis?"

Francis was disinterested in exploring the subject of Kurtz's family life as an adult with a wife and kids, and was content to say nothing more on the subject for now.

"You've got nothing to say about this?" asked Marlon after allowing Francis sufficient time to answer.

"Well, I haven't given Kurtz's home and family life as an adult much thought."

"What about in the days leading up to his departure for Southeast Asia? What was that like for him?"

"I don't know, Marlon. Perhaps this is something that you should explore in your writing."

"I have," said Marlon hesitantly and after a brief pause. He feared that whatever he says on this subject might be construed as stories and episodes of his own personal experiences of leaving his wife and kids to go off to some far away movie set at various points in his career. Marlon was not sure if he wanted to share these oftentimes painful memories, not even with Francis.

"You have? Then why are you asking me, Marlon?"

"I don't know," replied Marlon, stalling for time.

"Just tell me, Marlon. If you have stuff you want considered for the script you can't be self-conscious about it."

Marlon took a deep breath, cleared his throat, and then spoke.

"Well, I would suppose that Walter tried hard to espouse a certain amount of confidence and certainty, the same kind that his father did before leaving for war in the Pacific during World War II, in an attempt to allay the fears of his family."

"But he's confident in regard to what he's about to do, right?"

"Well, of course, Francis. I mean, he requests and goes through Special Forces training, for Christ sake! This guy is serious about what he's doing. Nothing is going to hold him back."

"Yes, I get all that, Marlon. But there must be some sadness, maybe some doubt, and perhaps even regret. After all, he is leaving his family behind to go off to war."

"Well, of course. He's not a robot. But Kurtz is a man going out on a military mission, one that he believes is noble. So yes, Walter does leave with a certain amount of sadness, knowing that he will miss his family. But he has no regrets."

"Okay, so you just mentioned the word *mission*, as in, Kurtz's military mission…"

"Right."

"What exactly is Walter Kurtz's mission?"

"As he sees it, or how the U.S. military and American government see it?"

"Ah, good distinction, Marlon. I would like to know Kurtz's mission, as he sees it."

"To defeat the communists," replied Marlon in a very matter-of-fact sort of way. "To protect the American way of life," he added. "At least initially, that is. And this would also be Kurtz's mission as understood by the U.S. military as well, I suppose. But eventually, after being in Cambodia for a while—in the jungle—Kurtz is awakened to something much bigger than this, something entirely different, something much more complicated than the defeat of communism and preservation of the American way of life."

"And just what is this *something*, Marlon?"

"Ha! Well, that's what we need to untangle and figure out, Francis."

Marlon looked coyly in the direction of his director. Francis knew that look. He understood it to mean that Marlon would want to talk about Walter Kurtz for days-on-end, which was something that Francis neither had the time nor the inclination for, much less the money. Suddenly Francis' mood turned. The reality of being over-budget and behind-schedule hit him.

"Marlon, I know you believe that actors and producers are always rushed because of budgets and the fact that on a movie set there are hundreds, and in this case thousands, of people on the payroll. And I agree with you completely. But we cannot construct every detail of Walter Kurtz's life."

"Perhaps this should have been done before you put a thousand people on the payroll."

"Yes, that would have been the prudent thing to do, I suppose. Or at least have it done before one very, very expensive and reluctant superstar actor came on-set thinking he has to know every detail about his character's early life, beginning from the moment of conception."

Marlon smiled.

"Also, perhaps this very expensive and reluctant superstar actor—one Marlon Brando—could have done his homework and read the book I gave him. And then maybe he, on his own time, could have worked through the issues and questions he might have had about the character, again, on his own time, and not when he is on his director's payroll, making about three million dollars for a couple weeks of work."

Again, Marlon smiled. Not because he was amused, but rather because he was annoyed by the accusatory tone of his director.

CHAPTER 13

"The term 'body count' infiltrated the American lexicon at some point in the late 1960s, becoming almost commonplace on television and in the newspapers, and even in everyday conversation. I don't think that people were even aware that such a grotesque and barbaric word and concept lived in their midst, side-by-side with them and their families as they ate dinner, watching the evening news on those little TVs so many people had in their kitchens back then. Little children would talk about their day at school while the news anchor would give the day's body count report, followed by the videotape of dead and wounded American and Vietnamese men and women passing before their young eyes. It was much different than how people experienced World War II. Back then they talked about battles and land won and lost, not the tally of dead enemy bodies. There was something dark and ominous about this strategy. People say that the Vietnam War cast a dark cloud over America. When I hear this I laugh out loud and tell them that the dark cloud was already there."

* * *

Back at Tigerden, I reviewed the many pages of documents I was supposed to have been looking over while in Danang. There too the term 'body count' seemed to be everywhere, the number of dead Vietnamese communists apparently becoming the primary indicator of victory or defeat for America in Vietnam. Put into plain terms, what the new directive meant for Green Tiger was that we were to be even more aggressive, to actively search out and kill any suspected communist sympathizer, Vietnamese or Cambodian. There would be no time for interrogations, much less trials out in the jungle. I-Core had given us the authority to be judge, jury, and executioner of any and all Southeast Asians living along the Vietnam-Cambodian border.

  I filled Wilke in on the contents of the documents, but not before waiting a day for him to come in from out of the jungle. In his usual candor, the sergeant looked at me sheepishly, chuckled to himself, and said, "Good God, a war of attrition. Things must really be bad out here."

  "What do you mean, *bad*? And how has this become a war of attrition?"

  "I mean *bad* as in *not good*, as in we're *losing* this war. A war of attrition, colonel, because, according to this new directive, it sounds as if the big boys have finally come to accept what we out here in the bush have been trying to tell them for years…that to win this war we're going to have to wage a full-scale slaughter of the North Vietnamese, something akin to a genocide, because the North Vietnamese will never give up!" I shook my head in disbelief. Not from what Wilke said. I accepted his analysis because it was the exact same thing I told the Joint Chiefs and Lyndon Johnson back in 1964, but because I could not believe that things had come to this.

  "This isn't something new to warfare, colonel, not even for American warfare. Remember the Indian wars? It's a method used for thousands of years, intended to render the enemy incapable of fighting simply because they don't have enough men, even women and children for that matter, to take up arms."

I had the same sinking feeling I experienced when initially told that neither the army nor the American government would claim knowledge of Green Tiger should our activities be exposed.

Despite my apprehensions, Green Tiger would take a more offensive approach to its mission. Moving quickly through the jungle, we came across people on both sides of the border whom, without a proper interrogation, were indistinguishable as Vietnamese or Cambodian, much less communist. All caution, however, was thrown to the wind, allowing instinct to take over. Most were deemed Vietcong and shot dead right on the spot. We would then melt back into the jungle, but not before burning all livestock and rice supplies as well as huts and shelters.

Tactics like this sickened me. The indiscriminate killing of peasant farmers and the destruction of their property were not why I came to Vietnam. The difficult time I began having dealing with the realities of this war made me wonder if I had grown too soft since Korea, that now as a forty-year-old man with a wife and two children, maybe I no longer had the stomach for this kind of thing.

* * *

It was during the filming of *The Godfather* when Marlon really started to notice a change in regard to how movies were being made. The production was getting much larger, the production crews bigger, budgets were becoming exorbitant. In his earlier films people in the production company often took on dual roles. For example, sometimes the script writers helped with hair and makeup, and vice-versa. There was a time when it was possible to know the names and even the life story of everyone on the movie set. On the set of *The Godfather* there were so many different people and experts and all their assistants and staff people that Marlon did not know whom he was supposed to be consulting with or answering to. His next two films were almost as bad, but nothing could have prepared him for what he would experience on the set of *Apocalypse Now*, where the production crew was almost as big as all his previous movies combined. It was like living in a small city, one filled with everyone from cobblers to special effects artists.

Marlon likened it to an enormous orchestra with its maestro, Francis Ford Coppola, at the center of an inferno of sight, sound, and fury, running around, flailing his arms, talking into his walkie-talkie, ordering, figuring, plotting, scheming, anguishing, running, walking, dancing, laughing, crying.

Even though he did not like this side of himself, Marlon's ego was suffering a bit. He was used to always being the center of attention on any given set. Marlon was like a prince, or even a king, someone everybody pampered and waited on so he could be made happy and comfortable in order to elicit the best possible performance from the actor who had reached the stature of icon while only in his twenties. Marlon usually, albeit passive-aggressively, controlled whatever set he was on. In contrast, Francis Coppola was definitely the alpha-male in charge of this set, but he was not a king or even a prince. Francis was its head grunt as well as its top executive. He would one minute be shoveling mud or moving brush, and then crunching numbers and data over the phone with production company executives and sometimes even representatives of the Filipino government. This was a world too fast-paced and complicated for Marlon Brando. He could not wait to get this movie finished and go back home to Tahiti, or at least this is what Marlon told himself.

* * *

```
After the death of Quac, the South
Vietnamese soldier, there was one thing that
everyone in Green Tiger understood and
agreed upon, and that was the fact that
```

Tigerden was no longer safe for us to inhabit. Even though I was the high-ranking officer, Sergeant Wilke would plan our next move. He told me this was a time for Green Tiger to retreat, to fall back and be absorbed by the jungle. We would hide in the places our enemy would not dare go so we could lay down and quietly bleed for a while. There we would grow strong again by acclimating ourselves to the jungle's most dangerous and unpleasant elements and conditions, ones that our long-suffering enemy could not even tolerate. What Wilke had in mind was for Green Tiger to emulate the jungle, to feed off death, to once again become the hunter instead of the hunted.

Wilke would lead a limping Green Tiger to a new basecamp situated even deeper inside Cambodia, leaving the jungle to devour what the Vietcong could not swallow of Tigerden. He pushed us further into the darkness and away from the enemy, insisting that a hunter hunts from behind and not in front of its prey. The new basecamp was seemingly twice as thick with foliage and vegetation as the previous one. The tops of the fir and bamboo trees formed such a dense canopy that the otherwise exceedingly bright rays of the tropical sun managed only a diffused glow by the time they reached the jungle floor, making everything appear as if engulfed in a green luminescent haze.

Two days after we arrived, about twenty montagnard soldiers dressed in green and brown American tiger-striped uniforms walked in virtually unnoticed as if the jungle suddenly took human form. Apparently, we'd been expecting them.

"Those are the Jarai, an ancient tribe of hill people from the Vietnamese highlands. They're tenacious jungle soldiers, and have been giving the Vietnamese fits for two-thousand years. Tough son-of-a-bitches!" proclaimed Wilke who has been witness to their tremendous skill and resilience on several occasions.

A people of dark complexion with long black hair, the Jarai resemble the American Indian in many ways.

"The VC are afraid of the highlanders, especially the Jarai. Always have been. They think the hill people possess special powers, that they can cast spells and all that shit. We're going to use them to harass and hit-n-run the VC up and down the Ho Chi Minh trail. What do you think, colonel?"

"It'll be nice to have the manpower," I said in non-committal fashion, somewhat leery at the prospect of having twenty non-English-speaking men under my command.

Since Wilke brought Green Tiger to the place of our new basecamp, he was given the privilege of naming it. Not only a great soldier, Wilke is also an astute student of philosophy and ancient history, including various religious traditions from many parts of the world, culling certain aspects from each of them to form the enigmatic amalgamation that is Wilke. He named the new basecamp 'Artemis', believing that its namesake, the Greek huntress and goddess of the wild, and the new basecamp, mirrored one another so perfectly that he felt compelled to dub Green Tiger's new home after the beautiful yet deadly Mediterranean icon, whose appeasement required endless human sacrifice.

Later that night a celebration of sorts took place at basecamp Artemis. Some of the montagnards had killed a couple of wild boar and were roasting them over an open flame. They were now out of their tiger-striped jungle gear issued by the U.S. Army, and were wearing their more traditional Jarai attire complete with loincloths and large amounts of bodily adornment consisting of brass earrings, necklaces, and bracelets. They began chanting and banging on tin gongs in an attempt to summon certain animistic gods and the spirits of their ancestors, but not before they dulled their bodies and heightened their senses by smoking mild hallucinogenic herbs and drinking an alcohol made from rice. Soon the Jarai were chanting very loud and boisterously, as well as dancing to the beat of the drums with the hopes of eliciting otherworldly assistance in their time of war.

This was not what I expected in our first night at Artemis, but would sit back and watch the fascinating cultural experience unfold, nonetheless. In fact, everyone was getting into the festivities, drinking the alcohol and feasting on the wild boar. Wilke looked like he was at home there, like most people of his ethnic background would at their favorite bar or restaurant. Wearing nothing but a pair of olive green boxer shorts and black army boots, sitting on the ground next to the fire with his legs crossed, Wilke ate, drank, and celebrated in the intense humidity of the tropical evening.

At first Lebetre refused to take part in the activities, thinking he was above such 'primitive' merrymaking, but after a couple jars of the rice alcohol he too was chanting, and even dancing around the fire. This episode was a small microcosm of how LeBetre's persona was changing or evolving out in the jungle. If asked his nationality, LeBetre would still say 'French' without hesitation. But the longer he was in the bush the less use he had for things inherited from his father, and the more of a necessity he had for the survival skills and instincts his maternal ancestors cultivated and honed for thousands of years.

As the night's celebration wore on, and the alcohol took effect, everyone from Green Tiger seemed to be hearkening back to their own primeval ancestral roots. By now we had all donned the brass necklaces and bracelets given to us by the montagnards as a sign of brotherhood, some even putting on a black face-paint made from water and ash.

Once the wild boar was eaten, and thoroughly washed down with the rice alcohol, the Jarai huddled together to again smoke the hallucinogenic plant through a long bamboo stem pipe, but more voraciously this time with obvious intoxicating effects. They then proceeded to turn the occasion into a raging prayer ceremony for their hoped-for messiah, the 'Python God'. Born out of a religious movement started in the highlands of Vietnam in the 1930s, the Python God, it is anticipated, will one day come and rid all Jarai lands of outside invaders, including the Vietnamese, cursing them with misery and various afflictions.

Each of us were offered a smoke of the pipe. All of us except for Wilke and LeBetre refused. The fact that Wilke indulged in the hallucinogens did not really surprise anyone, but we were all astonished when LeBetre agreed to partake. Wilke, looking as if he had done this before, took a deep drag, coughed slightly, then joined in with the rest of the Jarai as they danced and chanted in the world of the Python God, transported there by the thin wafts of smoke they exhaled into the thick atmosphere. LeBetre, looking like he had *not* done this before, coughed most of his drag up, but the sensation seemed to hit him almost immediately, making it all he could do just to find a place to sit down. With his eyes suddenly bloodshot, LeBetre engaged the swirling fire in a long inert stare-down. Inside his mind drunk with alcohol and herbs, the chanting, cadence of the drums, and outline of the dancers burned in the flames his eyes were absorbing, melting the sights and sounds into visions of his Indian ancestors. These subconscious introspections poured out of his heart and soul as if they had been lying dormant in his ancestral blood, awoken by the external stimuli of the ceremony and set free by the hallucinogenic. It was not the Python God that LeBetre saw, however, but rather the North American Indian Paiute messiah, Wovaka. Nor was it the Jarai he saw dancing in the firelight, but the Ghost Dancers of the American Great Plains who shook their bodies in exaltation of Wovaka with the hopes that they too would be saved from their invading enemies. As LeBetre experienced this vision, he could feel the deep faith of the Ghost Dancers that Wovaka would free them and their world from the European invaders, restoring and uniting them once again. So much so, at least for that moment, anyway, that this became his desire as well. But in his vision LeBetre would witness their dream die, however, as the Ghost Dancers were consumed by fire until the illusion burned itself out in the cauldron of flames coursing through LeBetre's mind. When the hallucination faded, he found himself dancing next to the Jarai, and so overwhelmed with emotion that he clutched his heart and cried for the sad faces that would haunt him from this day forward.

On the other side of the fire, I could see Wilke engaged in a meditative standoff with his shadow, created by the firelight. He seemed to be lost within himself, yet entranced by the crude orchestra of thundering drums, rhythmic chanting, and clanking of brass jewelry. Wilke twisted and churned his body in an odd manner, giving the impression he was trying to slide off or maybe even slip away from the conformity that he and his shadow have shared with one another all his life. Wilke has always feared that on some brightly lit night his dark silhouette would be his Judas, delivering him into the hands of his enemy. The battle-hardened sergeant understands his shadow to be the black antithesis of his living being, death carved in the shape of his likeness, stalking him, waiting to pull him into the black void. The two inseparable beings, but not by choice, one of flesh and blood, the other a one-dimensional hollow outline, stood face to face in front of the fire and prepared to wage battle. They circled one another warily, trying to find an opening, a weakness that they could exploit. Each move was systematically countered by the other combatant. Wilke rushed his shadow, but it retreated in perfect time. When he struck with his right arm, his shadow raised its left arm simultaneously to thwart it. Sweat rolled down the sergeant's face, his nostrils flared, and mouth grimaced with anger, but his adversary remained a dispassionate enigma. Several times Wilke thrust his shadow into the fire, only to make its way out unscathed, a fate Wilke knew would not be afforded his fleshly body. The Jarai cheered as the American soldier and his black reflection tumbled to the ground,

Wilke's antagonist temporarily disappearing underneath him. Believing he had won, and that the battle was over, Wilke made it to his feet, his arms raised in exaltation only to have his shadow emerge from the ground at the same time, claiming victory as well. The epic battle would end in a draw and a coming to terms between the two that they would forever walk side by side.

A couple hours into the celebration the sky became filled with dark, heavy clouds, poised to burst open with rain, making the stagnant atmosphere hot and wet. The smoke from the fires billowed into the sky very slowly in the sedentary air.

At one point during the hysteria, myself and Wilke, who had since calmed, sat together a short distance away from the festivities to talk. The alcohol and spirited nature of the celebration put both of us in a very open-minded, philosophical mood with each willing to let our respect for the other show. I was especially looking forward to using this moment to pick the brain of Wilke and find out a little more about what makes him tick.

Amidst the background noise of a Jarai celebration and the faint sounds of the jungle behind us, with jars of alcohol in hand, we began our chat with both of us anticipating that it would evolve into a discussion, and perhaps even a debate.

I talked in such idealistic terms as faith, honor, and duty. Wilke spoke of instinct, fear, and aggression. It was a colossal meeting between a man who adhered to a combination of Enlightenment philosophy and a Judeo-Christian world-view, and one who obeyed the Law of the Jungle. But out here I was in Wilke's neck of the woods, his lecture hall, his 'church', and would try to defy all that surrounded me physically with the power of that which filled me intellectually and even spiritually.

"What is it that you believe in, Colonel Kurtz? Everybody over here is fighting for something they believe in. The Jarai are fighting to throw out the Vietnamese, whom they consider to be Chinese invaders. The North Vietnamese are fighting to throw out the Americans, whom they consider to be imperialists. And the Americans are fighting to throw out the communists. But what are *you* fighting for?"

"Well, I'm fighting for freedom and democracy."

"Well, yes, me too, but those are very standard answers, colonel. You are a son of the Enlightenment, and so am I, to a certain extent, as most Westerners are. Are there reasons, apart from those ideological, for your presence here, colonel, perhaps reasons metaphysical?"

I initially hesitated to answer, believing that Wilke was simply trying to draw out my religious beliefs in order to criticize them, but then decided to proceed, albeit cautiously.

"Yes, I had a Christian upbringing, and I do believe in God."

"And, so, what does fighting a war in the jungles of Southeast Asia have to do with one's faith in God, from a Christian perspective, colonel?"

"The preservation of the Christian faith from the threat of atheistic communism. The preservation of the Western philosophical and political system...Western tradition and culture, to be more precise."

I thought for a moment and then continued, but would soon regret it.

"And the eventual realization of God's

Kingdom," I added.

"So, thy kingdom come, thy will be done, on earth as it is in heaven?"

"Yes, that is how the prayer goes."

"On earth as it is in heaven," repeated Wilke back to himself slowly. "What does that mean—-thy Kingdom come, on earth as it is in heaven?" Wilke of course had his own ideas, but wanted to hear my opinion.

"Well, I'm sure a learned man such as yourself understands the concept of the Kingdom of God."

"I've certainly heard the term before, but have never really gotten a clear explanation."

"It's not a difficult subject to understand. In fact, it's very simple, something I believe most people would agree is quite logical if they would simply open their mind to it."

"You're not talking about a world governed by the papacy, are you? Because that'll never work," said Wilke with a sarcastic tone intended to take some of the self-righteous piss out of his younger and less worldly counterpart in what was in fact quickly becoming more of a debate than it was a conversation. Quick to correct what I perceived as short-sightedness on the part of Wilke, I wasted no time rebutting.

"No, not an earthly government, not a world ruled by men nor their guns or ideologies, but a world ruled or governed by reason and by God's will."

"Hang on there, colonel, but those two concepts—-reason and God's will—-were considered by the Enlightenment thinkers to be at cross purposes with one another."

"Well, yes," I conceded, "but they have been reconciled since then."

"Oh yeah? By whom?"

"By philosophers and theologians."

"Uh huh," said Wilke, unconvinced.

"The point is, sergeant, that in such a world, the point of convergence for all mankind would no longer be that which makes us different, but instead what makes us alike. And our greatest commonality would be that we are all reasonable and rational human beings, all of us children of God, and we are all hoping for a peaceful world in which to live. So, yes, a combination of reason and faith, sergeant. Where the Enlightenment thinkers went wrong was in relying too much on human reason, just like the medieval church relied almost exclusively on faith at the expense of reason. Admittedly, in both cases the end result was catastrophic."

"So, you're saying, colonel..." Wilke attempted to interject, but I quickly cut him off because I was not satisfied that I had made my point clear enough.

"I know that sounds a bit fanciful and maybe even naïve, sergeant, but what's so hard to believe that a world adhering to God's law of love, and God-given reason, can live in peace?"

"So, what you're saying, then, is that in God's Kingdom...you're calling this impending peace, God's Kingdom, right, colonel?"

"In the West, yes. Many people in the West believe that true peace can only come with the realization of God's Kingdom, and not through any form or type of human contrivance such as an ideology or form of government. It's called other things in other parts of the world and other cultures, but in the part of the world and culture that I come from it is called the Kingdom of God."

"Will the Kingdom of God, colonel, exist here, on a transformed earth?"

"Well, again, admittedly, sergeant, it is a theological concept open to debate among many theologians. Some believe it will exist here on a transformed earth, while others believe it will exist in a separate plain or realm."

"Okay, but isn't there a general consensus among theologians that when it comes to pass, there will be no distinction between race or social and economic class, and that it will be a beautiful little utopia?"

"Well, yes, in a sense, but…"

"That kind of sounds like what we're fighting *against* over here," exclaimed Wilke, returning the favor of being interrupted.

"I know what you're trying to do, Sergeant Wilke, but what the communists don't understand is that this kind of 'utopia', as you called it, cannot be forced by the barrel of a gun, as Vladimir Lenin, Mao Tse Tung, and Ho Chi Minh seem to think, nor can it be erected upon the frail, fallible thought of mortal men such as Karl Marx. Mankind must be allowed to come to the Kingdom of their own free will. There should be no coercion of God's will, just as there should be no obstructions for those who seek it."

"But isn't that what we're doing over here…forcing our will, mainly political, but also religious, upon the North Vietnamese, with the barrel of a gun?" quizzed Wilke in another attempt at sidetracking my thesis.

"I would argue that we're tearing down obstructions rather than coercing, Sergeant Wilke," was my brief response, not wishing to indulge Wilke any longer in his role of devil's advocate.

"I don't think the North Vietnamese would see it that way," came one last word on the subject from Wilke, a baited path I chose not to go down, which was followed by a brief moment of silence used to absorb some of the tension that had built up between us while I tried to figure out how Wilke, who was still visibly stoned from the herbs he smoked earlier, could be so clear of mind. Then, deciding that I would be the one to determine the course of conversation, I looked out into the same direction of darkened jungle as Wilke, and asked him what he saw out there, metaphorically speaking.

Sounding introspective, less confrontative, and more like a man indeed under the influence of a mild herbal intoxicant, Wilke began answering my question that had been purposely left open to the sergeant's own interpretation.

"What do I see out there? I see a lot of things," he began to say, then paused for a moment to allow the plethora of thoughts and ideas evoked by the inquiry to come together as an ordered conceptualization. "I see a little bit of us all in there--you, me, the Jarai, the Vietnamese--we're all in there. It's our womb, it's where we were born and bred," explained Wilke to his senior officer who was more confused than convinced, perhaps because I was taking the sergeant's words literally instead of as the analogy they were meant to be.

"And when you look at us?" I asked in a manner that sounded almost patronizing, convinced once again that Wilke was not in his normal frame of mind.

"When I look at us I see the jungle, our real creator who shaped us in its own primeval image, endowing us with primitive instincts for procreation and survival. Like the jungle, we birth and kill by means of copulation and bloodletting. You see, colonel, the jungle is where we come from, it's where we still live to some extent, while the heavens are a place that we can only hope and pray to someday get to."

"I'm picking up a little Nietzsche, some Darwin in there…"

"These aren't secondary observations that came to mind after reading somebody else's ideas from a dusty book, Colonel Kurtz. They're simple deductions made from living for many years in the bowels of the jungle, being reminded every day that I, like the other creatures living here, am kept alive by my inborn ability to imitate the jungle, my capacity to evolve and adapt to my every situation. We've all inherited this primordial knowledge from the jungle. It permeates our flesh and flows through our veins, our internal nature reflecting the outward likeness of our creator. For the jungle to be deposed by the kingdom of God, colonel, these ancient instincts for survival that we possess would first have to be subdued. We've been able to conquer most everything on this earth, even the jungle to some extent with our bombs and napalm, but we have never been able to tame ourselves. Maybe subconsciously we know that to do so would be to die. Instinct, my friend, is true wisdom, endowed by our true maker--the jungle, the wilderness, whatever you want to call it--who has been battered but remains unbroken."

Confident he had proved his point, and uninterested in arguing any further about things he knew to be true, Wilke got up to get another jar of alcohol and rejoin the rest of the group.

I had had my fill of talk as well, but

remained where I was, deciding to watch the remainder of the celebration instead of participating in it. I was by now very drunk and sluggish from the heat and alcohol. Everything seemed to be moving in slow motion to my tired eyes. The smoke rolled even slower up from the fires, and the chanting and drumbeats sounded deep and guttural to my intoxicated mind. Through the wall of smoke and sound, I noticed Wilke was now dousing his head and body with water the Jarai had been praying over, a form of self-baptism intended to protect him from evil spirits. With the purification rite complete, Wilke and his shadow disappeared into the darkness and unseen foliage. Even though I did not think we were a whole lot alike at this moment, upon seeing this I realized that me and the sergeant were not all that different, either.

CHAPTER 14

"Would you say, Marlon, that the jungle is the antithesis of Walter's father in all his God-fearing, spar-spangled glory?"

"Well, no. I think for Walter the jungle is the antithesis of God, and that the jungle supplants, not his father, but rather God or the Christian religion as that which helps him understand the world."

"But, is Walter really *that* religious? I don't think I want Walter to be all that religious. I see Walter Kurtz, and his father for that matter, like we talked about earlier, to adhere to a kind of American patriotic-like religion. You know what I mean, Marlon? And they do so kind of unwittingly, as a lot of Americans do. It's kind of like…oh, how the hell can I describe it?" Francis paused for a moment to think. "Oh, I know. It's kind of like the system employed by the Roman Empire, with its cult of the emperor, and even cult of the empire itself."

"Right. Right."

"So, you know what I mean, then, Marlon?" asked a skeptical Francis Coppola.

"Of course I do, Francis. I learned all that from my role as Mark Antony."

"Ah, yes, I love that movie."

"Really? I hate it."

"Of course, you do, Marlon. You hate all your old movies," remarked Francis with a laugh. "So yeah, Marlon, I can see Walter adhering to a kind of cult of America type thing. And it's a cult that includes God, but it's more of an Americanized God, if you will. It's the idea that God is on the side of America, in war, and in all times and seasons for that matter. But Walter, as his dad did, and as a lot of Americans do, gets this idea of God mixed up with the Christian God, the God of the Bible. He thinks the Christian God—a God who is believed by many to be a universal God—is on the side of America."

"Yes, I think that's the right approach, Francis. Walter replaces the cult of America that he is unwittingly adhering to, with the law of the jungle, for lack of a better term, as the lens through which he sees or understands the world."

"Yes, Marlon. I think we're on the same page here. Say more about this."

"I will, Francis, but I want to comment about something else first."

"Sure."

"I find it interesting how this kind of 'becoming one with nature' thing that we've been talking about started getting big in America in the 1960s, and how it was thought of then as some kind of hippy-dippy, new-age bull-shit. But in reality, this manner of understanding man's relationship with nature is quite ancient, literally thousands of years old."

"Yes, good point Marlon. These are, as you said, ancient ideas, especially in the East, but new to Americans, entering the American lexicon and psyche by way of the hippy culture."

"Yes, but I would argue that there's another layer underneath all this Eastern and hippy-dippy metaphysical stuff."

"Such as?"

Marlon looked at his director in mild disbelief.

"Francis, you know this stuff better than I do."

"No, I don't think I do. Besides, I want to hear you explain it. I imagine, though, that you're going to mention Walter's contact with the montagnards of Vietnam and Cambodia."

"Yes, Francis, the montagnards—the highlanders—teach him their ancient methods of becoming one with the natural world—the jungle—its ebb and flow, its shifting tides, and so forth."

"Okay, so frame this thing for me, Marlon."

"What?"

"In a few sentences—a paragraph—put Walter Kurtz' religio-philosophical transition into words."

"Okay. I'll give it a shot." Marlon cleared his throat in jest for dramatic effect. "Walter goes to Vietnam, believing that every situation and circumstance, including the things of nature, can be mastered by man. Uh…he believes that God-inspired American ingenuity and know-how can triumph over any and all things. However, after a while, from living in the jungle and watching both the Vietnamese and the montagnards, Walter begins to see things differently. The world is no longer so ordered and reasoned…in the Western sense, that is."

"Right. I can see that."

"He now sees the world through the filter of the jungle, and he sees the jungle as this kind of amalgamation of dissimilar living things competing with one another to stay alive. And that the jungle blinds all these living things of this reality by keeping them embroiled in constant warfare. The various parts are too busy fighting, killing and devouring one another to realize how much they rely on, and serve, their...their...uh...their amorphous lord or master—the jungle—who rewards and gives sustenance to those who worship—those who kill—at the foot of the altar of nature's slaughter bench," said Marlon, looking and sounding as if he was trying hard to remember these pre-formulated words.

"That sounds like a trailer for a Cornel Wilde film, Marlon."

"Which one, *The Naked Prey*?"

"Yes, Marlon, *The Naked Prey*. What a weird fucken movie!"

"It was a stupid movie, and totally perpetuated some of the worst, most racist stereotypes of Africans."

"Well, yes, but it wasn't stupid. There was an edge to it. More than just an edge, actually. It was unnerving, and uncomfortable to watch. The movie takes these wealthy white, college-educated Westerners, who are in Africa on a big game safari, and pits them in a life and death struggle against the native Africans, who capture the white men, then set them free so they can hunt them down."

"Yes, but despite the fact that the Africans are in their own element, and have been hunting and killing with spears and knives their entire life, the Westerners are able to outsmart, outrun and outfight them at nearly every turn, for no apparent reason other than because they are Westerners. It's completely unbelievable, and quite racist."

"It was just the one white guy who was formidable, the in-shape guy, who was actually played by Wilde himself. All the other

Westerners were easily captured, mocked and brutally killed, much of which was extremely difficult to watch. The cinematography and mood created by Wilde was amazing. It had the look and feel of a documentary, at least in certain spots, more than it did that of a movie, which I really liked."

"They actually killed those elephants in the movie. Did you know that, Francis?"

"No. I can't say that I did."

"Shot them dead, with the cameras rolling."

"I always assumed they tranquilized them, or something."

"No, Francis. There were a lot of animals being killed in that movie, for real. Animals killing other animals. People killing animals. There was a lot about that movie that was difficult to watch, as you said. I'm not a fan of killing animals for the sake of making a scene look realistic, but in terms of creating a tense, uncomfortable mood, Wilde certainly did that. It was all very real, a little too real, if you ask me. I just didn't like it."

"Like the scene of the white man being burned alive."

"Yes. I had a kind of visceral reaction to it."

"Me too, Marlon! Let me ask you something."

"Okay."

"Do you think you found some of the scenes difficult and unnerving because the white men had lost control of the situation to the Africans, and were then completely at their mercy?"

Marlon paused for a moment to think.

"I know what you're saying, Francis, and unfortunately I think that you might be right."

"You said you had a *visceral* reaction to what you were seeing."

"Yes, it was visceral…"

"Mine, too, was visceral. And I think it was visceral because the people who looked like me up on the screen—the white men—were not in control of their environment, and were being victimized and brutalized by people who *didn't* look like me. It was all very primal."

"Yes, it was," said Marlon reflectively. "That's a very interesting perspective, Francis. I never considered it in that way."

"Not only that, Marlon, but the movie also makes a point about the jungle, too."

"It does?" replied Marlon upon realizing his director was

waiting for a response.

"Yeah. And I think it's the exact opposite of what you've been telling me for the past week or so."

"Which is?"

"If you think about it for a moment, you'd know what I'm talking about, Marlon."

"I don't want to think."

"Okay. I'll tell you. Wilde is trying to make the case that if you put a man in the jungle, even the most educated and civilized of men, he becomes a beast. He's not saying that it's the beast that makes the jungle, but rather it's the jungle that makes the beast."

Francis starred at Marlon, waiting for his response.

"Well, that might be true, too, Francis. It's a complicated subject, and I'm not saying I'm right, or that I even know what the fuck I'm talking about for that matter."

"Right. I get that, Marlon. I just find it interesting."

"You find what interesting?"

"The contrast between what you and what Cornel Wilde are saying about human nature, and human instinct, because I think that you're saying the opposite of what Wilde is saying."

"Not necessarily, Francis."

"But you are, Marlon. And I'm not saying who's right and who's wrong. You have been alluding to the idea or notion that the beast makes the jungle, and that we are really all just beasts, which is something we have managed to hide—to cover up—with the thin veneer we call *civilization*. And Wilde puts it the other way around. He's saying that the jungle *makes us* into beasts."

"I think we're both right, Francis."

"How can you both be right?"

"We just are. It's not something so clear-cut, Francis, and I think your movie is trying to make this very point, am I right? Things are not always so black and white, so clear-cut as a lot of people like to believe they are, right?"

"Yeah. That's what I'm trying to do, Marlon. You're right."

Marlon shrugged his shoulders. He wanted his director to at least understand this much, but he was not interested in wading into the nature vs. nurture argument at this particular moment, and neither was Francis.

"I've got to go, Marlon. We'll talk more about this later.

Wonderful stuff, Marlon, wonderful stuff!" said Francis loudly as he was already almost out of ear-shot.

Marlon watched Francis as he bounded away, then looked out into the jungle.

* * *

The men of Green Tiger were hunters, hunters of men, stalking our prey through the jungle, no matter where. Borders, countries and their governing laws meant nothing to us. The jungle acknowledged no man-made boundaries or legal processes, and neither would we.

I used to spend my nights asleep, lying next to my wife. Now the nighttime hours find me scouring the jungle, searching out the enemies of my God and my country so I can kill them. As I performed this nightly duty, I wore a crucifix around my neck intended to keep me safe from the darkness—literal and figurative. Everywhere I walked or crawled, the crucifix went ahead of me, the figurine of the crucified Son in effect claiming for the Father, and for the Western world, the lands until now held by the clutches of the infidels.

I did not like killing, but I knew I had to, and that the only way to defeat the communists and preserve freedom was to eradicate those spreading the Marxist poison. I believed that death was the choice the communists were making for themselves.

I knew what needed to be done, and I stood up like a man and did it. I could have taken the easy way out and requested to be rotated back to the states when the going got tough, but I didn't. Instead, I chose to carry out this horrible task asked of me by my country, doing so with great confidence and determination.

Like big-game hunters, me and the rest of Green Tiger relentlessly pursued our prey in the thick vine forests of Cambodia and in the swampy marshes of South Vietnam, worming our way in and out of the two countries, but all the while remaining inside the jungle. We pursued our quarry slowly and methodically, then hit with violent pugnacity, always making sure to count the dead. The numbers climbed into the hundreds, yet there was no end to our charge.

For some members of Green Tiger, the more they killed, the greater their bloodlust became. Edwards was a prime example of this. Killing gave him a rush the likes he never experienced before. It was a sensation the Texan could not get enough of. He collected the teeth and ears from the dead North Vietnamese, and even began joining the Jarai in their practice of carving the flesh off the skulls and placing them around camp, a method used by the Jarai for thousands of years to harness the physical and spiritual power of their enemies. On his helmet Edwards drew a confederate flag, and wrote 'Black Death', a reference to our own scourge of plague and pestilence we were spreading throughout eastern Cambodia.

CHAPTER 15

"How do you think Walter fairs in Vietnam, as a soldier?" asked Marlon. "I mean...he is sent there to kill."

"Yes, he is. And he is a professional, so he does reasonably well in regard to his mission, I would assume."

"Yes, but he is only human. And killing is not a natural human instinct, much less a natural human act."

"Are you sure about that, Marlon? Human beings seem to be pretty good at killing, and killing for a variety of reasons, many of which the animal kingdom does not even know exists, much less utilizes."

"I see your point. I still don't think that killing is natural for human beings, except perhaps in self-defense."

"Well, it might not be natural, but people kill for a lot of offensive reasons as well, such as greed, lust, for reasons of hatred and revenge."

"What about in war?"

"What about it, Marlon?"

"Is killing in war self-defense?"

"Well, that depends. The grunts out in the field are in effect killing in self-defense, even if they are on the offensive, because they have been ordered to do so. The commanding officers are just carrying out orders as well. It's actually the politicians, I believe, who are really the ones guilty of killing, because they are the ones making war, for reasons of greed, pressure from various interest groups, including the military-industrial complex, big business, their own personal and business interests, and the like."

"Have you ever wanted to kill someone, Francis?"

"I'm thinking about it right now." Francis waited for Marlon to comprehend his joke before continuing. Marlon rolled his eyes in acknowledgement of his director's attempt at levity. "No, I'm kidding, Marlon. You know I love you." The two men laughed. "Uh, let's see…I've been extremely mad at people before, but I've never wanted to kill them, I don't think."

"Are you sure? How about your wife?"

"My wife, Marlon?"

"Yes, your wife."

"Why do you ask me that?"

"Because I, at some point, have wanted to kill all my wives and lovers. You can't live in that kind of close proximity with someone, and not get so mad that you just want to kill them, especially one's spouse or lover. There is something very primordial going on between two people who are in a sexual relationship…lust, love, hatred, jealousy, hurt—all these things—and sometimes those passions boil over to the point that we just want to wring their neck."

"Marlon, I must admit, and this is why I wanted you to be a part of this project, you are getting me to think about certain things which are uncomfortable for me to think about. And this is where I want this movie, and the dialogue for this movie, to go. I want it to go to those places that are uncomfortable for people to talk about, and even uncomfortable for people to think about."

"Like *Last Tango*."

"Yes, like *Last Tango in Paris*! For God's sake, Marlon, you were fucking that girl up the ass. Marlon Brando, the biggest movie star in the world, a middle-aged Marlon Brando, is having anal sex on screen with a girl half his age! People are intrigued. They are shocked. They are horrified. Marlon Brando!"

"They shouldn't have been shocked. I had been playing controversial characters for two decades before that movie. My characters raped women and beat up men for no apparent reason other than to simply quench their animal lusts of sexual gratification and violence."

"I thought you said that it wasn't natural for humans to kill and do violence?"

"Well, it is for me," said Marlon, causing both men to chuckle.

"And a lot of the characters you played, too, apparently."

"Yes, I guess so."

"Can you explain this, Marlon? Is this just Hollywood sensationalism, or is there something more Darwinian at work here?"

Marlon thought for a moment.

"Well, Francis, let me preface what I said earlier about how it is not natural for human beings to kill one another."

"Alright."

"What I meant was that it is not natural for human beings to kill and do violence to one another, if, Francis, if, and when, humans understand themselves from a Christian-centric perspective."

"What does that mean exactly?"

"What? Which part?"

"Well, the whole statement, Marlon. But more specifically, 'Christian-centric perspective'."

"To understand one's self, or to understand humanity, from a Christian-centric perspective is to assume that human beings have been endowed with some kind of spiritual, and perhaps even physical ascendancy over and above that of the animal kingdom and all its sexual and blood lust. But when you consider humans as part of the animal kingdom, then violence becomes a very natural thing, both sexual and protective violence. There is no real love in the animal kingdom. It's all instinct. The males in effect rape the females in most animal species. So, in that regard, rape is more natural to humans than is the concept of consensual sex or lovemaking."

"Haven't you ever loved any of your wives or lovers, Marlon?"

"I don't think so. I think I have simply lusted after them. And when those feelings of lust subsided I lost interest. It is only after I stopped lusting after my lovers that I no longer wanted to kill them."

"So, the point that you're trying to make here, Marlon, is that human beings are really just animals, following their animal instincts. But that mankind, by way of certain religious and/or philosophical and even political ideas and ideologies, like Christianity, have come to believe we are something more akin to gods, or at a minimum that we have been created in God's image, which affords us an ascendancy over and above the animal kingdom?"

"Precisely. And I can see Walter, at war out in the jungle, first coming to unearth, and then accept his true nature, including his animal instincts. He even tries to utilize them in order to accomplish his mission, even though the reason why he took this mission—the ascendancy of his species and even his tribe—was something he no longer believes in, or at least he no longer understands this concept in the same manner that he once did."

"What do you mean by that, Marlon?"

"By what?"

"When you said that he 'no longer understands this concept in the same manner that he once did'. What do you mean by that?"

"He no longer believes in the spiritual ascendancy or superiority of his species. More specifically, Kurtz no longer believes in the spiritual ascendancy of white people, people of Western-European Christian descent. He no longer believes they are gods on earth."

"So why does he keep fighting the war if he no longer believes these things? I mean, if the reasons why he is fighting the war in Vietnam—God and country—are no longer things that he believes in, then what is his motivation? Why does he keep fighting, and perhaps even with more tenacity, more viciousness, more savagery than before?"

"Well, having been lost of the religious and/or mythological justifications for war, Walter is left with only his primordial instincts…"

"But doesn't he also have a lot of disenchantment, resentment, and perhaps even anger that he is now carrying around as a result of becoming so disillusioned, of in effect having the truth sift its way to the surface, just like his father said it would?"

"Ooh, that's good, Francis!" said Marlon, aware that his director was referring to his earlier description of the talk Walter's father had with him upon returning home from World War II.

"Yes, it is good, if I do say so myself. But let me ask you this, Marlon. Do we want Walter to be struggling with the revelations that his past is not what he thought it was? Or do we want him to have moved on rather seamlessly, and to be very sure in what he is doing now?"

"Explain more about what you mean, Francis."

"Well, when Walter first comes to Vietnam he is sure about why he is there. He believes in the cause, so to speak. But after he's there for a while he goes through the process of losing his patriotic and religious compass. Again, he is very clear-headed when he initially goes to war in Vietnam. But while there, he becomes lost of those initial reasons or motivations, and subsequently finds different motivators, whatever those might be."

"Yes, I see where you're coming from, but…"

"And I think the movie must be clear, Marlon, that Kurtz does find another motivation, because his fanaticism, his willingness to kill, his *capacity* to kill, and even to commit horrific acts, grows in its immensity and proportion, or at least that's how I want to have him portrayed."

"And, so, you're asking what this *other* motivation might be?"

"Well, yes, for lack of a better term."

"I was trying to tell you a few minutes ago before you interrupted me."

"I'm sorry, Marlon. That's what we Italians do. We're loud and we interrupt one another. I thought this was made clear to you when we were making *The Godfather*."

"Yes, but it doesn't make it any less problematic and annoying."

"Sorry, Marlon. Can you retrace that line of thought?"

Marlon took a deep breath and exhaled slowly in order to make his director understand the difficulty his interruption had caused him.

"You see, Marlon, as I said, Kurtz is no longer all about God and country, but he is certainly not a hippy, either, even though he has freed himself from certain social, moral, and religious constraints. So why is he fighting *now*? What is his motivation *now*?" I mean…why is he doing all this crazy, weird, and even horrible shit out in the Cambodian jungle?"

"I'm trying to fucking tell you, Francis."

"Sorry, Marlon. I won't interrupt again."

"I bet you will."

"Yes, I probably will. But please proceed before I do."

"Actually, Francis, in addition to his primordial instincts, I think Kurtz is a man who is at least somewhat motivated by his own personal celebrity and his ego. He is a proud man who became drunk on the accolades heaped upon him and the freedom that this allowed for. He is a man who had things come easy for him when he was younger. But now, getting older, coupled with the frustrations of the Vietnam War, Kurtz begins to question things, to question himself, his past, to just question everything."

"And so now he's kind of charging hard down some bizarre path, cutting sharply against the grain of all that he knows."

"Yes, I guess he is."

"What's he trying to accomplish, Marlon?"

Marlon paused to think.

"Hell, I don't know. Maybe he's just trying to survive," said Marlon, suddenly disinterested.

Francis shook his head. He hated it when Marlon would mentally drift off. He ran hot and cold, and did so throughout the filming of *The Godfather*. This was not anything new to Francis Coppola.

"If that's all it is, Marlon, then we don't have a movie."

"Maybe he's trying to expose all the lies."

"What lies, Marlon?"

"The World War II and post-World War II bullshit, which says that good and evil are so clear-cut, that the United States is always the purveyor of right over wrong, and good over evil, that God is on our side, etc., etc."

"So, some of this is about the stuff conveyed or articulated in the post-World War II war and military movies?"

"Yes, that's part of it. But that's an over-simplified explanation of it, Francis. He just wants to fight the war outside of the phony, over-hyped, glossed-over world of the American propaganda machine, and Hollywood has very much been a part of that machine, unfortunately."

"Are we still talking about Kurtz, or are we now talking about Marlon Brando?"

"Is there a difference?"

"I don't know. You tell me, Marlon."

Marlon paused for a moment to think.

"I think we're talking about both of us."

CHAPTER 16

Basecamp Artemis was near some ancient Khmer ruins close to the lost city of Ankor Thom, built some fifteen-hundred years earlier, but long since abandoned and overgrown with jungle. Underneath its massive entanglements of vines and other vegetation are elaborate temples, pavilions, and sculptures rivaling the best that ancient Greece and Rome had to offer.

The local Cambodians are deathly afraid to enter what they call the 'forbidden city'. The lost or forbidden city was built by the Khmers—ancestors of present-day Cambodians—who left behind their story as told by the statues they carved from rock as well as the paintings on the city's walls. On the walls of corridors built during the twelfth-century reign of Suryavarman II are endless paintings and etchings chronicling continuous, bloody battles between the Khmers and a wide array of enemies fought throughout Suryavarman II's living tenure as Khmer king. Suryavarman II's reign of terror not only sparked fear in his battlefield adversaries, but in his own subjects as well. So much so, that the ruthless dictator who insisted upon being worshipped as a god while alive, continued to be exalted in such a manner after he died, the lingering effects of a regime that maintained power by slaughtering all dissenters.

Eventually the Khmer people grew tired and weary of worshipping self-proclaimed man-gods such as Suryvarman II and his successors who continually led them into warfare and the worship of worldly things. Instead of leading his people to Nirvana as promised, Suryvarman II, as indicated by the wall carvings, forced the peasantry into the underworld when they died to be judged according to their fealty for him and other earthly kings. Those deemed unworthy of the promised place of eternal bliss would be dragged off to a fiery hell by demons for all eternity.

Saving them from this earthly drudgery and afterlife torment was the Buddhist monk, Jayavarman VII, who helped the Khmers build a society based on peace and charity as opposed to war and greed. When Jayavarman VII died, the Khmers repeated the mistakes made by those who worshipped Suryavarman II by building statues of their beloved spiritual leader and luminary so they could continue to adorn Jayavarman VII in death. Soon they forgot his message of humility, even fighting amongst themselves over the right to represent the legacy he left behind.

So distraught were Jayavarman VII's followers over his death and the degradation of his dream of an earthly heaven that they decided to leave their great city en mass, and some to leave this world altogether in order to search for their redeemer and the heaven he promised them, because neither could be found there in Ankor Thom, which was left for the jungle to devour, and roaming armies to destroy and pillage. Thick vines now grow through the cracks in its walls, slowly breaking apart the abandoned city. The statues of Vishnu, Buddha, Suryavarman II, and Jayavarman VII can be seen only by peeling away hundreds of years of jungle growth. When unveiled of their green shroud, it becomes obvious that centuries of wet humid air have slowly decomposed the expression and detail from the faces of man and god, time and nature rendering both equally vulnerable.

Various myths and legends regarding the lost city eventually reached the Vietnamese highlands, making the already superstitious Jarai deathly afraid to go anywhere near the ruins. But with Wilke's encouragement, and the fact that the ancient city soon became covered with the bodies of dead Vietcong, the Jarai eventually felt very much at home there. With the help of us Americans, they created their own scenes reminiscent of the bloody wall paintings describing Khmer life during the reign of Suryvarman II, a time of incessant slaughter and butchery as well. Bodies of dead North Vietnamese were propped up on rocks or hung from vines like trophy mounts on a hunter's wall. Once their teeth and ears were removed to make necklaces, the corpses were positioned along the city walls, both inside and out, believed by the Jarai to ward off evil spirits and keep one's enemy away. Once again stories were spreading from the Forbidden City out into the jungle. Its new inhabitants were described as demons and ghosts of such people as the Chams, slaughtered by the Vietnamese hundreds of years ago during their now endless war. Others claimed they were the restless spirits of the deceased French empire seeking their revenge.

The black ash that certain members of

Green Tiger made into a paste and wore on their faces during nightly forays ignited the spread of even more wild stories by those Vietcong who happened to see Green Tiger and escaped to tell about it. Our black appearance, and the fact we moved as quietly as dusk's creeping gloom, led many Vietnamese to believe that the darkness itself had taken human form and was hunting them down.

Like the Cambodians, the Vietnamese avoided the Forbidden City of walking dead and wrathful spirits. From their more northerly outposts, the Vietcong could smell the evil emanating from the jungle city as the dead bodies rotted and stank in the humid air. At night the Vietcong listened in horror as the sounds of chanting, drumming, wailing, even screaming resonated from the Forbidden City. From miles away they could see the sacrificial fires that the Jarai danced and prayed around in preparation of going out on a hunt, the orange braziers leaping high into the night sky and illuminating the outline of the Khmer architecture.

Basecamp Artemis reeked of dead bodies, the smell easily overtaking the many and varied exotic perfumed aromas coming from plant and animal enticements intended for mating purposes as well as the means of luring unsuspecting prey into one's general vicinity. Flies of many varieties ascended upon the basecamp in droves, their larvae quickly devouring the flesh of the Vietcong. Huge carnivorous crows flew in and out of Artemis as well, consuming their fair share of flesh. Even they have stayed away from the Forbidden City for hundreds of years, returning for the first time since the wars of Sayavarman II when dead carcasses littered its city streets in great abundance as well. They swarmed the skies over Artemis, creating a black cloud of hungry, screaming, bloodthirsty fowl, further blocking the sun's penetration.

The killing and desecration of the North Vietnamese no longer bothered me. I hated the communists. They were why I was in this God-forsaken place. It was my job to kill them. I would even pray for more kills and the end of my enemy so I could return home to my family.

* * *

As I requested while back in Danang, a priest was flown in periodically to pray with and counsel Green Tiger, and even celebrate Catholic Mass, usually at dusk inside one of the ancient Khmer temples. There the priest hung a large bamboo cross on a stone wall and lit an array of candles during the services to illuminate the former Hindu and Buddhist shrine.

Some of the Jarai attended the Christian vigils, and even Wilke could be seen sitting in from time to time, albeit appearing bored and restless. Being inside the stone-walled building made him feel trapped. Wilke spent most of his time in the shrine pondering possible escape routes should the situation warrant. A crack in the ceiling, created by an expanding vine, was just enough space to allow a beam of moonlight to peer its way into the temple, casting a lunar light among its worshippers as if the Lord himself was present, or so Father McDuffee told his congregation.

Army priest, Colonel Jerry McDuffee, would give rousing sermons on the evils of communism, and on the importance of being a loyal servant of God. "It's better to fight with God than against God," Father McDuffee would always say.

   Intrigued by the consecration of bread and wine into the body and blood of a man who was also believed by his followers to be fully divine, some of the Jarai would attend the services conducted by the Catholic priest. They had their own worship and rituals, however, ones in which they too would drink blood and eat flesh, albeit not those of a god, nor a man, but rather a wild pig. Their ceremonies would usually turn boisterous, the blood sacrifice and centerpiece of the Jarai celebration reaching almost orgasmic heights in contrast to the solemn Catholic Eucharist.

   A mixing of cultures ensued within Green Tiger as some of the Jarai began developing a taste for American beef, Budweiser beer, and Marlboro cigarettes, while a few of the Americans, especially LeBetre, preferred the rice and mango wine, and wild boar provided by the Jarai.

   Basecamp Artemis was not only an awesome display of devastating military effectiveness, but one of religious and spiritual fanaticism as well. The sight and smell of the numerous bodies of dead Vietcong scattered throughout lent a clear understanding as to the potency of both. The Vietnam War was considered modern in terms of the sophistication of military technology, but it was still fire, steel, and the will of the divine realm which were its means to an end, the same determining factors that have been in effect for thousands of years.

   Flame, weaponry, and the will of God were all at my disposal whenever I needed them, but I discovered something else that was of great service to me while fighting this jungle conflict. It too was an implement of war, one hiding just beneath my civilized exterior. Although confidant in the purpose and reasons for my involvement in this horrific war, I still searched for justification and even answers for all that I had become a part of out in the jungle. As I prowled the sublime foliage in search of my quarry, sometimes the hunter and sometimes the hunted, I unwittingly awakened my feral instincts for survival, ones lulled to sleep in my ancestors by thousands of years of civilization. It would be there, in that dark ancient void, a place forbidden by my Western Judeo-Christian enculturation, where I would stumble across my true nature, a part of myself so obvious yet so well hidden I had to turn myself completely inside out before I could see it. It was the adrenaline-induced fear and excitement from perpetually preying and being preyed upon, from living so close to death both night and day that I could literally hear the silent screams coming from the decomposed world of the jungle floor, that revived my carnal instincts for self-preservation and a remorseless desire to stay alive. I in turn became a conscienceless killer, playing right into the hands of the jungle, a mere extension of its death-ridden floor. And the harder I fought to free myself, the tighter the jungle's grip on me became.

The human civility so needed to survive for the first forty years of my life in Western society was being squeezed from my mind and body, the violent environment in which I currently live forcing me to adapt or die. I now learn my social graces and etiquette from the jungle, which has been Wilke's mentor for the past quarter-century, and that of the Jarai's since time immemorial.

It has literally been millions of years since my ancestors walked upright out of the animal kingdom to dominate the earth. Since then, the human species has occupied much of its time trying to further distinguish itself from the animals it once foraged amongst. The desire to place ourselves far above the earth's lowly creatures has inspired many explanations of mankind's past. Western civilization has developed doctrines, dogmas, and credos centered around the belief that mankind is formed in the likeness of God, inheriting the divine spark of our Creator, and given 'dominance over the fowl in the air, fishes in the sea, and hoofed beasts in the field', and that God is our Shepherd, who has led us out of the wilderness and away from our primal as well as sinful past.

The Christian would say that sin is an iniquity caused by the Fall. The Darwinian would contend that it is a residue of our animal instincts. The Christian world has bowed its collective head to the cleansing power of baptismal waters in return for the forgiveness of their Original Sin, offering their bodies and souls up to an all-powerful God in return for the destruction of our primal, sinful origin. But God could not kill man's carnal knowledge without killing man, because man is creature, not God. Subsequently, God buried it deep inside the subconscious mind of the creature he created in his own image, forbidding man from going there, making man feel shame and remorse whenever reverting back to the ways of the wilderness.

I found my way back to this forbidden knowledge by slaying the pangs of guilt that kept watch over it. Once in, I could not find my way back out. And although gutted of much of our human emotions, neither I nor the other members of Green Tiger had become animals. Animals do not pick up weapons and march off to war to kill for gods and governments. Nor do animals need to justify and find ablution for their brutal nature. These are things exclusive to man. The truth is, however, that we are neither man nor animal, but something in-between. But like animals, we killed our enemy without guilt, remorse, or personal judgment upon ourselves. Whatever we are, we look more dead than alive. Our faces have grown thin and gaunt, but wear the look of determination, and not defeat. We are like an apparition. We were there one minute, then gone the next, but not before taking the lives of the living with us.

    The pursuit of an elevated status has led man to aspirations of godliness, shackling ourselves with ambitions we could never attain. The human animal has proved itself incapable of being tamed, much less perfected to the likes of God. Western man eventually came to resent their God, one who has left us frustrated and embarrassed of our earthly imperfections that we could never overcome. We became jealous of our Maker and covetous of the subservience and adulation that God receives, as well as the wealth and power this kind of exaltation could bring us. God's children would slowly wrest away their Father's authority, using it to promulgate the same earthly empire that first killed the Father's Son, and then exalted him as God incarnate.

    Mankind is no longer constrained by the wrath of their judgmental God. We have freed ourselves from the expectations of perfection we were unable to attain. But in the process mankind has become a slave to our own greed, jealousy, desire and lack of restraint. This has become mankind's cruelest fate of all, proving ourselves to be more demanding and vengeful than our God ever was. No longer was mankind the servant of a wrathful and condemnatory God, but rather slaves to our own lusts and longings. The fiery hell promised by God to unrepentant sinners at the world's end instead became a this-worldly reality, lit by the kings of Western Europe and inflamed by their armies sent out to conquer and pillage the world of its riches for the greater glory of crown and country.

I am merely one in a long line of Christian soldiers, sent to Southeast Asia to expand the size and sway of God's Kingdom, only to find that I am but a mere errand boy negotiating the increase of Caesar's Empire. Being out in the jungle, far away from the civilized world in which I knew and understood, provided me the space and freedom for excesses of the mind and body. In addition to the North Vietnamese, the jungle became the other object of my wrath, seeking its destruction in the still-burning hell-fires ignited over a thousand years ago. I was given the means to rain fire from the sky and fill the air with sounds of thunder, the power over life and death and the authority to administer final judgment in what has become my own little corner of the empire. I fear I am a man deteriorating back into the wilderness, but with the weapons of a god at my disposal.

Just as godliness has eluded mankind, the animals ran from us, having little in common and even less of an understanding of their fellow life form that has reached so low in an attempt to sit so high. In our desire to leave the scavenged feeding grounds of the wilderness for the banquet tables of the gods, man became nature's deadliest enemy, destroying the habitat we once shared in joint dominion with the animal kingdom, burning it to the ground, laying waste to the evidence of our ancient communion. With the destruction of the wilderness would come the hoped-for death of mankind's primitive self, making man free to seek immortality.

   The jungle is a world in and of itself, one of natural selection in which all the plants, animals, and other living organisms form a brutal yet harmonious ecological community that has been in place for thousands of years, a congregation in which Green Tiger has yet to find its rightful place. When we walk through the diverse assembly, animals scatter to each side of our invisible wake, birds flock to the skies, and the reptilian creatures crawl and slither away from the encroaching humans. The only ones who are not afraid are the mosquitoes that buzz relentlessly around our heads and bodies in search of blood. Their lives are short, the species barely clinging to life. They are not afforded the time to be afraid. Though large in numbers, mosquitoes are a dying race. They must quickly procreate, repeating the birth and death cycle on a daily basis. Mosquitoes are forced to frantically fight for the life-sustaining blood flowing through the veins of the warm-blooded mammals, including us in Green Tiger, in order ensure the continuance of their kind. We were hunting for blood too. But we do not consider it precious. Instead, we spill it on the ground as if vile.

CHAPTER 17

"Marlon, you have done a lot of work in the area of Native American rights over the years, haven't you?"

"I have always wanted to, but my problems—my personal and even professional issues—always seem to get in the way."

"What would you like to do or accomplish in this area?"

"Well, there is not a whole lot that can be done for the Native Americans at this point. No, I take that back. In regard to reparations, and so forth, yes, that is something that can be done."

"By our government?"

"Yes, by our government. And I don't think it is asking too much for the government to offer up some monetary compensation to the descendants of the original inhabitants of North America."

"I agree with you, Marlon, but we are a nation that just recently spent about eight to ten years, billions of dollars, killed millions of people, and even sacrificed fifty-eight thousand of our own young men, in an attempt to take over Vietnam. And that's what it was, too, Marlon, it was an attempt to literally take over all of Vietnam, under the auspice of a so-called democratic South Vietnamese government. So, unfortunately, that will not happen, not even with Carter in the White House."

"Well, I don't think that will happen any time soon, either. I would, however, like the people of the United States to at least have an understanding of the atrocities committed against the native peoples."

"I think a lot of people have a pretty good understanding, Marlon, but they just don't care. It's totally an issue of race. Here, listen to this: I overheard a conversation between two women not that long ago. One was telling the other about a terrible car crash that killed something like five teenage kids, or something like that. The second woman was horrified! Absolutely horrified! Then the first woman told her that the five teenagers were Indians. The second woman then was not so horrified. It was as if she breathed a sigh of relief when she heard that. It was no longer such a terrible tragedy. 'Oh, they were Indians,' the second woman said. So, you see, Marlon, most Americans know what happened to the Native Indians, but they just don't care. Most white people consider the Indians to be inferior to them, and that they are savages, and all that shit. Most white Americans still believe the Indians merely stood in the way of progress, and so their removal, and even their destruction, was justified."

"Yes, but I would like to...to...to..." stuttered Marlon.

"You would like to be the messenger, wouldn't you, Marlon! You would like to somehow make it clear to Americans the terrible things that were committed against the native peoples, and that their lives are just as valuable as their own, that they have the same hopes, fears, dreams, desires as people of German, or English, or Scandinavian descent. Am I right?"

Marlon was annoyed that Francis interrupted him, and was in effect speaking for him, even though it was the very point that Marlon was trying to make.

"Yes, Francis, you are correct in your assessment. I would like to expose the United States as the murderous, tyrannical, two-faced, lying, stealing, cheating empire that it is."

Francis laughed loudly. Marlon looked at him with a grin on his face.

"Why do you laugh, Francis, you know it's true."

"Yes, I agree with you. What you said reminded me of your interview with Dick Cavett a few years ago."

"That imp!"

"You were speaking in these very same terms, like you're doing now. You were blunt and to the point, and you made Dick very nervous."

"I made him nervous because I was making his audience nervous—the people there, and those at home."

"And probably the sponsors, too."

"Yes, certainly the sponsors."

"Dick Cavett is a smart man, and very liberal, and I believe he considered what you were saying to be true, but..."

"And that's the point I'm trying to make, and you were trying to make, Francis. Americans can't stand the truth of what we did to the Indians. And that's because it is so fucken ugly. But it must be acknowledged, and looked at from a perspective other than the whole Manifest Destiny bullshit—the preposterous notion that God willed it to happen, including the death of untold millions, the destruction of their way of life, their culture, etc."

"The American people can't handle it all at once. They can only deal with it in small bites. Too big of a piece, like you were giving Cavett's audience, and the American public will literally choke on it."

"That's a bunch of bullshit, Francis! People just don't want to deal with the issue. Period!"

"I know. I agree with you, Marlon. Don't get mad at me."

"I'm not."

"Well, it sounds like you are. I'm just telling you why your appearance on the Dick Cavett show went over like a lead balloon. He got nervous because he knew his viewers didn't want to hear about America's war of attrition against the Indians."

There was a pause in the conversation as Marlon pondered his director's assessment.

"What do you mean by 'war of attrition'?"

Francis looked at his star actor, unconvinced of his claim of ignorance.

"You know what a war of attrition is, Marlon. Don't bullshit me."

"I do, Francis, but I just want to hear your interpretation of it. I want to hear you describe it."

"A war of attrition, Marlon, as you already know, is when one side inflicts so much death and destruction upon their enemy, that they simply cannot continue to fight, physically or even mentally."

Marlon thought for a moment.

"Well, then it certainly was a war of attrition, because the American government apparently wanted to kill all the Indians. I'm glad you understand this, Francis, because most Americans will not accept this charge."

"What, are you testing me, Marlon?" asked Francis with a

detectable amount of annoyance in his voice.

"No. Not really," said Marlon sheepishly. "The Vietnam War was a war of attrition, too," he added.

"Well, yes, all wars are wars of attrition. But you're absolutely right, Marlon. The United States inflicted a ton of damage on Vietnam, from its infrastructure in Hanoi, to the rice paddies, to the jungle. They indiscriminately killed men, women and children. But the North Vietnamese simply would not give up. They never stopped fighting!"

"No, they didn't. But the Indians didn't stop fighting, either. So why did things turn out so much differently for them than the Vietnamese?"

"Well, things were still pretty terrible for the Vietnamese. I mean, in the end they didn't lose, but they suffered unfathomable losses and hardships at the hands of the Americans."

"And I would like to believe, uh, Francis, that the tactics of attrition, at least initially, sickened Walter. The indiscriminate killing of peasant farmers and the destruction of their property was not why he came to Vietnam."

"So, Walter goes in with good intentions?"

"Well, he's going to war, so I don't know how good his intentions can really be. But I don't think he initially planned to adorn his camp with dead bodies and heads on pikes."

"And I'm sure he never anticipated that victory would be so elusive, either."

"No, he doesn't. Walter Kurtz has been denied victory, first in Korea, and now in Vietnam. And he desperately wants to see victory, at least initially. He wanted to feel like his father felt after World War II. He wanted to know the feeling, that sense of accomplishment, that good has prevailed over evil."

"Does Walter believe that Vietnam is *his* war, Marlon, like World War II was his father's war?"

"Yes and no. Walter believes that the *Cold War* is his war, and that the *Soviets* are his real enemy, just like the Germans and the Japanese were his father's real enemy. The North Koreans, and now the North Vietnamese, are peripheral or proxy enemies."

"Does this affect Walter's motivation to fight and kill his enemy? More specifically, is it possible for him to hate the Vietnamese like his father might have hated the Japanese? I ask that because the Japanese were expansionist and tyrannical to their neighbors, and a direct threat to the United States, whereas the Vietnamese were not."

"Yeah, I think it would be safe to say that Walter doesn't really ever grow to hate the Vietnamese. He went to Vietnam to win 'hearts and minds', even though he knew he would have to kill people. But I don't believe he hates them like people in America hated the Japanese and the Germans. I could be wrong, and maybe as Walter's story progresses, perhaps he will develop a hatred for the Vietnamese, but at least initially he does not consider the Vietnamese to be his true enemy, but rather a proxy enemy, as I said a minute ago. The Soviets in Russia are his true enemy, and Walter has been told this since the late 1940s, immediately after World War II."

"I can see that, Marlon, and it makes perfect sense. But that's the easy, uncomplicated part of the equation, so to speak."

Francis paused to catch the reaction of his star actor. Marlon looked confused.

"What I mean by that, Marlon, is that, yes, initially Walter Kurtz understands the Soviet Union to be his ultimate enemy, and yes, the North Vietnamese are pawns of the Soviet Union. But what about later, during the time that this movie is going to be covering? Once he becomes disillusioned with America's religio-political mythology, are the Soviets still his enemy? Or is the American religio-political mythological landscape his new enemy?"

Marlon breathed in deeply and then exhaled loudly through his mouth.

"Well, Kurtz isn't out in the jungle, doing what he's doing because he hates the Vietnamese, or even the Russians for that matter. I think it has more to do with his disenchantment of the American mythological landscape."

Now it was Francis' turn to breath in deeply and exhale loudly.

"That's how I see it too, Marlon. But we'll have to untangle that later. I've got some things I need to tend to. Keep thinking about this stuff, Marlon. What we have so far is fantastic!" added the director as he hastily walked away.

CHAPTER 18

From living together and experiencing the same brutal conditions day after day, Green Tiger, even though comprised of different ethnic backgrounds, began to don many of the same physical traits. Protruding cheekbones, deep lines on our faces, a permanent frown, and eyes tired and distant are descriptions that fit each one of us. And if the eyes truly are the window to the soul, then it was disturbingly obvious that many of us no longer had one, as if there was nothing but a black hole where our souls used to be. The jungle has gutted us of our former selves. The men born into these bodies no longer inhabited their carcasses. The transformation was one of necessity as human emotions are a detriment to the jungle soldier, the equivalent of having an open wound.

Even though Green Tiger was void of much of its humanity, it still managed to creep its way back in from time to time. The blood from all the death and killing was not able to completely wash away our humanness. There were even days when I could feel the sweet throes of love wrap their arms around me with comforting thoughts of my wife and kids, only to have them make a hasty retreat as soon as the reality of war again stared me in the face.

You could see the same look of pain on each of our faces as the human emotions passed in and out of our bodies. If there were a few quiet days of inactivity the smiles would return, as would the occasional laughter. But then the killing would start and we once again became a conscienceless pack of man hunters.

Everyone was affected by shifting tides of emotion, but LeBetre seemed to be the one suffering the most from an internal duality of the psyche. He now preferred to hang out exclusively with the Jarai, to the point of almost ignoring some of his American counterparts. He began speaking the language and participating in their customs. When the Jarai took off the tiger striped uniforms and put on the more traditional loincloth, LeBetre followed suit. With his black hair and dark skin he did not look out of place. He became adept at using a spear, which incidentally became an often used implement of the Jarai once it was demonstrated to me how effective a silent weapon could be. LeBetre's whole persona was changing. He even walked different, ambling through the jungle with his back slightly hunched and head tilted up just like the Jarai. He smoked the hallucinatory herbs almost daily, becoming more and more intrigued by the visions that put him in touch with his Indian heritage. LeBetre and the Jarai hunted together, ate together, and prayed together, further exasperating his already deteriorating relationship with Edwards.

By now the Texan was drinking heavily every day, contributing to his notions of invincibility, bragging openly that nobody or nothing could kill him. Wilke would listen to his tirades without making a comment, knowing that in time Edwards' arrogance, most of it gulped from a bottle, would collide with the law of the jungle, and the jungle would have the last word. Even though Edwards spent a lot of time laying around getting drunk, making fun of the rest of the men, he quietly admired Wilke and aspired to be like him. He resented it when Wilke paid more attention to LeBetre than to him, even going so far as to try and discourage it by berating LeBetre in front of Wilke, pointing out his weaknesses and blowing them out of proportion. Edwards made fun of LeBetre's newfound interest in his Indian ancestry by dancing around with feathers stuck in his bandanna in an attempt to mock him. Poor taste was a constant with Edwards, the kind of guy who never knew when to quit. As long as Wilke was around, however, he would not let himself get too out of hand. But when Wilke was elsewhere, Edwards would push things to their limit.

One night, just after sunset, the entire camp started to get a little nervous and edgy because both myself and Wilke were over three hours late in returning from separate patrols, each accompanied by a couple of Jarai. It was common for a group to occasionally come in an hour late once in a while, but two patrols simultaneously running over three hours late was thus far unheard of, leaving Edwards and LeBetre unprepared about what to do next. Edwards handled this situation like he did everything else, by drinking whiskey. When LeBetre started throwing around the idea of sending a group out to look for us, Edwards promptly challenged him on what he believed to be an attempt by LeBetre to put himself in charge. Words were exchanged and soon the two men were up in one another's face. The smell of booze filled the air around Edwards as they raised their voices and pushed one another around in the middle of basecamp, drawing the attention of the Jarai who began making their way over to get a better look. When Edwards spit in the face of LeBetre, a full-scale fight broke out. As the two combatants rolled around on the jungle floor, the Jarai formed a circle around them and began cheering wildly. The majority of them were on the side of LeBetre, but there were a few Edwards supporters as well.

Just when it seemed that LeBetre was gaining the upper hand, Edwards would regain the advantage. Henderson screamed loudly for LeBetre to kill Edwards, and it became clear that most of the Jarai felt the same way. Both men somehow made it back onto their feet. Edwards then brandished a knife, inflaming the excitement level of the crowd even further. With the stakes now considerably higher because of the introduction of the steel blade, the two combatants began to cautiously circle one another. Deciding to take advantage of his weapon supremacy, Edwards lunged at LeBetre, missing badly and falling to the ground. Now in a rage, he sprung off the ground, tackling his opponent and landing on top of him. Edwards proceeded to thrash and swing the knife wildly at LeBetre's face. Although missing, he left no doubt in anybody's mind that his intentions were to kill. The half-French/half-American Indian skillfully avoided Edwards' vicious attack. A few swipes of the knife did, however, manage to graze his flesh, sending tiny streams of blood flowing down the sides of his face. Becoming frustrated with trying to deflect

LeBetre's defense with one hand and stab him with the other, Edwards set the knife down and grabbed his wiry foe by the hair with both hands and began repeatedly smashing the back of his head into the ground until nearly unconscious. Straddled over LeBetre's limp body that was no longer able to defend itself, Edwards picked the knife back up and held it high in the air as if about to thrust it into the chest of his fallen opponent and kill him. The crowd of Jarai and a few Americans screamed and cheered in a crazed frenzy, both for and against the seemingly impending death of LeBetre. Edwards raised the tension level with every second he held the knife in the air, appearing to relish the power he had over life and death at that particular moment. Passions were running high, and certain divisions among the Jarai that until now had remained hidden were starting to show themselves as some screamed for Edwards to kill LeBetre, while others begged him not to. It surprised everyone, however, when Edwards chose not to pound the knife into LeBetre's chest, but instead cut two lines in the shape of a cross in the flesh over his heart. It was Edwards' way of telling LeBetre that no matter how much he wanted to shed his Euro-Christian skin, he could not. The cuts he made were deep and jagged, and LeBetre would wear them as a permanent scar that would offer a constant reminder to himself and others who he really was and where he came from.

  With his knife stained crimson from a mix of French and Indian blood, Edwards walked through the crowd of Jarai who had become silent, stepping aside and making a path for him to walk through. He strutted over to his hut as everybody stared at him, some loathing Edwards, others admiring him. LeBetre, on the other hand, had to be carried back to his quarters, and his wounds tended to.

Both myself and Wilke would return later that night, unaware that in our absence the seeds of dissension had been sown within Green Tiger. The incident spawned a noticeable rift within the camp based upon cultural preference. LeBetre hung out with those Jarai who desired to maintain their cultural identity while serving the Americans. He felt comfortable with them. Together they wore Jarai garb and practiced ancient Jarai rituals, and were definitely in the majority at Artemis. There was also a small faction of Jarai who were influenced by Edwards. They wore the tiger striped uniforms, and a few even cut their hair despite the fact I made no requirements that they do so. Edwards and his Jarai followers would sit up late every night, smoking Marlboro cigarettes, drinking bottles of Jack Daniel's whiskey, and doing their best to antagonize LeBetre and the other Jarai. The ancestral religion and spirituality that permeated their minds, bodies and souls since birth was being replaced by the things Edwards would do and say while in their presence, emulating his words and deeds until they too were without connection to the natural and spiritual world of their ancestors. Although Edwards considered himself to be a Christian, Christianity was never an inspiration for him. It was instead an easy way for the Texan to decipher who his enemies are. The act of killing was his real religion, and now the religion of his Jarai friends as well. Their prayer sessions consisted of heavy drinking, smoking, and talk of previous and impending hunts. They gave thanks by adorning themselves with the ears and sometimes the scalps of those they killed.

Wilke began referring to Edwards and his Jarai followers as the "mohawks". He approved of them even though they were a bit reckless, and seemed to be getting worse all the time. Wilke understands that jungle warfare can and often does bring out the worst even in the best of men, and the mohawks were no different. He believed that this happened for one simple reason—survival. But on the other hand, the twenty-year veteran of the jungle also knows the jungle's uncanny ability to weed out heedless and rash individuals, like Edwards, who succumb to their own arrogance and conceit. This would not concern Wilke at the present time, however. He would allow Green Tiger's current evolution toward dissimilarity to continue as long as they were still effective. Just to be fair, Wilke dubbed LeBetre and the rest of the Jarai, the "apache".

At first glance the mohawks and apache may have seemed easily distinguishable by their different culinary tastes as well as preference of booze and tobacco, the latter developing a pallet for things Western while the former preferred the ancient Jarai mainstays. But just like the blood that flowed through their respective veins, these things too were very much the same. Even though the slaughtering, fermentation, and harvesting were performed by different methods on separate continents, the bottom line was that they each ate animal flesh cooked by flame, drank intoxicants, and smoked dried plants. What set them apart was not necessarily the manner in which they dressed, but the fact that the apache followed the ways of the Jarai ancestors while the mohawks followed the ways of the Americans. Henderson fell in with the apache. Wilke called him the "black Indian" as a term of affection, and Henderson took it as such. The apache and the mohawks both tried to win the favor, and even the allegiance, of Wilke. But in reality, the sergeant was a swirling, inconstant, changeable-as-the-weather mix of both, and would never become one or the other, much less allow himself to be played-off between the two sides. Although he wore a United States Army uniform, Wilke belonged to nobody, except maybe the jungle. He made an effort to spend an equal amount of time working with each flank of Green Tiger, finding the ongoing competition between Edwards and LeBetre to impress him with acts of bravery and brutality to be healthy for the ultimate success of Green Tiger. As the rivalry grew increasingly fierce between apache and mohawk, the higher the body count.

    The apache walked barefoot and carried spears, while the mohawks wore boots and toted M-16s. Both clans were effective, but becoming increasingly more incompatible. I, unlike Wilke, was not quite so comfortable with the split in Green Tiger. I could not argue with the results, though, and so I tolerated it, but feared we would soon implode, nonetheless.

CHAPTER 19

"Before Vietnam, Walter's heroes and influences would have been his father, General Patton, General MacArthur, Audie Murphy, President Eisenhower, Joseph McCarthy...that whole crowd," explained Marlon.

"But would Walter have been so completely transparent? I mean...he's a very heady person, in Conrad's portrayal, and hopefully in ours. Kurtz in this movie is going to be a man who thinks very deeply and very clearly. I can't see him going from worshipping Audie Murphy to suckling from the tits of Nietzsche. I don't think it can be that clear-cut for Walter. He's got to be kind of hovering somewhere in the gray area before he gets completely turned inside out."

"Well, I don't think in the gray area, per se, but I would agree that things are not quite as clear-cut as they are for his father, who had no doubts about the fact that he was on the side of good fighting evil."

"But what about that look, Marlon, that look Walter sees on his father's face down by the river when he was a kid? Wasn't there some doubt?" asked Francis.

"Perhaps. And Walter always wonders about it. It affected him. It was something he remembered, because, other than for that brief moment, his father always seemed so clear-headed about the world and his place and role therein."

"Was seeing that look on his father's face something akin to what happens when a person reads Nietzsche for the first time? Because when I first read Nietzsche in college it blew my mind."

"That's an interesting way of explaining Walter's experience the one time he sees doubt and pain on his father's face—that it had the impact of absorbing one of Nietzsche's nihilistic diatribes in one fell swoop. I don't think it made that big of an impression on him, though. Things don't change for Kurtz until he's been in Vietnam and Cambodia for a while, but maybe that earlier episode does come back to haunt him on top of everything else he's experiencing while in the jungle."

"Do you think Kurtz would have read Nietzsche, Marlon?"

"No, I don't think Walter would have read one of Nietzsche's books, at least not before his time in the jungle. He certainly would have heard of Nietzsche and his kind, but his line of thinking is so far from his own that, no, I don't think there would have been any interest on Walter's part."

"Would it have been blasphemous for him to read Nietzsche?"

"Yes, reading Nietzsche would not have been acceptable in his world. But again, we're talking about before he went to Southeast Asia during the Vietnam War. Perhaps he reads Nietzsche while he's there, along with Frazer's *Golden Bough*. Maybe we could include Nietzsche's *Will to Power* in Walter's library?"

"That's actually a really good idea, Marlon, but of course this is not necessarily about reading Nietzsche."

"No, Nietzsche is just a metaphor here. I realize that, Francis. I'm just trying to figure out how he got to such a state, and what that state is, exactly."

"Yes. Good point, Marlon. Thank you. We're still trying to figure out exactly what his state of mind is. I mean, is he simply nihilistic, ala Nietzsche? Or, are his issues related more to the fact his primordial instincts have been awakened?"

"Which is also a Nietzschean concept."

"Yes, it is. Good catch, Marlon. So, perhaps both, then."

"Yes, Francis. Perhaps both."

"That said, I'm not so sure we're any closer to figuring this out, Marlon."

"Me neither."

* * *

```
     I chose to distance myself from the
dangerous internal politics of Green Tiger
by going out on patrols alone. I learned
```

from Wilke how to blend in with my surroundings by moving with the grain of the jungle, making easy targets of those Vietcong who were unwittingly moving against its flow. Entwined with the jungle, I systematically administered my own brand of natural selection by killing off those Vietcong unable to match my own skill at adapting to their surroundings, picking off unassuming Vietcong traveling in ones and twos on their way south.

Another tactic based purely on deception that I learned to employ was one where I would allow the Vietcong to pass without disturbing them in order to initiate a false sense of security for a particular pathway. Eventually, like ants following the scent of those that passed safely before them, the Vietcong would converge on the seemingly secure passage en masse. When their numbers increased, and concerns subsequently became only that of battling the mud and foliage, Green Tiger hit and a slaughter would ensue. Like a roving band of carnivorous animals hungry for the taste of blood, we would emerge quickly and violently from our impersonation of the jungle and its surrounding darkness. Fire and steel would burn and tear apart the tired and startled Vietcong. What this did not completely devour, the horrific explosions of napalm would.

When I wanted to get away from everything for a while, including the Vietcong, and just hide, I would go to a place that reminded me of the spot by the Willow River where I would spend many hours as a child, sitting and pondering my world. It too was a quiet little niche where I would sit and think, a place where I could forget about the war for at least a little while.

Early one evening while preparing to leave my river retreat and rejoin the rest of Green Tiger who were getting ready for a hunt, I laid back in the tall grass one last time in an attempt to summon a surge of strength intended to get me through yet another night of killing. I looked once again at the same white puffy clouds hanging overhead that I had been watching all day, ones that were moving only by means of the earth's rotation because there was no wind. The grass around me stood still as well. There had been no sight or sound of the war for hours. When I closed my eyes and listened to the sounds of nature uninterrupted by machine gun or artillery fire off in the distance, I found it easy to imagine myself down by the river of my youth and those days of childhood innocence. I would even catch an occasional whiff of a familiar odor such as the sweet smell of green reeds, so ripe they would ooze a milky nectar, transporting my mind back to some long lost mid-summer's day.

 Like I have many times in my life, I began to ponder that now infamous day of my childhood, the one soon after my father returned home from war in the pacific, a day that has haunted me ever since, when my father suddenly melted into despair. I have always likened it to watching my father suddenly die right in front of me.

 My recollections of that day on the bank of the Willow River with my father were quickly dissolved by distinct sounds coming from the time and place in which I now lived. My pulse raced, eyes opened wide, and my ears drowned out all other jungle noises. My instincts were telling me that something was not right, yet of what species or genus I did not know. I could not see anything from the horizontal position I was in, and was not about to stick my head up in the air to find out, so I just laid there. After about three minutes of waiting for one of my senses to identify the abnormality, my ears finally detected the sound of men speaking a northern dialect of Vietnamese. I then stood up high enough to see two black-pajama-clad Vietcong crossing the knee-deep river, eventually walking into the jungle and disappearing.

 My heart was pounding so hard I feared it could be heard outside my body. But my biggest worry was that a Vietcong scouting party was perhaps getting away with valuable information pertaining to Artemis, things that could be used to formulate an attack on Green Tiger. I knew I had to find the two Vietnamese and kill them. I swam underwater across the river, then followed the fresh footprints down a muddied trail. Deciding to outflank the Vietcong instead of trying to sneak up on them, I ran around the outside of the trail and waited for the two Vietnamese communists about a quarter-mile up the pathway. There I carefully examined the footpath for fresh tracks, and when satisfied nobody had passed through within the last couple minutes, I crouched down in the jungle foliage to wait for them, certain they would be coming along at any moment. My heart was beating even faster from running in the intense heat and humidity. Sweat beaded up on my forehead and ran profusely down my face as I sat in the dark, greenish hue of the jungle. I waited and watched for the Vietcong, quietly, intensely, focusing on the steamy pathway with my rifle at the ready. Five minutes passed and they did not come. Fifteen minutes and still no sign of them. I began to get very nervous. I started to think that maybe *I* was being hunted, that I was the prey and the two Vietcong were somewhere waiting for me. I gave it another ten minutes, but still nothing. I knew the area quite well, and geographically speaking, this made no sense. The trail was by far the easiest way back east to North Vietnamese controlled territory. To the north and south were impenetrable swamps. If a person managed to avoid being sucked into the bog, a feat that was virtually impossible, the snakes were certain to get you. All Vietnamese know not to go into the swamps.

Darkness began creeping its way into the jungle as I remained crouched in the same position, terrified to even adjust my stance, fearing my movements would be detected in the still air. Trusting my instincts and more willing to error on the side of caution and live, rather than to die a reckless fool, I proceeded as if I knew for a fact the two Vietcong were waiting for me somewhere in the thick foliage that separated me from Artemis. I wondered if they would attack me as I made my way through the jungle, or wait until I was in the river where I would be a sitting duck.

I waited until dusk fell completely over the jungle before embarking on my journey westward. Aware that survival hinged on my ability to go unheard as well as unseen, the jungle seemed quieter to me than it really was. To my ears, every noise I made sounded as if it was reverberating endlessly through the jungle.

Determined to make it back to basecamp even if it took all night, I slithered my way through the mud much like a snake. Down on the ground, alongside the small crustaceans and tiny organisms, I crawled for my life. The jungle floor is a world within a world, its inhabitants fighting the same daily battles for survival as Green Tiger and the Vietcong. I was a strange aberration to this world, using it as a gateway back to my own. Trying to stay all the way down on my stomach, I was forced to propel myself forward with my arms, my legs becoming like dead weight that only served to slow me down. They were useless, even a detriment to me in this situation as I pulled my legs along like two completely purposeless appendages.

Mosquitoes hovered around my sweaty head, taking complete advantage of my unwillingness to make any movements other than those necessary for immediate survival. They flocked to the usually topmost portion of my body as if it were an altar, or even a god that could sustain their lives, one from which they ravenously drew blood in their haste to save themselves. My arms and back ached from crawling on my stomach for what added up to an hour now. I would have done anything in order to get back up on my feet, but heeding Wilke's warnings that even the smallest amount of moon or star light can cast a long shadow, I stayed down as low as I could.

I was trying hard to think of all the other survival lessons Wilke had taught me, wishing I had paid better attention to the man who seemed to know every trick of the trade. Minus the things I learned from Wilke, as well as my rifle and the crucifix worn around my neck, I was all by himself. I did not expect anybody from Green Tiger to come looking for me, especially since I was on the other side of the river. But I did hold out hope, nonetheless, that somehow Wilke would figure out what was going on and come to my rescue. Wilke reminded me a little of my father in that he had a special gift for saying or doing the right thing, for always being there to save the day. Even though it seemed impossible at this point, I did not think it was out of the question that at any moment I would hear the reassuring voice of Wilke telling me he had killed the Vietcong and that it was all right to get up and follow him back to camp. But in the meantime, I prepared myself for the likely possibility that this would not happen, and that I would have to get out of this all by himself.

Every ten yards that I slogged through the mud seemed like a mile, and every noise I heard sounded as if someone was approaching. At one point in my journey, mostly out of frustration, I decided to take more of an offensive approach, reasoning that if I could kill the two Vietcong pursuing me then my uncomfortable situation could finally end. From down in the mud I watched for strange movements and odd shadows that may have been out of place on the jungle floor. The first thing I noticed was that strange movements and odd shadows seemed to abound *everywhere* in the jungle at night. Night is when the jungle hunts and preys upon itself. It is when the creatures too ugly and hideous to show themselves in the daylight battle one another for the unwanted refuse left behind by those things beautiful. I may have considered myself one of God's children, but on this night I was no more privileged than the jungle's vermin and reptilian creatures. The jungle mud is a damp clammy hell filled with tiny cold-blooded monsters and beasts slithering their way around, many with eyes that bugged out of their heads for better vision and forked tongues used to taste the air. Some were physically disproportionate, with heads too big for their bodies and legs too small.

It took me several hours, crawling then stopping every so often to assess the situation before I reached the edge of the river. Still on my stomach, I dragged my body into the brown, stagnant water. I made only tiny waves on the river's surface, but they shimmered bright in the moonlight. Once in I slowly submerged myself, intent on making it the rest of the way underneath the water. With my arms already exhausted from crawling on the ground, I now used them to thrust myself forward through the water, finding the going much easier than in the mud. My arms and shoulders burned with fatigue as I propelled myself to the other side. I thought I would never get there, that my lungs would explode first. I had no way of gauging my progress, much less knowing if I was even moving at all because the water was so black, making it impossible for me to see anything at all. The only thing I knew for certain was that I was still alive. The arms that pained me, and my heart that beat frantically in a vain attempt to replenish my body with oxygen, were my two best indicators.

At one point, I felt the sensation of weeds rubbing against my hands and face, then underneath my body, telling me that I was nearing the edge of the river, giving me some much needed hope. My body almost completely spent, I could only manage a few more thrusts, hoping and praying with each propulsion that it would be the one to get me there. I was able to kick out four more thrusts when in fact I thought I had none left, but I was still not on the other side. My heartbeat began to slow down, the burning sensation in my arms subsided, and my mind started to feel as if it was rising up from my body. It was all very peaceful, an almost welcome change from the intense pain I was feeling only moments ago. Suddenly, possibly a last gasp of cognitive function, I realized I was drowning. Aided by an intense shot of adrenaline, sparked by panic, I would forsake my earlier desire to stay underneath the water and hurled my body to the surface. Thirsting for air, my corpus pushed a large spray of water up with me as I leaped at the oxygen, my lungs immediately heaving in and out the humid night air, replenishing the life back into my body. I was only a few feet away from the bank so I walked over, but did not yet have the strength to pull myself up, so I laid there for a moment, still frantically sucking oxygen into my lungs. I was thankful for the muddy ground, of which I cursed only minutes earlier. Once I finally caught my breath, I extricated the rest of my body from the clutches of the murky water and moved back into the concealment of the jungle. There I decided it was safe to get back on my feet and walk the rest of the way to camp. It felt strange, even unnatural, for me to be walking upright. My lower back was ached by this, causing me to hunch over a bit.

  It was still dark when I arrived back at basecamp. Edwards and the mohawks were preparing to go out on a patrol. LeBetre and the apache were just coming in. As they walked past one another, apache and mohawk sneered in one other's direction. The sight of them moving in opposite directions was very emblematic, symbolizing more about the situation within Green Tiger than any amount of words could. Nobody noticed their haggard, bent-over colonel, who was busy surveying the camp in an effort to find Wilke and inform him of the two Vietcong I saw on the east side of the river. During my search of Artemis I would again see the two Vietcong, only this time they were laying on their backs, dead with their throats slit.

"Got these fuckers on the other side of the river," announced a shirtless Wilke, half his body illuminated orange from a small fire he was standing next to, his other half blackened by the night. He looked surreal, disproportionate, like a Salvador Dali painting. "Snuck up and killed 'em right where they stood," said the sergeant while testifying with his right hand how he cut their throats.

I simply shook my head in astonishment of the sergeant's hunting prowess, and the fact that I spent the entire night hiding from two Vietcong who were already dead, wrecking my back and nearly drowning in the process. I thought I detected a hint of smugness in Wilke's demeanor as if the sergeant somehow knew he had saved the life of his colonel. Everyone in Green Tiger, including me, were by now painfully aware of Wilke's superiority in all aspects of jungle warfare, and believed Wilke was capable of just about anything, and knew better than to ever underestimate him.

CHAPTER 20

"You know, Marlon, it was by strange fate and circumstance that the Americans and the montagnards came together in the jungles of Vietnam and Cambodia to fight the North Vietnamese."

"What do you mean?"

"Well, montagnard civilization may have trailed behind that of the Americans in terms of technology, but it took nearly two-thousand years for Western civilization to catch up with the montagnards and join them in the fight to expulse the Vietnamese from parts of Southeast Asia."

Marlon chuckled at Francis' attempt at both profundity and levity.

"Well, yes, Francis, but…" Marlon hesitated because he was not sure if he wanted to add more profundity or levity to the conversation, opting for the latter. "I do know a certain amount about the various indigenous peoples around the world, Francis. And it is amazing how similar their basic, core understandings of the world are. They all have a certain connectedness with the natural world, one that has either been lost to the Western world, or one that perhaps was never a part of it to begin with."

"Oh, I believe that we Westerners once lived more in a state of nature, too, but that we, because of technological advancements, have in effect left the natural world."

"The montagards have not left, nor do they desire to leave. From what I've learned it seems that they consider themselves to be almost an extension of the water, ground, and sky. They are one with, or a part of, the natural world, living within and through the soil, fauna, and water. They have literally grown into an integral part of the jungle, which they believe manifests itself in human form as the kings of water, fire, and wind."

There was a pause as Francis thought about what Marlon had just said.

"So, these are actual people—these kings?"

"Yes. They exist simultaneously."

"Marlon, where in the hell did you get all that from?"

"Well, I was talking about the Tahitians, actually. But as I alluded to earlier, much of what I said pertains to many of the world's indigenous peoples and their cultures, and this is what many of the Ifugao people here on the set have confirmed to me."

"Let's talk about the Vietnamese for a moment. What do we know about them?"

"You probably know more about them than I do, Francis."

"I did study them a bit in preparation of making this movie, and I get bits and pieces from other people who are involved in this project, but I don't know what to believe sometimes."

"What do you mean?"

"Well, there's such a stigma about the Vietnamese and Vietnam, on account of the war, in the minds of a lot of Americans."

"Yes, I don't doubt that. And it's of course going to vary depending on one's position on the war."

"Yes, it does. It's amazing...I have people who are working on this project, in various capacities, who come up to me with a story about their brother, or their father, or their husband, who fought in Vietnam, and they all have some story to tell me. And usually it centers around the toughness and the tenacity of the Vietcong, and how their dad, or brother, or husband had such respect for them."

"Who's told you stories?"

"Oh, you wouldn't know them. One person, this woman, a cook...her husband fought in the Vietnam War, and she seems to know a lot of history about Vietnam."

"Don't you have advisors who can tell you about the history of Vietnam, the Vietnam War, and whatever else?"

"Ah, shit, these so-called experts that you can hire as consultants on movie sets are a waste of time and money, and they don't give any real insight that I can't get myself by reading a history book. I can do better research on my own. Actually, the writers I have on the set can do better research and provide better information. You,

Marlon, can provide me with better information than what I can get from the so-called experts."

"So, what are people telling you about the Vietnamese."

"Actually, some interesting things. Again, it's nothing that I couldn't get myself from a history book, but in combination with some of the booze-fueled, late-night conversations, some tremendous insight has been reached. How I will use all this stuff, I haven't a clue."

"Why not?"

"Well, I don't know how it will translate onto the big screen. It's easier to make abstract points or observations in a book, but you really can't in a movie, you can't get too artsy or preachy."

"Well, from what I can tell thus far, that's exactly what this movie is intending to do."

"You're probably right, Marlon. A lot of *your* movies have been artsy and/or preachy."

"Yes, and most fell flat, because you're right...these things don't translate very well onto the big screen."

"What I didn't know, and this is what the cook told me, is that two-thousand years ago the Chinese ancestors of the would-be Vietnamese colonists migrated down into...oh Christ, what was the name of the place she said? Au Lac?"

"You're asking me?" said Marlon while shaking his head.

"Yes, Au Lac, or something like that, a domain in the northern mountains of what is now Vietnam."

"The Vietnamese are really Chinese?"

"Well, that's not so hard to believe, Marlon. China is just to the north of Vietnam."

"They started out like the English colonists in North America?"

"Yes, that's exactly how she explained it, Marlon. So, in the spirit of the English settlers in America centuries later, she said, the Vietnamese colonists struggled to free themselves and their newly adopted homeland from the heavy hand of the Chinese and the Han Dynasty. And, that for many years, again like the American colonists, they fought a series of wars for independence against China, spanning some fifteen-hundred years, or so. She said this is why Vietnamese society has such a distinct warrior mentality."

"So, for fifteen-hundred years the Vietnamese waged a war of liberation against the Chinese?"

"Well, the Chinese and other people who were already living in what is now Vietnam, yes."

"One-thousand and five-hundred years, Francis?!"

"That's what she said, Marlon. Fifteen-hundred years of warfare!"

"No wonder they gave the American military such a difficult time."

"Yes. Can you imagine, Marlon, the physical and mental fortitude and endurance it would take to literally wage war for a millennium and a half?"

"No. I really can't imagine. And yes, Francis, I'm sure they were forced to muster up a ton of physical and mental endurance," responded Marlon drowsily after a brief pause, making his director think the subject matter was boring him.

"You okay, Marlon?"

"Yes. Why?"

"I don't know. You suddenly sound like you're going to fall asleep."

"No, I'm fine."

"Okay, then. Let's expound upon this, shall we?"

"Sure," responded Marlin unconvincingly.

"So, it sounds to me like the Vietnamese, once free of the Han Dynasty, proceeded to create a nation whose culture was similar to that of the Chinese, but one with a history exclusive to themselves. What do you think, Marlon? So far, so good?"

"What? Ah, yes…sounds good, Francis."

"I'm going to start embellishing, so feel free to jump in, Marlon, okay?" said Francis, which only served to confuse his star actor even more. "And, so, early on they would proceed to erect their own empire, rolling back the jungle and taming its 'primitive' inhabitants, like the montagnards, who, of course were already there."

"Just like the Indians in North America," blurted Marlon, suddenly awake. "The Vietnamese were just like the English settlers. I'm starting to dislike them."

"Maybe you can go on Dick Cavett and tell him about it."

"That imp!"

Francis chuckled and shook his head.

"So, yes, Marlon, just like in North America, these Chinese colonists embarked on a kind of removal program of the area's indigenous peoples, because it was there—in the jungle—where they aspired to build their great cities and temples to house their own mandarins and seat their own emperors. She—the cook—talked about the fierce resistance they received from the various indigenous tribes, and even the jungle itself, which I found interesting. Neither was willing to cooperate with the making of a Vietnamese empire, she said."

"Well, of course the indigenous tribes they encountered would certainly have resisted Vietnamese subjugation and attempts at their destruction. But it is interesting that she mentioned the jungle doing the same thing. I mean, she's right, but it's just a really deep way of conceptualizing it."

"Yeah, it is, Marlon. What she said fits right in with what we were talking about earlier with Walter and his experience in the jungle and how it changes him over time."

"What did she say about the jungle? I'm curious."

"Well, she mentioned stuff like the difficulty it posed for the Vietnamese, with its impenetrable foliage, driving rains, searing heat...uh, relentless insects, predatory animals...did I forget anything?"

"Did you say heat?"

"Yes, I said heat."

"Because it's fucking hot out here."

"Yes, it is. It can't be any worse than Tahiti, though, Marlon, or am I wrong?"

"It's not this hot there. This is fucking oppressive!"

"I agree. But anyway...so neither the montagnards nor the jungle would give up or capitulate to the Chinese conquerors without a fight. And this is Walter's experience in Vietnam, too, because the Vietnamese so thoroughly utilized and incorporated the jungle—its thick foliage and difficult terrain—into their military strategy. The two became one and the same in Walter's mind."

"Okay, I can see that, Francis."

"That makes sense?"

"Yes. It does. Are you embellishing yet?"

"Maybe a little. It's more like taking 'artistic liberty' with the facts."

"I see. We actors do the same thing."

"Oh, you do? I hadn't noticed."

Marlon rolled his eyes, sensing his director's sarcastic tone.

"Please continue, Francis."

"Okay. I'm sure that in battling the Chinese for consecutive generations the Vietnamese not only developed a fierce warrior mentality, as the woman—the cook—said, but also great patience and resolve. I mean...they were fighting for over a thousand years! That takes a lot of patience, and a lot of resolve!"

"And fortitude."

"Yes. Thank you, Marlon. A lot of fortitude, too!"

"And the Americans certainly found out just how much patience, resolve, and fortitude the Vietnamese had."

"Yes, that's certainly true, Marlon. That's exactly what Dennis Hopper was saying last night."

"Oh, Christ!" Marlon rolled his eyes again. Francis laughed.

"I know you don't like Dennis. Hey, he frustrates me, too."

"He does more than frustrate me, Francis. He pisses me off. I hate him!"

"Well, he pisses me off sometimes, too. I don't hate him, but he pisses me off. He's a very good actor, though, when he actually calms down long enough to act."

"How often is that?"

"Not very often. Anyway, both Dennis and Marty seem to know a lot about Vietnamese history, and they were talking about how the Vietnamese fought the indigenous people, like the, uh, the Jarai, as Dennis was calling them…"

"Yes, the Jarai."

"You've heard of them?"

"Yes."

"But Marty was calling them the kemois, or something. I don't remember exactly. Anyway, Marty made the point that the Vietnamese fought the kemois with the same tenacity as they did the Chinese back when they were trying to win their independence. He talked about how the Vietnamese tried to drive the kemois from their land. And then Dennis would say stuff like, 'but the Jarai were as determined to stay as the jungle was to keep them, man'."

"Always with the 'man' thing. And then that nervous, diabolical laugh so many potheads have. Ick! He's not even of the hippy generation. Hopper's my age, for Christ sake!"

"Yeah, he does kind of have a Timothy Leary thing going on."

"No, Francis. Leary isn't psychotic like Hopper."

"But Leary was about twenty years older than all those kids he used to hang out with back in the '60s. He wasn't of that generation, either, but he did drugs and was down with the whole hippy vibe, just like Hopper."

"Yes, but that's where the comparisons end. Leary is a thoughtful, articulate, intelligent man. Hopper is a buffoon."

"Well, I wouldn't say buffoon, necessarily, but yeah, I know what you're driving at. So, there they were—the Vietnamese—in their push for empire, fighting wars in all directions, the kind that could bring them the great victories needed to construct their own glorious history."

"You must be embellishing now, Francis."

"Yes, I'm starting to embellish a little."

"Let me ask you something, Francis, before you continue."

"Sure."

"And maybe this is more of a statement than it is a question..."

"Go ahead."

"Why do people and nations need victories in war in order to have a glorious history?"

"Ha! Yes, I see your point, Marlon..."

"I mean...why can't a nation have a glorious history based on how well they've treated their citizens? The standard of living for all its people...health care, education? Stuff like that."

"And perhaps we can try and answer that question with this movie. But I don't have a quick, easy answer for you right now, except to say that these are not the kind of things that inspire people to come out into the streets to cheer and wave flags."

"You're exactly right, Francis."

"I usually am."

"Yes, of course you are. But seriously, Francis...why is it always that way?"

"I don't know, Marlon. That's a big question. Maybe we can answer it with our movie."

"Unlikely."

"Yes, that probably won't happen."

"So, anyway…the Vietnamese, Francis."

"Yes, the Vietnamese. Okay, so they continued to fight off the Chinese, pursued the destruction of the kemois in northern Vietnam, and ventured south into Champa to conquer yet even more lands. In the process…and this was pointed out by Dennis…Marty mentioned it first, but Dennis would expound upon it in the way that only Dennis can. And yes, I think Dennis was stoned out of his mind, but it enabled him to give a more colorful and vivid description. I wish you could have heard him, Marlon. He was standing up, running around, flailing about."

"And no doubt spitting while he was quacking away like some duck."

"Yes, I do recall a few volleys of spit being lobbed. Anyway, so Dennis is standing there, pacing around, making everyone kind of nervous with that weird laugh and the way he stares at people in an inappropriate manner. He is talking about how in their struggle, they—the Vietnamese—learned it was not an attitude of self-reverence or exaltation of a dynasty yet to be constructed that vanquished people and fashioned empires. He said that the Vietnamese came to understand that they were built by men who had no fear, felt no pain, and lived without the weight of conscience or remorse weighing them down. They learned this through hundreds of years of observing the jungle maintain its own imperium without displaying even a hint of regret or lamentation."

"I can just see him in all his glory, using his tirade to justify the use of drugs, because he thinks he is coming off so lucid, so clear of mind."

"Well, he actually did come off very clear of mind. He started reeling off the names of all these different peoples the Vietnamese have fought over the centuries, tying it in with the Vietnamese desire for their own homeland, how it led them into hundreds of years of horrific warfare with the Chinese, Mongols, Chams, and various montagnard peoples. And how living in this state of perpetual warfare slowed the Vietnamese aspirations of empire, bogging it down in the mud, thick foliage, and, uh, uh, stiff resistance from the people they intended on erecting their kingdom on top of. Dennis was using all kinds of symbolism, referring to the Vietnamese 'golden dream', and how it soon tarnished in the humidity of the tropical heat, or something like that, making it unrecognizable even to themselves, he said. And how generation after generation of Vietnamese fought their *endless war*, as he called it, numbing not only their bodies, but their minds, and eventually they knew not of those earlier aspirations of kingdom, but only that of war. And then Dennis pauses, bringing the energy level down for a moment before resuming in a very calm and even mesmerizing tone."

"Kind of like Hitler."

"What? Yes, kind of like what Hitler used to do, but in an aging-hippy sort of way. Dennis says...now, how did he put it? Something to the effect of, 'forgotten were their dreams of kingdoms and empires and Vietnamese emperors ruling all of Southeast Asia. Instead of walking bronze hallways in Annam and golden corridors in Cham, with silk draped around their bodies and jewels on their fingers, the Vietnamese trudged through rivers of blood and crawled over piles of corpses, with rags on their backs and dirt underneath their fingernails...'"

"How lovely."

"It was graphic, that's for sure. But it was good, Marlon, I'm telling you. Should I continue, or have you had enough?"

"Go ahead."

"Okay. Hopper then talked about how the jungle slowly lured the Vietnamese in with false promises of wealth and power, but instead took their minds, bodies, and souls without them even knowing it. In return the jungle made them hard and feral with the stamina to endure any and all pain and suffering their endless war would bring them'."

"Fascinating," said Marlon sarcastically. "Did everyone applaud?"

"They did, in fact."

"Probably out of fear."

"The man does have an incredible mind, though, you have to admit."

"And an imagination."

"And I think the drugs help him."

"When he gets the dosage and the combination right."

"That's true. I have seen him pretty screwed up and unable to think and even speak coherently on certain occasions, and then at other times come off as some kind of poetic genius, like he did the other day."

"He always comes off as some kind of baboon, as far as I'm concerned."

"So, after he again does the bit where he calms for a moment, he picks it back up again…"

"Oh, Christ, there's more?"

"Yes, yes, there is, Marlon. Dennis says, 'in the beginning it was the want of riches and glory that gave the Vietnamese the stomach to fight the endless war, but in the end their desire for these things had long left their conscious mind and the endless war became their empire'. Isn't that some good shit, Marlon!"

"Fabulous," said Marlon, rolling his eyes.

"Then he says…he says, 'back then, the Vietnamese pallet would have settled for nothing less than the prospect of dining on the likes of roast pheasant and a fine wine suitably served in an elegant dinner hall. But now, some rat meat and swamp water eaten knee deep in mud would better serve their fancy'."

"A real poet-idiot!"

"Well, I'm still not done. He also made the point that 'the future the Vietnamese once longed for has arrived, but not their empire. Those visionary, long-suffering plans have been replaced by their present thoughts consumed only with that of mere day-to-day survival'."

Once finished, Francis extended his arms and hands with palms up in Marlon's direction as if ready to receive an outpouring of praise from the star actor on behalf of Dennis Hopper.

"And?"

"And, what, Marlon? Isn't that enough?"

"He ended there?"

"Well, yeah, I guess he did. Everybody applauded, and patted him on the back, and everything else. It was really fantastic."

"I can finish this story, and I can do it better than what Hopper had done up until this point."

"Really, Marlon? Are you serious?"

"Yeah. Why not?"

"I don't know. I'm just kind of surprised, that's all."

"Surprised by what?"

"That you'd want to expound upon what Hopper said. You didn't sound too interested."

"I wasn't interested. And I'm not expounding upon anything that fool said."

"Okay. What will you be doing, then?"

"I'll be creating my own narrative."

"Okay. Fair enough. Take it away, Mr. Brando. Do it like Mark Antony."

"Yeah, right," said Marlon, rolling his eyes.

"That spiel you gave was brilliant, by the way."

"What spiel?"

"As Mark Antony...after the funeral of Julius Caesar."

"Oh, that."

"Do you like that performance?"

"No. I hated it then, and I hate it now."

"Do you like giving long speeches like that?"

"Do you mean in movies, or in real life?"

"Either one."

"Well, they're not the same thing."

"No?"

"No!"

"What's the difference, Marlon?"

"Well, with acting you're pretending to be somebody else, your words are not your own but from a script, and you get as many takes as you need to get it right. And when a person is speaking in public it's the exact opposite. It's you—your words, your beliefs and opinions—and you get one take. No thank you. I'm better at being a fake and a liar than I am at being truthful and sincere."

"Why the liar thing, Marlon? Just because you're a good actor doesn't mean you are a liar."

"My career has been a lie. My roles have been a lie. And Marlon Brando is a lie."

"You're a lie?"

"Yes, Marlon Brando is a fucking lie!" said Marlon in a manner that made it clear he wanted these to be the last words on the subject. "Hey, do you want me to finish up what Hopper so pathetically began, the dope-fiend hack of an actor that he is, or not? Talk about lies and liars...he takes the cake!"

"Okay, Marlon. Go ahead."

Marlon hesitated for a moment.

"I just need a minute to get my thoughts together. This is what happens when actors get old…and there's no fucking script to fall back on."

"But my understanding, Marlon, is that you are very good at ad-libbing. And that you've done it a lot during your career."

"I was much better at it when I was younger. I was much more clear-headed, and could talk much faster, and find my words quicker than I can now."

"That's true for all of us as we get older, Marlon."

"I suppose. You seem to do alright, though, Francis."

"I'm not as quick as I used to be. Plus, I'm younger than you, Marlon."

"Everybody's younger than me."

"Hey, you ready to go, Marlon?" asked Francis in an attempt to refocus his lead actor.

"Yes, I think so."

"Okay, then. Go ahead," said Francis after another pause.

Marlon cleared his throat.

"Warfare and its subsequent death, disease, and poverty have become a way of life for the Vietnamese…oh I can't fucken do this."

"No, no, no, Marlon. You're doing great. What's wrong?"

"Nothing's wrong. I just get so self-conscious when doing this kind of thing."

"What would help you? Should I look the other way?"

"No. Actually, I think it would help if I stood up."

"Alright," replied Francis as he watched Marlon struggle to get up on his feet, and then waited for him to get comfortable.

Marlon cleared his throat again.

"There is no time to mourn the dead. They are merely those who cannot fight anymore. The rest must pick up their weapons and continue on in search of the pain and suffering that they have become so accustomed to."

Marlon stopped to check the reaction of his director. Francis nodded his approval.

"Like the montagnards, the Vietnamese live in the jungle, carrying the same traits and armed with the same instincts as their home and creator, willing to bear any burden to protect who they are and where they come from. The Vietnamese now have for themselves that glorious history they so desired, and it is one that stretches further across the landscape of time than any empire or kingdom the world has ever known."

Again Marlon stopped to gauge his director. And again Francis nodded his approval.

"The history of the Vietnamese is also the history of the jungle, the two having coiled themselves around one another over the course of two-thousand years. The jungle generously shares this part of itself in return for a complete and unwavering obedience to its every will and desire. At the feet of the jungle the Vietnamese kneel, imprisoned in an endless war by the forgotten aspirations of their ancestors."

Marlon paused, making his director think he was finished.

"Bravo, Marlon, bravo!" responded Francis, who liked what Marlon said, but was not all that overwhelmed, knowing that his star actor would take offense if he did not receive praise.

"I'm not done yet."

"Oh. Sorry, Marlon. Please continue."

"It did not seem to matter to the Vietnamese who came to make war. Each was just another in a long line of enemies who never stopped coming. Their foemen once wore loincloths and carried spears, making their way on foot. Now they come in decorated uniforms, traveling from far-away lands by sea and air. The Vietnamese have been fighting wars in these jungles for two millennia, and will continue to do so until their enemies are no more…"

"Nice!" interrupted Francis, who was now genuinely impressed.

"You can kill their women and children, but not their will. Cut their eyes out and they will still see. Slice their ears off and they still hear. Sever his testicles and tear out his wife's womb and they will still multiply. Burn them with flame and they will not whither. Bomb their homes and they will find shelter in the dirt. Destroy their crops and livestock and they will subsist on vermin. Should you cut off his right arm, he will kill you with his left. If you cut off both arms, he will kill you with his cunning. Do not be satisfied with killing all but one of them, because that one will kill all of you. And never follow him into the jungle, for in that jungle you will surely die."

Marlon paused while Francis waited to make sure he was finished.

"That's it, Francis. I'm done."

"Bravo, Marlon. Or should I say, amen? That was really good. You definitely stole the show from Dennis," announced Francis sincerely, using the opportunity to stroke the ego of his star actor. "Too bad nobody else was here to listen to your performance. Could you repeat that later when we get back on the set?"

"Probably not," replied Marlon, while looking and feeling satisfied with himself.

* * *

"So, what about the Americans, Marlon?"

"What about them?"

"You just gave a magnificent explanation of how the jungle has affected the Vietnamese people, how it basically shaped and molded them into its own image. What does the jungle do to a guy like Walter Kurtz?"

"After that masterful performance, you're still not satisfied, Francis?" asked Marlon jokingly. "I think I will go back to my trailer."

"You don't have a trailer here, Marlon." The two men laughed.

"Oh, by the way, Marlon, I've been meaning to ask you something…"

"What?"

"Who was the worst director you ever worked for, the person who just kept demanding take, after take, after take, after take, the guy who just bugged the living shit out of you?"

"A guy by the name of Francis Ford Coppola."

The two men laughed.

"That's very funny, Marlon, and I knew you'd say that, by the way. But seriously…who?"

"Seriously?"

"Seriously!"

Marlon paused for dramatic effect.

"You!"

The two men laughed again.

"And they say you can't do comedy. Seriously, Marlon. Who?"

"Well, Francis, you do direct and produce much differently than a lot of other directors and producers. You expect a lot from your actors. And that's not a bad thing, necessarily. You treat us like artists, which is good. You give us the freedom to develop our own characters and to contribute to the dialogue. Some rule over their actors like dictators, never allowing them any kind of artistic freedom. But not you, Francis, you allow us so much artistic freedom that we end up doing much of what you are supposed to do."

Marlon's words, which were in fact intended to be jocular, made Francis laugh.

"Hey, listen here, Mr. Brando, I work my ass off on every movie I direct, as a producer and a director, and as a writer for that matter, as well as trying to manage and oversee the entire operation, from the actor's accommodation's, to where the dress and makeup people are going to eat breakfast, lunch, and dinner. Plus...plus...I think it's important to allow the actors some say in the dialogue and development of their characters. I could tell you exactly what to say, Marlon, and how to say it. Would you like that?"

"Yes, yes, I would," said Marlon, trying to get a rise out of Francis. "I would like more direction."

"Oh, the hell you would, Marlon. The hell you would!"

Marlon laughed.

"Are you done now, Marlon?"

"Done doing your job? No. Not even close, apparently."

"You're too damn funny, Marlon. I can't believe you haven't been cast in more comedies," said Francis facetiously.

"A lot of my most recent roles have been comedic, apparently, at least according to the critics."

"Ha! You do have a good sense of humor, though, Marlon. I think a lot of people don't know that about you."

"Probably not."

"No. They don't. Everybody thinks you're an extremely serious, super intense person, which you are, but you can also be very witty, too."

"If you say so, Francis."

"I do. But let's focus now on Kurtz and the men under his command. How does the jungle, and jungle warfare, change them? What does it do to them?"

"No, Francis, you tell me. I had my big scene. Hopper started this, then came me, and now it's your turn—the grand finale."

"No, Marlon, your dialogue was the grand finale. I just wish I had a tape recorder, or at least be able to remember what you said. You should have saved that spiel for one of the late-night talk shows."

"I wish I would have, but I can never be as articulate as I want to be on those damn programs. I can only do well in a setting that I'm comfortable in, like right now, here with you, Francis. I feel that, right now, I can speak about anything, and in an intelligent, articulate manner. But with all the lights, the live audience, the commercial breaks, as well as a snide, smirking host, like Dick Cavett can be, it's very hard to get my point across the way I'd like to."

"I can see that, Marlon. I have never done very well on talk shows, either. And I can only imagine how it's going to be making the rounds when this movie is finally finished. There is going to be so much criticism, especially after all the things I have already said about this movie, sometimes in confidence to certain actors, and even writers who have worked on this project."

"Like what?"

"Well, Marlon, my now famous, or infamous, statement about how this movie is going to win a Nobel Prize, has been a source of much ridicule."

"Who did you say that to?"

"Well, for one, I said it to you, Marlon."

"Yes, but I haven't repeated that to anyone. I knew you were being hyperbolic."

"And I said it to John Milius as well. I made this statement to Milius because I wanted to use the script he wrote many years ago."

"For this movie?"

"Yes. It's a long story, Marlon, but John Milius and myself, along with George Lucas, back when we were in college, wanted to make a movie based on Conrad's *Heart of Darkness*, but supplanting the nineteenth-century Congo with the twentieth-century Vietnam War. Milius actually wrote a script for it. And initially I wanted to use it. I hadn't read it in years, and back in the day I thought it was pretty good. Then I read it again in anticipation of making this movie and determined that most of it is not usable, but I didn't realize this until after I told Milius that this movie was going to win a Nobel Prize. And now he feels rejected, and he's been telling people in the press what I said, I think out of spite."

"It was no good?"

"No, not really. There's some stuff that's salvageable, which I will be using, and Milius will get writing credit, but most of it is just very amateurish. And that's not really a slag on him, necessarily. He was quite young and inexperienced at the time. And scripts are meant to be reworked and tweaked, but he doesn't want to do that, for some reason. He thinks it's great as it is."

"Why wouldn't he agree to rework the script? I ask this because every movie I've ever been in, the script was worked and reworked, over and over again. This is common practice. Everybody knows this."

"For whatever reason, Milius thinks he came up with some kind of masterpiece of a script, and he's never been open to reworking it, especially his characterization of Kurtz."

"How did he characterize Kurtz?"

"Milius envisioned Kurtz as a kind of psychedelic lunatic."

"A what?"

"The Kurtz in Milius' script is a kind of gung-ho type of soldier, but someone who is ingesting all kinds of drugs out in the jungle, as is everyone under his command, American and montagnard. He's only there to take drugs and have his mind blown during the fire fights, and by the sight of napalm ripping its way through the jungle. Milius' Kurtz is crazy and has completely lost his mind. Not because he's experiencing some kind of moral or philosophical crisis, but because there's so much stimuli he's simply succumbed to his desire for physical and sensory satisfaction. Milius' Kurtz is very shallow and uninteresting, at least in my opinion."

"It sounds like a B-movie script."

"That's exactly what it is, Marlon—a B-movie script. I think it would make a great B-movie, actually."

"I would have no interest in playing Kurtz as some kind of psychedelic-psychotic."

"No, I couldn't see you playing that kind of role, either, nor myself making a movie about such a figure. Actually, Jack

Nicholson would have been perfect for that role, or maybe Hopper, but I don't see the point in making a movie centered around a character who is really nothing more than some kind of hallucinogenic drug-tripper who's in Vietnam and Cambodia blowing shit up and killing people because it gives him a rush."

"So, whose script are we using, then, Francis?"

"Isn't it obvious, Marlon? We're not using a script."

The two men laughed.

"So now tell me about Kurtz and the men under Kurtz's command, Marlon, and what the jungle starts to stir in them."

"You mean, help you to write the script for your movie? Help you do your job?"

"Precisely, Marlon. Why the hell do you think I'm paying you so much?"

The two men laughed.

"I am trying to help you, Francis. But I'm not going to write the whole damn thing."

"I'm not asking you to, Marlon, for Christ sake."

"Well, it seems like you are."

"What?! I don't think so."

"Okay, then, Francis…like I said, me and Hopper had our say, and now it's your turn."

"Is this some kind of challenge, Marlon?"

"Perhaps."

"Perhaps? Either it is, or it isn't. There's no *perhaps*!"

"Okay, then. It is a challenge."

"That's better. I can relate to that. I like challenges. My wife always complains that I'm too competitive."

"Are you?"

"I'm pretty damn competitive, Marlon. Otherwise I wouldn't be out here in the Philippine jungle trying to make a Vietnam War-era adaptation of Joseph Conrad's *Heart of Darkness*, with all these big-name actors and huge egos to deal with."

"That's one way of looking at it."

"I don't mean you, though, Marlon," said Francis Coppola in jest.

"Right. Just get on with it."

There was a long pause as Francis sat pondering, seemingly unable to find a place to begin.

"I've got an idea, Marlon."

"What?" he asked, his inflection of the one-word answer pregnant with disinterest.

"How about if you get it started, and I will pick it up from there?"

Marlon sighed deeply. The seemingly haughty reaction might otherwise have caused Francis to regret asking his star actor to accommodate him in this regard, but it was actually the response he was looking for.

"Okay…"

"No. Never mind, Marlon," said Francis, feigning annoyance. He wanted Marlon to be confident, bold, even cocky in his sense of responsibility and worth to the movie, including the writing process.

"No. I'll do it. I'll get things started, Francis. I've got a lot of ideas."

"I'm sure you do," said Francis sincerely, hoping to tap into what he believed was a veritable goldmine of ideas, perspectives, and opinions lying deep within the mind and psyche of the legendary actor and consummate reader, a man who has experienced so much of what the world has to offer.

"Okay, Francis. And like you, I'm pretty sure I can do better than Milius."

"I'm sure you can, Marlon."

Marlon thought for a moment with his head tilted down. He then cleared his throat.

"Okay, well, Kurtz and his men are hunters, hunters of men, stalking their prey through the jungle, no matter where they were—Vietnam, Cambodia, Laos—borders, countries and their governing laws mean nothing to them. The jungle acknowledged no man-made boundaries or legal processes, and neither would they."

"Excellent, Marlon, excellent. You see, why should I hire writers and these over-priced consultants when I have smart, worldly people like you, Marlon, who can do a much better job?"

"But look at my price tag, Francis. Are you really saving any money?"

"Good point, Marlon, but at least I've got you doing something for your money, other than sitting around and waiting for a script to be written. You're actually writing the script."

"Right. But will any of this get used?"

"Hopefully. But who knows, Marlon. You know how these things go."

"So, then, probably not."

"Yeah, probably not." There was more laughter. "What else can you say about this, Marlon?"

"Okay. Well, because he's married, I think the point can be made that Walter used to spend his nights sleeping next to his wife. Now the nighttime hours find him scouring the jungle, searching out the enemies of his God and his country so he can kill them."

"I spend my nighttime hours scouring the jungle, too, Marlon, but I'm not searching out the enemies of God and country so I can kill them. I'm usually up, searching for some Brandy and a way to end this fucken movie."

"Ha! That's good, Francis," said Marlon with a big grin on his face. "Let me ask you something."

"Sure."

"If Walter is a religious man, Francis, wouldn't you think he would wear a crucifix around his neck, or at least a cross, some kind of talisman intended to keep him safe?"

"I suppose. I mean, we've established that he is a Christian, but not overly religious, if you know what I mean. And he would only be wearing a crucifix if he were a Catholic. I don't think Protestants wear crucifixes."

"Then Walter must be a Catholic."

"Why?"

"Because he wears a crucifix."

"Do you want him to wear a crucifix, Marlon?"

"I think I want him to be a Catholic."

"Why?"

"Because I don't want him to be an Evangelical."

"Yes, I agree. I'd rather he be a Catholic, too. So, okay, he wears a crucifix. But does that mean, Marlon, that you, as Kurtz, will be wearing a crucifix in the movie, visible for all to see?"

"No, this would be before he slips the bonds of Western rationalism, not after, which is when I come in. The crucifix has long since been discarded."

"Wouldn't that make for an interesting moment in the movie,

when Kurtz discards his crucifix?"

"Yes and no," answered Marlon with noticeable trepidation. "Then you run the risk of having this become too much about religion, and perhaps even be an anti-religion movie, or simply about a man who loses his faith. I think you want this movie to be something much bigger than just that. Am I right, Francis?"

"Yes, you're right, Marlon. It was just a thought."

"I'll continue, then."

"Please do."

"And everywhere he walked or crawled, the crucifix went ahead of him, the figurine of the Son of God in effect claiming for the Father the lands until now held by the Buddhists and the Hindus."

"Oh, that's good, Marlon. Now you got me thinking we should do something with the crucifix."

"Okay, I'm going to stop talking about the crucifix."

"You probably don't want to wear one in the movie, do you?"

"No, I don't."

"Perhaps you shouldn't have brought it up, then, because it's a pretty good idea."

"Yeah, I wish I wouldn't have. I'll be more careful in the future."

"Does Walter like killing, Marlon?"

"No. Walter does not like killing, but he knew he had to, and that the only way to defeat the communists and preserve the American way of life was to eradicate those spreading Marxist ideology. He believed that death was the choice the communists were making for themselves."

"That sounds good, Marlon. Can I see what you have there?" asked Francis while casually reaching for the stack of papers Marlon was holding, and occasionally glancing at.

"I'd rather you didn't," responded the reclusive actor while playfully pulling his makeshift script out of the reach of his director.

"So, Walter knew what needed to be done," continued Marlon, "and he stood up like a man and did it. He could have taken the easy way out and made a request to be rotated back to the states when the going got tough, but he didn't."

"Why can't I see what you have, Marlon? You're a good writer. Having worked with you on *The Godfather*, and now with this movie, I'm convinced that you could make it in this business as a writer. Of course, you wouldn't be getting paid the kind of money you are now, but I'm sure you'd be okay with that," said Francis, hoping Marlon would get the humor.

"I'm not going to just hand my work over to you, Francis, because, first off, I'm not a writer. And secondly, I want to be able to explain it to you as you're reading it. I've seen how you dismiss most of the stuff your writers give you as useless garbage. I think if they had the chance to be present and explain their work, you might actually find more of it useful."

"Do I really do that?"

"Do what?"

"Quickly and easily dismiss a lot of the stuff my writers bring me?"

"Yes, you do, Francis. And a lot of it I don't think you really give much of a chance. I've seen you quickly scan over several sheets of material in a few seconds, and then just tear it up, or throw the sheets up in the air out of frustration. I don't want you doing that with my stuff."

"I really do that, Marlon?"

"All the time."

"Okay, I shouldn't be tearing stuff up and throwing it up in the air, but I don't need to labor over something very long in order to determine if it's any good…if it's something that I want to put in my movie or not, Marlon."

"That's fine, Francis, but…"

"Don't worry, Marlon. I wouldn't do that to anything you bring me. I won't embarrass you like that, believe me."

"I'd rather not take that chance, Francis."

"So, I really do that? Huh! What do the writers do when I so easily dismiss their stuff?"

"Most aren't present to witness it. But those who are usually skulk off with their tail between their legs. Most of the writers out here are afraid to bring you stuff."

"I didn't know that. The things you learn from your lead actor! No wonder we don't have a script."

Marlon and Francis stared at one another, both of them pondering the irony.

"Okay, well, anyway, Marlon…what else do you have there?

And don't worry, I'll let you read and explain it. I won't take the pages from you, rip them up and fling them into the air."

Marlon paused, letting a sufficient amount of time pass before proceeding in order to secure the proper mood. He cleared his throat.

"Yes, and so…like big game hunters, Walter and the rest of his men relentlessly pursued their prey in the thick vine forests of Cambodia and in the swampy marshes of South Vietnam, worming their way in and out of the two countries. And even though they were sometimes in Vietnam, and sometimes in Cambodia, they were always in the jungle. The jungle doesn't distinguish between, or recognize, man-made boundaries. The jungle is the jungle," added Marlon, deviating from his script. "Do you know what I mean, Francis?"

"I absolutely do, Marlon. Please…keep going with this."

"They pursued their quarry slowly and methodically, then hit with violent pugnacity, always making sure to count the dead. The numbers climbed into the hundreds, yet there was no end to their charge."

"Yeah, the whole body-count nonsense."

"Right. And the more they killed, the greater their bloodlust became, because there's really no end to the killing on account of the refusal of the Vietnamese to ever give up. Pretty soon, and you've seen the pictures of this kind of thing, Francis…pretty soon these young freckle-face American boys are collecting the teeth and ears from the dead North Vietnamese and wearing them around their neck. And some even begin to join the montagnards in their practice of carving the flesh off the skulls and placing them around camp, a method used by the Jarai for thousands of years to harness the physical and spiritual power of their enemies."

"I see Kurtz and his crew doing this, Marlon."

"What, exactly?"

"Adorning his Cambodian compound with skulls and dead bodies. It's a testament to his madness, and his genius, just like what the Russian says about Kurtz in the Conrad book. The place is rife with death. You can see it and smell it. It's everywhere, so we better start killing people, Marlon."

"Why?" asked Marlon, knowing his director was making a joke, but not understanding the meaning behind it.

"Because fake dead bodies cost a fortune, and cadavers are hard to get. Plus, they start to stink really fast. And in this humidity, they would have a shelf-life of only a few hours. But nonetheless, I like the idea. And it fits in with what Marlowe saw when entering Kurtz's camp in Conrad's book."

"How did Conrad explain it? What were all the heads about, according to him?"

"Like I said a minute ago…according to Conrad, the heads are a testament to Kurtz's madness *and* his genius."

"How so?"

"Well, on the one hand, it says he's mad enough to kill, conquer, destroy, mutilate—all these things—without remorse. And genius or smart enough to know that this is a necessary trait for men who are fighting a war, or pillaging resources, as in the case with Kurtz in *Heart of Darkness*."

"That this kind of thing is *necessary*?"

"Ah! Good point, Marlon. It's not *necessary* that men do this. But, rather, that they have the fortitude to do this if it *becomes* necessary."

"That makes sense. What about Nietzsche? How would he understand it?"

"Again with the Nietzsche, Marlon?"

"Yes, I find him interesting. And his perspective seems to fit in so well with what we're doing here."

"That's true, Marlon. But I think we've pretty much covered the Nietzsche perspective. What I would like to know is the perspective of the United States government, Marlon? What would they think of the dead bodies and severed heads in the Kurtz camp?"

"Something tells me that neither the United States government, nor the army, would see it in the same way as Nietzsche."

"Hence, Captain Willard's mission to kill Colonel Kurtz."

"Right."

"How would Marlon Brando see it?"

"Probably the same way Nietzsche would."

"Hence, your role as Colonel Kurtz."

"I'm afraid so, Francis."

CHAPTER 21

While the rest of Green Tiger hunted the enemy predominantly by sight, Wilke tracked the Vietcong by what he called "ancillary evidence", that is, things such as odors in the air, or the way in which the birds, animals, and insects were acting at a given moment. Wilke likes to make the analogy of this "ancillary evidence" to that of ripples rolling outwards in the water, such as those instigated by a rock that is tossed into a body of water. Once the rock has been submerged, the only evidence it was ever there are the ripples that flow outward from where it landed until they too eventually disappear. Likewise, if the Vietcong cannot be seen or heard, other means of ascertaining their presence is required. The 'ripples' for Wilke, so to speak, in regard to the Vietcong, are things such as the smell of their urine and fecal matter, the flying patterns of crows, the tone of shrieking monkeys, maybe even the level of determination emanating from a chorus of thousands of buzzing flies and mosquitoes from deep inside the jungle. These were the kinds of things which led Wilke to believe that the Vietcong were wandering in closer and closer with greater daring and frequency, much like they did with Tigerden.

"Hey, colonel…" blurted Wilke just as I, tired and exhausted, turned in the direction of my quarters to get some sleep. "Did your dad ever take you to a lake when you were a kid to do some fishing?"

"Yes," I replied, perplexed as to the nature of Wilke's inquiry. "Many times."

"Then you've probably sat on the end of a dock or in a boat and dropped a worm in the water for either perch or sunfish. Am I right?"

"Yes," I said again, more matter-of-fact this time, knowing Wilke was not merely interested in my childhood fishing trips but was probably going somewhere with this. Wilke often spoke in parables and even riddles to better get his point across. I, although exhausted, knew that Wilke never said anything irrelevant, and would hear the veteran sergeant out.

"Did you ever notice that when you first drop your bait in the water the fish are afraid of it, scurrying in every direction? Then, slowly but surely, they become more and more interested in it. Pretty soon they're all ripping and tearing at it without any fear whatsoever. But if you suddenly jerk the pole they all retreat from it again, the cycle repeating itself over and over."

"Yeah, I know exactly what you're talking about," I said, indicating I understood how the fishing scenario related to our situation. "We've got to jerk the pole before we get eaten alive, right?"

"That's right, colonel."

"Go ahead. Do what needs to be done," I said, conceding a certain amount of authority to the sergeant before turning back around.

Wilke knew every intricacy of jungle warfare, having invented much of it himself. He would be the one to devise a strategy intended to scare the Vietcong away from Artemis. It would be the kind of tactic they did not teach back at Fort Benning where Wilke had been trained to be a soldier over twenty years ago. Not even the jungle taught him this. When it comes to the art of terror, mankind, when pushed to the darkest recesses of its imagination, is a suitable rival for even the jungle. Wilke learned all he needed to know regarding terror from reading about the Medieval Christians who attained most of their knowledge, first by observing the Romans plunder their villages north of the Danube, then from reading about the warring Hebrews of the Old Testament translated into Latin by Christian monks who later regretted infusing 'an eye for an eye' into Medieval Christianity.

Wilke was neither Roman, Frankish, or Jewish, but the portent of doom that he would conceive on the edge of the riverbank would have made Caesar, Charlemagne, and the Hebrew Joshua envious. Just as the New Testament is believed by Christians to reveal and fulfill the books of the Old Testament, Wilke's impending master work would bring to light and make clear all things true and real about myself, the American involvement in Vietnam, as well as the jungle itself. And once illuminated and made bare, I would never see any of these things in the same light ever again.

* * *

About three weeks later, on orders from Wilke, the mohawks and apache hung twenty Vietcong bodies from tree branches and placed about one-hundred severed Vietcong heads on five-foot high pikes sticking out of the ground. As darkness approached they lit the bodies and heads on fire, illuminating the river's edge as if an array of lanterns. Once the visual aspect was put in place, one of the apache began banging loudly on a deep-resonating bass drum made from a hollowed-out tree stump and boar skin, calling out the attention of the Vietcong. Soon, apache and mohawk alike were pounding on drums, clanging brass gongs, screaming and whooping at the top of their lungs amidst the intensely hot and bright flames, beckoning the Vietcong to take notice. The orange and white-hot blazes emanating from the burning bodies and heads reflected off the river, and smoke billowed quickly into the darkening night sky while the blood-red glow of the setting sun still held its grip on the western horizon.

There was not any drinking, feasting, or smoking of hallucinogenic herbs at this ceremony, however. Its patrons were instead gorging themselves on the utter ease in which they defiled the bodies of their enemy, becoming intoxicated by the powers they had over life, death, and even desecration. It was an amazing display of both method and madness, and was about to get even more horrific.

Once the black of night completely enveloped the riverbank, the Jarai dragged out three living Vietcong captured only days ago for this specific purpose. They proceeded to hoist them up off the ground by their extended arms, pulled away from their bodies by means of vines and rope attached to nearby trees. Resembling crucifixion but without the wooden cross, the Vietcong were positioned alongside the burning bodies whose flesh was still being devoured by the flames, but much slower now, while a thick smoke dispersed the vile smell of burnt flesh into the air. The fire and intense heat that surrounded them immediately began chewing and clawing at the bodies of the Vietcong hanging by their outstretched arms about ten feet off the jungle floor. The three brave Southeast Asian men screamed and wailed as loud as their smoke-filled lungs would allow. The unintelligible bellowing was the only explanation necessary to understand what horrible means of torture they were enduring.

The Vietcong soldiers were in effect being cooked alive next to the hot flames leaping from the already dead bodies of their fellow countrymen. Their horrendous cries of pain and anguish resonated out into the four-corners of the jungle, begging the attention of any and all nearby creatures, both man and beast.

The symbolism of the three bodies hanging as if from a cross was obvious, but the fact that they were being burned and tortured into madness was Wilke's own personal enhancement. It was not quite an exact reproduction of Golgotha, but it was authentic enough to initiate observable anxiety in Henderson, the recipient of a God-fearing Southern Baptist upbringing. He tried to look stoic as if it was not bothering him, but inside Henderson could barely stand it any longer. The screaming terrified him. He wanted to run as far away from the riverbank as he could, which is precisely what Wilke was trying to do to the North Vietnamese. He was playing on their ingrained fears of the Christian God, the seed planted long ago in the minds of their forefathers by French missionaries. Even though some of them had witnessed the fall of the French in Southeast Asia only a generation earlier, and now in theory adhere to the communist ideal of atheism, many North Vietnamese still fear the wrath of the white man's god.

Unlike most of the soldiers from the Western world that he has observed and worked with, always in search of an immediate result from their actions, Wilke liked to sometimes sow seeds deep into the ground, giving them time to grow and flourish, knowing that he would reap their bounty somewhere down the line. He by no means expected every Vietcong in Cambodia to be peering across the river at his horrific display and then run off screaming in different directions never to be seen again. Wilke was confident, however, that it would be experienced by at least a few Vietcong and Cambodians, who would then spread word of it throughout the jungle, similar to what happened in the Forbidden City a century and a half earlier. He knew it would take a while, even welcoming the inevitable embellishments intended by individual storytellers to make their version of the events on the riverbank sound more foreboding than the one they themselves had heard. The harvest will come when the Vietcong, reminded of their ancestral fear of the Europeans--their weapons and their God--make a determined effort to avoid Artemis, retreating from the outpost instead of encroaching upon it. Green Tiger was more effective in their job of killing when pursuing and hunting their enemy, preferring that their quarry run and hide rather than stand and fight.

The black smoke billowing from the plethora of burning bodies was now ascending even more slowly into the night sky as the intensity of the flames continued to subside, some of it even beginning to float back to earth.

Against the backdrop of twenty smoldering bodies and a waning crescent moon that was taking on the same blood-red hue as the sun that had now finished setting, the three Vietnamese men continued to scream out their Jobian wails, unnerving everyone including me. By this time, Wilke had ordered all drumming and chanting to cease. Other than the quiet prayers muttered by Father McDuffee pleading with God to end the suffering of these men, the only other sounds coming from the riverbank were those of the three dying North Vietnamese. They were retching out incomprehensible curses at everything from the soldiers of Green Tiger standing there watching them, to their own resilient bodies that would not succumb to death.

It was not long before the sight, sound, and smell of what they were experiencing began to make everyone sick to their stomachs. This fact did not escape Sergeant Wilke who stood back and observed them. One by one, they all walked off to their beds for the night, each appearing mentally and physically infirm. Even Edwards could no longer tolerate the merciless screaming and went off to get drunk. Wilke was the last one to leave the riverbank, staying until all three North Vietnamese were dead. Their bodies never actually caught fire, the heat literally baking their insides. The bodies were left there to hang, much like the boar carcasses that the Jarai would keep on a spit for days even though the edible flesh and entrails had been completely devoured. In a sense the three Vietnamese too had been consumed, their bodies and souls served up as a feast for the gods of fear and terror.

Long after his human sacrifices gasped their final breath, Wilke stayed to survey the riverbank and the perpetual death scene he inserted there like carved statues amongst the jungle ruins. He was trying to get a feel for the mood of the jungle in the solemn afterglow of the night's events. The vibe received by the seasoned jungle soldier was mixed. The eerie quiet and desolate ambiance of the immediate area seemed like it went on forever, as if the entire jungle was dead silent and that there was not a Vietcong or any other living creature within miles of the riverbank. But things were too quiet, forebodingly so, and Wilke knew it. The rest of the men back in their beds may have considered this a blessing and a sure sign they had accomplished their goal of scaring off the Vietcong. But Wilke, as he always did, saw things a bit differently. Instead of the jungle being quiet, he thought it horrifically loud, screaming out in pain as well as anger. It was hurting, not just its pride, but from a gaping, bloody wound inflicted by one of its own trying to manipulate its ebb and flow.

Just as Wilke initiated his plan to expulse the Vietcong away from Artemis and its surrounding area with the hopes he would be compensated for his efforts at a later date, he knew the jungle would do the same to Green Tiger. Wilke contemplated the possibilities as he stood there in the darkness, studying the other side of the river. The jungle stared back at him with an enigmatic glare that Wilke knew he would not disentangle on this night, so he decided to go to bed.

Walking back to his quarters, Wilke went

past my hut and observed me on my knees praying in front of a candle and crucifix. Inside his own bamboo and leaf shelter Wilke prayed the way he knew how--by listening intently to the jungle's symphonic rhythm, performed by the jungle's ensemble of diverse living and even nonliving parts. On this night, the jungle's normal nighttime Wagner-esque thunder and tumult was preempted by a more steadied and reposed Beethoven-like introspection. The sergeant was by no means indulging his external senses with nature's sweet rhapsodies, but instead trying to find a place where he could get back in tune with the jungle's rhythms in light of its suddenly changing tempo.

CHAPTER 22

"When I was a younger man, I naively thought I was in the process of making my life better, improving it as if I were on some kind of permanent incline or progression...as if stagnation, much less regression, were not even possible. I always thought that the more movies and money I made, then the more houses and cars and nice clothes and extravagant dinners I could afford to buy, and subsequently the more women I could date, and ultimately the happier and more fulfilled I would be. I worked hard trying to get someplace, but now in hindsight I'm not exactly sure where I was trying to get, or where it is I've arrived at for that matter, because there is no happiness and no satisfaction here. I am fat and bloated. Not just my body, but my mind, my reputation, my legacy, my memories, my past, present, and even my future. I shoved things into myself and into my life, thinking I was building and accomplishing something. But in reality, all these things were an illusion, and so am I. There have been many Marlon Brandos, and therefore many illusions, or perhaps 'mirages' is a better way of describing all the different Marlon Brandos, each a fleeting glance, a blink of an eye, lasting only as long as the typical movie cycle of filming, promotion, circulation, as well as the review and reaction process. My looks change with each mirage, as does my age, my demeanor, financial situation, relationships, mood, health, etc., etc., but the name on the marque always reads MARLON BRANDO. And along with it comes all the problems and issues that every one of my illusions, my mirages—all those Marlon Brandos—carry."

* * *

"It certainly seems that both Vietnam and Cambodia have been fought over incessantly for many hundreds of years. And this brings me to an angle that I want to consider exploring in the movie, Marlon."

"Which is?"

"How history repeats itself. More specifically, how history is an endless cycle of rising and falling empires and conquests. I want to use the movie to dispel the whole idea that human civilization is progressing toward something more advanced and civilized, to the point that human and societal perfection is possible."

"Like the European Enlightenment thinkers believed."

"Precisely, Marlon. I want the movie to point out that we are not progressing toward anything, but that we are stuck in this kind of cyclical loop of endless conquest, and that there is this ongoing, seemingly endless cycle of rising and falling civilizations and empires."

"You could make the point that the Americans are just spinning their wheels in southeast Asia, that everyone who goes there ends up fighting the endless war, and accomplishes nothing."

"Like the French?"

"Like a lot of people."

"I am thinking of having some of the footage take place around some old Hindu and Buddhist ruins, like Ankor Wat or Ankor Thom in Cambodia."

"That will cost a ton to replicate, Francis."

"Yeah, I know. I was thinking of maybe doing some actual scenes in Cambodia, at least a few, so we don't have to try and duplicate all this stuff. But I agree. The logistics would be a nightmare, and it will never happen. Anyway, I would somehow like for the movie to convey a sense of the long, rich history of Southeast Asia, and of the Southeast Asian people themselves, because I think a lot of Americans believe that history began around the time of the American Revolution, or something like that. They do not realize that there have been many incredible civilizations built by non-Western people—by Asian people, Middle Eastern people..."

"By African people."

"Yes, African people, and so on. I want to have, perhaps as an underlying theme, the idea or notion that this part of the world—Southeast Asia—and the ancestors of the Vietnamese and Cambodians, have been here for thousands of years. And that American culture, American civilization, hell, even European culture and civilization, is something fairly new to the world. That there is a long, complicated history of peoples, cultures, and dynasties, and that this will continue long after the Americans are gone, and that America is but a mere blip on the map of world history."

"That will be very, very difficult, Francis. Isn't your movie ambitious enough just trying to tell the story of Walter Kurtz?"

"Well, yes. I suppose it is, Marlon. But it's bigger than Walter Kurtz. And the stuff I was talking about—American history and Asian history—are going to be subtle, underlying themes of the movie, conveyed by way of the things experienced by Walter Kurtz while in Vietnam and Cambodia."

Francis stopped talking in order to gauge Marlon's level of comprehension. Marlon understood what Francis was trying to say. He just did not think his director could accomplish something so ambitious.

"Why are you apprehensive, Marlon?"

"I'm not apprehensive, Francis. I'm just doubtful that you can pull this off."

"Well, that's being apprehensive. Why?"

"Why?! Because you're trying to do too much, that's why. People are going to go to your movie, expecting some kind of war movie with lots of fire fights and napalm scenes, and all that kind of shit. They don't want to be preached at. They don't want a history lesson. And they certainly don't want subliminal messages."

"Subliminal messages?"

"That's what it sounds like you're going to try and do."

"Marlon, I don't think people are expecting a normal or traditional kind of war movie from me."

"No, I'm not saying that…"

"I think people know that this movie is going to be much different than the stuff they're used to getting from Hollywood, especially when it comes to war movies."

"Like *The Green Berets*?"

"Yes, like *The Green Berets*. Terrible movie! Total piece of shit!"

"It has John Wayne in it, for Christ sake, Francis! What did you expect? It's very much in the same vein as all those World War II movies, the Audie Murphy stuff."

"You're right, Marlon. A total propaganda piece! It came out in 1968, I think, with the hopes of convincing the American public that the war in Vietnam was an honorable war."

"Yeah, that's why they got John Wayne to play lead. Actually, Francis, John Wayne directed the film, too."

"That's right. And his son, Michael Wayne, produced it. Oh Christ, no wonder there was such clear lines drawn in that movie. The Americans were of course the brave, young heroes, fighting evil. And the Vietnamese were the sly, cunning, deceitful, evil, treacherous Asians, much like the Japanese were portrayed. The Waynes really tried to play up the Japanese parallel with the Vietnamese, simply because they are both East Asian. Well, we're not making another *Green Berets* flick here, Marlon, that much I am sure of."

"The critics would be more kind to you if you did, as opposed to some kind of Fellini-esque thing that I think you're going to end up making."

"The box-office numbers would be better, too."

"It's not too late to get John Wayne in here, Francis."

"Oh, it's way too late for that Marlon. Way too late! You're not getting out of here that easy."

"I'm not sure I'm ever going to get out of here, Francis."

"I don't think any of us are."

CHAPTER 23

The torturous exposition on the riverbank seemed to work, at least for now, as no Vietcong were spotted anywhere near Artemis for the next couple weeks. It might have worked too well. Our kill numbers were way down for that period because we simply could not find our enemy.

In the meantime, Edwards and the mohawks began taking up residence down by the river where the sacrificial ceremony took place, amidst the burnt bodies and heads. The lack of contact with the enemy lent the time and opportunity for Father McDuffee to try and convert the 'heathen' Jarai over to Christianity. Even though they knew very little English, Father McDuffee was still able to excite the Jarai with thunderous sermons by the riverbank, causing several to plunge themselves into the water for a spontaneous baptism, coming out of the murky waters as Christians, at least in the eyes of Father McDuffee. But in reality, the Jarai had no clue what they had just done.

Born in Northern Ireland fifty-two years earlier, and making his way to America twenty years after that, Father McDuffee was a kind, good-hearted man who loved his God, but feared him even more. His sermons were filled with apocalyptic themes and imagery. According to Father McDuffee, the end was always near, and God was always on the verge of unleashing his wrath upon a world that had fallen into wickedness. Father McDuffee would visit regularly with his new converts down by the river, teaching them the Gospel stories, but he also spoke a lot about the Book of Revelation. Even though he understands the core of Christianity to be the life, death, and resurrection of Christ, Revelation held a very special fascination for the priest because it was Bible prophesy yet to be fulfilled, portents of an impending doom that he believed could still be avoided by mankind's complete submission to God. But like most men, Father McDuffee would have his dark moments, times when he felt that the whole world needed to be cleansed of its sinfulness in some sort of fiery hell, welcoming the very end-times he otherwise tried to stave off with impassioned sermons stressing the virtues of living a God-centered existence. His calling to spread the Word to 'heathen' and 'savage' has taken him to every continent and corner of the world. Father McDuffee fears not the jungle, spear, or rifle, only God's wrath.

Like the mohawks, LeBetre and the apache found their own place of refuge away from basecamp. There they would pray to the spirits living in the trees and rocks, and perform rituals passed down from their ancestors for thousands of years. They did not approve of Father McDuffee coming into their area, aware that the intention of the Catholic priest was to baptize them and abolish their native practices and centuries-old beliefs. Father McDuffee was not afraid or discouraged by the unfriendly and sometimes resentful displays the apache gave him. Rejection has not been a stranger to his career as an envoy of Christ. Persistent, he had to be literally chased from the apache's vegetation-dense place of worship numerous times before he finally got the message and stayed away.

The growing divisions, contempt for one another, and the anxiety stemming from these things were only exasperated by the ensuing month of inactivity since the sacrificial ceremony by the river. The lack of an external enemy caused some in Green Tiger to turn their hatred inward. Mohawk and apache were at one another's throats, as were Edwards and LeBetre. While LeBetre and the apache showed indifference toward me and nothing but respect for Wilke, the Edwards-led mohawks were beginning to challenge the authority of us both, especially Wilke. The sergeant was keenly aware of their increasing defiance toward him, knowing their motivations better than they did. Whereas the apache no longer wore uniforms or even carried rifles, they still followed orders from both me and Wilke. This is more than could be said for the renegade mohawks, who were starting to look only to Edwards for instruction.

Wilke was more concerned at this moment with the Vietcong to worry about Edwards' misguided power play. Green Tiger could not find its enemy from our current location. Our strategy has been to dictate the rules of the hunt, to stay close to the base, keeping the enemy in front of us, and Artemis to our backs. I found out the importance of this that time a while back now with the two Vietcong when I got turned around a mere fifty yards on the other side of the river, enabling the enemy to get between me and basecamp. Wilke has always been very adamant about not being drawn too far out into the jungle when trying to make contact with the enemy, and was proselytizing this point more now than ever.

"We hunt the Vietcong! We don't try to stumble upon the Vietcong!" was a frequent admonition he would use to remind everyone of this. This philosophy was just fine with LeBetre and the apache, but it did not satisfy Edwards and the mohawks. Father McDuffee was not helping Wilke's cause, stirring the mohawks up with stories of the Crusades and soldiers of Christ traveling to distant lands to kill the enemies of God. It was certainly no secret that Father McDuffee's sermons were filled with militaristic rhetoric and overtones, behooving his listeners to not just kill, but kill fanatically, all in the name of God. It got so bad that I eventually asked Father McDuffee to stop, but his cries of "holy war" were very convincing, perhaps more than any of us bargained for.

* * *

"Okay, people," screamed Francis through his megaphone.

"Captain Willard and his crew are entering the Kurtz compound."

There were about one-hundred heads strewn about the camp, some made by the costume department, while others were real. The real ones were still attached to their living bodies, which were buried in the mud and under other objects in order to give the impression they were detached. Francis wanted authenticity. And this meant using real human heads. The whole thing looked completely bizarre, which is exactly what Francis was aiming for. Instead of Africans as in Conrad's story, this version of the Kurtz compound was littered with dead Cambodians and Vietnamese, played by the Ifugao people of the Philippines.

Marlon was not involved in the early shoots of the Kurtz compound, but did, however, choose to hang around and watch from off to the side in order to get a feel for what was happening. Captain Willard's entrance seemed to go on and on, take after take. Martin Sheen was not the problem. He was a consummate professional. Dennis Hopper was the problem, much to the annoyance of Marlon. Dennis could never say his lines, no matter how brief, without first requiring a thorough explanation from the director. He wanted clarification on every sentence, and sometimes even on the choice of a particular word, often lobbying and arguing for alternative wording. This irritated everyone on the set, but Marlon's biggest aggravation was over the fact that Dennis Hopper started to monopolize all of Francis' time with his ranting and raving, his confusion over his character and his dialogue.

"What the fuck can he be confused about," asked Marlon in the general direction of Francis and Dennis, sure that they would not be able to hear him. But Martin Sheen heard him. He seemed to agree with Marlon, shrugging his shoulders while taking a deep drag off his cigarette, apparently frustrated, too, with the pace of the shooting.

"Dennis, you're a fucking American photographer. You're in Cambodia. You have stumbled upon Colonel Kurtz's compound and you think it's a big story, so you stick around and even get seduced by Colonel Kurtz and his perspective on things to a certain extent," yelled Francis at his seemingly uncooperative co-star.

"So, are we friends…me and Kurtz? Do we sit around and philosophize, and stuff like that? Are we pals?"

"No, you're not pals. Kurtz has no pals at this point. He likes the Cambodians and the montagnard people, but only because he thinks they understand the world the way he does, or maybe he believes he understands the world the way that they do, whatever the hell the case may be. But I don't think Kurtz likes your character, Dennis."

"Why not? You'd think that Kurtz would want the company of another Westerner. He needs somebody he can relate to, right?"

"But Dennis, that's Kurtz's problem. He can't relate to Western civilization anymore. He doesn't want to relate to it. He's grown above and beyond that world. He thinks your character is a fool, that he's an idiot, and that most Westerners are fools and idiots."

Francis and Dennis could now hear Marlon grumbling off to the side. He was pissed off. The Kurtz compound was his time. He was the big star here, and this part of the shooting was supposed to focus on his character. Marlon did not like Dennis Hopper, anyway, and was now really growing to hate him. Francis took note of the growing tension between the two stars and decided he would use it in the script.

"Dennis, your character loves Kurtz. He thinks Kurtz is an enlightened genius, of sorts."

"Uh-huh."

"But Kurtz actually hates you."

"He hates me? Why does Kurtz hate me?"

"Because he does. He's annoyed by you."

"Why wouldn't he just have me killed, then? He's got all this power, and he's a trippy dude the way it is, so why would he let me live if he hates me so much?"

"Well, maybe he will kill you, I don't know, Dennis. All I know for sure is that Kurtz and your character are not friends. You are a photo-journalist. You're here taking pictures and writing a story about Colonel Kurtz and what he's doing in Cambodia…"

"Wait, wait, wait, Francis, timeout…" said Dennis with arms flailing. "Why would this Kurtz guy, whose got all these heads and dead bodies lying around, want an American photo-journalist writing a story about him? I don't get that, man. You'll have to explain that one to me, Francis," he finished saying and then laughed nervously, holding his gaze tightly on his director in childlike anticipation of an answer.

Francis breathed deeply and sighed. Trying to appease Dennis Hopper was proving to be more difficult than dealing with Marlon Brando.

"Dennis, listen to me, okay?"

"Okay, Francis. I'm listening."

"Your character is a crazy hippy, photographer/reporter. You, or your newspaper or magazine, get wind of this Kurtz dude, whose doing all these crazy things out in the Cambodian jungle. You go there to see what's going on, and to write a story about it."

"Okay. Okay. Who do I work for?"

"I don't know. *Time. Newsweek. The New York Times.* I don't know. Something big. I mean, you're not working for some local newspaper back in the states, or something."

"Okay. I like that," replied Dennis and then chuckled. "But why would this Kurtz dude let some reporter from some big-name newspaper or magazine do a story on all the crazy shit he's doing out here, man? I mean, look at this fucking shit, Francis!" said Dennis with great enthusiasm, and then laughed in the druggy, diabolical sort of way that his director now expected from him when finishing a sentence.

"That's what I want you to say to Marty—to Captain Willard—when he arrives in Kurtz's camp, after you've talked to him for a while. You are in awe and even a bit excited about Colonel Kurtz and what he is doing here. This is like Woodstock meets Charles Manson for you. I want you to tell him what you just said to me. I want you to say, 'look at this fucking shit!' And do it dramatically like you did with me in an attempt to get the point across to Captain Willard that something big is happening here."

"That's funny, Francis, Woodstock meets Charles Manson. I get it. That's funny," laughed Dennis. "But what *is* happening here, Francis? I don't think I understand. There's a lot of heads and dead bodies, a lot of the local folk all painted white, which is fucking blowing my mind. And Marlon Brando, the greatest actor of all time, is here too, standing off to the side. The whole thing is crazy, Francis, but I don't know what any of this means."

"To be honest, Dennis, I don't really know what's happening here either. We're kind of making it up as we go along."

"That's cool. I'm down with that," laughed Dennis. "But I still don't understand why Kurtz allows me to be here. Do we know why, Francis?"

"That's a good point, Dennis. We should probably try to figure that out, because, yes, it seems more logical that Kurtz would not allow such a thing, considering all the crazy shit he's got going here."

"Hey, I've got an idea, Francis," announced Dennis while chuckling gleefully.

"Okay, Dennis, but we really don't have time to delve too deeply into this."

"Okay, okay, I'll be brief. How about if..." started Dennis, and then began to giggle.

Francis starred hard at Dennis Hopper, which only made him giggle more.

"Please, Dennis. We need to get back to the shoot."

"Okay, okay, Francis. I'm sorry. How about...if..."

Again, Dennis started to giggle.

"I've got to go, Dennis," said Francis in an attempt to move things along.

"No, wait, wait, Francis. My idea is so good...I'm just really excited about it. Uh, okay, uh..."

Dennis began to giggle again.

"Dennis, for Christ sake! I don't have time for this shit, so I'm going to tell *you* what's going on here. Okay, here's why Kurtz doesn't kill you," said Francis with his voice raised enough to draw the attention of most everyone on the set, including Marlon and Martin Sheen. "Kurtz doesn't kill the photo-journalist because he wants the American government, and the American people, to know how he's conducting the war, and how successful he is, in contrast to the conventional American war effort."

"Yeah, that's pretty good, too, Marlon," said Dennis, and then giggled. "But my idea is better."

"I'm sure it is, Dennis, but for whatever reason you seem unable to convey to me what that idea is. So until that time comes, we are going to go with my idea."

"Okay, that sounds fair, Francis. But there's something I still don't understand."

"What's that, Dennis? But please keep in mind that my patience is wearing thin."

"Okay, I do get that, Francis. But I just don't understand why Kurtz hates me. I would feel much more comfortable if Colonel Kurtz at least liked my character."

"Well, to be honest with you, Dennis, I don't think Marlon would feel comfortable doing scenes with you in which he has to be your friend."

"Yeah, I don't think Marlon likes me much, does he, Francis?" Dennis laughed nervously.

"Look, Dennis, I like you. You know that. You are a brilliant man and a brilliant actor. But you're very eccentric. I can say that to you, Dennis, because I'm eccentric, too. I am sometimes hard to take, or so people tell me. I know how to handle Marlon, and you don't, Dennis. I know when to tone things down for Marlon, and when to rev things up, and you don't. Hey, it's not a big deal. Don't worry about it. It's not your job. It's my job to deal with Marlon Brando. But we're not going to try and make your two characters into friends. I just don't think it will work. It will be much more believable if Kurtz doesn't like the American photo-journalist."

"Okay, I get it now, Francis. I think I'm starting to understand this whole thing."

"I'm glad to finally hear that, Dennis."

"Yeah, me too, Francis. Uh, so, what I think you're saying is that the photo-journalist thinks that this Kurtz guy is enlightened, and that he has some kind of grand insight into all this fucking death and killing and shit, the war, and everything that's going on in the world. He thinks that Kurtz is the man who has figured it all out. Not the fucking hippies with all their peace and love bullshit. From listening to Kurtz talk, he's come to realize that the truth is something much darker and more sinister, and that Kurtz is going to blow the fucking lid off of everything."

"Yes, Dennis, even though I didn't quite say it that way, I think you're on the right track."

"Far out, man. This is really far out, Francis."

"I'm glad you like it, Dennis."

"I'm not saying I like it, Francis," said Dennis while giggling. "I'm just saying it's far out."

CHAPTER 24

After about the fifth week without a confirmed kill, Green Tiger seemed poised to implode from tension and nervous energy. Around dusk on one particular evening, I stepped outside my hut to watch and listen how the men under my command were dealing with the tedium of being finely-tuned killers forced to let their skill and instinct lie dormant. They were like a pot ready to boil over. The apache banged their drums off to my rear, the sound muffled by the fir and palm trees that separated us. The smell of wild boar flesh cooking over an open flame was also noticeable from their direction. The mohawks were down by the river getting drunk, becoming more enraged and anxious the more that they drank, arguing and fighting among themselves as they did whenever the apache were not around. Even Wilke was nervous and unable to relax, still uneasy about the possibility that he might have angered the jungle much in the same manner a devout Jew or Christian would worry about offending their God. He could be seen pacing around Artemis, stopping periodically to sit down and meditate in an attempt to communicate with and try again to understand the jungle that he now felt so estranged from. Like a once gifted magician lost of his powers, Wilke tried over and over to recapture what used came so easy for him, but the jungle refused to open itself up to the man it once gave great insight, relegating him to that of mere human like the rest of Green Tiger.

Even the animals were restless. All heads turned toward the direction of a bunch of chimpanzees shrieking and screaming wildly as they fought over the flesh of a gibbon monkey, killed after a relentless pursuit. The mohawks howled back in their direction, sounding envious of the apes and their successful hunt. The apache stopped what they were doing to take note for only a brief moment before refocusing their attention back on the feast they were enjoying. It seemed both man and beast were hungry for blood on this night.

By the time the full moon had ascended to its highest point in the night sky, Edwards and the mohawks had wandered away from the edge of the riverbank, and away from Artemis and the rest of Green Tiger for that matter. Seemingly as angry as the chimpanzees that they listened to earlier, tearing apart and devouring their kill, Edwards and the mohawks made their way north in search of Vietcong, using machetes to chop their way through the dense jungle foliage. They could wait no longer. Whether it was Father McDuffee's sermons, the full moon, their own internal instincts, Wilke's diminished authority, or a combination of these things, something in their bodies and minds told them to hunt their enemy, and they obeyed.

Edwards and the mohawks were not even sure where they were going, or what they would do when they got there. But if the manner in which they were hacking away the vegetation in front of them was any indication, the end result was going to be violent and bloody. Like men-possessed, they ripped their way through the dark steamy jungle, wearing strings around their necks garnished with dried ears taken from the heads of their enemy in days past, an item increasing in value now that the enemy was scarce.

In his reckless abandon, Edwards could have unwittingly led the mohawks into a Vietcong stronghold or ambush, even a boggy marsh that might have sucked them up in a matter of seconds. But what they did stumble upon instead was a quiet Cambodian peasant village consisting of about eight huts, its occupants resting quietly in their beds at this late hour, unaware and completely unprepared for the approaching nightmare. When Edwards and his men first saw the village, they stood still and silent for a brief moment. Then, as if they were all of one mind, in groups of twos and threes, they stormed into the huts swinging their machetes, slashing away at any and all inhabitants whether they stood up to challenge them or not. A few did offer some resistance, but it turned out to be an instinctive reaction that only made them an easier target.

Whatever kind of madness that had come over this renegade offshoot of Green Tiger, Edwards seemed to have it the worst. He screamed and yelled wildly as he gashed and chopped at helpless men and women abruptly awakened only to be slaughtered where they lay. One thing was for certain about this murderous rampage: its perpetrators were not going to let anyone live to tell the story of what happened. Edwards was completely fearless in what he was doing, all guilt and inhibition gone from his mind. It was a moment in which he was completely free of any moral shackles placed on him by the ideal of 'civilization' from whence he came.

When Edwards and the mohawks were finished with their massacre, they laid the bodies out in the middle of the village like they normally would at Artemis, then feasted on what food and drink they found as a continuation of their gluttony. Once their stomachs were filled with rice and goat's milk, which steadied their anger and adrenaline, some of the Jarai started to get scared over what they had done. A few of them cried and became sick, vomiting onto the ground what they consumed only moments earlier. Edwards too was sickened, but it was because of the weakness the Jarai were showing.

He walked around chiding and even slapping a few of them on the side of the head as if it would knock some sense back into them, serving to only make them more scared. They knew enough English to understand Edwards when he gave them the option of going back to sit around with the rest of the "cowards", or stay with him where they could hunt and kill the Vietcong. He did not care if some went back and told the rest what happened. In fact, Edwards wanted me, and especially Wilke, to know how he successfully took it upon himself to get kills while our leadership had rendered Green Tiger impotent.

Most of the mohawks, about fifteen of the twenty, abandoned Edwards, only about ten of those making it back to Artemis. The rest tried to return to their homes way over in the Central Highlands of Vietnam, but in their haste they did not take into consideration the fact they had several hundred miles to cover. Meanwhile, Edwards and the few mohawks who remained proceeded northward, certain that one of their many enemies would soon be in pursuance of them.

When the returning Jarai, who were now no longer mohawks as far as they were concerned, came running back to the safety of Artemis in the middle of the night, they were terrified and in search of an American to whom they could confess their sins. Some woke up Father McDuffee, receiving a scolding in a thick Irish brogue for their efforts. Others sought me out, while still others ran around basecamp in a frenzied search for Wilke. Those who went to Father McDuffee fell to their knees at the foot of his cot, praying the 'Our Father', and begging the Catholic priest for ablution of their heinous deeds. Unable to make any sense of the Jarai's manic behavior, and even a bit frightened by it, Father McDuffee walked past the Jarai who were still on their knees, and out to the middle of basecamp in search of either me or Wilke, the Jarai following behind him with hands still clenched together in prayer. Soon I was there, too, a few terror-stricken Jarai tagging behind me as well while the rest were running back and forth like crazy men, trying to find Wilke.

All of them were too scared and nervous to concentrate long enough to speak the limited amount of English they did know in order to explain themselves. They instead tried to speak in their native Jarai tongue, but with such rich accent and so fast that neither I, whose understanding of it is limited, nor Father McDuffee, who converses often with them, could understand a word. We both stood there looking equally confused, becoming almost as nervous as the Jarai who were now repetitiously performing the sign of the cross on themselves while again down on their knees.

When Wilke came walking in with his own small entourage of incoherent, terrified Jarai, myself and Father McDuffee breathed a sigh of relief, convinced things would finally get straightened out. Showing signs of frustration over his recent inability to negotiate the jungle and find the enemy, and complete disdain for the Jarai's display of paralyzing fear of Father McDuffee's God, Wilke shot his rifle into the air a couple times, then screamed at the Jarai in their own language for them to sit down and shut up. They did so, but wept like children. He waited a moment, allowing the silence to calm everyone, then pulled one of the Jarai aside and had him explain what the problem was.

"There's been a massacre to the north," was Wilke's paraphrased explanation to the other English speaking members of Green Tiger. In the jungle it was understood that the word 'massacre' had an entirely different meaning than that of 'bodycount'. In this instance, it meant Edwards and the mohawks slaughtered a village of neutral peoples, those off-limits in this zero-sum game of dead bodies. "Congratulations, father, you taught these men Christian guilt," he said sarcastically. "The rest are presumably still with Edwards, heading northward, capable of who the hell knows what."

Wilke and I immediately began making arrangements to visit the sight of Edwards' barbarity as described by the Jarai who had witnessed it. Wilke rounded up the apache from out in the jungle. He was initially going to make Father McDuffee stay behind with the still unnerved Jarai, but I overruled him after the priest became adamant about going along to pray for the dead. Henderson and some of the apache did stay behind with the now former mohawks who were too physically and emotionally distressed to go back to the place where their blind obedience in Edwards took them so willingly only hours earlier. Back then they were mohawks, soldiers employed by the Americans to kill their enemies. Now, they were once again Jarai, confused and terrified at the end result of having served their fellow man as if he were God.

Carrying torches to light our way, the rest of Green Tiger were escorted by one of the more composed participants of the slaughter over to where it was carried out. We followed the trail of mangled vegetation, felled and bleeding from the lacerations inflicted upon them by shafts of heavy steel en route to administer the same type of carnage on human flesh. We traveled single file with Wilke bringing up the rear. Several of the apache were carrying small army shovels, while LeBetre brought a can of gasoline, and Father McDuffee his Bible. All three items were an intended means of making the night's bloodbath go away.

"Cambodians!" announced Wilke ominously upon the arrival of Green Tiger to the village Edwards and the mohawks laid waste to a few short hours earlier, the sergeant pushing his way to the front. Cambodia was theoretically an American ally in the effort to expulse the North Vietnamese from the officially neutral country. The Americans had the tentative, secret permission and support of the Cambodian government to be there, but maybe not for long once word got out that American and American-led Jarai soldiers were killing Cambodian civilians as they slept.

After a brief discussion between myself and Wilke while the rest stood silent, staring at the dead Cambodians made visible by the light of the moon and burning torches, the Jarai were ordered to dig a shallow pit about thirty yards away from the small jungle village. Wilke was able to convince me that they should not burn the bodies, but instead bury them underneath the vegetation in the mud. Wilke was attempting to use the opportunity as a sacrificial peace offering, giving the jungle the death it had been cheated out of as a result of his adverse manipulation of the jungle's natural harmony.

The torches were now shoved in the ground, arranged in a circle to illuminate the large green leaves, stems, and roots the apache had to first chop and dig their way through in order to get down to the mud where they would burrow out the mass grave. They, like the mohawks did earlier near this very spot, hacked and slashed with machetes, cutting their way through the vegetable kingdom's living veins and capillaries on orders from the Americans. Once the hole was sufficient enough to conceal the dead Cambodians, the apache carefully placed the carcasses within its boundaries like pieces of a puzzle.

Before they covered the bodies with jungle and earth, Father McDuffee was allowed to say a prayer for the dead Cambodians. In his typical dramatic fashion, the Catholic priest called out to the heavens, his head tilted back so he could gaze at the sky, and his arms stretched outward with palms cupped to receive the Lord's blessing should God decide to offer any.

"Lord, grant these departed souls forgiveness of all sin—Original and those of their own will—and accept them into your heavenly kingdom, in peace. Amen."

Then in a manner that seemed to underscore the respect given them during the short prayer, the apache threw leaves and mud on top of the Cambodians until covered. The huts and other visible remnants were dismantled and strewn about the jungle in an effort to deny the very existence of the village, much less the slaughter of its inhabitants. The jungle then commenced its digestion of the offerings of desecrated human flesh in its usual slow, deliberate manner.

Once the task of feeding the end result of Edwards' anger and frustration to the jungle was complete, Wilke began to prepare himself for the impending hunt of the young and out-of-control Texan. I wanted Green Tiger to go back to Artemis and plan strategy there, and then send out a hunting party to track Edwards down. Once again Wilke would overrule me, designating himself the sole pursuant of the dangerous defector. The truth was that Wilke desired to take Edwards out himself, wanting to prove a few things to his brazen would-be usurper, and perhaps to himself for that matter.

* * *

Francis walked over to the man who was about to begin playing the role of Colonel Walter Kurtz. Marlon pretended to be disinterested. He was still perturbed at all the time Francis has been spending with Dennis Hopper.

"Okay, Marlon, Captain Willard and his crew have entered your camp. They are of course awe-struck with what they see. There are all these dead bodies and severed heads, Marlon. They have met the photo-journalist." Marlon rolled his eyes. "They have met the photo-journalist, and he has only served to add to Kurtz's mystique. He talks about how you have enlightened him, and how you are such a great and misunderstood man."

"Like in the Conrad book."

"Yes, like in the Conrad book. That much is the same. Marty's character—Captain Willard—is taken captive by some of your people, your followers. They're taking him to you. It kind of has the look or feel of someone being taken and placed at the foot of a medieval king or something. Kurtz's followers definitely understand him to be a kind of king or a god, and this will play into the whole *Golden Bough* theme we talked about earlier, the idea of the dying and rising god."

"Is Kurtz seated on some kind of throne?"

"No. He is more of a philosopher-king. He's a thinker. Besides, it's exactly this kind of thing that he rejects, the notion of royalty and other pretentious forms of protocol. I envision Kurtz sitting there, perhaps reading something. He pays no attention to Willard when he's brought in. Kurtz won't acknowledge his presence. He doesn't even look up at him. And he probably won't for a long time, I don't know. He just goes about his business as if he's disinterested."

"If Willard is there to kill Kurtz, then why does he basically announce himself by floating right up to the front steps of the Kurtz compound for all to see, and then proceeds to allow himself to be captured? After all, somebody else had been sent earlier to kill Kurtz, but is now *with* Kurtz, according to what you've told me, Francis, and Willard knows this. So, why does he do this?"

"Right. Good question, Marlon. And I'm pretty sure I will keep the earlier failed mission in the movie. I think it adds to the allure of Kurtz if a previously-sent assassin has been absorbed into the Kurtz fold. So, if Willard knows that Kurtz is aware that he is a marked man, then why would Willard basically enter right through the front door into the camp, right?"

"Right. It doesn't sound believable."

"Well, Willard is concerned about the prospect of assassinating an American, an American army officer, to be precise. And, so, he's curious about Kurtz. Willard wants to find out a little more about the colonel before he carries out his mission. He's not afraid of being taken into captivity. In fact, he expects it, perhaps seeing it as the only way to get close to Kurtz, because Kurtz, according to the photo-journalist, is supposedly out in the jungle with his people when Willard and his crew arrive. And what this means for Willard is that he will not get to see Kurtz until Kurtz was good and ready, and Kurtz would probably be good and ready only after Captain Willard has been captured."

CHAPTER 25

"Okay, let's shoot this thing. Marlon, there will be a voice-over with Marty right before Colonel Kurtz's first appearance. Willard has been taken prisoner by some of the montagnards. He is brought before Kurtz as if Kurtz is some kind of king or god. Finally, when he is good and ready, Kurtz begins to address Captain Willard. He's trying to figure out why Captain Willard has come here. He of course suspects that Willard is there to kill him, but wants to talk to the captain in order to determine if this is something he really wants to do, or if he's just following orders. In the meantime, Kurtz is going to try and turn or convert him to his way of thinking, just like he did Colby…"

"Who?"

"Colby. The man sent before Willard to kill Kurtz. You, Marlon, are just going to begin by making calm, quiet conversation with Captain Willard."

"Yes, I know. Tell me again what the voice-over will say."

"The narrative given by Willard is one in which he gives a brief description of Kurtz's quarters, the place where he runs his operation. It's also his living quarters. He says it is a place full of the smell of death, of malaria, of nightmares. Willard's narrative will indicate that it is definitely the end of the river, the end of his journey."

"Francis, I really think that Kurtz should be a shadowy, mysterious character, much like Conrad's Kurtz."

"Marlon, I agree with you to a certain extent. But we need to showcase you and your talent at least a little bit. I mean...c'mon, Marlon, I'm paying you, what, four million dollars to do this?"

"The money is for the name, and you know that, Francis. My performance will be panned no matter what, so how about if we don't give the critics a whole lot to pan?"

"Marlon, you are still an incredible actor, and I didn't bring you onboard just for your name. I brought you here to the Philippines to help make this a great film. I brought you here to act, Marlon."

"And act, I will. God, I hate that word—*act*! But sometimes less is more."

"Yes, I understand this. Don't worry, Marlon. I will not overexpose you, but I'm not going to underexpose you in this movie, either. Your role is not going to be some mere cameo, Marlon. Granted, your character comes in very late, but once we get to the Kurtz compound, your role is going to be very prominent."

"That reminds me, Francis…"

"Of what?" asked Francis Coppola somewhat tersely.

"A question I wanted to ask you."

"Okay," said Francis, who was barely able to refrain from rolling his eyes, knowing it would upset Marlon and slow the progress of the scene even more.

"Is this movie more about Colonel Kurtz, or is it more about Captain Willard's trip up the river?"

"I'm not following you, Marlon. Why are you asking me that?"

"Because this almost seems more like some kind of *grail search* on the part of Captain Willard, than it does an examination of Colonel Kurtz."

"Well, that's because it's not simply an examination of Colonel Kurtz, Marlon. It's much broader than that. But that's a good point. This is kind of a grail search. But I don't think it's limited to Captain Willard. We all go on the grail search with him. He's trying to find the truth. Now of course Willard isn't really thinking of it in these terms, but he's trying to figure things out, just like we all are, right, Marlon?"

"Well, yes…I suppose."

"There's a reason why he doesn't just come in with guns blazing in an attempt to kill Kurtz, and it's more than just strategic. Willard is intrigued by Colonel Kurtz. He perhaps even holds out the possibility that Kurtz really isn't insane, but has maybe tapped into something, that he has somehow become enlightened in some sort of way. Does that make sense, Marlon?"

"Yeah, it does, I guess," responded Marlon in his usual non-committed fashion.

"And, so, a question I have, Marlon, and one that the movie might need to answer, is whether or not Kurtz has anything to offer Captain Willard, and for the rest of us? More specifically, is there any real wisdom or insight in what Colonel Kurtz is doing, or is it all just madness?"

"This is the same question posed by Conrad, to a certain extent."

"Yes, it is, Marlon. And in your opinion, does Conrad answer this question?"

"Yes and no."

"Okay. In what way, yes?"

"Well, by means of Kurtz's final statement, of course."

"Say more."

"It's not until Kurtz's final statement of 'the horror' at the very end of the book that we gain an understanding of the man."

"Yes, well, more specifically it is Marlowe's understanding or analysis of Kurtz's final statement in which we finally get an evaluation of Kurtz. Let me get the book."

Francis got up to fetch his copy of *The Heart of Darkness*.

"The Conrad book?" shouted Francis. "Where is the Conrad book? Can somebody bring me my copy of the Conrad book?"

"I think I've got the book, Francis, unless you've got another."

Francis turned back around and looked at Marlon.

"That's right. I gave it to you. Can somebody please go get Marlon Brando's copy of *The Heart of Darkness*?" yelled Francis in the direction of an amalgamation of stage hands who were coming and going.

"Is it in your boat, Marlon?"

"Uh, yes."

"Where in your boat? I can have somebody go get it?"

Marlon hesitated.

"I'd rather that nobody goes into my boat, Francis."

Francis sighed deeply.

"Would you mind going to get it, then, Marlon?"

"Alright," replied Marlon, who then too sighed deeply to express his irritation with the request.

"We need a driver for Mr. Brando!" announced the director through his megaphone.

* * *

"Okay, here it is, Marlon. Marlowe makes the claim that in the statement of 'the horror, the horror', Kurtz is summing things up, as well as judging."

"Judging what?"

"Well, judging *everything*, apparently," announced Francis while studying the page. Marlowe says, 'all truth, all wisdom, all sincerity are compressed into that moment in which Kurtz steps over the threshold of the invisible'."

"'Threshold of the invisible'," repeated Marlon. "Is he talking about the world beyond
death, the mystery of what lies beyond this world?"

"Perhaps, Marlon, because he—Marlow—suspects that Kurtz is in fact on the precipice of death."

"Or is he referring to Kurtz having ascended to a higher level of consciousness or understanding of this world?"

"I'm not really sure, Marlon. But that's a really good distinction."

"Well, either way I think it's brilliant. I love the fact that he remains a mystery to the very end."

"I wouldn't say that's completely the case."

"No?"

"No!"

"Well, we don't really know what he's talking about, or referencing."

"You mean, Kurtz's 'the horror, the horror' statement?"

"Right."

"I don't think it's really that big of a mystery. He's referencing what the Western world has done in places like the Congo, the world-condition as it stood at that time as a result of the West in effect imposing its will on the rest of the world for the past four-hundred years."

"But that's your opinion, Francis. That's your opinion as a fairly liberal-minded American man living in the latter-half of the twentieth-century. And I agree with you, but a right-winger might see it differently."

"How might a right-winger understand this, Marlon? If nothing else, just to hear Marlon Brando's interpretation of a right-wing person's understanding of Kurtz's 'the horror, the horror', statement from Joseph Conrad's *Heart of Darkness*. Let's hear it."

Marlon was slightly taken aback, unsure if Francis was flattering or mocking him, but went ahead anyway.

"A right-wing person, Francis, might understand Kurtz, and Marlowe's subsequent veiled interpretation, to mean that Kurtz was abhorred at the 'uncivilized' elements of the world, such as the jungle, and the Congolese themselves. The 'horror' that Kurtz is talking about, as a right-winger might interpret it, is a reference to the inability of Western civilization to completely wipe away and destroy every last vestige of the wilderness, the remnants of man's primitive beginnings that we in the West have tried so desperately to forget about, and even tried to kill and destroy."

"That's interesting, but not the angle we are going to take here, obviously, Marlon."

"No, I didn't think it would be."

"But all kidding aside, Marlon, what we can't do is have Kurtz say nothing, and leave everything for the viewer to infer, like Conrad does. I can hear the critics now. They will grill me for bringing in Marlon Brando, paying him a few million dollars for three or four weeks of work, and his character doesn't say anything. I'm already being criticized for the amount of money I'm paying you."

"You are?"

"Of course I am, Marlon. You know that."

"Yes, I agree, Francis. Kurtz needs to say things both interesting and profound, but I do think that less will be more."

"And I agree with you, too, Marlon. But everybody is expecting this Kurtz guy to shed some light on things, to perhaps offer up some kind of great insight or wisdom. We've already established that this is why Captain Willard doesn't just burst in and kill the colonel, but rather wants to meet and talk to him, even if it means being captured. I think that in the back of Willard's mind he is hoping to be enlightened by Colonel Kurtz, and so will our audience, I'm afraid. And that's why we need to have Kurtz do something in this regard, otherwise everybody will be disappointed."

"Yes, but the problem here, Francis, is that the profound things Kurtz is going to say will be nothing more than the personal philosophy of Francis Ford Coppola and Marlon Brando—our outlook on the world, our opinions on history, politics, religion, and all that stuff. Nobody is going to want to hear what you and I think about these things. We can't simply give our political perspective, and pretend that it is coming from Colonel Kurtz. People will see right through it, and the critics will be unforgiving."

"But there is going to be such buildup to Kurtz. And, of course, part of the reason for the buildup is because everybody is going to be anticipating your appearance, Marlon. Everybody is going to be waiting for the great Marlon Brando to finally appear on screen, which doesn't happen until at least two-thirds of the way through. And when you do appear, Marlon, we need to have something for the poor, starving masses, who are going to be looking to you for some kind of philosophical nourishment."

"Ha, that's funny, Francis."

"Maybe so, but it's not that far off."

"I don't think your assessment is accurate."

"Why not?"

"Because at this point in my career, people are not looking to me for some kind of philosophical insight. Hell, nobody ever has, really. People used to look to me for good, even great acting. Now they look to me to see what kind of weird, bizarre character I'm playing, and how much my acting skills have deteriorated. Yes, Francis, there will be a buildup to Kurtz. But if this movie pretends to have all the answers, then it will get panned. You will get panned. I will get panned. We have to leave some of what we're trying to say to inference, to conjecture, even to individual interpretation."

"I see what you're saying, Marlon. We can't get too preachy. We can't just have the whole movie be a long set-up for a Kurtz monologue, or sermon, which is really just a Francis Ford Coppola and/or Marlon Brando-inspired liberal sermon, right?"

"Right, Francis. It will be pegged as left-wing, anti-war propaganda, and won't last in the theaters more than a couple weeks."

"But we can't have this big build-up to Kurtz and then have the whole thing end in a whimper. In reality, though, Marlon, we don't even know if Willard is going to kill Kurtz, or what's going to happen to him."

"No, I guess we haven't talked about it. I was just assuming that Willard would kill Kurtz, I guess. What are the chances that Willard gets converted, like the Colby fellow?"

"Not likely. I'm pretty sure that Kurtz is going to die. There has to be a resolution to the story, like in the Conrad book."

"Yes, but Kurtz simply dies because his health is so bad."

"Right. Nobody is sent to kill Kurtz in Conrad's book. But in our movie, Willard has been sent to kill Kurtz, and so I think it would be anti-climactic to not have Kurtz killed. To have Willard get converted, or even to have him refuse to kill Kurtz, would leave the story too open-ended."

"But, would having Willard kill him be too predictable?"

"Well, perhaps it would. Maybe we could have Kurtz kill Willard."

"But that doesn't resolve the Kurtz situation, which is what the movie is really all about. Am I right, Francis?"

"Yes, you're right, Marlon. And, so, you see my dilemma with the ending. Do I have Kurtz say a bunch of really interesting, profound and enlightening things, but risk making the movie come off sounding too preachy? Do I have him get killed, which is probably too predictable? Or do I find a way to end the movie with Kurtz still alive, which would probably leave it too open-ended? What should I do, Marlon. Please tell me!"

Marlon shook his head and looked away.

CHAPTER 26

"Marlon, I think that this movie is going to change the way the world sees war, certainly the Vietnam War, and maybe even the way the world sees the United States and the last four-hundred-plus years of Western imperialism. I know that sounds a little optimistic on my part, but I really think this thing is going to be big. My wife says I'm having delusions of grandeur, but why can't a movie do all these things? Why can't a movie be so brilliant, so illuminating, so enlightening, that it causes a shift in world perception? Why not, Marlon, why not?"

Marlon did not answer his friend and director, but then noticed Francis looking at him in a manner suggesting he expected a rebuttal.

"Is that a real question, Francis?"

"Yes, it's a real question. I didn't intend for it to be rhetorical. I in fact do want to know why, Marlon. Why can't my movie do all these things?"

"Okay. Well, that's the question I have been asking for years. And I've tried to do just that—to create movies that are going to educate, enlighten, and even change people's perception, but they've always failed miserably. *The Ugly American, Sayonara*, even *Burn* did not do much of anything in that regard. People—Americans—don't want to have a finger wagged at them, especially not by Hollywood. They don't want anybody, much less us Hollywood left-wing wackos, telling them that their history is a lie, that their perception of themselves is a lie."

"Are you calling us 'Hollywood wackos', Marlon?"

"That's what a lot of people think about Hollywood, that we are all left-wing wackos and communists."

"So, we can't, or shouldn't, use movies to enlighten people?"

"Well, what we would call 'enlighten', Francis, right-wingers would call communist propaganda, and we want to make sure and not create something that is going to be labeled as communist or left-wing propaganda, because it will fail right out of the gate."

"Okay. So, then, tell me, Marlon, what do you want this movie to do? I mean...you know the plot, for the most part now. I think you have an idea of where I'm trying to take this film. Let's pretend that this is your project and that you are in control of its message. What should that message be?"

"But it is my film, Francis," said Marlon with a big grin on his face.

"Well, yes, to a certain degree it is. Any time your name is on the marquee, it doesn't matter who else is in it, or who the director is, it's Marlon Brando's film, yes. But let me ask you this, Marlon...what would you like this movie to do for you, for your career, for your public image?"

"I would like it to make me a big Hollywood star."

"It's too late for that, Marlon. *Streetcar* did that, over twenty-five years ago now. What else?"

"Seriously, Francis?"

"Of course, seriously."

"I want it to be a rebirth, of sorts. I want it to cleanse me of myself, to wash away my past."

"Everything? Your whole past, Marlon?"

"Yes, everything, Francis. I want it to destroy the young Marlon Brando and all those early characters that nobody seems to be able to let go of. I want it to destroy the weirdo, eccentric Marlon Brando who did strange and crazy things because I was so uncomfortable with myself and the roles I've been so closely associated with."

"I definitely get the sense that you want to shed your old skin, Marlon, that you are tired of who you have been, maybe even who you are now, but most definitely that you are sick and tired of being what, and who, people want you to be, or who they think you are."

"Well, yeah, that's pretty much what I'm saying, Francis."

"Marlon, I think this is perhaps the very same way that Colonel Kurtz feels."

Francis paused, waiting to see Marlon's reaction. Marlon looked over at his director, his interest piqued.

"Kurtz was born into a very patriotic, military-minded, American family. His was a very strict, conformist, and narrow existence, and the same can be said about his world-view. Here in Cambodia—in the jungle—he eventually sees and understands something bigger, something different than all that. And because of this, he can no longer embrace the old ways. He can never again be the old Walter Kurtz. And it's not necessarily because he's tired of being pigeon-holed, tired of being, or trying to be, what everyone expects or wants him to be. No. He has come to understand that the old ways—the pre-Vietnam War America, and pre-Vietnam War Walter Kurtz—are a lie, and he can't play that role or live that lie anymore."

Francis paused, waiting to see Marlon's reaction. Marlon nodded in agreement. Francis continued.

"Walter does not want to be the hero figure, at least not as Americans understand heroes. He doesn't want to be a savior. The world he came from doesn't exist in his mind anymore, and maybe doesn't even exist anymore at all. He can't save it, nor does he want to save it, because he's come to realize that, alive or dead, it's just a myth anyway, and it's always been a myth. Or, Marlon, how about this? Maybe he wants to save the myth, even though he doesn't believe it anymore. Maybe he thinks the American mythological landscape gives meaning to time and history, and that it staves off nihilism, not just for him, but for all Americans, as well as those around the world who have been Westernized, or perhaps see America as some kind of beacon of light and of hope."

"Wait a minute, Francis. You've just talked yourself into a circle."

"I what?"

"You've come full circle. That last part…Kurtz wanting to save the American myth. It doesn't fit into what we're doing here. It's my understanding that Kurtz is in Cambodia and cut off from the American enterprise precisely because he no longer believes in the American mythological landscape, and doesn't think it's worth saving."

Francis laughed.

"Yes, I guess I did do that. What I want is for Kurtz to become nihilistic…"

"Right."

"But not too nihilistic."

"Not too Nihilistic? Is there such a thing?"

"Well, yes. Of course, there is, Marlon. Let me tell you what I mean by that."

"Please do."

"Kurtz no longer believes in the American myth, but he doesn't come to believe that there is absolutely no meaning to life, that there is no truth."

"No?"

"No! He believes there is truth, but that it's something so different, so unfathomable, so bizarre, strange, and even abhorrent to the American psyche and to our Western sensibilities, that most people would not recognize it anyway, much less accept it as such."

"You're making a lot of sense to me, Francis."

"I'm making sense to you, Marlon, because these are the very same things you are feeling or experiencing as Marlon Brando. Am I right?"

"So now you're going to tell me how I'm feeling, and what I'm experiencing?"

"As long as you're on my payroll, then, yes, I am going to tell you what you're thinking, how you're feeling, and when you can take a shit, Marlon," said Francis with a grin on his face, which was met with a grin from Marlon because both men knew it was not true.

"So, let's talk a little more about you, Marlon, because I think you could use this as an opportunity to work out a lot of personal issues. Just like when you played those roles in *Streetcar* and *Wild One*, which were kind of an extension of who you were at the time, Kurtz can be an extension of Marlon Brando, circa mid-1970s, Marlon Brando at fifty."

"I can relate to that, I suppose."

"No, Marlon, this could be huge! This could be as much of a statement about Marlon Brando as it is about Colonel Kurtz and Western imperialism."

"Francis, I don't think you want your movie to be a statement about Marlon Brando. Don't try to do too much with this movie, Francis. I'm telling you...less is more. Trust me. I have learned this the hard way."

"Okay, okay, Marlon. You're probably right. But you...you, Marlon, can exercise your own personal demons in a way that enhances the Kurtz character, and subsequently enhances the movie."

"Are you trying to give me motivation, Francis, provide me with an inspirational spark?"

"Well, of course I am, Marlon. That's what director's do. We try to get the best out of our actors."

"I don't need incentive, or coaching, or coaxing, or anything else for that matter, to act, and act well."

"I have no doubt, Marlon, that you don't need much, if any, incentive to act. I'm just trying to help you find that *thing* or that *something* about Kurtz that Marlon Brando can relate to, that *thing* or *something* that helps you put yourself smack dab in the role of Walter Kurtz, to help you find that point of convergence in which you and Kurtz can merge into one."

"I told you, Francis, I don't need you to say or do anything for me to merge with my character. I can just do it."

"As I said, I don't doubt that at all, Marlon. Not at all. But I can see something potentially very big here, and I'm trying to find a way to bring it out. Marlon, you have a chance with this role to right everything you believe you have done wrong. You can steer your personal life, and your professional life, back on course. You can take these things back. You can redefine yourself with this role, Marlon. The opportunity is that fucking big!"

Marlon looked at Francis with a certain amount of disbelief.

"This role can do all that?"

"If done right, then, yes."

"Well, then what are we waiting for, Francis?"

"Somebody to write the script."

"Ha!"

CHAPTER 27

    Much like a young tiger challenging the supremacy of an older and established leader, Edwards had been moving in on Wilke for some time now, questioning the sergeant on every decision he made as well as the mental and physical capabilities of the aging soldier. Edwards would make the case that his eyes and ears were keener, his body stronger, and his intellect clearer and sharper than that of the man he took orders from. With this in mind, and nothing but his rifle, machete, and twenty-plus years of experience as a jungle soldier to accompany him, Wilke embarked on yet one more hunt.
    Not knowing which way Edwards went after slaughtering the village, Wilke allowed his instincts to point him in the right direction. Once afoot, he methodically sifted his way through the jungle, collecting the tiny bits and pieces Edwards would leave behind of himself, hoping they would eventually lead to the sum of Edwards' whole.
    Edwards and his men were surviving on animal flesh that took time to kill and prepare. Wilke subsisted on plants and an occasional small reptilian creature he ate on the run. Edwards took time to rest when

he got tired. Wilke simply did not get tired. Edwards' sloppy aftermath was making it very easy for Wilke to track his prey. Dead Cambodians, animal carcasses, smoldering fires, and empty alcohol jars littered his path. But instead of haphazardly chasing Edwards through the jungle and in effect running to be killed by his own quarry, Wilke probed, studied, and analyzed every action taken and not taken by Edwards and the mohawks, maintaining his distance to encourage the reckless mode they were already in.

Meanwhile, up ahead, Edwards was still hitting his mark. Vietcong, NVA, as well as the bodies of more innocent Cambodians were strewn along their spiraling trail that seemed without destination, serving as proof to his one-time mentor that he learned how to kill, if nothing else. Edwards' intention, and Wilke knew it, was to lead the 'old king' to slaughter on the altar of his very own domain, and seat himself upon its throne. But the ideal of a flesh and blood king of the jungle was a notion that existed in Edwards' mind, not Wilke's. Wilke was not going to force the inevitable culmination of the hunt, but instead let itself play out, knowing that Edwards would eventually exhaust his desire, resources, and maybe even the loyalty of his followers. Then, with his nemesis bled white of motivation and wherewithal, he would go in for the kill. But Edwards had learned a few things from Wilke over the past year and would not make it that easy for him. In fact, Wilke was taking the extra time in order to brace for what perhaps might be his greatest challenge ever. Never before in his military career has he been considered the old, tired soldier, the keeper of the status quo, the relic of a bygone-era who somewhere along the line became comfortable with merely not losing as opposed to winning. It was always him who taught the officers as well as the enlisted men how to be innovative, how to keep their tactics fresh and new, how to keep the enemy off balance and always on the defensive. In Wilke's opinion, he never stopped doing all these things, and would once again have to prove himself, or die.

Craving kingship, and running out of patience, Edwards stopped the forward momentum of his war party to engage the man whom he believed held claim to the title. Edwards already killed off his fear, guilt, and the limitations they were intended to impress upon mortal flesh. Now he would attempt to do what the North Koreans, Vietminh, Vietcong, and the jungle could not do—-kill Wilke.

Edwards' killer-instinct and his royal aspirations were not incompatible. Instead, they complimented one another nicely. Although lofty in his conceptualization of himself, Edwards was not a man who tried to ascend above his brutish nature. He was not embarrassed by his occasional fits of rage, nor the violent acts that usually followed. Edwards never tried to repress his anger, because it did not offend him. He used these primitive reactions as a means to kill and survive his enemy, free from mankind's contemplation of morality. The culture in which Edwards was reared taught him that the path to godliness led out of the wilderness and up to the heavens. He never understood this logic. Rather than looking up at the stars and constellations, wishing he could emulate their perfection, Edwards instead took notice of himself and the world in which his species currently lives. From this point of view, he could see that they were not simply kings, but gods, gods of this earth. And that it was mankind's ruthlessness and animal cunning that delivered them to this lofty position on this otherwise gravity-bound place. Edwards chose to let his primordial instincts live and breathe, to bring him the power and glory he so desired right here, on earth, in the jungle, not somewhere up in the heavens.

Edwards may have chosen the sight in which he would attempt to slay the old king, but Wilke would be the one to decide the moment in which the epic battle would begin. In the meantime, the mohawks lit a big fire, illuminating for Wilke the place of his impending overthrow and sacrifice. They then banged on drums constructed from bamboo and animal skins, in a slow, continuous beat, intended as a message for Wilke to come forward and be stripped of his crown along with his life. This went on for a couple hours, the tension building with each passing moment as the sun set and darkness permeated the soon to be contested jungle kingdom.

Youthful exuberance getting the best of him, unable to wait any longer for what he believed would inevitably be his, Edwards stood in front of the fire, cupped his hands around his mouth and howled into the jungle--a crude gesture for the old king to come forward and accept his fate. But Wilke would not be provoked by such presumptuous measures. He would make Edwards and the mohawks await his entrance as if he in fact was a king, choosing the moment that best suited him to confront his court that had turned against him.

Alas, the time was ripe, the soldier-king emerged from his garden castle, walking past the mohawks whose drumbeats trumpeted his appearance, as well as portended his doom. There in the firelight they stood. Machetes held tightly in their vascular hands, looking indeed more like tigers preparing to wage war for territorial supremacy than two men about to fight over a mythical throne.

Edwards was shirtless, his tattered tiger-striped pants cut off at the knees, and his face wore a full beard. A green headband made from the since discarded shirt served the practical purpose of keeping the sweat from dripping in his eyes, but in this instance looked more like a make-shift, provisional crown. His wrists were encircled with brass bracelets, jingling whenever he moved. Wilke, for the most part, was adorned in much the same manner, but sporting a few gray hairs and some lines on his face. Neither wore, nor had any use for medals, both considering them to be a meaningless 'pat on the head' given to those who follow blindly.

Eye to eye they mast themselves, Wilke looking at the face of what he once was, Edwards at that which he would someday be. Both seemed to be waiting for the other to concede peacefully, but it would not happen that way. The two men raised their machetes to an offensive position and began circling one another, trying to find an opening or weakness to exploit. Suddenly, without warning, the young man physically engaged the old man, flesh and steel crashing together, the final stage of the coup d' tat had begun. Sparks flew from the colliding machetes. Groans emanated from their bodies. Edwards lunged and slashed wildly, taking advantage of his quickness while Wilke cunningly countered. Edwards charged Wilke, swinging the sharp-edged metal from side to side in an attempt to decapitate the sergeant. In the process, he gave Wilke an opening which he quickly took advantage of, hitting Edwards in the ribs, forcing him to reel backwards and scream out in pain. The sight of his own blood incensed the younger of the two, sending him into an all-out, frenzied attack. He again swung his machete wildly, badly missing its intended target many times over before finally downing Wilke with a hit to the thigh, causing him to fall to one knee. Going in for the kill, but overcompensating because of excitement, Edwards fell on top of his intended victim, pinning Wilke on his back. He then relentlessly tried to decapitate the sergeant, but repeatedly missed Wilke's head which was skillfully moving from side to side. The old man heroically fought off Edwards' ferocious onslaught. He and his shadow both eventually made it back to their feet. With his mobility limited, Wilke soon found the cold steel thrust into his left shoulder, the pain inciting him to send a thunderous roar out into the jungle. His rage then subsided and his eyes grew distant, taking his mind away from the battle at hand. Ceasing the moment, Edwards slammed his machete against the side of the dying king. Again the old man roared and his eyes faded some more. For a second time, Wilke crumbled to the ground, his shadow disappearing in the mud underneath him.

  The mohawks began banging their drums a little faster and cheering their soon to be victorious king a little louder. But before thrusting his sword across the throat of the old king as a final act of the succession process, Edwards took the time to laugh in gleeful anticipation and dance over the body of his fallen adversary. He then raised his machete high in the air and gave the heavens a defiant snarl. With his eyes and machete still fixed on the stars in the night sky, the wanton king screamed out in pain and unexpectedly fell to the earth with a hard thud where he lay writhing in pain. The sudden turn of events was so swift and abrupt it stunned the mohawks into silence. In what was perhaps a last gasp effort, Wilke had whirled his machete around in a counter-clockwise circle, hitting and breaking both of Edwards' shin bones with a sound as loud as thunder on lightning's immediate impact. Wilke climbed to his feet and chopped at Edwards as the young man rolled from side to side, now trying to avoid his own slaughter. Wilke broke Edwards' arms and ribs, inflicting deep wounds into his flesh. Still the young man fought on. He struggled to make it to his feet, but failed. With each aborted attempt, Edwards would fall, rendering himself unprotected from Wilke's assault. His body of flesh and blood that he thought to be indestructible was no match for hard steel guided by desperate determination. Edwards' blood flew from the carcass that once securely held it in. Some splattered onto Wilke while the rest spread itself on the ground.

   Edwards lived by the sword, and would die by the sword. The young man was too negligent and heedless to live. He had to die. It was the law of the jungle. With the trustee of this unwritten edict of nature standing over him, Edwards panted for air, but instead choked on his blood. The young man was now dead. Leaving the body for the jungle to do with as it pleased, Wilke

```
started walking back to Artemis, the mohawks
following him. Long live the king!
```

* * *

"I wish I could just kill off my younger self, my haughty, arrogant, self-righteous, hot-headed, oh so-handsome, talented, charismatic, and idiotic younger self. I would like to take a machete and beat him into a bloody heap. He was such a lie. The role of Marlon Brando was my greatest acting performance of all time, my greatest lie. If I ever deserved an Oscar, it was for playing that rogue. I was none of those things. I was scared, unsure of myself, and talentless. I wasn't even arrogant. I just acted as if I was. It was all just posturing and saber-rattling. And to top it off, I was actually ugly. But I knew just how to physically carry myself and to pose for the camera, and in everyday life for that matter. I figured out a way to somehow make myself appear attractive. But that, too, is a skill I have apparently lost. It's much harder now, with less hair, all these wrinkles and this weight. I've now been exposed as the average-looking man with average acting skills that I've always been. I've tried to tell people this much, but they don't believe me. They just want to talk about Streetcar, and Waterfront, and Wild One. People think that shit's real. Me, those characters, my persona—they think that was really me. That man—that person—never existed. Yet he's more real than I am now. If I could kill him, I would. But he's a ghost, an illusion. Yet there have been monuments erected in his honor in the minds of millions of people, in books and magazines, on thousands and thousands of feet of film, perpetuating the lie. He lived fast and hard, and now I am left here to pay for all his sins. Die, you bastard! Die!"

CHAPTER 28

Marlon was stewing in his houseboat, pacing around, mumbling to himself, picking up the Conrad book that he brought back to his riverside living arrangement, thumbing through its pages, and then setting it back down. He liked what Francis said about using his role as Kurtz to redefine himself. Marlon so desperately wanted to set the record straight about his career and his activism, and to get these things back on track. He has always hated the fact that the tabloid media seemed to have the power to determine what and who he is, if his movies and acting are any good, and whether his social activism is sincere or not.

Marlon kept picking up the *Heart of Darkness* book, reading Kurtz's final words—"the horror, the horror"—and then tossing it back on the couch, repeating the process over and over. The words echoed inside Marlon's head, reverberating in such a way that it reminded him of certain, weird special effects used in movies during the late '60s and early '70s.

Marlon walked over to the window and peered out into the darkening western horizon. He could see the palm trees swaying in the wind against the dimly-lit skyline. The mood of the jungle was ominous. From its outward appearance, the jungle seemed quiet and peaceful, but in reality, it was suffering and in great pain. The entire Filipino land was in great pain, as were its people, and Marlon could feel it pushing in on him. Marlon has sensed this feeling, this sensation, on many movie sets in foreign locations over the years, usually in places that had been colonized by the Western world, oftentimes those located in a tropical or jungle setting.

Marlon turned to look at Rafael, a Filipino man in his mid- to late-fifties, who was assigned to assist or serve him during his off-hours on the houseboat. Marlon now believed he understood the vibe he had been receiving from Rafael for some time now. It was all starting to make sense to him. The man's look—his stare—was something all-too familiar to Marlon, yet he could not place it, until now.

Whether he knew it or not, Rafael carried with him, espoused, and even emitted, the collective memory of the Philippine conquest, colonization and repression at the hands of the Western world, especially the United States, flowing out through his personal demeanor, mannerisms, and vocal inflections. These were things picked up on by Marlon, who was not oblivious nor unfamiliar with Rafael's subtle undertones of anger and bitterness, which were hitting Marlon with powerful thrusts as if the past was rushing toward and hitting him like ocean waves, their momentum building with each oncoming tide. Marlon could sense their two worlds intersecting there on the houseboat, and that they were on a collision course. He could glean from the things Rafael said, the way he looked at him, and through his body language, that he held the American actor in high esteem, while at the same time resenting and perhaps even hating him, and all that he represented. Marlon felt very much like the gluttonous Western colonial overlord that he feared Rafael perceived him to be. This was only fomented by Marlon's perception of Rafael as the stereo-typical short, dark-skinned, servant-boy of a white Westerner who was in his country to extract its wealth and riches. Marlon did not really know the history of the Philippines in great detail, but knew the history of other tropical nations and peoples who have been affected so negatively by the encroachment of the Western world. And in this moment, on a houseboat on the Pagsanjan River in the Philippines, Marlon felt that he represented and encapsulated all the injustice, the atrocities, the crimes—the horrors—committed by the Western world in the last four-hundred years.

Marlon did in fact expect to have a servant, perhaps even several servants, to assist him with his day-to-day needs. He did not necessarily expect them to be Filipino, but in hindsight what else should he have expected? It always amazed Marlon how blind he was, and how easy it was for him to unwittingly promulgate the colonial system. It did not even occur to him that he was in fact perpetuating it by demanding a servant in his houseboat. He felt like a hypocrite. No wonder the American press criticized his Native American activism, he surmised. Here he is, on a movie set in the Philippines, a place reeking of American imperialism, where he is making millions of dollars for just a few weeks of work, while his Filipino servant is making just pennies waiting on him hand and foot. And at least initially he saw nothing wrong with this. But now it bothered Marlon, to the point that he had to talk to his director about it.

* * *

With Edwards gone, the schism between mohawk and apache began to mend, commencing the process of their restoration. Nobody referred to any of them as mohawk or apache anymore even though, at least initially, it was still easy to discern the Jarai who were baptized and introduced to Christian theology by Father McDufee, from those who were not. Those who had, the mohawks, were still having a difficult time finding peace with past sins as a result of their fear of an eternal damnation for those who sin against God, inculcated by the apocalyptic preaching of Father McDuffee and expounded upon during the drunken fireside ramblings of Edwards. As these former mohawks assimilated themselves back in with the former apache, they were in effect, through the retelling and even embellishments of the stories and tales of suffering, torment, and flame, advancing the Christian acculturation of the Jarai begun by the Irish priest whose Bible is earmarked to the pages spewing fire and brimstone.

These now second- and third-hand accounts of an all-powerful God and afterworld infernos consuming seas of sinners at the end of time's linear progression were once again falling upon ears unsullied of any such concepts or ideas, piercing the ancient convictions of the ex-apache with the force of a spear thrust into human flesh. Some of the Old and New Testament stories were so foreign and abrasive to their traditional understandings of the world that the subconscious mind of the ex-apache immediately launched an effort to expulse them. But for most of them it was already too late. The seeds of Judeo-Christian thought, scattered by the Americans, had grown into long vines permanently wrapped around the mindset of all the Jarai.

The Jarai were in the process of becoming whole again, but not as the same Jarai they once were. These Jarai were nervous, paranoid, and deathly afraid of what the future held for them as long as they continued to serve the Americans. The once confidently devout animists from the mountains of Vietnam, along with LeBetre who was now one of them, would sit for hours and even days in a makeshift council, debating and philosophizing, trying to piece back together the world they knew and understood before the Americans came and blew it to smithereens. The Judeo-Christian view of time and history had split the world they inherited from their ancestors—temporal and spiritual—in half, forcing them to either choose between the two halves, or somehow reconcile them. The Jarai gravitated toward what was familiar to them, choosing the old ways, hoping it would make them forget the ways of the Americans.

In an attempt to reaffirm their ancestral beliefs and wash away the frescoes of an enfleshed God consuming the world in a flaming inferno, painted in their minds by the artful words of Father McDuffee, the

Jarai held one of their ancient ceremonies to praise the gods, spirits and ancestors who rule over the world they come from, a place they wished to go back to in order to flee the impending wrath of the angry, jealous God only recently introduced to them by the Westerners. A nervous tension resonated from their chanting and drumbeats as they drank rice alcohol, smoked intoxicating herbs, danced and prayed around a wild boar cooking over a fire. The more the Jarai drank and smoked, the louder they chanted until it evolved into gut wrenching screams, the intensity of the dancing increasing along with the volume. They were soon visibly drunk, including LeBetre, who along with the rest of the Jarai cut his body in several places, sending streams of blood flowing down his arms, torso, and legs as a sacrifice to the spirits.

As the ceremony raged, the Jarai danced and shook themselves free from the thorny sty of fear the Catholic priest incarcerated them in, their self-inflicted lacerations perhaps symbolic representations of a literally tight exit. But just as fast as they freed themselves the Jarai were abruptly frightened back into their allegorical pens. This time it was their sanity that was ripped to shreds as they witnessed the wild boar shake its dead body voraciously as if trying to escape the metal rod pierced through its body. Upon noticing Father McDuffee observing them from atop a stone mound, his thinning hair and black robe blowing ravenously in the strong night wind, in a surge of fright the Jarai began vomiting and heaving up the alcohol and whatever else they consumed earlier in the day. Even after they realized it was probably the wind that shook the stuck, glorified pig, its tusks a crown to the boar's elevated status among swine, the Jarai were still scared, paralyzingly so. Their ceremony stopped dead in its tracks, the drums fell silent, and the dancing ceased as they watched to see if the wild boar would move again.

Once their stomachs were cleansed, each of the Jarai reacted differently. Like a herd of wild animals running in different directions on an open plain to avoid the pursuit of a relentless predator, the Jarai scattered themselves cerebrally, each having a different explanation for what they had seen. Some mumbled while others annunciated loudly their theories in an entangled buzz that was incomprehensible to anyone except themselves. Ultimately, however, they all came to the same conclusion that it was time to flee the American enterprise and their God, no longer sure anymore where one began and the other ended.

* * *

"Marlon, where have you been? You were supposed to have been here two hours ago," asked the agitated director. He and the rest of the cast and crew had been waiting for Marlon with the hopes of getting some of the Colonel Kurtz footage shot. There was an eerie silence as Marlon, having just walked off his houseboat a few moments ago and then driven to the movie set, entered the Kurtz compound. Everybody stopped what they were doing to watch as Marlon appeared out of the jungle. Even Francis watched in awe at the stage presence Marlon possessed, his personal charisma. It was as if Colonel Kurtz had materialized out of thin air. It was kind of a 'moment' for everybody there on the set, but something altogether lost on Marlon Brando. Instead of understanding that he was the focal-point of the awe and unmitigated respect of everyone on the set, American and otherwise, Marlon felt like a child, shyly approaching one's father to inform him that something was amiss or not quite right in his world.

Francis noticed Marlon's apprehension and made his way over to him so they could speak in private.

"What's wrong, Marlon? I know that look. You're not ready. What happened?"

There was a long pause. Marlon looked around, and then back at Francis.

"There's a lot going on here, Francis, that I don't really like."

There was another pause as Marlon looked up at Francis, hoping he would immediately know what his star actor was talking about, but Francis had absolutely no clue where Marlon was coming from.

"Uh, what don't you like Marlon—your contract, your houseboat, your lines, what?"

Francis was annoyed with Marlon and was not afraid to show it. Marlon was taken aback a bit with Francis' terse response to his concern, turning away instead of answering his director. Francis threw his hands up in the air as a display of his frustration, but then quickly realized he needed to be very careful with Marlon lest he run the risk of him walking off the set.

"Marlon, what happened? Do you want to go somewhere and talk?"

"I think we'd better, Francis," said Marlon after yet another long pause.

"Okay, then that's what we'll do."

Francis walked back to the set to inform everybody that there would be no shooting on this day. Marlon could hear the boos and other sounds of disappointment coming from members of the cast, the extras, as well as the stagehands. He grumbled a few words to himself as he limped his way from the Kurtz compound with the assumption that Francis would soon be in tow. The director did catch up with the lead actor, but not before having to explain in some detail the reason for shutting down the set for the day to about five different people, including Dennis Hopper.

"Francis, Francis, I'm ready for this, if you know what I mean," begged Dennis with a firm hand on the director's shoulder.

"Dennis, I can't help it. Marlon is apparently having a problem. We'll try again tomorrow."

"Well, I'm having a fucken problem here, too, Francis. I got myself in the perfect frame of mind. I'm poised. I'm ready. I'm on the cusp of nailing this thing, man. Nailing this thing!" Dennis ended his plea by giving Francis a desperate look, still holding onto the director's shoulder.

"Dennis, I have to go and talk to Marlon. I can't make him act. I can't force him."

"The hell you can't, Francis! Why in the fuck are you letting him dictate the terms of this movie? We're all going to be out here until we fucking die, Francis!"

"Dennis..."

"If you're waiting for that fat-ass, over-the-hill has-been to feel like acting, we are all going to decompose into the fucking mud. Look around you, Francis. The jungle...it's closing in on all of us. It's...it's...fucken swallowing me up, man. I can't be out here much longer, Francis, before I'm completely devoured by all this fucken shit, man!"

"Dennis, I'm sure you will survive for a few more weeks," said Francis while walking away and in the direction of his wife, knowing he must also make it through her inquiry before reaching Marlon.

"Francis, you can't let Marlon keep doing this," she said.

"What can I do? I can't make him act."

"But you can make him stay on the set."

"Can I?"

"Well, you can at least not indulge him on every little issue or problem he's having."

"I know how to deal with Marlon, dear. If we lose Marlon, this movie is done. It's that simple."

"We can replace Marlon. We've already replaced a big-name actor out here, Francis."

"You can replace a Harvey Keitel, dear, but not a Marlon Brando!"

CHAPTER 29

Back at Artemis, Wilke started noticing signs that the Vietcong were once again venturing into Green Tiger's area of operations, close enough that the hunt could resume, and on our own terms. But we would need soldiers, the Jarai in particular, who were still around, but acting very much like they were no longer a part of Green Tiger. Wilke knew where they were, discernable from the dim glow of the small fire they would light each night, and went to talk to them. LeBetre still trusted Wilke as did the Jarai, and after a couple hours of sitting alongside them, talking about how he and many of their fathers fought the Vietminh together, LeBetre and the Jarai agreed to come back to Artemis the following day. But when they failed to make good on this promise, myself and a couple newly-arrived South Vietnamese soldiers, weapons in hand and against Wilke's advice, went to get them, literally forcing LeBetre and the Jarai back at gunpoint. They came, but were now completely alienated, and distrustful of anyone wearing a uniform.

At the pre-hunt briefing, not only did the Jarai seem despondent, but so did Wilke. It was not necessarily because I did something against his wishes. He understood and accepted the military's chain of command system. Wilke was withdrawn and distraught because he knew the Jarai had been lost, that they would never hunt the Vietcong for the Americans again, not after being forced to do so. The Jarai would probably still follow orders and go out looking for the Vietcong, but they would not *hunt* the Vietcong anymore. There is a difference, and Wilke knew it. A soldier, whether an American, Jarai, or North Vietnamese, has to be motivated, they have to believe in what they are doing and they must *want* to kill. Wilke could see it in their eyes and in their body language, the Jarai no longer believed in the Americans, nor wanted to kill for them. They just wanted to go home. The squawks and shrieks of a nearby field radio, used to stay in contact with I-Core, seemed to rip their stomachs open every time it erupted with static-laden chatter. The presence of Father McDuffee did not seem to help matters either. His piercing glare tended to unnerve even those of the most steadfast faith, much less those outside of the Church.

Despite his insistence that he does not meddle in areas outside the ecclesial realm, Father McDuffee adheres to the school of thought that says the Catholic Church and its leaders should still have a certain amount of authority regarding what are otherwise considered secular issues, including that of war. More than a great admirer of Pope Urban II who launched the First Crusade from Clermont, France in 1095, Father McDuffee liked to be in the mix during strategy sessions, taking very seriously his duty of blessing the men before going into battle. He had long since worn out his welcome with Wilke, however, who blamed Father McDuffee for "ruining" the Jarai with his attempts at Christianizing them.

It was precisely because they were Jarai—a people who have lived and fought in the jungles of Southeast Asia for thousands of years, and whose natural enemy was the Vietnamese—that the Americans sought their services in the first place. Not only could they never really be Christians in the Western sense, they could never again be the Jarai that they once were. Instead, they are now a frightened and confused lot, a mere shell of their former selves, neither American nor Jarai, with only their own failure to resist eating and drinking from the trough of a medieval-apocalyptic version of the Christian religion to blame for their infirmities.

The resumption of Green Tiger's war against the Vietcong was scheduled to begin at sundown. But a few of the Jarai had other ideas as some of them began a quiet diaspora from Artemis amidst the chaos of a pre-hunt preparation and the coming darkness. They walked away in pairs as well as individually into the vast expanse of the jungle, another sign that their like-mindedness was gone. The fact that they left at all was an indication of their fear-stricken panic. Artemis was too far from their ancestral homeland for them to even think they could find their way back. The sudden exodus was apparently more out of a desire to simply leave Artemis than it was to actually go home.

Once gone from Artemis, the frightened Jarai scattered in all directions. Nobody, not even Wilke would have known about this development except for the fact that

Henderson was manning the outside of the perimeter at the time, witnessing several of the Jarai scamper away, the sound of heavy breathing and bare feet slapping the mud alerting him of what he could not see through the foliage. He did not bother trying to stop them, but instead reported his observations to me right away. This news immediately put a halt to the offensive Green Tiger was preparing to embark upon, as well as sounded an alarm amongst both myself and Wilke.

The idea of scared and unhappy Jarai running loose in the jungle was an extremely unpleasant prospect for those still at Artemis. They could be picked up by the North Vietnamese and forced to divulge critical information about Green Tiger, setting Artemis up for a deadly attack. Or they could even stumble across one of the many American journalists scouring Cambodia for U.S. indiscretions of one kind or another. Wilke has told me many times in the past that he feared the American press finding Artemis more than he did the North Vietnamese. Simply stated, once the story broke, Wilke believed the government would have Tigerden, Artemis, or whatever name our basecamp was going by at the time, turned to ash in an instant in order to destroy the evidence of any such existence. At least against the North Vietnamese we would have a fighting chance.

Aware that we had to move fast, Wilke and I quickly debated about what to do regarding the Jarai gone AWOL, as well as with those still there. It was determined that the remaining Jarai could not be trusted to hunt down the deserters, and that ordering them to do so may result in a full-scale mutiny, something neither of us wanted to risk.

Wilke brought up the idea of going out by himself to try and coax the fleeing Jarai into coming back, but then dismissed the notion, further evidence of his growing lack of confidence. His initial instincts were to save the Jarai, but the ideas he came up with on the spur of the moment were all void of working possibility, none taking on life for even a moment.

  Without any practical alternatives from Wilke, I was forced to radio I-Core for immediate assistance. It was something I really did not want to do, but if I failed to inform them now, and Jarai began turning up in North Vietnamese propaganda, I-Core would have my head. Before doing so, I looked over at Wilke, giving him one last chance. In disgust at his seeming increasing inability to perform his own organic brand of miracle, Wilke got up and walked away.

  Feeling a bit like a young boy let down by his father, I turned in the other direction to go do what I knew was necessary. First, I ordered the South Vietnamese soldiers to disarm the remaining Jarai and tie them together at the feet so they could not run, including LeBetre, who along with the rest of the Jarai had now become the enemy. Even as I was calling headquarters, and the South Vietnamese were rounding up spears, knives, and M-16s from the Jarai, Wilke was still trying to think of a way to avert what he knew was inevitable. He felt responsible for them. After all, it was he who lobbied to get the Jarai involved again in American operations in the first place. The Jarai have always been there for him, risking their lives, leaving their homes and families to help him. Now, when they needed Wilke, he was not able to reciprocate. The mighty Wilke, a man whose legend of invincibility and battlefield conquests have grown to mythical and god-like proportions in the minds of the Jarai, sat on the ground in quiet resignation of the fact that everything he'd built was collapsing around him, a personal domain whose breadth he was not fully aware of until it began falling down.

* * *

It was only a matter of about forty minutes after I informed I-Core of the recent developments that the sounds of Huey helicopters became audible in the distance, the low hum of rotating helicopter blades evolving into a steady heart-thumping beat as they approached. Immediately out of the first of three helicopters, each with barely enough room to land, came two army military policemen. With their rifles held in a ready but non-threatening position, the first of two asked me where he could find Sergeant Wilke. I pointed to the distraught man on the ground.

"Sergeant Wilke, I'm here on orders from I-Core to escort you back to Danang, sir."

Except for the three helicopters taking a brief respite from waging war against gravity, but still loud in repose, a silence fell over the rest of basecamp as even the jungle had a stake in this. Wilke rose to his feet in an almost conciliatory fashion.

"Your weapon please, Sergeant Wilke," politely requested the MP, but whose courteous manner was overshadowed by his abrupt grab for the M-16 and ensuing pat-down by his counterpart. Wilke was not being arrested. There would have at least been *some* dignity in that. He was instead being stripped of his Caesar-esque aura in front of everyone and led away as if a common pleb. His arms and legs were free to resist which was perhaps the greatest of all insults to someone once considered by many to be the greatest soldier in the world.

As Wilke was being escorted to the awaiting helicopter about fifteen yards away, those witnessing the events unfold—myself, Henderson, Father McDuffee, the South Vietnamese, LeBetre, and the remaining Jarai—were all looking on as if it were a dream. Some of them wondered if this might be the impasse that would afford Wilke the opportunity to orchestrate a final masterpiece, one that would secure his place in the pantheon of history's greatest fighters. But those who hoped he would do something to save himself and the Jarai would be disappointed. Wilke instead accepted his fate, and the fate of all the other men of Green Tiger for that matter.

As he prepared to board the helicopter that would take him out of the jungle, Wilke stopped to take one last look around. It was then, as he stoically scanned what had been his home for the past thirty years, that everyone watching expected Wilke to perform something akin to a miracle, perhaps something even reflective of the Exodus event. He had the kind of mystique in which nothing seemed impossible for him, even in my skeptical mind's eye. But just as I suspected all along, Sergeant Wilke was not only just a sergeant, but a mortal one at that. He was not a king, not some demi-god of the jungle who could finesse his realm whenever he pleased.

It was hard for Wilke to leave. He did feel certain loyalties to the Jarai, as well as the rest of Green Tiger. And if this had happened just a few years earlier, Wilke probably would have single-handedly, defying man, machine, and the forces of nature, found a way to lead the Jarai back to their ancestral home. But if the truth be told, Wilke had not only grown old out in the jungle, he had grown wise as well. Wise, because he was smart enough to realize that he had grown too old to carry out such an ambitious task. Once again Wilke chose not to defy that which was bigger and more powerful than he is, and would live another day to perhaps fight again. On this occasion, it was Father Time that he bowed down to, the first instance in which he acknowledged supremacy to anything other than the jungle.

When the army was teaching Wilke how to survive the duress of war some twenty years ago, his commanders had no way of knowing that there was very little they could have done to improve on what nature had already given him. When he received the news that some of the Jarai had left camp, Wilke knew right away they were going to die, as would the Jarai who were still there, and anyone who tried to assist them for that matter. So, knowing he would probably die too if he got involved with trying to save the Jarai, Wilke's deeply embedded, well-honed, and often-exercised instincts to stay alive would not allow him to help the Jarai. And perhaps this is what bothered him the most.

As Wilke stood next to the helicopter that in a few moments would take him away, the sergeant smiled wryly at me, then nodded his head at all the faces staring at him as if he were some kind of tragic figure. Having a flare for the dramatic, and not letting anybody down at least in this regard, Wilke bowed to each of his now former comrades, a final curtain call for the multifarious group of people he did not believe would make it out of Cambodia alive. Already feeding on itself, everything Wilke knew told him the jungle was poised to devour what remained of Green Tiger. He fended it off as long as he could. Now it was my turn.

At least in theory it seemed as if Wilke had finally been cornered. But it was not the Vietcong or even a bloodthirsty Asian tiger that had him trapped. Those things he could fight off. It was instead the abstract concept of army politics as well as the bureaucracy and red tape propelling it that had him pinned down, something he could not escape by pulling the trigger on his rifle, swinging his machete, or with a sleek run through the jungle. Never one to buck the oncoming tide, always finding it more prudent to jump on the back of a charging elephant than out in front of it, Wilke decided to hop on and live rather than be trampled underfoot by something he could not control. I was always critical of, and never quite understood, Wilke's insistence on determining the flow of natural and cosmic momentum, and moving with rather than against its grain. But remaining loyal to his instincts and gut feelings instead of rules and regulations would get him out of the jungle alive, a feat not yet accomplished by me.

* * *

"Some men are cut down in the prime of their lives, which I will always believe is a man's youth, probably mid- to upper- twenties. Maybe early thirties, depending on the person. James Dean will forever be the young, handsome, free-spirit. He was not as good of an actor as people give him credit for, nor was he all that good looking, either. Like myself, he was a master at creating an illusion. He perfected that illusion, and then he died while it was

still potent, and will forever remain potent and intoxicating. Whenever his name is mentioned, or when people see his picture, people think they are hearing the name of a god, and even seeing a god for that matter. My earlier characters are gods. I used to be a god. Oh, I'm still kind of a god, I guess, but an old, vulnerable god. I am no longer Hercules, Dionysius, or Apollo. Those are young gods who burn bright and fast. I once burned like that, too. To look at me too long was to risk becoming blinded, or even immolated. Yet people still looked at me. They couldn't help themselves. I was beautiful, dangerous, sometimes even vicious and vile. Yet people could not look away. People now look away. Some are disinterested in me, while still others are uncomfortable to look at me. They are embarrassed for me. When you are young, talented and beautiful there are such high expectations for you. But it's not the young man who has to fulfill those expectations. No. The young man merely represents the potential of what is possible. It's the old man, the man who no longer has the looks, the self-assuredness, the energy, the will, the drive to do great things who is left to carry out all those great expectations. Here I am, trying to carry out all those things promised by my younger self. Where is Stanley Kowalski? Where is Johnny Strabler? Where is Terry Malloy? Where is Marlon Brando?"

CHAPTER 30

"Marlon, what the hell is going on? I just had to explain to both Dennis Hopper and my wife why we cancelled today's shoot. I wouldn't wish that on my worst enemy, which right now is you, Marlon. So, what gives this time?"

"How much time do you got?"

"Oh, good God. That bad?"

"Yes, it's that bad."

"Where do you want to go and talk about this, other than back to L.A. or Tahiti?"

"I don't want to go back to L.A. or Tahiti. Not yet, anyway, but we'll have to work a few things out in the meantime."

"Where do you want to go to discuss this, Marlon? Your houseboat, my hotel, a bar, a restaurant? Where?"

"The jungle."

"The jungle?"

Marlon nodded.

"Yes, the jungle."

"Marlon, we're in the fucking jungle!"

"No, out there." Marlon whirled his arm around to indicate he wanted to go out beyond the area in which the movie was being shot.

"Out where? What do you mean by 'out there'?"

"Out in the jungle. Away from all this bullshit."

"What bullshit? You mean the movie? It's not as if I can walk away from this thing, Marlon."

"That's not what I'm saying, Francis. I'm talking about this...this town, this city, all the ghosts and demons of its past, the history of this country, the lies...the...the stench of lies, the cover-ups, the false histories."

Francis looked away and shook his head, knowing full-well the difficult time he would have trying to fix all that was wrong in Marlon's mind.

"Do you mean here, in the Philippines, Marlon?"

"Yes, here in the Philippines. It's the same here as in the rest of the world."

"What is?"

"Imperialism. Racism. And we don't even know we're doing it."

"Doing what, Marlon? What is it that we don't know we're doing?" asked a now visibly exasperated Francis Coppola.

"Oh, for fuck sake!" said Marlon after a brief pause and look of disbelief aimed at his director. "My *house boy*, for one thing." Again, Marlon stared at Francis, waiting for him to understand or see things the way he did.

"*House boy*, Marlon? I don't follow you."

"I have a fucken house boy on my boat!"

"You wanted a house boy on your boat!"

"Exactly."

"Exactly what, Marlon?"

"I wanted a house boy. And you provided me with one—a Filipino. And neither one of us thought there was anything wrong that."

"I still don't get your point, Marlon. What is wrong with that?"

"Don't you see, Francis? This is how blind we are."

There was a pause before Marlon continued.

"We ugly Americans come over here to the Philippines, and we're completely ignorant of its history, and what we've done to the Filipino people. And then we proceed to make them our servants and slaves, and we don't even realize what we're doing. It just comes very natural to us."

"Ugly Americans? Marlon, we have employed a lot of Filipino people here, but we are in fact *paying them*. They are not our servants and slaves. They are our employees, Marlon. Nobody is forcing them to work for us. Nobody is forcing your house boy to be your house boy. In fact, *house boy* isn't the proper term. That's something you came up with, Marlon. He's an employee of American Zoetrope, the studio sponsoring this fiasco of a movie."

"But we're here in *their* country, in positions of power and authority. Us, we Westerners—you, me, American Zoetrope—stand to make millions of dollars from this endeavor, while they are all making a mere pittance. We are doing here what Conrad's book and your movie are trying to illuminate."

"Oh, for Christ-sake, Marlon, I hardly think so. You can't compare our movie set with the rubber and ivory harvest of the nineteenth century, or with the Vietnam War for that matter."

"But it's in the same spirit as those things, or better yet, an offshoot, a direct correlation of white racism."

"How is what we are doing here a direct correlation of white racism?"

"We are the overlords of the Filipino people. They are in a position in which they need us. We don't need them."

"I think we do need them, Marlon. Look at how many Filipinos I've employed here. This movie is helping the Filipino economy. I'm even paying the Filipino government to use its helicopters and air bases."

"That's not what I mean, Francis."

"Then what do you mean, Marlon, because I don't really understand?"

Francis smiled in a conciliatory fashion upon saying this, knowing it probably came off sounding a little too condescending, which he knew would only cause Marlon to turn inward, making him completely impossible to deal with. Marlon was in fact hurt by Francis' tone, choosing to look away instead of answering his director's question.

"We need to talk," said Marlon with a very serious and dead-pan look on his face. Francis recognized that look. He knew the Kurtz compound scenes were days, perhaps weeks away from being shot.

* * *

"There's something I want you to listen to, Francis," said Marlon in his all-too familiar somber, semi-despondent, garbled voice.

"Okay," replied Francis, unsure yet curious.

"Take up the White Man's burden--Send forth the best ye breed--Go bind your sons to exile. To serve your captives' need; To wait

in heavy harness, On fluttered folk and wild--Your new-caught, sullen peoples, Half-devil and half-child." Marlon finished and then waited for Francis' response.

"I've heard that before. Wait, don't tell me. Kipling?"

"Right."

"And the name of the poem is...*White Man's*...uh..."

"*White Man's Burden*," announced Marlon, wanting to move beyond the formalities. "Kipling is talking about the Filipino people, Francis."

"I didn't know that, Marlon."

Marlon stared at Francis, perhaps waiting for him to say more. Francis, confused, stared back at Marlon.

"Don't you see what's going on here, Francis?"

"To a certain extent I think I do, but something tells me that I'm not grasping this in the manner that you want or expect me to."

"*New-caught? Half-man, half-devil?*"

"Terrible, racist words, Marlon. Again, you're preaching to the choir."

"The point I'm trying to make here, Francis, is that you can see these words, or at least the sentiment behind the words, on the faces of the Filipino people. I can see them on the face of my house boy. He thinks that I, as a white man, automatically perceives him in this way. And do you want to know what's even worse?"

"No, but I'm afraid you're going to tell me, Marlon."

"Worse yet, Francis, is that the manner in which I perceive him has much to do with how he perceives himself."

"What? I'm not following."

"Having been forced to see himself from the perspective of the white man has not only given him a disdain for the likes of me because I'm white and Western, but a disdain for himself because he's *not* white and Western. You see what I mean, Francis?"

"Marlon...I think you've read way too much into this, and the so-called *look* your house boy gave you."

"Francis, I think the very fact we're referring to him as a 'house boy' lends a certain amount of credence to what I'm saying."

"Those are your words, Marlon. To me he's an *employee*."

"But you called him a 'house boy', too."

"Only because you did. Marlon, stop. Just stop. What is this really all about? What?"

"We're trying to make some kind of a statement here with this movie, and yet what we—us white Westerners—are doing here is...is...what we are doing is..."

Marlon was looking around, trying to find the right words. He sensed Francis' restlessness, which only caused him more consternation.

"Would you just give me a god-damn minute to finish one of my thoughts, Francis? Jesus Christ! I'm trying to convey to you my concerns, and what I'm getting from you is your usual impatience. I'm sorry that I don't talk fast enough for you, Francis."

"Oh, for fuck sake, Marlon!" interjected Francis.

"Francis, I just want you to listen to me, and to be patient, and to not start fidgeting, or looking around, or trying to finish my thoughts for me."

"Marlon, no other director in the world would allow one of their actors to pull them away from the set for days at a time to discuss their concerns. I'm not showing you enough patience? For God sake, Marlon! What more would you have me do?"

"You could listen to me, Francis. Really listen to me."

Marlon's words evoked silence between the two men. Francis donned a conciliatory look on his face.

"You're absolutely right, Marlon. I need to be a more patient, better listener. Hell, my wife tells me this all the time, so there must be something to it. Marlon, please continue. You will have my full and undivided attention."

Marlon gave Francis a look of skepticism.

"Marlon, right there! That look! I'm sorry, Marlon, but that look you just gave me...that is the face of Walter Kurtz. That's the expression that you should wear when we film. Can you do it again?"

"No!"

"I know what I just said about giving you my undivided attention, Marlon, but that look is so perfect for the Kurtz character. It's a cynical 'I've seen and heard this bullshit a million times before', kind of look."

"Touché."

"Touché? Oh, that's hysterical, Marlon. Don't make me out to be the enemy. I'm on your side, here, remember?"

"Yes, I know you're on my side, but you won't let me talk, for fuck sake, Francis."

"Okay, Marlon, I get it. I understand. I just needed to point that one thing out before the moment was gone. Please continue."

Marlon stared at Francis, unconvinced.

"There! There's that look again, Marlon! It's Kurtz! I'm sorry, Marlon, but Colonel Kurtz just passed through you again."

Marlon, still staring Francis down, smiled and then even chuckled, which was reciprocated by Francis. Soon the two men were laughing out loud together.

"Would you just shut the fuck up, Francis, for fuck sake!"

Marlon yelled these words loudly, but were intended to be fun and jovial. Both men waited for the laughing to die down before anyone attempted to speak again. Francis knew it was Marlon's turn and he must cede the floor to him or risk Marlon's newfound good nature turning sour again.

"Francis, we need to talk about the Philippines."

"Yes, Marlon," conceded Francis with exaggerated sincerity.

"We could use the movie to cast a light on what the United States did here."

"I guess I don't even know what the United States did here, to be quite honest, Marlon."

Marlon rubbed his eyes and groaned as if the task of trying to explain what America did in the Philippines was too daunting for him right now.

"Well, it's like this, Francis," began Marlon, who said these words using a slow, whiny voice, one that Francis cannot stand, a voice and cadence that told Francis the forthcoming explanation was going to be long and perhaps even directionless. Francis squirmed and contemplated trying to moderate what Marlon was about to say, but knew to do so at this point would only risk alienating his star actor even further. Marlon continued to rub his face, and then the top of his head as if massaging it, perhaps even trying to draw out an explanation to offer up to his director.

"I like that, Marlon." Francis could not resist. The way in which his lead actor was rubbing his head prompted his director's instincts into action yet again.

Marlon gave a look of stunned surprise.

"What?"

"That thing you're doing. I like it. The rubbing your head thing. It's something that I can see Colonel Kurtz doing. Try to remember that, too, okay?"

Marlon paused for a moment. He was trying not to get upset with Francis for once again interrupting him while attempting to give an explanation of his concerns.

"Okay, I'll try to remember that, Francis."

Marlon looked the other way, shaking his head in disgust, and now lost of his desire to explain what was bothering him.

CHAPTER 31

"Colonel Memmington, reporting from I-Core," said the tall newcomer, his thick English accent and well-groomed exterior complete with beret, medal-laden uniform, shiny black boots, and clean-shaven face, pulling my eyes away from the black night sky that only moments earlier swallowed up the helicopter taking Wilke out of the jungle. "Colonel Memmington, reporting from I-Core," said the British soldier a second time now that he had my full attention, his mannerisms indicative of someone waiting for a salute even though we held the same rank.

"Welcome to Artemis, colonel," I said, obliging the British officer in the universal military ritual denoting respect and even dominance.

"Artemis, you say?" responded Memmington dryly as he looked around the jungle basecamp now silent of Huey helicopters. "Seems you have a few Jarai that have flown the coup, eh."

"Yes, uh, colonel, they've been gone, uh…" I responded, stumbling for words as a result of being a bit uneasy in the presence of Colonel Memmington, a man I knew I-Core would be sending, nonetheless. "They've been

AWOL for about four hours now. And if we don't waste any time…"

"All right, then," interrupted Memmington. "We'll go inside your quarters and plot strategy. Artemis, eh. She must be a real bitch to have that kind of name," he added, then chortled at his own attempt at levity, considering it successful.

Inside my hut, Colonel Memmington firmly packed his pipe with tobacco then lit it, taking three hard drags then proceeding to puff it slowly. He waited patiently for me to offer him something to drink, but when it became apparent that none was forthcoming, the colonel inquired himself.

"I'm a bit parched. How 'bout a belt before we get started, my good man."

I pulled out an unopened bottle of Scottish whiskey, one that Father McDuffee gave me.

"Cutty Sark. Excellent!" declared Memmington.

Standing in front of a map illuminated by the soft glow of a kerosene lamp, his slow burning pipe filled with an aromatic Columbian blend of tobacco clenched between his teeth, a glass of Scottish whiskey in his hand, and an audience to spin his tales to—-this is the kind of moment that Memmington lived for. He considered the planning of military strategy to be an art-form much along the same lines as painting a fresco, sculpting a statue, or even making a fine wine. In other words, a trade that requires time, creativity, and planning. While crafting one of his artistic abstractions, Memmington liked to smoke, maybe have a drink or two as on this occasion, debate, and share war and adventure stories with whomever happened to be in his presence.

    In practical terms, however, Memmington's battle plans were usually something far less than a Van Gogh or a Picasso. Once an extremely competent and well-respected military strategist, the now fifty-nine year-old World War II hero and relic of a bygone-era has been in effect put out to pasture for the past ten years. Like a once champion race horse retired to endless fields of green grass and clover, the British army has trotted Memmington out into the third-world as a sort of soldier of fortune, a trouble-shooter in the war against communist insurgencies anywhere they might pop up. In no way a vital cog in the West's Cold War arsenal, Memmington was given this assignment more as a reward to an aging soldier for his many years of dedicated service, a man who could not bear the thought of dying without his boots on.

In the years since assuming this role, Memmington has become more and more of an eccentric embarrassment to be pawned off from one unwitting country to another. Political and military leaders who received him would not only be burdened with ridding their nations of communist insurgents, but also Colonel Memmington, who in short order never failed to disaffect those around him. His biggest problem was his inability to adapt to the strategies and nuances of guerilla warfare, which were commonplace in the world's various Cold War conflicts, as opposed to big, set-piece battles prominent in World War II. Insurgencies and counter-insurgencies, as well as the kinds of strategies employed therein, were things that Colonel Memmington refused to even try and understand, thus contributing to his own antiquation by not willing to change with the times.

Not only was the colonel of virtually no practical use wherever he went, he would usually hurt the cause by acting as an extreme reactionary, sauntering himself around and barking out orders as if he was a nineteenth century British colonial overlord. His Anglo-centrism literally got him run out of the Congo in the early 1960s, a friendly hand from a hovering helicopter pulling the misfit colonel out of the clutches of some angry Congolese who had their fill of Memmington. In 1967, the Colombian government, acting on the recommendations of the country's military leaders, told the British "no thanks" regarding Memmington and his so-called 'expertise'. It seems that Memmington, with the help of a small band of locals that he recruited, took it upon himself to rid the Colombian countryside of coca plants, but instead burned down several large tobacco plantations in the process. Memmington was actually detained by Colombian authorities for two weeks until the British government made reparations.

When I radioed I-Core for help, Memmington just so happened to be in Danang, sent there by the British a few months earlier with the hopes that either the Vietcong or the Americans would kill him and put everyone out of their misery. Having long since worn out his welcome, I-Core sent him to Artemis, partly because they were short on officers willing to leave the comforts of Danang for the Cambodian jungle, but mainly for the reason that he was driving everyone there crazy.

"Colonel Memmington, I remind you that time is of the essence here," I said politely, interrupting the colonel's lengthy story about one of his tiger hunting expeditions in India that took place over twenty-five years ago, rambling on for over fifteen minutes, yet unable to move the story beyond the first day of a three-week hunt.

"Yes, I suppose you're right, colonel. Well then, I'll just have to finish that one later, won't I," he conceded, delighting in the prospect of future storytelling. Then, with a quick turn of his wrist, the colonel threw back what remained of his whiskey, placed the glass down on the table, patted his stomach then headed out the door. Confused, I followed him.

"You say the Jarai were seen running to the north? And that's the direction you assume them to be going, back to the highlands?" asked the colonel who was only now starting to assess the situation. Then, with an air of assertiveness that was becoming more prevalent, Memmington made a circular motion with his right hand, a signal for the two remaining helicopters to fire up their engines. It also prompted the ten Cambodian soldiers who arrived with him to a readied position. Speaking over the sounds of helicopter blades slapping the humid jungle air, Memmington hollered out his design for retrieving the runaway Jarai, the plan's simplicity a clear indication of its spontaneity.

"We'll all get into Hueys and drop the Cambodians off a couple miles to the north. They'll fan out and do a ground sweep back to Artemis while we fly overhead scanning the jungle with the searchlight. Then, after the bastards flush like a covey of quail, we'll bloody their asses with hot lead." Memmington capped off the description of his plan with a quick but thundering diabolical laugh. The man was a living, breathing cliché.

It was midnight by the time the Cambodian soldiers were in a straight-line formation and properly distanced to suit the British colonel, who was annoyingly barking out orders through a loudspeaker from inside his helicopter. Once their southward march through the nearly impenetrable jungle foliage commenced, the two Hueys began buzzing back and forth at such low altitudes in order to see through the jungle canopy that they at times forced both the vegetation and the Cambodians to the ground.

I knew immediately that this strategy was going to end in catastrophe.

Memmington continued to yell out orders to the Cambodians who could not hear over the helicopter blades anyway, halting his verbal onslaught only to take an occasional potshot with his rifle into the chaotic mess of shadows, swirling plant life, and Cambodian soldiers down below.

After an hour of this confusion, the Cambodians, having been able to work their way through only an eighth of a mile of jungle, suddenly lost two men within five minutes of each other. The first one falling victim to a booby trap, the second to the reckless gunfire of Colonel Memmington who blamed it on the Jarai even though I assured him they were only carrying spears.

With the Cambodians unable, and quite possibly unwilling to go on, and not one confirmed Jarai sighting, Memmington wisely decided to salvage what was left of his already badly tarnished reputation as a military strategist, putting an immediate halt to the failed operation.

The helicopters were lowered as far as they could without getting tangled in the jungle in order to allow the tired and beleaguered Cambodians to be hoisted in before heading back to Artemis, minus the two casualties we would leave behind. Even more folly would be waiting for us when we got back on the ground, however. There, a scared and hesitant Henderson had the daunting task of informing Memmington and myself that LeBetre had apparently picked up Wilke's skill for subtle illusion. He and the rest of the Jarai somehow freed themselves from the ropes binding their legs and arms, and ran off into the jungle.

"What's that you say? The rest have escaped too?" interrupted Memmington from about ten yards away and then quickly strutted toward us in an attempt to forcibly include himself in the conversation.

The new development did not really upset the British colonel. He saw it as an opportunity to divert attention away from his own fiasco. And because I was hesitant to do anything at this point, it enabled Memmington to maintain control over the situation.

"God damn it! I want everybody who's still in this bloody fucken camp, right here," screamed Colonel Memmington, pointing to the spot in which he was standing as if talking to dogs. "And somebody bring me a bloody fucking radio," he added.

There was a brief pause in his tirade as he waited for Henderson to get I-Core on the line.

"How long would it take to get some Stieng out here?" barked the colonel as if whomever he was speaking to would automatically know who he was. He then turned to me and in a very pleasant tone said, "marvelous fighters, the Stieng. I worked with them in Laos. Nasty lot! Oh, for God's sake, man.

This is Colonel Memmington," he then yelled, resuming his phone call to I-Core. "We're in a bit of a quandary out here. I require the assistance of about twenty Stieng. How soon? Before the sun comes up. Splendid! I will also need some napalm. That's right. Keep a couple bombers at the ready. Thank you, my good man. That's right. I'll have this mess cleaned up by tomorrow," he then assured me.

After the colonel was finished making demands of I-Core, I stood there like a fool, waiting for Memmington to brief me, but not before the British soldier first dropped the radio receiver on the ground for somebody else to pick up.

"They won't live to see the sunrise," announced the British colonel while gazing up at the black sky. "Let's retire to your quarters for a moment, Colonel Kurtz. I fancy another belt of that whiskey." This was Memmington's polite way of saying he did not want to discuss his latest round of strategy in front of Henderson, Father McDuffee, or the South Vietnamese who were all still standing in the middle of camp at his behest. The colonel of the British Royal Army did not like to "cast pearl upon swine," as he would later put it.

Back inside my quarters, Memmington had a look of intensity and determination that he did not have the first time. He sucked hard from his pipe then threw back in one gulp the two fingers of Cutty Sark that I poured for him.

"The bloody savage bastards will die this time, I guarantee it!" assured Memmington in a calm but serious matter-of-fact sort of way. "There will be no escape for man nor beast out there in light of what's coming," added the colonel coyly in a manner that invited inquiry, but which was temporarily preempted by a sudden question from Memmington.

"You say there's an American out there?"

"So, what do you have planned, colonel?" I asked, ignoring what I believed to be an attempt at diversion on the part of Memmington.

"Whatever possessed him to run wild with the savages, anyway?" the painfully upright British colonel wanted to know before divulging his plans on how he would kill him.

"I don't know," I replied, enunciating each word carefully in order to sound convincing.

Now it was Memmington's turn. Slowly puffing his pipe, the colonel strategically positioned himself next to the map in a manner he assumed made him look dignified and authoritative.

"One word, my good man: fire!" Something you Americans seem to have forgotten over here, all hell-bent with your damn guerilla war. Why do you waste your time hunting your enemy, killing them one at a time, taking so many casualties when you have the power to kill them quickly and cleanly?" rebuked the Englishman.

"So, you're going burn them out?" I asked in a tone indicating I was in agreement with the plan if indeed this was Memmington's intention.

"Like I said, Colonel Kurtz, there will be no escape for man nor beast with what's coming." The colonel gazed at me with a certain intensity that told me it was his desire to napalm the entire area. I did not know how this was going to affect the future of the mission, or even if there would be a mission for that matter, but I understood the necessity of killing the Jarai, as well as LeBetre, and that guerilla tactics would not get it done, just as Memmington said.

"What do you need the Stieng for?" I inquired, asking only because their inclusion hardly seemed necessary if Colonel Memmington was going to raze the entire area.

"They'll be the teeth of this operation, going in first to chew up the Jarai for the flames to devour," was his reply, an answer that satisfied my curiosity even though I was not exactly sure what it meant.

On a night already filled with chaos, and more destined to come, Memmington and myself sat in the calm silence of my hut as we waited for the Stieng to arrive.

"Do you play chess, Colonel Kurtz? Wait a minute, here they come," said Memmington before jumping to his feet and heading out the door to greet the in-coming Stieng arriving aboard three Hueys. Everybody backed away until the helicopters were on the ground and the blades given ample time to slow down. Out of the first helicopter came about ten more Cambodian soldiers. Then the twenty or so Stieng stepped out of the other two Hueys and onto the jungle floor while everyone watched in curious amazement. They looked different than the Jarai. They were much darker and their hair was long and frizzy. Native to the swampy lowlands of Cambodia, the Stieng are well known throughout Cambodia and Vietnam for their prowess as hunters of man and animal. They are feared and reviled by the Khmer, as well as various other Cambodian ethnic groups, for their brutal and bizarre practices, with cannibalism purported to be one of them.

To everyone's surprise Memmington walked right up to the Stieng, who were unarmed and wearing only loincloths, and began conversing with them in their native tongue. After a brief exchange in which even laughter rang out into the miserably hot night air, the British colonel told me, Father McDuffee, Henderson, and the South Vietnamese to gather everything of necessity that could fit aboard a helicopter because we would be departing immediately.

"Five minutes, people. You have exactly five minutes," declared Memmington as we each went off in a different direction to gather up our things.

The Cambodians were ordered into the helicopters as well, but the Stieng were staying on the ground.

Memmington tried to create a sense of urgency for our departure, sounding as if Hitler's Luffwaffta was about to lay waste to London, or some other calamity.

"Father! What in the name of God Almighty have you got there?" screamed the English colonel at the Irish priest who was hoping to go unnoticed as he scurried to a waiting helicopter with a large box of prayer books in his hands.

"They're prayer books! The men need them," replied the priest, purposely masking his Irish accent so not to prompt the colonel into making a final decision based on certain age-old prejudices evoked by the sound of his voice.

"More than ammunition? More than food? Look around you, Father. Do these men look like they need prayer books?"

Memmington grabbed the box and threw it into the fire burning in the middle of the camp, the priest making a dash for them.

"Leave 'em," scolded Memmington as he pushed Father McDuffee away from the fire.

"You wicked bastard!" screamed the priest after performing the sign of the cross on himself and bowing to the pages of God's Word being devoured by flames, his Irish accent clear and unmistakable.

   I did not appreciate what Colonel Memmington did either, but was more concerned with the impending second attempt to get rid of the Jarai to make a big deal out of it. Despite evidence of a quickly expanding powerbase for the British colonel, I was hoping that Memmington would simply do what he was sent here to do, and then leave. But in the meantime, however, I could not help but feel like some kind of prisoner with him around.

CHAPTER 32

"What about Tahiti, Marlon?"
"What? What do you mean?"
"Tahiti, Marlon. Isn't that where you live?"
"I have a home there, of sorts."
"Aren't you the fucken king of Tahiti, Marlon?"
Marlon chuckled.
"And isn't your home a fucken castle?"
Marlon sighed.
"I have a very modest residence there, yes."
"Modest, Marlon? I've seen pictures of your home. It's a fucken palace!"
"You must be thinking of somebody else's island home, because I live in a grass hut. And just so you know, I live on Tetiaroa, and not Tahiti-proper, my friend."
"I know that, Marlon, but it's still Tahiti, right?"
"Yes, it's a part of Tahiti."
"How far is it from the mainland?"
"It's about thirty-five miles."
"Thirty-five miles? I had no idea it was so far. So, you can't just get in a canoe and row over there. Maybe you can have some of your subjects paddle you around."
"*Subjects*? Fuck you, Francis! What the fuck do you mean...*subjects*?"
"Why are you getting upset, Marlon?"
"Why are you getting hostile with me, Francis?"

"Well, you were getting hostile with me earlier, Marlon, with all that talk about how my movie production is some kind of quasi-colonial endeavor, or something."

Francis paused to gauge Marlon's reaction. He looked mad.

"The point I'm trying to make, Marlon, is the exact point you were trying to make."

Again, Francis paused to gauge Marlon's reaction. Marlon shook his head, indicating he was not tracking.

"Which is what, Francis? What's the point that we are both making, or trying to make?"

"The point that you were trying to make with me, Marlon, and that I'm trying to make with you, is that the Western world, and even we as Westerners, no matter how enlightened we consider ourselves, are oblivious to how far-reaching and all-encompassing Western colonialism and imperialism have been. We tend to think of Africa, and North America with the Indians, and even Vietnam in more recent times. But places like the Philippines, as you were pointing out, and even tropical paradises like Tahiti, have felt the effect of Western exploitation."

Francis paused to again gauge Marlon's reaction to his statement.

"You see, Marlon, Tahiti was conquered by the Westerners, just like any other non-white country or people. That movie didn't give an accurate portrayal, Marlon. The English didn't come and civilize Tahiti, and then everybody lived happily ever after. That's Hollywood fantasy-land circa the 1950s."

Marlon gave Francis a confused look, indicating that he needed to further elaborate.

"In the movie, *Mutiny on the Bounty*…the movie you were in, Marlon?"

"Yes, I remember," said Marlin defensively.

"Remember how the mutiny happens because the British sailors fell in love with the simplicity of Tahiti?"

"Yes, I know how the movie goes."

"I'm sure you do, Marlon. But the story of course doesn't end there. No. The English and the French would lie, steal, cheat, and eventually take the island by force from the native peoples."

Marlon, looking surprised, perked up a bit.

"Does that surprise you, Marlon?"

"Does what surprise me?"

"The fact that the Tahitian people, and Tahiti, were subjugated by the Westerners."

"Nothing that Western civilization does surprises me. It's just that when you put it in those terms...I guess I never really thought of it in those terms."

Marlon put his head down as if ashamed.

"Marlon, I'm not trying to make you feel bad."

"Well, I do feel bad. I've been living there very much as some kind of king or monarch, whatever, living my Hollywood lifestyle, and then retreating to the ways of the native peoples when it is convenient for me. Me and my family have been like a bad soap-opera, on full display for the Tahitians. I went there trying to emulate the Tahitians, but have held on to my Western mindset and all my vices, as well as my lame-ass excuses for why I'm so fucked up."

"We're all fucked up. And you're right, Marlon, that even in the midst of trying to create a movie that speaks to the evils and the pervasiveness of Western imperialism, we come in here, and yes, we act like the imperialist dogs that the rest of the world thinks we are. We come in with all this fucken money...I mean...I'm like a fucken conquering king, Marlon. Whatever I want, I'm able to get. It's fucking ridiculous! But am I going to complain? Fuck no! I'm not going to complain. I'm trying to accomplish something here, and I won't be stopped. And there are certain things that I need in order to make this thing happen. Am I being an imperialist? I don't know. Maybe I am. And therein lies the tension, Marlon. Therein lies the tension! The white man has a kind of...oh, I don't know what to call it...a certain mentality, or spirit, or something. For whatever reason, we are conquerors...creators, builders. I don't know. There's some good, and some bad in there. I know that myself, personally, I love to do things, to create things, to create big things like major motion pictures. Is this kind of ambition bad? Please tell me, Marlon, because I don't know the answer to that right now."

Marlon turned his attention away from the ground and up at Francis.

"I don't know what to think, Francis."

"Marlon, can we be ambitious without exploiting other people?"

"You mean you and I?"

"Anybody. I mean...I'm running over a lot of people trying to make this movie, Marlon, and I know this. I'm talking about my wife, staff people, actors, the Filipino people, the tribal peoples on the set—they all in effect are here to cater to my every whim. But I have to be hard and aggressive in order to get this thing done. And just to be fair, I too am being run over and given the shaft over here."

"By who?"

"The Filipino government, the banks, the production company..."

"Well, as much as I was complaining earlier about what we're doing here, I'm really not comparing it to colonialism, or imperialism, and all the killing and violence these things have wrought upon various peoples from around the world at the hands of the Western Europeans and the Americans. I'm not saying that."

"I know you're not, at least not on that grand of a scale. And neither am I, but the point I'm making is that there is *something*, I don't know how to label it, but there is some propensity on the part of people who descend from Western Europe to seek and create, which has sometimes resulted in conquest and exploitation and mass killings justified by notions of racial, cultural, and religious superiority—that type of thing. And I'm not trying to say that people from other ethnic groups are not ambitious, and talented, and driven, and I know that exploitation is not something exclusive to the Western world, but at least in the recent past, the Western world has in effect lost its place in the natural world. We have tried to transcend it, and that might be part of the problem here, Marlon. Would you agree?"

"Yes, the Western world seems to hate nature, and only wants to destroy it, whereas many of the world's native peoples desire to live in harmony with it."

"Precisely, Marlon. And it seems that the world the West is trying to create, and has created for that matter, is something void of the natural world. And we've been trying to drag the rest of the world along with us, or perhaps *down* with us is a better way of putting it."

"With a gun pointed at their heads."

"Yes, with a gun pointed at their heads. Or with a boot on their face?"

"A what?"

"It's a quote from *1984*."

"From what?"

"Orwell's book. *1984*. That quote about how the future of the world will be one visualized as a boot on a human face, or something like that."

"I can't say I remember that, Francis."

"Well, perhaps gun to the head is a better way of putting it, anyway."

There was a pause in the conversation as Francis looked around, nervously slapping the side of his leg. He looked over at the movie set, which was about twenty yards away, and all the hub-bub going on over there, and then out at the large expanse of Philippine jungle.

"Hey, let's do it, Marlon!"

"Do what?" asked Marlon, genuinely confused.

"Let's get out of here, like you said, away from all this shit for a few days, a week, maybe. Whatever it takes."

"What?"

"Let's split. Let's get out of here."

"I thought that's what we're doing now."

"No, let's really get out of here. Let's go somewhere where we can get our heads right...where we can figure all this shit out. Let's go out into the jungle, like you were saying earlier!"

"You mean, *completely* abandon the set?"

"Why not, Marlon?"

"Because it's going to cost you thousands, perhaps millions, depending on how long you do so," said Marlon, who no longer sounded so keen on the idea he vigorously brought up and advocated earlier.

"I don't care, Marlon. I need a fucking vacation. Jesus Christ, Marlon, this was your fucking idea. And now I'm trying to convince you to do it. Plus, Marlon…plus, I don't know how I'm going to end this damn movie. And nobody, none of my fucken writers are able to come up with anything worthwhile. I really think that you and I, Marlon, can do a better job than these guys anyway. So, let's leave for a few days, go out into the jungle, and try to figure out how to end this move. What do you think, Marlon?"

"Are you going to pay me for writing the script and give me writing credits?"

Marlon was smiling when he said this. It was a joke, and Francis took it as such.

"Ha! I'll pay you writer's wages, Marlon, and it wouldn't be enough to even cover the interest on what I'm paying you for actor's wages. And as for writing credits, if this movie flops, Marlon, you don't want to receive blame for both your acting and your writing, do you?"

The two men shared a brief laugh.

"So, what do you say, Marlon? Let's get out of here for a few days. I feel I need an epiphany of some sort in order to finish this movie. And I can't go alone. Nobody will allow that. My wife wouldn't allow it. She would think I was off somewhere with one of the female staff people."

"Maybe that's what you should do instead of going with me."

"Yeah right, Marlon. I'm in enough trouble the way it is. I don't need to add a pissed-off wife and a vindictive staff person to my list of problems. Besides, I can justify taking off for a few days if I say I am trying to help my big star work through his role."

"Why me? Why not Hopper? Or Sheen?"

"Why not Hopper? I'm not going out into the jungle, or anyplace for that matter, with Dennis Hopper. My God, I would be running back within the first hour. Are you kidding me, Marlon...Dennis Hopper?"

"How about Marty Sheen?"

"He's too quiet. Marty's a smart man, but it's all internal. He's not good at verbally communicating his ideas. What, don't you want to get out of here for a while, Marlon, and go find yourself out in the jungle? This was your idea in the first place, as I keep reminding you."

"First of all, I haven't done any work since I got here, so I'm not burned out or anything just yet. Plus, everybody is going to think that I'm being some kind of a head-case, and that you're putting a halt on production for several days, perhaps a week, in order to deal with your overpaid, temper-mental, over-rated actor."

"Precisely, Marlon. That's why the plan is so brilliant. It's so fucking believable!"

CHAPTER 33

At about four-thirty in the morning, with the jungle still engulfed in darkness, the helicopters lifted off from Artemis. The Stieng, as planned, were left behind, standing poised, holding onto the same machetes once carried by the Jarai. When the Hueys were a safe distance away, Colonel Memmington radioed for the air strikes. Minutes later three American bombers roared in from the west, dropping three lines of napalm, each approximately a mile and a half long, forming a triangle that encircled the Stieng and presumably the Jarai, eventually becoming a circle of flames once it started burning inward. After the jets finished heaving their fury onto the jungle that surrounded Artemis, the helicopters flew back in to dance atop the flames, allowing those inside to get a birds-eye view of the hell down below.

Inside the intensifying abyss, LeBetre managed to round up a few of the Jarai while the rest ran around panic-stricken in ones and twos trying to find a way out of the building inferno. He led those who followed him along the edge of the giant wall of fire in an attempt to find an opening, or at least a spot where the flames were not as intense, a weak link in the fiery chain that might allow their escape. But the more time it took to find such a spot, the more saturated the whole area became with the gasoline induced blaze, and the farther inward the encroaching bulwark of flames crept. It did not take long for LeBetre and the Jarai to become disorientated and lost in a maze of fire and smoke. Some began to scream and even cry as their death by conflagration seemed inevitable.

   Biding their time, hoping for a miracle, LeBetre and the Jarai, for now, could only retreat from the onrushing tide of flames ripping its way through Artemis. As they were pushed closer to the center of the camp, silhouettes of the frizzy-haired Stieng started to become visible against the orange backdrop raging in from the other side. Once the Stieng saw the Jarai they began howling and dancing, waving their machetes in the air in eager anticipation of the slaughter to come.

   Off in the distance, the tormented moaning and bellering of Jarai falling prey to the hot flames was becoming audible from every direction. Those still alive must have thought they had fallen into the hell Father McDuffee meticulously described to them on many occasions, its demons, fire, and suffering all a vivid reality for them now. Faced with the prospect of being butchered by the Stieng whom they thought to be devils, a few of the Jarai began opting for the wall of flames, their bodies expulsing cries of agony before being devoured.

   Seemingly unafraid of fire, and not bothered by smoke, the Stieng approached the now completely hysterical Jarai, some huddled together and some running around in circles, and began hacking at their flesh with the machetes. Blood spattered and flesh was ripped from its bones as the Stieng cut off arms, legs, and even heads during the brutal onslaught.

Refusing to let the sword be his fate as well, LeBetre, knowing he would die one way or another, chose the wall of flames to that of cold steel as his means of passage out of this world. He lunged into the angry mass of hellfire, and was instantly overcome by heat and fell to the ground. Everything went black. LeBetre then felt the sensation of someone grabbing his hand. And even though he could no longer see, LeBetre sensed it was the Paiute messiah Wovaka, pulling him into the next world. There he would no longer feel the flames searing his body, or hear the screaming Jarai being burned alive. Freed from the flesh that caused his physical pain and inner consternation, LeBetre's soul went back home. He may have been born and lived his life as a French-American, but LeBetre died a Lakota Indian.

The remaining Jarai ran back and forth between the Stieng and the encroaching wall of flames, trying to determine whether or not they should follow LeBetre into the fire or let the Stieng chop them to pieces. Most would let fate decide this for them, dropping to their knees somewhere in the middle of their two relentless pursuers, allowing whatever or whomever got there first to take their lives. There on the ground, as a last resort, they prayed one final time for Father McDuffee's God to save them, or perhaps to just have mercy on them. But before this could happen, and in front of the still roaring flames, the Stieng got there first. With their already bloodied machetes, they tore open the skin and crushed the bones of their fellow jungle animists who chose to beckon the help of the white man's God instead of defending themselves. From one of the helicopters hovering above, Father McDuffee repeatedly recited the 'Our Father' as he watched the Stieng massacre the 'washed' as well as the 'unwashed' Jarai, leaving both to lie in the same heap of blood and guts.

Dawn began to break by the time the Stieng finished their butchery of those Jarai who opted for death by steel instead of the walls of fire, which were now diminished to that of smoldering mounds of burnt jungle debris. The helicopters sat back down on what was the western edge of Artemis, the leaves on the trees and the smaller vegetation now gone, giving the Hueys more than sufficient space to land.

Against a backdrop of the sun rising in the eastern sky as well as the charred remains of Artemis and the blackened and disheveled Stieng walking in behind him, Colonel Memmington stood tall and haughty in what looked to be a meticulously choreographed stance. His fists were dug into his sides, chest puffed out, and chin held high. The Englishman seemed to have little doubt that the image he cast at this moment was one of mythological proportion, one that would be indelibly burned into the minds of all who stood before him, on this, his finest hour.

"I'll need a radio!" demanded the British colonel, subtly breaking his portrait-like pose by holding out his hand, awaiting fulfillment of the order. Once carried out, he proceeded to boast to I-Core that the objectives had been met. In turn, Memmington was told to re-locate the entire operation, Stieng included, to the north and resume Green Tiger's previous operations.

"Load 'em up, we're heading to the north!" exclaimed Memmington now sure in his earlier assumption that he had been put in command of Green Tiger. He repeated this order to the Cambodians and Stieng in their native tongues as best he could before bothering to brief me in greater detail by means of the vernacular common to both of us.

His self-aggrandizement did not end there on the edge of the scorched piece of jungle. Memmington's own personal chronicle of heroism and righteousness would be repeated again and again to the English and non-English speaking members of Green Tiger over the course of the next several weeks. In his version, Memmington's heroic exploits very much resembled those of Lord Chelmsford who defeated the Zulus at the Battle of Ulundi in 1878, while LeBetre would be reduced to a nameless "savage" who was responsible for a violent uprising that threatened what he called the "Allied enterprise" in Southeast Asia.

* * *

Nestled next to a major tributary of the mighty Mekong River, the new basecamp was littered with palm trees and an array of colorful flowers that gave it the appearance of a tropical paradise. Golden sunsets shimmered off the river every evening, giving the entire basecamp a rich yellowish hue at dusk as majestic birds gracefully swooned amidst the bullion backdrop while feasting on the plethora of bugs that came out at night.

I never enjoyed the jungle's natural beauty. To me it was merely an obstruction that concealed my enemy. I saw it as death and darkness even though it teamed with life and bright colors. The jungle was also the place that held my darkest secrets, things so horrific I tried to bury them, but always under more of the same sort of iniquitous deeds. It did not take me long to expunge myself of all guilt I may have had following the violent deaths of LeBetre and the Jarai, however. To me they were heretics, savages, denizens of the darkness, their animism and spirit worship the continuation of mankind's refusal to leave the wilderness and join the civilized world. Everything I had seen while in Cambodia thus far indicated to me that the jungle was not only a refuge of evil, but a source of it as well.

As the days and weeks passed since Wilke's departure, I came to understand that the sergeant was right about a lot more things than I ever realized. Mainly, that the jungle was indeed a place untouched by the spread of European Christendom, as well as Enlightenment philosophy. I further expounded upon Wilke's theory, considering it a living empire in its own right, one of wickedness, inhabited by heathens who remain heedless prisoners to the pangs of their sin-ridden bodies.

Even though I included the Stieng as well as the Cambodians into the category of heathen, I was tolerant of their animist and Buddhist practices in exchange for their help in destroying the jungle and killing the Vietcong. This sort of sufferance was not the case between the two native-born Cambodian peoples, and newest members of Green Tiger, however. Whereas the Cambodian Khmer *Serie* would often worship at the feet of the venerable statues of Buddha found interwoven with the jungle, the Stieng would knock over the idols erected by their ancient Brahman and Buddhist oppressors who had cut a path from India to the villages and homes of their ancestors thousands of years ago, assimilating some and scattering the rest. For their part, the Cambodians would rather die than admit they share a common history with the Stieng, or any of the other montagnard peoples native to Cambodia. They instead claim to have descended solely from that of Hindu princes, spurning any suggestion that they have a cultural affinity or common origin with that of the *phongs*, as the Cambodians of Khmer stock refer to the montagnards.

Most of the *phongs* fled the Indian Hindus to the high and lowlands of Cambodia and Vietnam, resisting them and their complex pantheon of gods. Those who didn't flee were absorbed into the civilization of colonizing Hindus, the two cultures melding together as one to be called Khmer. The *phongs*, including the Stieng, consider the Khmer a race polluted with the gene of cowardice from their own kind, those who were too weak to resist the seductive words of the Brahman priests. Much like the apache and mohawk did before them, Stieng and Khmer Serie would keep their distance, watching one another with suspicion and contempt from separate sides of the camp.

CHAPTER 34

It would be a few days before Marlon and Francis officially began their working vacation of sorts, one intended to resolve Marlon's inability to shake-off his own imperialist tendencies, as well as conjure up an ending to Francis' movie. Meantime, they would first commandeer one of the many PBRs being used, taking it down river while the cast, crew, the production company, family, friends, and a host of others were left behind, wondering when the two most vital cogs of the *Apocalypse Now* film production team would return.

For his part, Francis actually welcomed the interlude. He wanted to get away from all the chaos and craziness of the movie set with all its egos and complications, at least for a little while.

For Marlon, however, this was something much more serious. He believed that all the injustices that he has been fighting throughout his career, the very reason he joined this particular project, were in fact on full display in the country hosting the movie he hoped would make things right, or at least help set the record straight.

"Everybody is mad as hell at me, Marlon, for embarking on this little journey of self-discovery, or personal enlightenment, with you out in the jungle. My wife is fit to be tied. She said we're both a couple of self-indulgent idiots."

"But you're the king here, Francis. You can do whatever you want."

"No, you're the king here, Marlon."

"This is your realm, Francis. It's your gold that is funding all this. We're here to carry out your will."

"Yeah, yeah, yeah, Marlon. C'mon...please. If I'm the king out here, then why doesn't anybody do what I tell them? Plus, it might be my gold that is funding most of this project, but it will be my blood that's spilt if this thing fails, nobody else's."

"Well, I beg to differ with you, Francis, on both counts, especially the second one."

"How so, Marlon?"

"If this thing fails, Francis, I will lose yet another pound of flesh, as I have with every movie I've done since *On the Waterfront*."

"Except for *The Godfather*."

"Yes, you're right, Francis. *The Godfather* was the first successful movie I did in over a decade."

"I just wanted to set the record straight, Marlon."

"Thank you for doing so. Anyway, where were we? Oh yes, you were complaining about how nobody here listens to you, Francis. But from what I can tell, everybody here is waiting on your beck and call."

"Well, everybody except you and Hopper."

"Yuck! Hopper. I don't want him anywhere near me, Francis."

"Marlon, how in the hell are we going to shoot the Kurtz compound scenes if you and Dennis are not on the same set, engaged in dialogue with one another?"

"Must Kurtz have dialogue with this man's character?"

"Yes. Dennis' character is a photo-journalist who has been with Kurtz for a while now. He is enamored with him. He thinks Kurtz is a genius, and he is going to try and convince Willard of this exact same thing."

Marlon thought about it for a moment while Francis gauged him.

"Okay, Francis. My character will engage in dialogue with Hopper's character, but that's it. I will not speak to him on a personal level, not even about our dialogue. And I will remain in his presence only long enough to shoot the scene."

"Okay, fair enough."

"Where are we going, anyway, Francis?"

"Nowhere in particular. We're going to take the PBR a little further down the Pagsanjan River for a few days."

"Why don't we take my houseboat down the river?"

"Because, Marlon, we—you and I—are going to try and find out who in the fuck we are as white, American males of Western European descent, so we can better know who this Colonel Kurtz guy is, and how we should end this fucken movie, because I am at a loss. And unless you can whip out a really fucking good ending, right here and now, Marlon, we are going down the river together for a few days, and in a PBR."

"I'm fine with going down the river, Francis, but why do we have to rough it?"

"Are you just fucking with me, or what?"

Francis looked at Marlon, waiting for a response, but none came.

"Marlon, you are the one having the problem with this enterprise—my movie—being such an imperialist endeavor, and when I propose that we go into the jungle in an attempt to shed our imperialist skin, you start complaining because we aren't going to be surrounded by all the comforts of Western civilization. Next, you're going to ask if we can bring some Filipino servants, or perhaps some of the indigenous Ifugao to scrounge up food for us."

"You mean we're not bringing any…uh, guides?"

"Guides? You expect a guide, Marlon?"

"I'm joking, Francis."

"That's so damn Western, Marlon!"

"That was my point."

"Guides, Marlon, are nothing more than servants who walk in front of the white guys because they're more familiar with the terrain. It conjures up images of those old 1930s movies about the British in India and Africa. You have the native people hauling the British around on some kind of cart, or literally carrying them through the jungle because, heaven forbid, the Westerner should soil his clothes or exert himself too much in the hot, tropical climate and terrain, primitive in its absence of cement sidewalks and tarred roadways."

Marlon always liked the jungle. Or at least he thought he did. But in reality, he liked the tropics. The jungle and the tropics are two different things. Marlon liked locations such as Tahiti, places that are beautiful and possess at least the most basic of creature comforts that Western civilization has to offer, which the jungle has none of.

"These fucken bugs!" announced Marlon while swatting fcrociously at them.

"This is what happens, Marlon, when you leave the white-sand, windswept beaches of Tahiti."

"The sand in Tahiti is black, Francis."

"It is?"

"Yes, because of the volcanoes."

"Oh, that's interesting, because the sand in *Mutiny on the Bounty* looked very light. It certainly wasn't black."

"They brought in white sand in order for it to look more aesthetically appealing to the viewer, or some kind of bullshit like that. It was all a lie. And why must you always chastise me about Tahiti, Francis? For Christ sake!"

"Well, you were criticizing my movie set here as if it were some kind of nineteenth-century sugar plantation, Marlon."

Marlon grumbled something that Francis could not decipher, and then walked over to the other side of the boat.

* * *

"So, tell me, Marlon, as we sit out here along the river in the Filipino jungle, tell me again about some of the things you said earlier regarding those first acting roles, like *The Wild One*. What was the name of the guy you played, Johnny Stabler or something?"

"Johnny *Strabler*, Francis, *Strabler*."

"I know. I was just kidding. Stabler is the name of the quarterback for the Oakland Raiders—Kenny Stabler."

"I wouldn't know anything about that, Francis. I don't follow sports."

"So, this Johnny fellow, Marlon..."

"Yes. Johnny. One of my many alter-egos...my many nemesis. What do you want to know about him?"

"How has your perception of these roles changed over the years, between then and now? Or better yet, how has your perception of these characters, like Johnny, changed over the years?"

"Do you mean the way in which I played these characters? How I now critique my performance?"

"No, Marlon, the characters themselves. The message conveyed by these characters. For example, Johnny Strabler was cutting-edge back in the day, the outlaw motorcycle guy with the leather jacket and bad attitude. Now, Johnny Strabler is passé. He's a cliché, a caricature, almost. I mean, hell, look at the Fonz on *Happy Days*. He's what the greaser, leather jacket wearing, motorcycle riding hood has been reduced to. The Fonz isn't even counter-cultural. In fact, he's very much a part of mainstream society, and so is that whole image."

"Well, yes, because all the hoods got old. We've been replaced by the hippies."

"So, you consider yourself a hood, Marlon?"

"Well, not completely, but I certainly identified myself more with the hoods than I did the hippies."

"You were a little too artsy for the hoods. I mean...you had hood tendencies, but you could not have been pigeon-holed as a hood."

"What do you have there, Francis?" interjected Marlon in an attempt to change the subject.

"Oh these? I brought some books with me, Marlon."

"I can see that. What are we going to do out here, Francis, read?"

"Well, maybe a little. But in all seriousness, I really think that these books can help us figure this shit out. I mean...we're trying to determine who Kurtz is and how he got the way he is—the whole 'slipping the bonds of Western rationalism' thing. The truth is, Marlon, I don't really know exactly what that even means. My head is literally spinning, and has been spinning for months now, trying to figure out how to end this damn movie. I'm afraid, Marlon. I'm pretty damn scared right now!"

"Afraid of what?"

"What am I afraid of, Marlon? Isn't it obvious? I'm afraid of this damn movie I'm making. It's become a god-damn monster. It's a fucking beast, Marlon, and it's poised to swallow up both of us."

"I think you need to calm down, Francis. It's not quite as bad as all that."

"Marlon, it's not your fucking money, your assets, your professional reputation that's on the line here…"

"I beg to differ, Francis!"

"Okay, yes, your professional reputation is also on the line here. I acknowledge that. But everybody wants a piece of this thing, Marlon, because they think it might be big, but nobody wants to put up even an ounce of their own flesh, except for you, Marlon. Other than that, it's my ass, and my head that are on the line here. I'm either going to fail miserably, or succeed in such a big way that this thing could actually change the fucking world. I mean...why not? Why can't a movie change the world? Painters and philosophers have changed the world! Why can't a movie change the world?"

Upon the conclusion of his director's rant, Marlon sighed loudly.

"Francis, as I told you earlier, I've tried to say important things with the movies I've been in, and nobody's taken those movies, or that message, serious."

"But why is that? You're the great Marlon Brando! I don't understand why you're not taken serious in this regard."

"To be honest with you, Francis, I don't know why anybody *would* take me serious in this regard."

"What? Why not?" asked Francis while shaking his head as an indication he did not agree with Marlon's assessment.

"Well, for a lot of reasons, Francis, from my personal behavior over the years, to my private and family life, but mostly because I've played characters that are now seen as such archetypes, like Johnny Strabler and Stanley Kowalski. They now seem silly by today's standards. None of the young people can identify with them, and so they can't identify with me."

"I can't believe it's because of your previous roles."

"Well, but as I said, there are other reasons, too, like the fact that I'm known as a weirdo and a sexual deviant."

"Perhaps, Marlon, but I also think it's because people know that you're a bit of a bull-shit artist."

"Well, yeah, I guess," replied Marlon, hesitant to acknowledge the statement. "But it comes with the territory."

"What territory?"

"The acting profession."

"I don't necessarily agree with that, Marlon. You've always been the guy who's pulling shit on people…fucking with them. You're always in character…some character. You're never just Marlon Brando, and so nobody knows who the hell Marlon Brando really is."

Marlon nodded his head as if in agreement with his director.

"Yes, you're right, Francis. And when I do try and be serious about some subject, everybody is wondering what kind of stunt I'm trying to pull. Nobody wants to get fooled by me. And because of this, I've never been allowed to make a statement with my roles or the movies I've been in. So, if that's what you're trying to do, Francis, I'm the wrong person to have in your movie. I'm damaged goods."

"I get what you're saying, Marlon. And even though I do agree that you are damaged goods, you are still a huge Hollywood actor. You always will be a huge Hollywood actor no matter how fucked up your off-screen life has been, or even how many bad movies you've been involved with. This movie cannot say what I want it to say without the notoriety of a Marlon Brando. And I believe the fact that you are damaged goods is actually kind of a good thing here."

"How so?"

"Because you're real, Marlon."

"A real what?"

"A real asshole. No, I'm kidding. I'm sorry. I couldn't resist. You set yourself up for that, though, Marlon."

"I did, Francis."

"On purpose?"

"Yes, on purpose."

"You see what I mean, Marlon? You're always pulling something."

"Yes. You're right, Francis."

"But in all honesty, Marlon, people know you as a brilliant actor and a flawed human being. People know that you have fought for equal rights—the rights of black people and American Indians. Your reputation goes beyond the big screen, Marlon. You're kind of like a Hollywood ambassador, of sorts, on various social issues."

"Yeah, right," said Marlon cynically.

"No, you are, Marlon. And just let me say this…you have made more of an impact on social issues than you give yourself credit for. You have brought a lot of things to the attention of white Americans that they otherwise never would have heard of."

"Perhaps, but mostly it's been fodder for the tabloids."

"But everything you do is fodder for the tabloids, Marlon. Take this movie for example. The tabloids are making a big deal of your salary, and the fact that you're supposedly only going to be in the movie for a brief moment, and not until the very end. And according to the tabloids, there's supposed to be tension on the set between you and me, and between you and some of the other cast members. They apparently know that I have no idea how I'm going to end the movie, and all kinds of other shit, Marlon. Hell, I should ask these tabloid assholes how to end the movie if they know so damn much."

* * *

"Are the eyes of the world upon us, Francis?"

"Well, I wouldn't say *the eyes of the world*, but there's a hell of a lot of people watching and waiting to see what we're going to come up with out here. I mean…the expectations for this movie have transcended Hollywood and the simple notion that movies should be entertaining, and nothing more. I know that this isn't the first time that somebody has tried to make some kind of political or social statement with a movie, but I believe, simply because there is so much attention on this project, that we stand at the cusp of…well, of something that could be big. I don't know, Marlon. Maybe the eyes of the world are upon us. Hell, I don't know."

"I agree, Francis, but the problem you have here…"

"What do you mean *you*? I thought you were in this with me, Marlon?"

"Francis, you just told me, not more than a fucking minute ago, that you're the one who is bearing the brunt of this project, how you have the most to lose, and all that self-indulgent kind of shit."

"Self-indulgent? You—Marlon Brando—are calling *me* self-indulgent?"

"Yes, you're self-indulgent. You should listen to yourself talk, Francis, for Christ sake."

"Well, you should listen to *yourself* talk, Marlon. Jesus Christ! You'd think you were the only fucking person on the planet."

Immediately an awkward silence filled the air around the two men.

"But I think all people are self-indulgent and self-centered, for that matter," conceded Francis in an attempt to reconcile.

Marlon looked over in Francis' direction in a manner indicative of someone who was expecting an apology. Francis sensed this.

"I'm sorry, Marlon. You're not any more self-indulgent than I am. I mean...classic case of the pot calling the kettle black, right?"

The director's admission was met with only silence.

"So, let me ask you, Marlon, how would you change or alter the script?" inquired Francis, trying to change the subject. "I know you've said in the past that the script, what there is of it, is terrible, and maybe you're right. I don't know. And I'm not being critical of you, or trying to be a smart-ass, but I really want to know how you, Marlon Brando, a man who has seen and experienced a lot of things, how you would add to the script, and most importantly, how you would end the movie."

Marlon stared at Francis in disbelief at all he just laid on him, especially on the heels of such a scathing critique of his personality, but one he knew was true, nonetheless.

"Well, Francis, I would need quite a bit of time to think about these things before I could even begin to formulate anything," said Marlon, sounding uninspired and still irritated.

"Well, we don't have a lot of time to figure this out, Marlon," chuckled Francis, trying to lighten the mood. He knew that Marlon's mind did not work well unless constantly prompted and given direction, perhaps even agitated, and that he was good at taking existing ideas and breaking them open, going deeper with them than he himself could.

"Marlon, I really think that if I knew how I was going to end this movie that I could improve the quality of the rest of the script. The problem is, Marlon, that I don't really know how this thing is going to wrap up, so therefore everything else that comes before is just kind of hanging in limbo, so to speak, because it could all change once the ending has been determined. Do you know what I mean, Marlon?"

Marlon sighed loudly. He was not exactly sure what Francis was asking him to do. Confused, he stared at his director, looking for insight.

"Marlon, I'm not literally asking you to write the ending for me. What I'm looking for is a conversation, something that will inspire me, something that will illuminate how this thing will end. What I believe, Marlon, is that there is a way that this thing *should* end, the way it's *supposed* to end, if you know what I mean. There's a message, or a story, that needs to be told. I just don't know what it is exactly, or how to articulate it. Do you understand what I'm saying, Marlon?"

Marlon said nothing.

"Marlon, it's kind of like how the Conrad book really spoke to you. You were inspired by its overriding message. Well, I want my movie to do the same thing. I want it to make a statement, a bold, relevant statement. I want people a hundred fucking years from now to be talking about my movie, or at least the message that we are conveying, whatever the fuck that is going to be, just like we are doing right now with Conrad's book. I'm really feeling the pressure, Marlon. The press has blown this thing out of proportion. They've really upped the ante. I'm horrified, Marlon. I'm terrified. This is an important fucking topic—the Vietnam War. But it's even bigger than the Vietnam War. It's about imperialism, colonialism, racism, history, religion, God, sex, drugs, rock n' roll. All these things, Marlon."

"I think you're putting a lot more pressure on yourself than you need to, Francis."

"I'm not putting pressure on myself. The press is. The press and the critics."

"You can't concern yourself with the things that they write. They're going to hate your movie no matter how fucking good it is, or how profound of a statement it makes. And the more profound you try to make it, the more they will hate it."

"You're right, Marlon. So, what you're saying is that I can't win either way."

"No, you can't. The expectations are already too great. The key is to say something profound, yes, but also something enduring, like Conrad has done with *Heart of Darkness*."

"I agree, Marlon. But the movie—the acting, the scenery, the subject matter, the cinematography—are going to be grandiose. How can the message be subtle?"

"The imagery and the topic can be grandiose, but the message, in order for it to be enduring, in order for it to be timeless, must be somewhat subtle."

"I agree, Marlon. I know what you're saying. Conrad's message is quite subtle. But the problem is that I don't think a lot of people understood the message when the book came out, and probably still don't. It was ahead of its time."

"I think a mistake that a lot of people make is to assume it's simply a story about Kurtz, that the whole book is just a story about this Kurtz fellow."

"Yes, while it is a story about Kurtz, told through the eyes, or filter, of Marlowe, I believe that Kurtz actually represents Western imperialism in terms of what it looked like, and how it was perceived around the turn of the century. Would you agree, Marlon?"

"Yes, that's certainly how I understood it."

"So, let me ask you something, then, Marlon..."

"Okay."

"If Kurtz represents Western imperialism, does Marlowe represent the Western world coming face-to-face with the ugliness of Western imperialism?"

"Uh, I haven't thought about it like that, I guess. But yeah, that's a good analysis."

"I think so, too, Marlon. I think that while Kurtz represents Western imperialism, Marlowe represents the whole of the Western world, a Western world that is in that moment coming face to face with what it has done, and who it has become. And Marlowe is in effect doing this by way of experiencing Kurtz and Kurtz's camp—seeing the horrible desecration and violence that has been carried out there by Kurtz, as well as both seeing and hearing Kurtz the man. And the sights and sounds that Marlowe is experiencing are not pleasant. Kurtz and his camp both reek of Kurtz's 'the horror'. Marlowe comes to realize that Kurtz's pursuit of wealth and power has transformed him into something horrific and wretched, both inside and out."

"Does Kurtz want to die, Francis?"

"Do you mean Kurtz the man, or Kurtz the symbol and manifestation of Western imperialism?"

"Ah, brilliant distinction, Francis! But I thought you didn't want Kurtz to be an archetype?"

"You're right, Marlon. I don't. So maybe *symbol* isn't the best choice of words here. How about *symptomatic*? Kurtz is symptomatic of Western imperialism."

"What's the difference?"

"Symptomatic implies that Kurtz is indicative, or the end result of Western imperialism, that is, an example of how imperialism affects the imperialist, the colonizer, the oppressor."

"I still don't see the difference. And you really didn't answer my question, Francis."

"I guess I don't know the answer to the question, Marlon. I don't know yet if Kurtz wants to die, literally or figuratively. I'm not quite sure yet what he wants, or what he's trying to accomplish. Maybe you know what Kurtz wants, Marlon?"

"I'm not sure, either, Francis, but maybe we can figure it out."

"Okay, Marlon. Good. This is what I was hoping for. Let's figure this out."

"Okay, well, to begin with, I think that Kurtz is a man who has seen too much. He knows too much about the world, and its ugly realities."

"Okay, good. So, is our man Kurtz looking to change this ugly reality, come to terms with it, or just simply trying to forget all that he has seen, and perhaps even all he has become?"

"Well, he knows he's not going to change the world…"

"No, and now that I think about it, he's actually contributing to this ugliness. I mean…he's out in the Cambodian jungle, killing, and even desecrating with such tenacity, and with such clarity. How can this be an appeal to rid the world of its ugliness?"

Marlon looked confused. The cynical tone of his director's voice made Marlon feel like he was being challenged, making him feel uneasy.

"Are you asking *me* this question, Francis? Because this is not the point I was going to make before you interrupted me."

"I'm not saying you were, Marlon. It was a rhetorical question. Yeah, I guess I did interrupt you, Marlon. Please continue with what you were going to say."

Marlon was uncomfortable.

"C'mon, Marlon. I need you to think. I need your insight."

"Okay, Francis. Don't rush me."

"I'm not."

"Yes, you are."

"Well, I'm not trying to."

Marlon paused for a moment to gather his thoughts.

"Kurtz has done the horrible, nasty things that he believes he needed to do in order to win this war. They're not the kind of things that people back home in the United States would ever understand, but they are things that need to be done, for better or worse, to preserve the American way of life."

"And Kurtz steps up and does the nasty things that most people don't even know, or want to know, goes on during war time. Okay. I get that. Things like what, Marlon?"

"Well, he's certainly killed, but killed in the most ruthless, horrific kinds of ways. His intention has been to intimidate the enemy, to spread fear, to show the North Vietnamese that he and his kind are able to inflict more savagery than they are, the very people whom the Americans call savages."

"Yes, yes, Marlon! This is Kurtz trying to bust through, or expose, the 'timid-line morality' of the United States, which is so front and center during the Vietnam War. He's not trying to cover up or change the ugly truth, or 'ugly reality', as you called it, Marlon, but rather expose it. Kurtz is trying to illuminate the hypocrisy of so-called human civility! Look at some of the tactics employed by U.S. servicemen in Vietnam. Some of them indiscriminately killed North Vietnamese civilians. They killed women and children. They destroyed a lot of private property. They cut off ears, noses, and heads, all in an attempt to intimidate the enemy, to scare the hell out of them, to get them to quit. And, unfortunately, these are the kinds of things that sometimes need to be done to win a war, to get your enemy to give up. But, this is the kind of stuff the American public back home doesn't want to know about. They don't want to hear about ears and heads being cut off, do they Marlon!"

"Of course not. But this kind of thing does go on, and more often than people realize, and not just in Vietnam."

"Precisely. And Kurtz knows this, and understands this. He knows what he has to do as a soldier fighting a war. Kurtz knows that war is a dirty business. He knows it's not like the World War II-era movies, which were nothing more than propaganda pieces that both glamorized and sanitized war."

"So, what's Kurt's problem, then? What's his issue, Francis?"

"Kurtz's issue, Marlon, is that…well, for one thing he doesn't like the hypocrisy of it all. And what I mean by that is that he has grown sick and tired of all the 'good guy' imagery of the United States when in fact everybody knows that U.S. soldiers were killing civilians, many of them women and children, and that the U.S. was bombing the shit out of Hanoi, again, killing innocent women and children. But what he really hates, Marlon, what Kurtz cannot stand is the fact that the United States is not, at least in his opinion, really trying to win the war."

"Why does he think that the United States isn't trying to win the war?"

"Good question, Marlon."

"Do you have a good answer for me, Francis?"

"Well, I have an answer. But I don't know how good it is. The answer is, and this is something a lot of Vietnam vets had a problem with…the answer is that he didn't believe the United States, despite all the brutality it was inflicting upon the North Vietnamese, was doing all it could do to win the war. That is, the United States needed to be even more ruthless than it already was in order to win the war. And not for the sake of simply being ruthless and killing people, but to force the enemy to give up, to capitulate."

"And part of the problem for the U.S. was that this war was basically being televised for the American public."

"Right. And so whenever a village was destroyed, whenever a hospital or a school was bombed, whenever innocent women or children were killed, it was on the evening news for everyone in America to see, which would only serve to hinder the war effort."

"So, what you're saying, Francis, is that Kurtz is looking for victory?"

"Yes, Marlon, he wants to win the war and get it over with. He's tired of the U.S. being held hostage, not just by the media, but like I've been saying, by America's own 'timid-line morality'. And, again, what I mean by this is that the United States is willing to be ruthless and brutal, but only if it doesn't tarnish its image too much, which made the war drag out longer, while in the meantime the Vietnamese were not constrained by these things. Kurtz believes the North Vietnamese were so successful because they did anything and everything needed in order to win the war, something not afforded the American soldiers."

"So, Kurtz is not afraid to be ruthless, to let his dark side control his actions."

"Right. He's not. But I don't believe that Kurtz considers this to be his 'dark side', Marlon. I would say that Kurtz, because he has freed himself from this timid-line morality, considers this to be more of his 'primordial' or 'instinctual' side."

"Does he love or hate this *side* of himself, the side of him that is willing to carry out all those horrible, nasty things that need to be done to win a war?"

"I think he accepts this primordial side of the human species. He doesn't relish the things he does. He doesn't find pleasure in them, either. But he accepts it. He can, to a certain extent, live with himself, but I think the bigger question here, Marlon, is whether or not Kurtz can find peace with it, or will it tear him apart, like Kurtz in Conrad's book."

"Well, if I may, Francis…"

"By all means."

"I don't think Kurtz can find peace with it. He might be able to live with himself, but that doesn't mean he has completely accepted who he is and the things he's done."

"Okay. Then let's explore this topic. Why can't he find peace with himself and what he's doing? Well, maybe we should first establish what he is doing, exactly, that is so horrible. So, he's killing. What of it? There's a lot of killing in a war."

"He's killing without remorse, without conscience…without judgment."

"Without judgment of whom?"

"Of himself."

"So, he's accepting of the fact that he has to kill, and in a manner which could be considered brutal and violent, even in wartime, but he's okay with it. Is that what you're saying. Marlon?"

"Yes, it's all very primordial to him. He's of course a Westerner who lives in the twentieth century, but he sees through all the rhetoric and all the propaganda, the sterilization of American society that really began in earnest after World War II, in which everything is so perfect and pure."

"The *Ozzie and Harriet* thing."

"And *Leave it to Beaver*."

"Yes. *Leave it to Beaver*. He knows that post-World War II American society and its commercialized happiness and perfection are a sham. But Marlon, is there a part of Kurtz that wants, or seeks, this kind of 'purity', if you will? I mean…he must have experienced some of this when he was a child, just like most of us did, only to have the real world trample it underfoot, just like it does for all of us."

"Oh, I don't know, Francis. I wouldn't say *purity*, because he knows that world is not real. I think he's looking for a new beginning, a rebirth, or something like that. He's trying to move away from the extremely violent and unforgiving world he lives in as an American soldier in Vietnam. He wants to end the war—to win it—so he can resume a somewhat more conventional existence. He's not a fan of the world's brutal realities. He doesn't love killing, but he doesn't hate it either."

"Does he wish he could lose himself of the things he knows? Because I think that Kurtz is a man lost of all inhibition. And like I said earlier, a man now void of self-judgment."

"Yeah, I think he would like to be a little more naïve and a lot less familiar with life's dark underbelly."

"But I also get the sense that he doesn't respect, and perhaps even loathes those who remain naïve and fail to understand the dark complexities of the world and of human nature."

"Yes, I can see that too, Francis. It's perhaps also true that the people who can't see 'life's dark underbelly', as you called it, consider people like Colonel Kurtz to be a little weird, or strange, perhaps even crazy to a certain extent, because they themselves see a different reality—the naïve post-World War II *Ozzie and Harriet* thing. And they think a guy like Kurtz is mad, or insane, because he sees something other than what everybody has been spoon-fed by the American propaganda machine."

"That's a great point, Marlon. Kurtz sees through all the bullshit. He thinks the majority of people are either naïve or they are just lying to themselves, while at the same time these people would consider a guy like Kurtz to be crazy or insane."

"Yeah, that's how it always is with *avant-garde* thinkers. They are always dismissed as crazy or even dangerous."

"Are you an *avant-garde* thinker, Marlon?"

"I'd like to think so, actually. I've never bought into all the American rah-rah, yankee-doodle-dandy crap. And people have always considered me crazy, and even dangerous, to a certain degree."

"Dangerous, how?"

"I don't know. I just make people uncomfortable."

"Your lack of convention?"

"Yeah…my anti-establishment persona, my anti-conformist rhetoric. I'm the guy other fellows don't want to see a cock-tail party, especially if your wife or girlfriend are there."

"Why not?"

"Because women have always found my *avant-garde* persona sexy and seductive, something out of the ordinary, and most women are bored with ordinary. And, of course, this made all the men hate me, because their women would flock to me."

"When was this, Marlon, the sixties?"

"No, the fifties. I became passé in the sixties."

"The sixties had people like Timothy Leary, musicians like Jim Morrison and Bob Dylan. The list goes on and on…Charles Manson."

"Why do you keep bringing up Charles Manson, Francis? Why?"

"Well, I think it's because Kurtz has the same dark understanding of the world that Charles Manson does, one that the status-quo finds so dangerous, so unnerving."

Marlon grumbled, but did not say anything. Francis then continued.

"And Kurtz is a colonel in the fucking army. He's out there, commanding troops. And he's not only defying orders, he's giving out his own orders. He's conducting the war according to his own perception of reality, not the reality of his commanding officers or even the American government. This is kind of what Manson was doing with his little enclave of weirdos out there at Spahn Ranch."

"And that raises another question, Francis," said Marlon, trying to steer the conversation away from Charles Manson.

"Oh, God, not another question, Marlon. There are so many loose ends already."

"Okay, I won't bring up another issue that I have."

"Well, now you have to, Marlon. Please tell me. Who knows, this could be *the one*."

"*The one?*"

"Yeah, the big idea of how we're going to end this movie, Marlon. Let's have it!"

"Okay, well here's hoping. Oh hell, I forgot what I was going to say. Shit! Something about…"

"We were talking about how Kurtz's perception of reality perhaps wasn't the reality of the military brass, or of the government…something like that. We were also talking about Charles Manson," added the director in jocular fashion, knowing that it would irritate the star actor.

Marlon closed his eyes as if trying to unhear what Francis had just said.

"Yeah…okay," began Marlon while his director chuckled. "So, um…so the high brass, the high command of the military, maybe, Francis, maybe they do perceive things the same way that Kurtz does…"

"Oh, interesting!" interrupted Francis.

"Yes. I mean…these are men of the world, too. Many have seen combat. They've fought and killed, and have seen many different kinds of horrors and terrible things, and have been privy to all kinds of hypocrisy in the various military and political circles that they've been a part of, and experienced."

Marlon was talking too slow for Francis. The director had some things he wanted to add.

"Yeah, okay, Marlon. But what's the end-game with this?"

"What's the end-game? You know, when you do that—when you interrupt me or try to rush me along—I tend to lose my train of thought, so you really shouldn't do that, Francis."

"You're right, Marlon. Sorry. Please proceed."

"My end-game, if you want to call it that, is that maybe the military brass, and everybody else, is of the same opinion as Kurtz, but the grand façade, if you will, must be preserved."

"The grand façade?"

"Yes, the whole notion that…"

"Yeah, I know what you mean, Marlon. The whole idea that human beings—Americans, white Americans—hold a place of preeminence, and that America holds some special place in God's plan, and that there's really some meaning to everything that's unfolding throughout history, and that our current reality is not just the random result of millions of years of human and social evolution, right?"

"I don't know why I bother, Francis!"

"What? What do you mean? That is brilliant, Marlon."

"I think you're referring to what you yourself just said."

"No. Your whole assessment, everything *you* said. Brilliant, Marlon! Brilliant!"

"I really wasn't finished."

"Okay. Go ahead. I promise I won't interrupt this time."

"Uh huh. I really don't believe anything you say anymore."

"Please, Marlon. Continue before you forget what you were going to say."

"I already forgot."

"No, you didn't, Marlon. C'mon."

Marlon laughed, followed by Francis.

"I was just going to mention that Kurtz, and those like him, are so easily dismissed by the so-called established order as crazy or insane. Some are ostracized or marginalized, while others are institutionalized or incarcerated, or even put to death depending on how dangerous the established order considers them to be."

"Like Christ."

"Yes, Francis. Christ is a perfect example."

"And an obvious one at that."

"Well, not always, Francis, because most people now associate him with the established order, whereas in reality he was a counter-cultural freak."

"Like Charles Manson."

"Yes, like Manson," sighed Marlon, "but without the killing."

"Who knows, though. Maybe the story has been drastically changed. I mean…much of the historical record regarding Christ has probably been distorted. Even a lot of theologians acknowledge that. But let's get back to Kurtz."

"Okay, Francis. I have a question about Kurtz."

"Me too, but you first."

"Okay," said Marlon, rolling his eyes. "So, the military is dismissing Kurtz as insane, right?"

"Well, that's in effect how it's being sold to Captain Willard, yes."

"So, do the military guys really believe Kurtz is insane, or is their real problem with the fact that Kurtz is thinking outside of their strict, narrow philosophy?"

"Yeah, I see what you mean, Marlon. Kurtz is thinking for himself, and therefore becomes a threat to the military establishment."

"And how is it that a group of military officers are going to make that kind of medical diagnosis, anyway?"

"Well, the charge of *insanity* is an oft-used and convenient accusation against one's political and military opponents for centuries now."

"Insanity is a very complex issue."

"Well, yes, it is, Marlon. Have you ever wondered if you've gone insane?"

"Why? Do you think I'm insane, Francis?"

"No, I didn't mean it like that. I mean...I've sometimes wondered this about myself, Marlon. And I've certainly questioned my sanity during the making of this movie because of some of the decisions that I've made. And a lot of people, I can tell, have questioned my sanity throughout this process. Hell, my wife has been calling me crazy for the past year or so. And I think she really means it."

"Okay, Francis. Let's use you as an example."

"Alright," said Francis, somewhat leery about what he was agreeing to.

"So, you are doing the things that you need to do in order to make this movie happen, and to make it the way you want it to be made, right?"

"Okay, I think I know where you're going with this, Marlon."

"Good, then I don't have to finish what I was going to say."

"No, please do, Marlon."

"Then don't interrupt me, Francis. You know I have trouble staying focused and completing my thoughts."

"Right. Sorry, Marlon. Please continue."

"Now I forgot what the fuck I was talking about, Francis."

"You were talking about how insane you are."

"Oh yeah, I forgot," said Marlon, playing along, deciding to use the opening as an opportunity to talk about some of his own concerns, unaware that his director had successfully sidetracked his analysis of Francis' own sanity. "Well, I honestly don't believe I am insane, or anything like that. I may be a little crazy, though. But what I do know for sure is that I am frustrated."

"Frustrated with what, Marlon?" asked Francis quickly.

"Frustrated with my life. And I know that it sounds like bellyaching, because I have been blessed, truly blessed, and I know that. But my frustration is with the fact that I could have been so much more, and done so much more. Francis, I have wasted so much time doing…oh, I don't know what in the hell I've been doing sometimes."

"Do you wish you could do more in the way of charitable causes, or…"

"Well, yes! I just wish things had turned out differently."

"How so?"

"I wish that my past—both on-screen and off—wasn't such a fucken monster. It seems to follow me around, haunting me, like some kind of fucking Frankenstein, or something."

Francis began to chuckle.

"I'm sorry, Marlon. I don't mean to laugh, but I have this image in my head of all the previous roles and characters you've played, following you around, not as Frankenstein, but as a bunch of fucken zombies, and you're trying to get away from them."

"Well, yes, that's what I feel like sometimes. And it's not just those old characters. It's my own personal past that haunts me as well. You see, Francis, I'm not all that proud of my past."

"But you're a fucken icon, Marlon, an American Treasure, even."

"An American Treasure? Oh, for Christ sake, Francis, don't try to flatter me."

"I'm not flattering you, Marlon. Why would I need to flatter you? I already got you out here, starring in my movie."

"I don't know, Francis. Why would anybody need to flatter me?"

"Probably because they want something from you, Marlon."

"Precisely, Francis. People have always wanted something from me, whether it be money, or to use me to gain fame and notoriety for themselves, or..."

"I get that shit too, though, Marlon. People flock to me because, well, not because I'm a great looking and talented Hollywood actor, but because I can maybe make them into a famous Hollywood actor. Sometimes it's like moths to a flame, my friend. Hollywood is full of opportunists and phonies."

"We're all opportunists and phonies, Francis. And that never changes."

Francis thought about Marlon's words for a moment.

"Well, yeah, you're right, Marlon. I've had to wear many hats as a producer and director, including that of con-man. I see what you're saying."

"But an actor is perhaps the consummate con-man, because we make a living faking it, and even lying to people. We pretend to be someone or something that we're not. And people heap accolades and all kinds of praise upon us when we are good at faking it and pretending to be something we're not. Everyone bows down to the liar."

"Aren't you being a little hard on yourself, Marlon?"

"Francis, for most of my career I've been put up on a pedestal, like some type of god or something, some type of Dionysian god, because of my good looks and so-called acting ability. I was even called the 'savior' of Hollywood after my first few movies, because people believed I was going to save the motion picture industry."

"So, *you* saved Hollywood, Marlon!"

"Hollywood didn't need a savior. It just needs the newest and latest so-called 'great actor'. I wasn't the first 'great actor', and I won't be the last. James Dean was supposed to take my place as the next 'savior' of Hollywood. But in reality, Hollywood 'saviors' and 'great actors' are a dime-a-dozen, Francis. They just need to be young, good looking, and have a certain amount of acting ability, which in my opinion, means they need to be great fucking liars."

"You know, Marlon, that reminds me..."

Francis paused, long enough that it caused Marlon to look in his direction.

"Reminds you of what, Francis?"

"Of the books I brought."

Marlon rolled his eyes and looked away.

"No, Marlon, these are important."

"Books, Francis? I don't see how a bunch of books are going to be of any use here."

"Earlier, when you wanted to change the subject, you seemed very much interested in these books. Don't think of them as books, Marlon, but ideas, important ideas. And all this talk about younger Hollywood saviors replacing the old guys, and all that, reminds me of the James Frazer stuff we talked about a while back, the *Golden Bough* stuff. I'd like to get back to that, if we could, Marlon."

Marlon looked blankly at Francis.

"I don't recall," he said in reply while shaking his head.

"I think you do, Marlon. It's the idea, and it's a prominent one found in many cultures throughout history, that gods get old, or become weak and ineffective, and are subsequently replaced by younger gods. The theory also speaks to the notion that sometimes the old gods are in effect reborn, and that they go through a kind of rebirth, a resurrection, if you will. They are reborn or resurrected as a new, youthful version of themselves. Their powers have been restored."

"That sounds wonderful. I wish I could do that."

* * *

"Have you ever had delusions of grandeur, Marlon, especially when you were younger? Did you ever buy into the hype and adulation to the point that you considered yourself some type of god?"

"When I was young I'm pretty sure that I did..."

"And when I say *god,* Marlon, what I mean is someone who has a rather inflated opinion of themselves, and for whatever it is they do, such as acting."

"Yes, I understand what you're saying, Francis," said Marlon, annoyed. "I was arrogant. I was haughty. I was, and always had to be, the center of attention. I really thought I was the coolest, most important person walking the face of the earth."

"I know what you mean, Marlon—the whole youthful invincibility thing. And for you, Marlon, you were great looking and a great actor, and everybody told you this all the time, and you started believing all the hype about yourself. Right?"

"Yes, Francis, but there is more to it. It's much more complicated than simply falling into some kind of ego trap set by the fans and the media."

"No, I agree, Marlon. But I do believe that the hype can cause delusions of grandeur, which in turn becomes an almost unhealthy sense of self, which often crosses over into such an inflated image of oneself that we do start to think of ourselves as god-like."

"Yes, Francis, I agree with that."

"And, so, I think that Kurtz, as a white man, a white Westerner living among the Cambodians or montagnard tribes, with the power to kill and rain fire down from the sky in the form of napalm and whatever else…I do think that Kurtz sees himself as a god, and that his cause is transcendent, both before and after he goes insane, or goes native, whatever perspective you take."

"Both before and after?"

"Yes."

"How so?"

"Well, initially he thinks that the American cause or effort in Vietnam—to stop the spread of communism—is of paramount concern and importance."

"Right."

"But then when Kurtz becomes disenchanted with that cause, or at least the American approach to that cause, he takes things into his own hands, and then considers himself—his mission as he now understands it—to be of paramount concern and importance. Kurtz thinks he transcends the American war effort in Vietnam. He thinks he transcends the United States, even the Cold War itself. Kurtz thinks that what he is doing—his personal philosophy, the reasons for his actions—transcends time and history."

"Transcendent, perhaps. But I would argue it is also primitive, or primeval, rather."

"Say more about that, Marlon."

"Because, as I said earlier, Kurtz is following his animal instincts, the very ones which kept his ancestors alive for millions of years, the ones which enabled or allowed his kind—the human animal—to dominate the earth. This is what Kurtz allows to live and breathe. Yes, he's relying on technology—guns, bombs, and all that shit—but these things mean nothing if the person possessing them is afraid to use them without concern for what is considered or deemed moral or appropriate by the so-called 'civilized' world."

"I like the comparison you're making between godliness and primal instinct. Even though people don't realize it, or at least don't want to think about it, despite having the power of God, or of the gods, in our hands, we are still very much guided by our primordial instincts."

"Yes. That's what I've been trying to tell you, Francis."

"I know you have, Marlon. And I've liked that angle from the beginning, but now it's really starting to resonate with me. It's one of those things that…and you're right, Marlon…it's one of those things that people don't like to think about. And that's because our animal instincts—our ruthless, barbaric, savage nature—is an embarrassment to us. It's something we have to hide or even pretend doesn't exist. But in reality, it is the very thing that has put the human species on the top of the evolutionary pyramid, as well as enabled the Western world to dominate the rest of the world's peoples and cultures. And, yes, I know it's because the Western world is technologically advanced in terms of its capacity to conquer and kill, but it has also been savage and barbaric enough to use that technology. The Western Europeans have been fucking remorseless in their pursuit of wealth and riches, as well as in their destruction of other peoples in their pursuit of these things."

Marlon nodded his head in agreement, but did not respond.

"So, yes, Marlon. I think we've established this whole idea that the Western world is both powerful and ruthless, and that Kurtz is a kind of bright, shining example of this. And that the American people, for example, are comfortable with the notion or idea of power, but not of ruthlessness and savagery."

"Yes, that is America's dark, dirty secret. Americans don't want to know how ruthless and downright savage its history is."

"Most Americans are not able to comprehend it in those terms. Most people have bought into the World War II-era mythology, most of which has come from Hollywood, those damn propaganda pieces that we've been talking about. The kind of thing that you have been associated with, Marlon, simply because you've worn a military uniform in a lot of your movies."

"Actually, it's not as many as you might think. And I really never played the stereo-typical American hero. People just think I did."

"What role are you most proud of, Marlon?"

"None."

"None? Oh, c'mon, Marlon. You've had a lot of amazing roles. You've received a lot of accolades. Oscars. All that stuff."

"All shit."

"Shit?"

"Yes, shit, Francis. You know I don't give a damn about accolades."

"But you do give a shit about acting, right?"

"I thought I did, way back in the day when I believed it meant something to act well and to make good, meaningful movies."

"What happened between then and now?"

"I came to realize that good and meaningful movies are a lost cause."

"Why is that?"

"Because they don't make any money. They don't sell tickets, and subsequently nobody wants to direct or produce them. None of the production companies want to fund them, and no actor wants to act in them."

"But you made some movies that are considered meaningful, such as *Sayonara* and the *Ugly American*, and *Burn*, which made a very powerful anti-colonial statement."

"Crap, crap, and crap!"

"How about *The Godfather*, Marlon? Was it crap, too?"

"No, but that movie didn't try to do anything other than entertain people. And it accomplished that task. The other movies were intended to make some kind of a social or political statement, but in the end they failed."

"Why did they fall short?"

"I don't know. I think the studios that produced these films would only let them go so far in terms of making a social or political statement, which left them stuck in the middle between saying something important, and being entertaining, but ultimately did neither. Oh, and because I was in them…that's another reason they failed."

"The first part of your analysis makes sense to me, but not the second. I mean…why would having the name of the great Marlon Brando atop the marquee be a detriment to a movie?"

"Let's hope you don't have to find out, Francis."

"Touché. But really, though, Marlon, why? You're the great Marlon Brando! Your name alone should have catapulted those movies to at least some sort of respectability. If not in the eyes of the critics, then in terms of ticket sales."

"They were panned and didn't do well because people will only accept me in the role of some kind of freak, not somebody who is trying to make a political or social statement."

"I agree to a certain extent, Marlon, but if playing the role of a freak is the sole criterion determining the success or failure of your movies, then so many of your other unsuccessful movies should have done much better than they did, like *Candy,* and *Nightcomers*, and *Last Tango*."

"Crap, crap, and crap."

"Well, *Candy* was crap. I liked *Nightcomers*. It was very gothic, which I kind of like. And *Last Tango* was, well, just not that interesting, other than your sex scene. In fact, when I heard that you did a rather graphic sex scene, I went to see it for that very reason. And I must admit, Marlin, I only sat through the movie to see that cute little co-star of yours having sex."

"These movies only contributed to my reputation as an aging, weirdo actor, whose skills are rapidly declining."

* * *

"Can I ask you a crazy question, Marlon?"

"Okay, I guess so. I consider most of your questions to be crazy, though, Francis."

"Well, this one is extra crazy."

"Go ahead."

"If you could, Marlon, if you could…would you want to be born again? Born again as a new and refreshed version of yourself, one shed of all your past indiscretions?"

Marlon stared at Francis as if he had lost his mind.

"I am starting to think you are mad, Francis, and quite mad at that."

"It's just a hypothetical question, Marlon."

Francis and Marlon stared hard at one another.

"What, Marlon, what? Just answer the question. I know. It's silly. But what if you could truly have a fresh start, a new beginning, to in effect shed your old skin? I'm referring to what Frazer writes about in *The Golden Bough*, the whole idea or belief that gods get old, die, and are then resurrected, born anew, so to speak, their power and energy restored. Would you do this if you could?"

"If only you could offer me that for real, Francis."

"But would you do it?"

"Of course, I would do it, for fuck sake, Francis. There's not a man alive who wouldn't. Wouldn't you? Of course, you would. Eternal youth and virility—these things are more sought after than gold."

"Right. Everybody would. So, let's do it."

"What the fuck are you talking about?"

"I'm talking about giving you new life, a new beginning, Marlon."

"Again, what the fuck are you talking about, Francis?"

"I've got an idea, Marlon, but you're going to have to work with me a little bit."

"Work with you? That's what I'm doing, Francis. I'm working with you."

"Marlon, I mean work with, as in *cooperate*."

"Isn't that what I'm doing now? I know I'm difficult at times, but…"

"What I'm saying, Marlon," said Francis loudly, interrupting Marlon, "is that we can create for you a scenario in which you can use this movie, or your role, rather, as a kind of means in which you can kill off and bury the old Marlon Brando. You can start anew."

"I still don't understand, but I'll play along, or *cooperate*, as you put it."

"I'm not really sure, Marlon, how or what this is going to look like but we can make a statement within a statement, if you will."

"Eventually you'll have to start clarifying this for me, Francis, because I don't have any idea what you're talking about."

"Okay, it's like this, Marlon. There's an image that both fans and critics identify you with, or have attached to you. And from talking to you, I get the sense that this image is unfair and unfounded. Am I correct so far, Marlon?"

"Yes. Pretty much."

"You started out your career as a youthful, handsome reckloose, with great acting skills, and you're now a middle-aged, over-the-hill sexual deviant recluse," said Francis with a grin on his face. "Did you see what I did there, Marlon?"

"Yes," said Marlon while rolling his eyes at Francis' attempt at levity. "Yes, that pretty much sums it up, Francis," said Marlon, playing along.

"But in all seriousness, Marlon, I think it's the image of you as an imperialist U.S. serviceman that you dislike the most. As you've said, Marlon, it's an image that you really haven't even portrayed, but yet you've been lumped into the category of post-World War II propaganda films simply because you've worn a military uniform in a certain amount of your roles."

"Yes, that's part of the problem, I guess, but..."

"We can try to free you from, or perhaps even kill this image, Marlon. My movie will expose this image as the post-war American imperial propaganda that it is. And I'm not just talking about you and your roles as a U.S. serviceman, but the whole idea of the U.S. serviceman as the archetype handsome crusader of good against evil. You know what I'm talking about, Marlon, right?"

"All too well, Francis. So much so that I'm one of those archetypes."

"So how do we do this, then, Marlon? How do we free you of this image, as well as unmask this image altogether?"

"You're asking me, Francis? This is your idea. I'm still not even completely sure what you're talking about."

"Well, yes, I'm asking for your opinion, Marlon. You need to provide input here, and you should welcome the opportunity. And I'll tell you why, Marlon...it's because the Marlon Brando story has been told by so many other people except for Marlon Brando. This is your chance to set the record straight, Marlon. Don't leave it entirely up to Francis Ford Coppola to do it, because I too might fuck it up. Okay? I think that we have the makings of an ending here. And we can make it even more powerful, I think, at least for you personally, Marlon, if we use the ending to help you exercise some of your demons."

"Okay, fine, Francis. However, it's one thing to say that we are going to create an ending that's going to resurrect me and unmask the false image of American servicemen as handsome good-guys and heroes, but it's another thing to come up with something functional, much less something believable."

"Well, that's kind of the problem here, Marlon. I really don't know what this will look like except for the fact that Colonel Kurtz will probably die at some point."

"Like in the book."

"Well, yes, but the death of Kurtz in Conrad's book is a quiet death. The first time I was reading it, my mind was wandering, and I actually missed the fact that Kurtz dies. It's that subtle."

"Yes, it's subtle, Francis."

"But we need something a little more dramatic than Conrad's sleeper of an ending."

"Sleeper of an ending? *Heart of Darkness* gives us one of the most dramatic endings of all time. Kurtz's last words—'the horror, the horror'—says so much. It's a brilliant ending!"

"Let me ask you this, Marlon. What is it exactly that Kurtz dies from?"

"In the book?"

"Yes, Marlon. In the book."

"My brain is starting to hurt, Francis. Can we talk about this later?"

"No, Marlon. Our time is limited. We need to work through this stuff now, even though we're tired and agitated. I agree with you that Conrad's book is subtle, and open to interpretation. I want to know your understanding as to why Kurtz died."

Marlon paused for a moment. He took a deep breath.

"Well, Francis. Kurtz is diseased. He's sickly. He represents the Western world, weakened and sickened by its own excesses. He slowly disintegrates from within, basically."

"Okay. I agree. Our Kurtz, Marlon, as we mentioned earlier, is not going to be the sickly, emaciated Kurtz of Conrad's book. He's going to be a big, strong, healthy, gung-ho military type. Not a robot, mind you, but a kind of *Ubermensch*, as Nietzsche proposed. He's physically and mentally strong, and cerebral, which makes him interesting, as opposed to a one-dimensional gung-ho soldier."

"So, Kurtz, because he's cerebral, because he's smart, has transcended the narrow post-World War II and Cold War propaganda and imagery of the United States at this time, the late sixties. Is that what we're saying, Francis?"

"Right. Yes. That's a good way of describing it, Marlon. He's no simpleton soldier. He's no archetype, either. I want him to have thoughts and feelings. I want him to be a real person, with real emotions."

"Okay. If Kurtz is a real person, with real thoughts and emotions, does he want to die?"

"This again? You tell me, Marlon."

"Okay. Yes, I think he does want to die. But he hates the hypocrisy more than he wants to die. He hates the post-World War II propaganda and imagery of America and of the American officer and soldier. And therefore, he wants that image to die more than he wants to die himself, I think."

"Precisely, Marlon. I think you're on to something. And I think you want this image of yourself to die, too, so you can shed your old, dead skin."

"I want a lot of my so-called 'images' to die."

"What I mean is that I think you want to be taken seriously as a humanitarian, and as an advocate on certain issues, like American Indian issues, and you would like people's preconceived notions of you to stop hindering your efforts. Am I right, Marlon?"

"Yes, pretty much, Francis. But how are we going to work this into the Kurtz character?"

"I don't know yet, Marlon. But let's start breaking things down a little to see if we can find some direction."

"Sure."

"Okay, so we've established that Kurtz wants to die, or at least is okay with dying, because he thinks that much of what he represents will die with him."

Francis said this and then paused.

"So, do we agree that Kurtz should die in the movie, Marlon?"

It was now Marlon's turn to pause for a moment. He studied the face of his director, and then began answering the question.

"Well, yes. He dies in the book, so we should follow suit, I suppose. But also, the death of Kurtz is a logical consequence, or better yet, a fitting ending."

"How so?"

"Well, I can't see any scenario in which he lives. Can you?"

"Not necessarily, Marlon. But tell me why you think that."

"I can't see Kurtz finding some kind of resolution to his problem. I mean, he's not going to live happily ever after, is he?"

"No, probably not. He's seen and done a lot of unsavory things, and he himself is an extremely volatile character. He's gone too far to ever come back. Plus, we have Captain Willard, a man sent to kill Kurtz. So, he's going to die. I think we've now established that."

"So, is it going to be Willard who kills Kurtz?"

"I would assume so. Either him, or maybe one of his crew, perhaps. It's an interesting idea, though—that somebody other than Willard kills Kurtz—and maybe we should explore it. How about if the North Vietnamese kill Kurtz?"

"The North Vietnamese?"

"Yes, the hero-figure—the American serviceman—is villainized and then killed by the people who are normally villainized and killed in American movies."

Marlon shook his head in disagreement of his director's scenario.

"We can't justify their cause, Francis—the North Vietnamese. If you do that, you will be making a pro-Communist movie, and that will be panned beyond all panning. You'll be absolutely lambasted. Your movie may even be boycotted."

"I realize this, Marlon. Believe me. It was just a thought. Yes, if we try to make the movie simply about how the Americans were wrong, and the North Vietnamese were right in resisting them, the movie will fail on many levels, especially at the box office.

Moviegoers will dismiss it as communist propaganda, and in the end the only point I will be making is that America's involvement in the Vietnam War was wrong. And that point has been made many times over, even by people who initially supported American involvement there."

"How about if the montagnards kill him?"

"Hmm...the montagnards. You know, Marlon, that would play into the whole dying and rising god thing that Frazer talked about. We could definitely work something like that out, but we would also have to figure out how and why the montagards would kill Kurtz rather than Willard killing him. We would have to answer the question of why Willard would decide against killing Kurtz, while the montagnards, the people following and worshipping the man like a god, are the ones to actually do it. I'm just trying to figure out why Willard, the man who travels all this way just to kill Kurtz, wouldn't be the one who kills him. You know what I mean, Marlon?"

"Maybe Willard gets word that the montagnards are unhappy with Kurtz, that they want him dead, and he simply waits for them to do it, or even encourages them to finish Kurtz off. Maybe Kurtz tyrannizes them, and so maybe they hate him, and Willard gives them the courage to kill their oppressor."

"Yeah, maybe. These are all good, that is, if we go with the idea that the montagnards kill Kurtz. I'm just not completely sold on that, either. I'm afraid it would be too cheesy in an almost Walt Disney kind of way."

"Yeah, I can see that too, Francis. It might give the movie a kind of *Jungle Book* quality."

"Yeah, I know what you mean. And perhaps part of my fear with this scenario is that I will just be making some hippy-dippy statement about how the native peoples have got it right, and the so-called civilized and technologically advanced Westerners are clumsy and clueless. And even though I do understand that whole thing, and actually agree with it to a certain extent, this is not the statement I aspire to make here. And that's why, Marlon, I think it best to have Willard, a white American Westerner, kill Kurtz."

"I agree, Francis."

* * *

"I want to illuminate the hypocrisy, the sheer madness of the United States during the Vietnam War, how it's gotten so big and gluttonous that it is literally devouring itself. I want to show how an advanced civilization, one which claims to be motivated and guided by reason and rational thought processes, is in reality still shepherded by primal instinct and even superstition, and how these things, too, are responsible for its world domination, even though most people are oblivious, or perhaps in denial, of this fact."

"Just like I was saying earlier, and have been saying all along, Francis."

"Yes, Marlon, just like you've been saying all along. I think this is the key to the ending, and maybe even the whole movie, for that matter. It is violence and destruction, the willingness to be ruthless and merciless based on some notion of racial and/or spiritual transcendence and superiority, which has enabled the United States to be the world's preeminent power. And we've talked, Marlon, about how America has portrayed and advertised itself and its motives, all the way down to its conquering soldiers, as some kind of wholesome, pure, freckle-face boy next-door enterprise. But in reality, it's much deeper than that. There is, as I just said, this kind of belief, or mythology, that the white Western-Christian world is on some kind of spiritual crusade to save, or civilize, the rest of the world."

"And this image—this mythology—held up pretty well until the around the time of the Vietnam War."

"That's pretty much true, Marlon. It was during the Vietnam War when everybody began seeing through the United States and its clumsy intentions."

"Yes, but I don't think anybody saw the debacle of the Vietnam War in its full historical breadth, though, Francis."

"Say more, Marlon."

"Well, I think the critics of the Vietnam War saw America's intentions only from the perspective that it was a large, rich, and technological advanced nation trying to take over a small, poor and technologically backward nation, and that they were doing it by way of their economic and military supremacy."

Marlon paused to make sure his director agreed with his assessment thus far. Francis initially nodded in agreement, but then decided to say a few words.

"Yes, it was seen as an imperialist endeavor, a quasi- or neo-colonial endeavor. Absolutely, Marlon."

"Yes, Francis, but nobody considers, or even knows, the ancient religious or theological roots of the Western colonial political system, and how its ghost—its Holy Ghost—hovers over every imperialist undertaking of the Western world, including the Vietnam War."

"Whew!" replied Francis after a long pause, knowing that his star actor just spit out a mouthful of information that could easily become a day's worth of conversation. "That's a pretty long, complicated, and winding path for us to go down, considering the fact we probably need to head back to the set tomorrow. Hopper, at least in his mind, has probably overthrown me has director, and is filming the final scenes even as we speak."

"Speaking of final scenes, Francis, I have a feeling that your much hoped-for ending to the movie can be found somewhere in what I just said."

"Oh, don't get my hopes up like that, Marlon. I've been praying for an ending to this movie. I've even sold my soul to the Devil in return for a way to end this damn thing."

"Well, your prayers might have been answered, Francis, but you'll have to bear with me, and hear me out."

"So, is this something you've been sitting on, Marlon? Or something that has just come to you?"

"It's just come to me, Francis," lied Marlon. Fact is, it is something that Marlon has been pondering and even writing about privately for years. He has always hoped for an opportunity to use his now well-formulated theory regarding the still on-going religious or Christian component of Western imperialism, one submerged in political and patriotic speak and rhetoric.

"Okay, good. Because if it's something you've been sitting on for all this time, then I would have to kill you."

"No, Francis. It's something that has just landed on me. It's not fully formulated yet, and it's barely hanging there in my mind, so you'll have to give me the necessary time and space, and to hear me out."

Francis knew that drawing the idea out of Marlon would be difficult, considering how slow he talks and processes his thoughts, and how easily he is distracted. He had to walk a fine line between steering Marlon too much and not enough. But the director was also aware that for Marlon Brando to make the claim of a possible ending to the movie meant the long-time actor was having a moment of inspiration that was worth exploring.

"Okay, Marlon, I will let you talk in order for you to formulate and unfurl your idea, but let me ask you a question before you get too far into it."

"Go ahead."

"Is this idea from God or the Devil?"

"What?"

"I'm asking, Marlon, because I want to know which one is answering my prayers, and subsequently where I'll be spending the rest of eternity."

Marlon thought for a moment.

"Well, just listen to what I have to say, and then I'll let you decide."

"Fair enough, Marlon."

Marlon paused before beginning.

"My fear is that this will be too tedious for you, Francis."

"Tedious? Why would it be tedious?"

"Because my inspiration for this goes back in time a bit. But like I said, just bear with me," begged a nervous Marlon Brando.

"How far back in time?"

"Ancient Rome and Medieval Europe."

"Really? Why so far back?"

"Because, whether anybody likes it or not, the point we're trying to make begins with the figure, or person of Christ, and the idea of an incarnate, or flesh and blood god."

"Oh, I can't wait to hear this. But we have to be careful, Marlon. I can't make a movie with either a pro- of anti-religious message."

"Yes, Francis. I know that. Just hear me out. I'm really not sure exactly where this is going to end up, but I better get started before I lose my train of thought."

"Then by all means, Marlon, please proceed."

"Okay," said Marlon, who then took a couple deep breaths and looked around.

"Now, Francis, it doesn't begin with Christ's life or even his crucifixion, *per se*, but rather when Christianity became the religion…the main religion, of the Roman Empire."

"When would that have been?"

"It was when Constantine was emperor in the early part of the fourth century AD."

"I don't think I knew that."

"The Roman authorities had already killed Christ-the-man over three-hundred years prior to that point, but this is when the anti-imperial religion of Jesus, the Galilean preacher, was subsumed into the Roman imperial system, becoming a pro-imperial religion, and Christ was transformed from a champion of the poor and oppressed to…"

"Wait, Marlon," interrupted Francis. "This is really good, but you're going too fast for my small brain."

Marlon grumbled.

"That's the first time I've ever talked too fast for you, Francis. I'm usually talking too slow."

"Right. And I'm sorry for interrupting you, but what you were saying was really good, but it was just coming too quickly. What were you saying, something about Christ being subsumed into the Roman imperial system, or something?"

"Yes. The anti-imperial religion of Jesus, the Galilean preacher—the historical Jesus, as many theologians now refer to his life on earth, before he was killed—that Jesus and his anti-imperial message was subsumed into the Roman imperial system, becoming a pro-imperial message and religion."

Marlon paused.

"Okay. I got that."

"And Christ was transformed from that of an advocate of the poor and oppressed, to a god, or *the* God, the human incarnation of the most powerful God, who willed and justified the rule of corrupt emperors and kings, and even church leaders."

"Okay," said Francis slowly after Marlon paused again.

"But whereas the historical Jesus tried to raise up the so-called meek, humble, and outcast, these corrupt emperors, kings, as well as popes, come the fourth-century and beyond, relegated them to penned-up swine, exiling Jesus' followers back into their cages of conformance to human law and doctrine."

"Okay. That's a pretty good beginning, Marlon, and some heavy stuff. Are you sure this is something you're just now coming up with?" asked the skeptical director.

"Well, it's something I've read about, and have given a lot of thought to over the years, Francis. So, no. I didn't just come up with this idea. It's just the first time I ever thought it might find relevance in a movie script."

"I see. Please, go on."

There was a pause. Francis looked away, knowing that when he stares at Marlon it makes him nervous.

"Like Constantine and those so-called Christian emperors who came after him, the kings of medieval Western Europe also appropriated or took possession of God and God's power with such theo-political contrivances as 'Vicar of Christ' and 'Royal Absolutism'…"

Marlon paused in order to gauge the comprehension, interest level and patience of his director.

"I'm with you Marlon."

"I'll say it again. The kings of medieval Western Europe appropriated or took possession of God and God's power…in the minds of the people, at least…with such theo-political contrivances or inventions as 'Vicar of Christ' and 'Royal Absolutism', both of which made the claim that the king was God's representative on earth, carrying out God's will."

Marlon stopped again and made eye contact with his director.

"I'm still with you, Marlon. Keep going."

"Eventually, as a result of the Enlightenment and the revolutions that followed—the French Revolution, the American Revolution—the rank-and-file, the masses, the peasantry, the meek and humble, all those who had been relegated to that of swine locked up in cages of conformance…"

"*Symbolic* cages of conformance, right, Marlon?"

"Yes, *symbolic*," said Marlon while closing his eyes to subtly show his annoyance. "All those who had been relegated to that of swine locked up in cages of conformance…symbolic cages, an imprisonment of their mind…broke loose, utilizing the ideal of 'democracy' to seize the God-like power and persona of the king, and appropriate it to themselves."

"Yes, Marlon. I like that. I'm not sure where this is all going to go, but…"

"Me neither."

"But it sounds good so far. If nothing else, I'm getting a history lesson."

Marlon smiled before continuing, talking even slower than usual in order to give Francis time to digest everything he was saying.

"So, to reiterate, or rephrase, that last point…"

"Yes, Marlon."

"By the end of the Middle Ages, the peasantry—the masses, the chattel, the swine, whatever you want to call them—had stormed the king's courts and seized for themselves the royal birthright to the access of power and wealth."

"Okay," said Francis, who was simply trying to encourage his star actor but not distract him.

"And this is where it would start to get difficult for most Americans, Francis."

"Well, that's kind of what we're shooting for, isn't it, Marlon?"

"I guess so, but we have to be careful, otherwise we'll piss too many people off."

"We can't make a movie that makes a profound statement, and at the same time be fearful of pissing people off. It just won't work."

"I agree. But we need some kind of balance…some subtlety."

"Yes. I agree, Marlon. Please continue."

"Okay, so, begun by the king's greed—and I'm talking the kings of England, France and Spain—European colonization of places like Africa, Asia, as well as North and South America, exploded into nation-building and a tyranny of the white Christian minority against the native peoples."

Marlon stopped to gauge his director, allowing him the opportunity inquire.

"That's good, but explain that last part a little more."

"The Divine Right. Are you familiar with the Divine Right of Kings, Francis?"

"Yes. You just explained it a few minutes ago," responded Francis, nodding his head. "It's when the king is assumed to be God's representative on earth."

"Yes. Well…yes."

"What, it's not?"

"No, it is."

"Then why did you hesitate?"

"I didn't. Just let me continue."

"Okay, Marlon."

"The Divine Right of Kings, once reserved for those of royal lineage—the royal bloodline—had been disseminated to all Christians of Anglo descent, a notion that would live just below the surface of American democracy, an ideal claiming a share of God's divinity for every white male. The hierarchical order of Western Christendom had been turned upside down. The so-called meek and humble—the chattel, the masses…"

"The swine!"

"Yes, the swine, as the peasantry have sometimes been referenced by certain aristocratic segments of European society. They had seized power. Every man—every white male—according to the concept of 18th and 19th century American democracy, was considered a god, or god-like, because it was believed that they alone were created in God's image, even possessing a share of the God's divine spark, if you will."

"Where do you get all this stuff, Marlon? It sounds like something from Tolkien."

"I read a lot. But I don't read that fantasy shit. This is directly from the writings of various European and American religious and political thinkers and philosophers from that time period."

"I've heard you are a voracious reader, and that you have a magnificent collection of books."

"I don't watch television, or go out drinking, or do much of anything out of the house for that matter. I spend most of my time reading."

"Which makes it all the more perplexing that you weren't able to find the time to read *Heart of Darkness* before coming over here."

"Truth is, Francis, it just didn't interest me. I can only read a book if it interests me."

"I can understand that."

Marlon waited a moment before proceeding.

"American democracy may have afforded the white Christians of the New World, life, liberty, the pursuit of happiness, and a share of God's divine nature, but they were still Old World swine…"

"I like the swine analogy."

"Medieval peasants were often referred to in this manner."

"So interesting! And disturbing."

Marlon paused before continuing.

"The Euro-Americans could not escape the dogmatic pens in which they were still confined despite their efforts. Willfully grazing on the same regurgitated truths as their ancestors—submission and fealty dressed up as nationalism—the flock was led to believe they were following their Galilean Shepherd, too feeble of mind and body to perceive that their veneration and toil were instead building Caesar's new empire."

Marlon paused.

"Here comes more of the swine analogy, Francis."

"I'm ready."

"Like the domestic pig, the Euro-Christian mindset of the white Americans unknowingly lived in cages of dependence for things familiar and facile. A fearful and guilt-ridden conscience can only imitate. It has castrated the seeking spirit, ending its search for truth. Subsequently, in the spirit of the monarchs whom they fled, a hatred of the natural world—of nature—and an exalted, puffed-up, inflated sense of self, ascended the mob-ruled throne in America."

"Mob-ruled throne! That's good!"

Again Marlon paused, taking a breath and looking around before continuing.

"By the turn of the twentieth-century the descendants of the European immigrants had harvested the American wilderness, one overgrown with mankind's imperfections, constructing what they believed to be God's Kingdom, but what they really fashioned was the New Rome. And what was their means or method of destroying the sin and wickedness of the New World in order to build a kingdom fit for themselves, a people reflecting godly perfection, a kingdom that in reality would be no different than the ones they escaped from back in Europe?"

Marlon paused for dramatic effect.

"I don't know," answered Francis, unsure if Marlon's question was rhetorical or if he expected a response.

"Fire! The flame, Francis! The flame has always been the great purifier, the means by which the Western Christians have obliterated the final vestiges of the primeval world and erased the literal tracks and footprints of our evolution, lest the narrative, the story of our existence, be a lie."

"Yes, Marlon!"

Marlon continued, but with eyes closed, trying to remember the words he has written down, and even spoken aloud to himself on many occasions over the years when trying to deduce this concept.

"Like a blacksmith forging iron with the blunt force of an anvil, the Western Christians have hammered out a world with a past, present, and future, distinctive to themselves. The Garden of Eden is from whence they came. The Kingdom of God is their perceived destiny. The apocalypse of their adulterated birthplace is the means of reaching this end."

Francis waited before saying anything, wanting to make sure Marlon was finished.

"And now, Francis, to try and bring it around, and make all this relevant to the 1960s and the Vietnam War…"

"Okay."

"Even though the term Manifest Destiny…and you know the religious overtones and undertones of the concept of Manifest Destiny, right, Francis?"

"Uh, yes, I think I do, but just quickly tell me how it fits in with what you're saying."

"Manifest Destiny was basically the name of the process of expanding American rule and Western-style civilization across the whole of North America, from east to west, in order to justify the destruction of the Indians, as well as put the wilderness under our power and sway."

"Got it."

"It basically said the destruction of the Indians and their way of life, as well as the taming of the wilderness or wild frontier, was willed by God."

"Divine Providence."

"Precisely. And I'm bringing that concept back around here, too, Francis, because we talked about Divine Providence a few weeks ago."

"Right."

"So even though Manifest Destiny was no longer a working definition of American governmental or military policy by the late 1960s, its legacy was alive and well in Southeast Asia. And no matter what name or conceptualization it went by—Manifest Destiny or the spread of freedom and democracy—it was still proliferated with fire and steel. That's how the Western world has always laid waste to the things it finds uncomfortable, primitive, revolting, frightening, and contradictory to our current belief system. They have burned it off, incinerated it, cremated, conflagrated, razed it as if it never even existed!"

Francis wanted to respond, but held himself in-check just in case there was more.

"Fire, Francis. The great purifying flame!"

Marlon stopped. Francis waited.

"That was really good, Marlon."

"Really?"

"Yes!" said Francis emphatically.

"Did it help?"

"I'm pretty sure I have my ending!" said the director with a grin from ear to ear.

"Really? What is it?"

"You'll see."

"You're not going to tell me?"

"Not yet. But what I can tell you is that we're going back to the set tomorrow."

"Okay," replied Marlon with a slight hint of dread in his voice. "Hey, Francis?"

"What?"

"So, was it God or Satan who answered your prayers?"

"Both, I think, Marlon. Both."

CHAPTER 35

In time, Colonel Memmington's relationship with me and Father McDuffee would become more amicable than on the night we met, yet laden with animosity and mistrust, nonetheless. The first few weeks at the new basecamp were for the most part uneventful. There was no contact with the enemy, nor anything to overtly trigger our hostility for one another, which lived just below a surface teaming with tension.

Amidst mine and Father McDuffee's personal distaste for Colonel Memmington, and vice-versa, we still found it palatable to dine together in the evenings on an ancient Hindu pyramid of rock overlooking the river. On one of its sides there was a set of steps that led up to a flat surface from where one could see the river unimpeded by jungle fauna. There, inside a tent of mosquito netting, the only three Caucasians in Green Tiger would feast by candlelight on steaks sent in from I-Core, while outside the crickets chirped loudly. From about twenty feet above the jungle floor we sat before plates of ambrosial Holstein flesh cooked to our specifications. Blood would ooze from the meat as we meticulously carved it with sharp knives into pieces small enough to chew and swallow. While eating we would talk of such things as war, peace, and the taste of the flesh and blood we were consuming. But before each of these dining episodes, we three Westerners would bow our heads and thank our mutual God for the bounty placed before us.

Outside the candle-lit tent, in the jungle, the animals foraged for their own taste of blood, having to kill for their life-sustaining nourishment. But they were the fortunate ones. Many of their own kind from the animal kingdom have been domesticated, lost of their survival instincts by the predictable consistency of pasture and pen, ending up on the plates of those who tamed them.

In the latter part of the twentieth-century, the world was still one in which we as white men of European descent were kings, gods almost, and all things wild were ours for the picking. It was this very jungle that harbored the most recent of those deemed the enemy of Western civilization-- the communists of North Vietnam. The jungle enabled the Vietcong to avoid their enemies, hiding and giving them shelter from the Western armies that have come to kill them. The jungle is a place unfamiliar to us, however, an abhorrence to our ideals of civilization, a garden of evil, and an obstacle to victory in Southeast Asia.

Father McDuffee spoke often, directly and indirectly, on the subject of the jungle, often quoting from the Old Testament.

"And God told the Israelites to increase in numbers, fill the earth and bring it under your rule, have control over the fish of the sea, the birds of the sky, and all the animals that walk on the earth. I shall

give you every plant on the earth that bears fruit."

He also liked to use his own words when justifying the jungle's destruction.

"The angels of God will fell the dark wilderness so the Light can penetrate this place so unclean with sin and wickedness."

Father McDuffee still believed his duties in Cambodia were important despite the fact that no one came to him for spiritual guidance. But he was still a servant of God, and even if nobody was listening he would persevere in his quest to make the Word of God available to anyone who wished to hear it. Father McDuffee would not waver in his lifelong desire to see the darkness, places like the very jungle he was in, destroyed by God's wrath, and the Kingdom of God, the new Israel, growing from out of the ashes. Trampled underfoot would be the carnality of the wilderness and the 'savage man' who lives there.

Little by little, piece by piece, American napalm methodically burned northeast Cambodia to the ground. Down came the flames in a burst of thunder, first exploding onto the earth, then climbing its way to the top of the jungle, the black smoke billowing up to the sky, serving as a testament to the inferno below. The gasoline-soaked napalm roared through the green albatross, spreading the fiery holocaust like a disease, killing the vegetative underworld in a plague of devouring heat and flame".

Both the Vietcong and the animals living there would scatter, fleeing the scourge decimating their home. Some escaped while others were eaten alive, unable to allude the man-made hell. Day and night the skies rained fire and steel onto the jungle, charring the once lush, supple foliage, melting away the colorful flowering that hid the Darwinian world below. But the jungle has stood for time immemorial, taking millions of years to spread itself across the whole of Southeast Asia, and it would battle its antagonist with a patient and long-suffering endurance until its last vestige was uprooted.

* * *

"Time is not of the same conceptualization or urgency for the Vietnamese as it was for the Americans. The cultural mindset or psyche of the North Vietnamese was unduly Taoist, possessing a cyclical rather than linear sense of time and history. Like a waft of smoke rolling through the air, time can advance, recede, or stay constant with no predestined intelligible plan. In the Tao all is united, blending things similar and different in harmony with the laws of nature."

"In Southeast Asia, mankind does not occupy the ascendant role we enjoy in Western thought as the protagonist of the natural order and prime object of creation. In contrast, man is envisaged as but a single part of nature's complex system, the human soul the same in essence as the water, fauna, animals, and air. The Taoist aspires to attain harmony with nature. Their relationship with it is organic and inseparable. No boundaries are drawn between the supernatural world, the domain of nature, and that of mankind. When mankind conforms to Natural Law, says Lao Tzu, society enjoys peace and tranquility. But if mankind resists Natural Law because of selfish arrogance, the delicate balance between heaven, earth, and mankind is disrupted. Concord of the three entities can result only when mankind surrenders to the 'eternal way' or Tao—-the rhythm of the universe—-and learns to harmonize with it."

"Having long since been absorbed into the Tao, the Vietnamese melded with the jungle a mere two thousand years ago, but have already attained harmony with its rhythms and cycles. Throughout their endless war, the North Vietnamese have held sway to the Taoist maxim of 'cling to the unity'. What this meant for the Americans in their war with the communists of North Vietnam was

that their enemy, like the jungle, would battle their foe to the very end, until the last drop of blood flowed from the last body."

"America's involvement in Vietnam was like a rapidly accumulating debt, time coming at an ever-increasing cost. Although certainly not free, time came at much less of a price for the North Vietnamese, the breadth of their struggle diluting the severity of sacrifice and loss during any one period of time. With each day that passed and every body-bag that left the jungle filled with another dead American, the urgency grew, but so did North Vietnamese resolve. The thinly veiled wanton perdition of the North Vietnamese and Cambodian countryside by the Americans revealed their desperation and the schism plaguing American society."

CHAPTER 36

"Look, Francis. It's Mr. Clean," said Dennis Hopper to his director, and then giggled in a manner that convinced Francis he was stoned. Dennis was pointing over at Marlon Brando, who just emerged onto the movie set with his head shaved.

"What the fuck?" responded Francis while starring at Marlon in disbelief. He was trying to figure out the implications of trying to fit, not just an overweight Kurtz, but a bald Kurtz as well, into the storyline.

"What happened to you, Marlon?" inquired Dennis with more than a hint of cynicism and the kind of nervous laughter that Marlon has grown to hate.

"Shhh! Dennis! Jesus Christ, don't piss him off."

Dennis laughed nervously. Marlon walked past both men without acknowledging either one, his not-so-subtle way of indicating he will not speak with his director while in the presence of Dennis Hopper.

"Marlon!" yelled Francis while stepping away from Dennis Hopper in order to have a word with his star actor. "Marlon, the hair? What's going on?"

Marlon stopped, prompting Francis to halt his pursuit.

"Don't you like it?"

"Well, I don't know yet. It's just that we already had to change the image of Kurtz from emaciated and sickly to big and robust. And now you've thrown another curve ball at me, Marlon, by shaving your head."

Francis waited for a reaction. Marlon did not say anything, but rather rubbed his right hand over the top of his head in a manner suggesting he too was still trying to get used to the fact that he was now bald.

"I mean, a crew-cut or a flat-top I could understand, and within a week or two you can have it at that level, but your head completely shaved, Marlon? You have to explain to me your motivation, and what it means for Colonel Kurtz to be bald. I mean, is it a kind of Zen thing, Marlon? Don't get me wrong. I'm not saying I don't like it. I'm just kind of surprised, and perhaps in need of a little bit of an explanation, that's all."

"Well, if I must, Francis. It's about the whole death and rebirth thing. I see Kurtz as a former gung-ho type, somebody who has, and we talked about this a while back, Francis, he is somebody who has thrown that whole thing off to a certain extent. He's not a hippy or a pacifist. Far from it. He believes in violence, but he believes that if you're going to be violent in order to win a war, then *be fucking violent*. Do whatever it takes to win the war and don't play politics, and don't try and hide behind the thin veneer of the concept of 'civilization' and all its hypocrisy, and all that shit that we talked about a while back. Kurtz believes that violence is our natural state. That peace and even restraint are both contrivances that cut against the grain of our true nature."

"Okay. But what about the haircut? Why the shaved head, Marlon?"

"He's trying to differentiate himself from the other American military commanders. He doesn't want to wear his hair like them. And, I have another idea."

"What? You're going to shave your legs, too?"

"Maybe you should shave your legs, Francis. You're the hairy one here."

"Hey, I'm Italian, Marlon. My whole family is hairy. Women too. So, what's your other idea, Marlon?"

"My other idea is to have Kurtz wear something other than an American military uniform."

"Like what?"

"I don't know exactly."

"Well, there can't be too many options out here. I mean...we can't have Kurtz dressed in something from Loro Piana, now can we!"

"Francis, I'm trying to be serious. I come out here today and that fucking idiot, Hopper, starts mocking me, that fucking dope fiend." Marlon started to raise his voice. Francis put his hand on Marlon's shoulder and gently turned him away from the rest of the crew, especially Dennis Hopper, the focal point of his tirade.

"If that fucker gets in my way one more time, I'm leaving this fucking set immediately and going back to Los Angeles."

"Okay, Marlon, okay. I'll talk to Dennis. I'm sorry if you think I haven't been receptive to your decision to shave your head. Let's go over there and talk," said Francis, pointing to a place off to the side. Francis picked up his megaphone. "Okay, everybody. We're going to take a break. Let's come back in thirty minutes," he announced.

"Okay, Marlon. The hair?"

"I was thinking, well, it's a combination of things, really. On the one hand, it's a way of preparing myself for my impending death here on the set and subsequent rebirth, like we talked about."

"Is it a kind of Zen or Buddhist thing?"

"Well, kind of, yes. But let me explain what I had in mind in regard to what Kurtz should wear. I see him wearing something black, something similar to the black garb, or pajamas, as they were referred to in the West, worn by the Vietcong."

"Hmm, interesting, Marlon. But my fear is that it will be perceived as Kurtz having gone over to the side of the North Vietnamese. I'm afraid he will be seen by the Western audience, for whom the movie is intended, as a man who has become a Buddhist because of his shaved head, and perhaps even a North Vietnamese sympathizer or collaborator because of the black pajamas."

"Well, here's what I think should be the intended message regarding Kurtz, and then we can figure out how to get there from here. I don't see him as switching sides by any means or any stretch of the imagination. He is still fighting the North Vietnamese, with the help of the montagnards, but he comes to respect and even admire the tenacity with which the North Vietnamese are fighting this war. They are not afraid of their violent selves. They are not startled at the notion that they are loving husbands and fathers, yet they are able to kill with great tenacity, and with little or no remorse."

"Ah, yes, Marlon. I do like that. So, it's almost something kind of neutral for Kurtz, the shaved head and black pajamas, right?"

"Yes, I would say *neutral* is a good way of putting it."

"He sees the American uniform and crew-cut as things fraught with too many limitations, too many rules that get in the way of winning the war, too much historical baggage. Kurtz just wants to be free to do the things necessary to win this war, so he separates himself from the United States to a certain extent. That's why he's in Cambodia, and he doesn't try to hide it or make any excuses as to why he is in Cambodia, when of course Americans weren't supposed to be in Cambodia. Is this kind of what you are shooting for, Marlon?"

"Well, yes, that sounds good to me. Once again, Francis, you're able to take my ideas, as small as they are, and bring them to full fruition."

"And Marlon, that's what I love and respect about you so much. That's why you are such an asset to this and any other movie set. It's because you come up with great core ideas. You don't always have them fully developed, and that's where I come in. I'm good at developing ideas. I'm just not good at coming up with them."

"Plus, Francis, I think the black will hide the extra weight I'm carrying, which I know is a concern of yours."

"That's a good point, Marlon. I know it's not a comfortable issue for you. I'm over-weight, too, and I don't like it either. My wife is always bringing it up, and I get defensive. It's not easy to lose weight, Marlon. I know this and I sympathize with you. I agree with what you said earlier about filming you in very low light. I want the Kurtz scenes to be shadowy. I want the Kurtz character to be shadowy and elusive, literally and figuratively. Kurtz's headquarters will be dark, like a cave or something, overgrown with jungle. Kurtz will rely on candle light. It will be thick with humidity, almost steamy."

"But do you agree with the black pajamas, Francis?"

"Yes, I think it's a good idea, actually. I like it because I can't see Kurtz wearing an army uniform at this point. He's moved beyond the pomp and pageantry, the superficiality."

"I'm glad to hear that, Francis, because I too have moved beyond the pomp and pageantry, the superficiality. And I will never wear a military uniform for a movie ever again. I would do just about anything for you, Francis, but I won't play GI Joe. Not for you. Not for anybody."

"Wow. I'm glad we were able to find a way to work around that issue, Marlon. I had no idea you felt that strongly about it. What would you have done if I asked you to put on a uniform?"

"I would have said no."

Francis did not respond. He instead donned a look of surprise and pondered the implications.

CHAPTER 37

The circumstances in Green Tiger contained much of the same ambiguities as those back in the states, with the Englishman, the Irishman, and myself, each with a different vision for the American war in Vietnam. The obvious odd man out was Colonel Memmington. Little by little he used the privileges afforded his higher rank to fashion an imperial realm for himself inside the Cambodian jungle. There the man enthralled by the concept of royalty could finally be a monarch, even if his kingdom and status therein were mere figments of his imagination.

Since having usurped me as both commander and strategist, Colonel Memmington has relied almost exclusively on air strikes to bring the Vietcong and NVA to their knees in Cambodia. And for the most part, I agreed with this tactic. I too wanted the jungle destroyed, but was also a believer that overt sweeps of the countryside were necessary, that bombs and napalm could not do the job alone. Memmington would eventually accept my rationale regarding the aforementioned sweeps, subsequently sending me and the Stieng out on daily patrols to rid his emporium of vagrants, keeping the

Cambodians behind to serve as his personal sentry.

Despite the well-documented misgivings about Colonel Memmington in various military circles, he was still considered a hero in the opinion of many at I-Core, his decisive action in handling the situation with the Jarai saving them from much possible embarrassment. It was mainly for this reason that he was given official command of Green Tiger in the first place. This was something I could not have foreseen the night I contacted I-Core regarding removing Wilke and sending in additional help. I was not impressed with the colonel's leadership abilities, or his grasp of the nuances of this particular jungle conflict. I oftentimes found myself assuming Wilke's old role of playing devil's advocate, trying to subtly point out to the colonel any misconceptions he may have. This only served to widen the gap between us, with Memmington becoming increasingly suspicious of both me and Father McDuffee. So much so that he made it a priority to keep us separated, continually sending me and the Stieng out into the bush on nonsensical errands, leaving little opportunity for the two Catholics to conspire against their Protestant commander.

Keeping in mind the end-result of his attempts to Christianize the Jarai, Father McDuffee kept his distance, at least theologically, from the Stieng and Cambodians. He constructed an altar in his small thatch hut. A bamboo cross, a couple candles, and the Bible that he carried with him were all the worldly possessions of his small church. The normally quick to proselytize priest stayed away from Memmington, even toning down the volume of his rhetoric, fearing he would send him back to Saigon the minute he rubbed the colonel's English brass the wrong way with his Irish rosary beads.

Whenever time and circumstance allowed, both myself and Henderson would join Father McDuffee in prayer, doing so in a quiet and subdued manner.

In stark contrast, the Stieng would hold loud boisterous sacrificial ceremonies down by the river. Their animal of choice for slaughter, like the Jarai, was that of the wild boar. But the festivities of the Stieng were noticeably more violent and bizarre than those of the Jarai, even to the point of unnerving myself and Father McDuffee, both of us never fearing the celebrations of the Jarai.

They would pray over the body of a living boar, offering it to their various gods and spirits before eating it alive. Tearing at its warm flesh with their long fingernails sharpened for this very purpose, the Stieng would indiscriminately devour handfuls of muscle, organs, and entrails, stopping only to drink the blood of the oftentimes still-battling beast by cupping it in their hands. Over the course of their flesh-feast, they would smear the bright red life essence on their face and bodies in a bacchanalian-like fit of madness to the unintelligible beat of drums and gongs.

None of this was any concern to Colonel Memmington. He was actually entertained by this sort of 'savagery', as he would call it. If the Stieng started practicing Catholicism, then he would worry. But the Cambodians were an entirely different story. The sudden eruption of drums that began each Stieng ceremony frightened them, terrified that eventually the fate of the wild boar would be their own. They were fast becoming uneasy and wary participants in Green Tiger, unsure if Colonel Memmington was a worthwhile reason for them to stick around and risk their lives.

While the internal differences within Green Tiger played themselves out, the bombs and napalm continued to fall on northeast Cambodia. Green Tiger no longer had to radio I-Core encouraging these maneuvers as a veritable aerial blitzkrieg pounded the North Vietnamese sanctuaries day and night. Green Tiger's mission was still to eliminate communist infiltration into the South via the Ho Chi Minh trail. But we were also concerned with hunting down those fleeing the American bombing raids with the intention of relocating. Memmington's biggest worry in all this was that the absconding North Vietnamese would overrun his kingdom and take it for themselves. He was consistent in his behest that the Cambodians stay close by, but could not decide whether he wanted the Stieng to form a human perimeter around his domain, or have them actively pursue the North Vietnamese before they could organize themselves against what he considered to be the 'Queen's Cambodian outpost'. As a result, Green Tiger became paralyzed and completely ineffective.

* * *

With all their glaring differences, it was perhaps the manner in which my two fellow officers of past and present—Wilke and Memmington—perceived the concept of 'basecamp' that distinguished them the most. As understood by the Englishman, basecamp was a stronghold, an established entity that needed to be defended and preserved above all else until the last man. As goes the basecamp, so goes the men who protect it. And ultimately, so goes the mission. Seen through his Anglo-centric eyes which still envision England's colonial preeminence, a basecamp was a symbol and source of pride, something worth fighting for, an island of civility amidst a sea of barbarism and savagery.

In contrast, basecamp for Wilke was whatever best served his needs at that particular moment. It was formless and fluid, something he would simply allow the enemy to have if they wanted it bad enough, sure in the fact that moral victories do not win wars. He would not fight for it, because as Wilke understood the concept of basecamp, if you had to fight for its very existence, then it was not a basecamp anymore. In the opinion of Wilke, a basecamp was a place where operations could be planned and launched undisturbed by one's enemy. If these things were not possible for any reason, it was no longer a basecamp, and need not be preserved. For him, a basecamp could be large and sprawling with a stone wall around it, or it could be a small hole in the ground covered with jungle leaves. It was whatever the situation warranted. Nothing more, nothing less.

Even though I probably would have better identified with Colonel Memmington in this regard when I was still fresh from the states, time and necessity have molded me into a jungle savvy jungle fighter, and I now see things much the same way Wilke did. I did not approve of Memmington's fortress-mentality, or anything else about his command of Green Tiger for that matter. Having long since questioned his competence,

I now began to wonder about the colonel's sanity as well. I still respected Memmington's rank even though I held very little regard for the man himself. I was aware of I-Core's recent love affair with Memmington as a result of the Jarai incident, making it improbable for me to execute a removal campaign over the radio, leaving only the priest to confide in.

Despite having his own problems with Colonel Memmington, Father McDuffee recommended restraint and lots of prayer. The more we discussed the matter, however, the more open Father McDuffee became on the subject, admitting his own displeasure for the Englishman and his desire to have him "fragged by the Holy Ghost" as he put it.

Memmington was where he had always dreamed of being, and was not about to let a 'Mick' or a 'Yank' take him down. Like many of his World War II era comrades, he too was in command of a military outpost in a far-off exotic part of the world, one with sufficient links to goods and services from the Western world. He saw it as something owed him for all the years of dedicated service to his Queen and country. Whether this was indeed the reason for him being there, or whether it was merely a means of getting rid of a 'sacred cow' who was no longer wanted, the Cambodian outpost was the kind of pasture that many career-types without a home, like Colonel Memmington, hoped to spend, not only the last days of service, but the last days of their life.

Instead of enjoying what he had, Memmington was in the process of driving himself mad with worry over losing what he considered the crowning jewel of his career. He quit calling for air strikes anywhere near his basecamp out of fear that the enemy would spill across its borders. The distant rumblings of B52s far to the north were enough of a concern for him. The meals he ate were not as satisfying as he thought they would be in such a situation, the cognac not as smooth, nor the wine as rich in bouquet. Memmington had nobody to share his stories with as he partook in these pleasures because he alienated everybody around him like he always did, leaving them without any interest in the past exploits of this slow fading soldier. Just like King George in the grips of losing the colonies, Colonel Memmington's consternation led to episodes of near psychotic behavior, as well as the ever-growing possibility of an insurrection among his not-so-loyal subjects.

Despite his arrogance, the colonel was aware that he did not have the respect, much less the admiration of those under his command. He could live without their affection, but not their obedience, concerning himself more with bending them to his will rather than trying to make them love him. Even though myself and Father McDuffee felt the adverse effects of this, as did the mission itself, the brunt of Colonel Memmington's megalomania was aimed at the Stieng. He once found their rituals amusing. But now he blamed them for his fraying nerves, a partial acknowledgement, at least to himself, of his mental unraveling.

The constant drumming and chanting caused Memmington's hands to shake and his oftentimes bourbon-soaked mind to flail in delusional thought. But the colonel never actually considered putting a stop to their celebrations until one night, while completely inebriated, when he suddenly came to believe that the drumbeats were merely a long prelude to the Stieng coming up from the river to kill him as he sat atop his jungle abode. The next day he ordered the Cambodians to throw the drums and gongs into the river while the Stieng were gone. Along the riverbank, the Khmer Serie, in their search for these objects of Memmington's pain, suffering, and even loathing, found many animal carcasses and the remnants of some North Vietnamese whose flesh they believed the Stieng might have eaten. The Cambodians hesitantly did what Colonel Memmington ordered, but were more than slightly nervous about the potential ramifications of their actions.

  Later that night the Stieng returned to find their sacrificial altar desecrated. They quickly and resourcefully constructed new percussion instruments and chimes, performing on them with renewed vigor. The already queasy Cambodians slipped away into the darkness, never to be heard from again. No longer did they deem Colonel Memmington's haughty arrogance worth saving.

  Once aware that the Cambodians were in fact gone, Colonel Memmington ordered me into his quarters. With the mood of the Stieng's musical composition going from celebratory to foreboding by its 'second movement', I sat down at a small table across from the British colonel. There was a candle burning in-between us, and a glass of cognac next to it. The colonel's shaky hands seemed unable to steady, much less raise the goblet of whiskey to his lips.

  Memmington looked much different than he did a couple months back at Artemis when he was at the height of his glory. He should have quit then and rode into the sunset knowing he was still a capable soldier.

Instead, feeling reborn from his success, the colonel stayed, wading ever deeper into the Cambodian jungle, believing he had found the fountain of youth. But Memmington soon found his aged body again drowning in a sea of incompetence and despair. Yes, Colonel Memmington should have stopped soldiering the morning he stood tall as both artist and focal point of that impressionist masterpiece, a self-portrait of strength and courage walking victorious out of the smoke and rubble. Conceived in victory, the once self-exalted figure now cast an image of weakness and capitulation, the ravages of time the artisan of this more objective portrayal.

The colonel looked very old and frail as he sat slumped in his chair. He and the candle, burned nearly to its end as well, were both putting up a brave front, each trying to look strong even as their spark of life was quickly extinguishing.

"Victory at all costs, victory in spite of all terror, victory however long and hard the road may be; for without victory there is no survival," mumbled the colonel while staring at the fluttering candle—a quote from Winston Churchill. "We shall defend our island, whatever the cost may be, we shall fight on the seas and oceans, we shall fight in the hills; we shall never surrender."

Saying these things aloud made Colonel Memmington feel confident enough to attempt a sip of cognac. But again his nervous hands failed him, spilling the precious nectar down the side of his glass and onto the table, aborting the attempt before any touched his lips. The colonel's inability to perform even this most simple of tasks epitomized his short stint as commanding officer of Green Tiger, as well as spoiled his brief enthusiasm gained from the previous recantations of World War II rhetoric.

Having said nothing yet, I sat and watched Memmington and the candle flinch involuntarily at the whim of their adversaries, ones apparently bent on slowly torturing them to death. Just as the subtle bursts of breeze made by the colonel as he spoke forced the candle to tremble and burn faster, hastening its demise, the Stieng continued to beat their drums, causing Memmington's mind and body to melt from the heat of his inflamed nervous system.

"We are never without the resolve of our…I will not die until my duties here have been…" The colonel tried to say something profound in his own words, but that too was beyond his capabilities at this point. "It pains me to my very core to say this, Colonel Kurtz, but our days are numbered."

I raised my eyebrows and prepared to listen intently at the first comprehensive words Memmington uttered since he sat down across from me.

"I'm not talking about Vietnam, or Southeast Asia, but the whole bloody fucken world. The Anglo-Saxon order, of which you are very much a part of whether you realize it or not, colonel, is what I'm talking about."

Colonel Memmington's eyes suddenly became clear and his voice once again authoritative and crisp.

"The white, English-speaking Christian…we are a dying race. And it won't be the Franks, the Bavarians, or even the Slavs that will take our place. They are all dying too. It's the colonial peoples—the Moslems, the Buddhists, and the Hindus who will build the next empires. The Western world is growing old and stagnant. It's crumbling to the ground just like Greece and Rome did before it. Someday the Arabs and Chinese will be studying us, trying to figure out who we were, what we believed, our decline and fall."

The colonel stopped to catch his breath. At that moment I realized I did not hate Memmington in the manner I initially thought I did. I still despised Colonel Memmington the officer, but not the man who was sitting across from me at this very moment. Stripped of his arrogance, Memmington was intelligent and insightful, someone who should have been at Oxford or maybe Yale teaching world and military history, not commanding troops in the jungles of Southeast Asia. It was when Memmington had an attentive audience to share his vast wealth of knowledge that he felt alive and vibrant. Little did he know that his uniform and the rank assigned to him, the very things he thought gave him life, were actually sucking out his lifeblood and decomposing his still-living body.

With the colonel once again slumped over, lost somewhere in his own thoughts, I, still having said nothing, got up and left. After walking about fifteen yards away from Memmington's quarters, I turned back around, prompted by the sounds of the colonel reciting what was unmistakably Shakespearean.

"O! that this too solid flesh would melt, thaw, and resolve itself into a dew; or that the Everlasting had not fix'd His canon 'gainst self-slaughter! O God! O God! How weary, stale, flat, and unprofitable seem to me all the uses of this world. Fie on't! O fie! 'tis an unweeded garden, that grows to seed; things rank and grown in nature possess it merely. That it should come to this!"

Against the background of the still raging Stieng concerto came the beautifully tragic act that would follow.

I turned back around and continued making my way over to the Hindu pyramid overlooking the river, joining Father McDuffee who was already there watching the sunset. With the majority of Stieng still down by the river, banging the drums in a slow, methodical manner, about three of them, faces colored red with pig's blood, walked up to Colonel Memmington's quarters. One at a time they entered through the doorway in calm fashion, their eyes immediately focusing on the Englishman who sat placidly in his chair, still staring at the candle. In a kind of delayed reaction on his part to what was an expected visit, Memmington rose from his chair, stood at attention and saluted the Union Jack hanging from the ceiling of his bamboo and grass hut.

"Take up the white man's burden…send forth the best ye breed, half devil and half child. For Allah created the English mad, the maddest of all mankind! Now English is on the anvil…hear the hammers ring. For this is the law of the jungle…as old and as true as the sky; those that keep it may prosper, but those that break it must die. Oh God, if I must die, please drive far off the barb'rous dissonance of Bachus and his revellers."

The Stieng allowed Colonel Memmington these final words—-a collage of Kipling and Milton that he pasted together to sum up the emotions of what he knew would be his final living moments. Once done, they quickly moved in on the colonel, grabbing him and carrying him off, the Englishman offering no resistance. Up over their shoulders, the colonel's horizontal body facing the sky, the Stieng ran with him down to the river. Once there, the drumming became wild and frantic again. Memmington was placed on the ground. The Stieng danced around him in the firelight.

Meanwhile, Father McDuffee and myself sat quietly atop the ancient Hindu temple, watching the river gently flow southward under the encroaching light of the moon. We were both aware what was happening just a short distance away up river, but pretended that we didn't.

Then, in a final scene more Homeric than Shakespearian, more reminiscent of ancient Pompeii than Medieval Europe, the Stieng ascended upon Colonel Memmington's body in an orgasmic frenzy, clawing and tearing him apart, devouring the flesh and blood of the Anglo-Saxon who had strayed too far from the empire that produced him.

"Like that of leaves is a generation of men," said Homer. "Let's carve him as a dish for the gods," added Shakespeare. Then fell the curtain on this life of an old Britannian soldier.

CHAPTER 38

"I liked the look and feel when The Bounty arrived in Tahiti, Marlon."

"Really? I thought it looked like something out of a Walt Disney movie."

"No, not at all, Marlon. Are you crazy? It was one of the best parts of the movie. I mean...talk about your clash of civilizations, for Christ sake. You have these British sailors from the Western world—from Britain—the hub or epitome of all that is supposedly civilized and enlightened at the time, entering into this tropical, jungle paradise, with palm trees and all these native peoples who look different, and dress different. There's fucking drums and all this tribal music, and it's just this amazing contrast."

"I guess a lot of that was lost on me, Francis."

"You were probably back in your trailer, being some kind of weirdo."

"Ha! More than likely."

"That was one of the few moments where there was a certain amount of edginess to that movie. It's a brilliant moment in an otherwise average movie. The idea is really good, though, the whole thing with these Westerners falling in love with this tropical island, its people, and their way of life, and all that. But, yes, I agree with you, Marlon, talk about a Walt Disney kind of parody!"

"Yes, Francis, another terrible movie that I was involved in, and another terrible role."

"Your accent was in fact terrible, Marlon."

"Yes, I admit that. It's hard to use an accent. It throws everything off, one's timing, just everything."

"Okay, all that aside, what I would like to do when Captain Willard and his crew are entering the Kurtz compound, is to create a similar kind of strange, edgy moment, a kind of clash of cultures, if you will, but much more bizarre, if you know what I mean. I want thick jungle with no sunlight penetrating through. I want it enclosed, encapsulated with jungle. I want it so humid that you can literally see steam rising up from the jungle floor. I want dead bodies strewn about, and severed heads on pikes. I want this place to look like Caligula meets John Wayne, or something fucking like that, but with a little bit of Nietzsche sprinkled in."

"How much of this is about Kurtz, and how much of this is about Marlon Brando?"

Francis chuckled.

"It's up to you, Marlon. How much of it do you want to be about Marlon Brando? I mean, whatever motivation you can draw from all this stuff is fine with me. I want to get an amazing performance from you. If you want the heads and the dead bodies to represent things from your past, perhaps bad movies or bad roles, or simply just bad decisions you've made, then by all means, Marlon, I want you to do that."

* * *

Memmington's absence allowed Father McDuffee to move his church out of the abstemious walls of his quarters to the openness of the fertile Cambodian atmosphere. The Stieng did not become Christians, nor were they encouraged to, unlike the Jarai. And the three remaining Christians of myself, Father McDuffee, and Henderson, certainly did not become animists. But somehow, in a mutual acculturation of one another, we came together, meeting in the middle, somewhere between Catholic Eucharist and pagan blood-letting until the lines separating the two became blurred beyond recognition.

Father McDuffee constructed an altar down by the river, becoming a place of worship for all in Green Tiger. He also made a large cross of bamboo and palms, which served as the gathering point for the varied strains of invocation emanating from its worshippers. The drab colored idol eventually became potent, imbued with a brilliantly radiant dye of intoxicating rapture that Father McDuffee cast upon the whole of his congregation, his amalgamating words melding all gods and higher powers with the palm-garnished cruciform.

   The Americans and Stieng, long-lost brothers whose mutual parents Father McDuffee's Bible says came from Eden, were reunited in the Cambodian jungle. Not stated in the priest's sacred book is the fact that a vineyard of Dionysian madness would be the birth-child of our re-gathering. The Stieng learned to speak more Old World Latin than they did the King's English thanks to Father McDuffee's fluency in the ancient church language and his desire to keep it alive. Together they chanted in the original tongue of the Roman Catholic Church for *Dei omnipotens* to help vanquish their common enemy.

   Father McDuffee's scriptural oratories, and the primal flesh and blood sacrifice of the Stieng fermented together in a bottle of madness and gluttony, which was drunk by all of us in Green Tiger until inebriated. Everyone, including myself and Father McDuffee, began painting our flesh with a combination of sacramental wine and pig's blood, intended to be a godly shield between ourselves and our enemy. These sacrificial rituals were much more than simple praise for our God. They were a mutual consumption between mortal and divine. Green Tiger and our God ate and devoured one another until full, each vomiting the other back out in the form that we desired.

"With Him, in Him, in the unity of the Holy Spirit, all power and glory are yours

Our labors, still presumed by myself and Father McDuffee to be the burden of the hallowed, led us to places of a continuously lower altitude where it seemed to get even hotter and more humid, the fauna thicker and more acrimonious. The bugs and reptilian creatures we encountered seemed to increase in abundance and hostility. The mosquitoes, thriving in this place of shallow muddy pools and nonexistent wind, were merciless in their assault. The snakes, perhaps fearing a challenge to their supremacy of the jungle underworld, lunged and bit at the invading army of mammals, slowing us down on occasion in order for one to suck the poison out of the other. In contrast, the flies welcomed Green Tiger and followed us closely, our frequent kills providing the carnivorous insects with a never-ending supply of flesh to feed themselves, and a womb to gestate their young.

* * *

For several days, Marlon did very little other than sit idly by on the set, waiting for his scenes to come up. In the meantime, Francis, occupied with trying to get the Kurtz compound portion of the movie up and going, was unable to tend to Marlon's needs. The director's main obstacle, however, was Dennis Hopper, much to the annoyance of Marlon Brando.

Marlon spent much of his time reading old *Time* magazine articles about the Vietnam War, provided by Francis. He tried to get Marlon to read *The Golden Bough*, but whenever Marlon made an attempt, it failed to hold his attention for more than a minute. Marlon also spent a lot of time playing with the local Ifugao children, performing magic tricks for them and just generally acting silly. He considered this something of a natural progression for both him and Colonel Kurtz. Marlon, like Kurtz, seeks a certain purity and innocence, one he knows doesn't really exist, but playing with the children helps balance this out, nonetheless.

Somewhere in the middle of all the activity and chaos, Marlon found a poem in one of the books that he could not stop reading or thinking about.

"*We are the hollow men. We are the stuffed men. Leaning together. Headpiece filled with straw.*"

Marlon, now adorned in his black pajamas, sat far off to the side, reading these first words from T.S. Eliot's, *The Hollow Men*, and then seemingly meditating on them. The Ifugao children who were playing around him sensed a different, more intense, contemplative vibe coming from Mr. Brando, allotting him sufficient space.

"*The hollow men. We are the hollow men. The stuffed men...*"

Marlon kept repeating these words to himself, over and over again. He found it mesmerizing to say them. They sparked his imagination.

"*We are the hollow men. We are the stuffed men.*"

The words were helping Marlon morph into the person of Kurtz, and perhaps even for Kurtz to morph into the person of Marlon Brando. Marlon was beginning to feel as if the story of Walter E. Kurtz really was the story of Marlon Brando, and vice-versa. Marlon believed that he and Colonel Kurtz are hollow men, leaning together, both having had been stuffed and propped up with the trappings of Western civilization, their headpieces filled with straw, things dry and dead. Marlon wanted to be loosed from all the things cluttering his mind and body, and he assumed Colonel Kurtz did too.

The old *Time* and *Newsweek* articles about the Vietnam War no longer interested Marlon. Instead, he found himself paging through and eventually reading the books that Francis recommended for him, the books his director envisioned being a part of Colonel Kurtz's library. Marlon would study Frazer's *Golden Bough*, ponder the *Faustian Bargain*, even explore the possibility of the Christian Apocalypse in an old copy of the New Testament Francis had brought with him to the Philippines, but it would be Eliot's

The Hollow Men that would continue to intrigue Marlon and be the motivation for his role as Kurtz.

"Our dried voices, when we whisper together are quiet and meaningless as wind in dry grass, or rats' feet over broken glass in our dry cellar. Our dried voices, when we whisper together are quiet and meaningless as wind in dry grass…"

Again, Marlon found himself repeating a section of *The Hollow Men* softly to himself, prompting those around him to stare and wonder what he was saying. Marlon did not care, however. His professional instincts had taken over, as well as his will and desire to break away from his public persona of both greatest actor of all time and Hollywood freak. Marlon was not sure exactly what some of these passages from Eliot's poem meant, but they resonated with him deeply, and he found himself performing a kind of exegesis on them.

Francis was torn about what his high paid actor should be doing as production moved closer to the moment of Colonel Kurtz's appearance. On the one hand, Francis wanted Marlon to be engaged and getting a feel for things leading up to the point in which he makes his debut. But on the other hand, Francis knew that he should limit Marlon's exposure to Dennis Hopper, as well as other on-set monotonies and distractions, as much as possible.

"Why is it, Francis," asked Dennis Hopper, "why is it that when Marlon sits off on the side, mumbling to himself, he's getting into character? But if I do it, I'm all fucked up. Why is that, Francis?" he added and then gave his trademark nervous laugh.

"Well, Dennis, it's because you usually are fucked up."

Dennis laughed again, then took a deep drag off his cigarette.

"So true, Francis. So true!"

"Dennis, I want you to leave Marlon alone, okay?"

Dennis laughed.

"Leave him alone, Francis?"

"Yeah, please leave Marlon alone. You know he's a bit temperamental."

"Temperamental? Next you're going to be telling me he's on his period."

Dennis laughed.

"Dennis, just give me your word that you will leave Marlon alone, alright?"

"You mean, don't pick on him?"

"Yes, Dennis, don't fucken pick on Marlon Brando, okay? If Marlon gets pissed and leaves the set, I'm going to fire your ass, and maybe even have you killed. Do you understand me, Dennis?"

Dennis laughed, and a big grin enveloped his face.

"So, let me get this straight, Francis. I'm supposed to film several scenes with Marlon, but I'm not supposed to talk to him or interact with him in any sort of way? Because if that's true, Francis, then I don't know, number one, how I'm going to do my job; and number two, if I even want to stay here and try to do my job."

Dennis gave Francis a very serious dead-pan look.

"You're fucking with me, aren't you Dennis?"

Dennis laughed.

"No!" he replied, and then laughed again with a big grin on his face. Francis rolled his eyes and walked away. He looked back over his shoulder at Dennis.

"I mean it," said the director.

Dennis laughed.

CHAPTER 39

The obvious difference between two of Green Tiger's remaining sons of Western Christendom—myself and Father McDuffee—besides our professional garb, was the way we enunciated the Anglo language. But the things that really contrasted us, however, were those not seen or heard. Pressed upon our mind and spirit by ancient lineal crests, emerging a little more with each day spent in the jungle, was each of our ancestral perceptions of the natural world around us, imbedded in our respective cultural psyches and passed along to each new generation via modern conceptualizations.

I, being of German descent, can trace my patriarchal past to the Germanic tribes, possibly the Ostrogoths or Visogoths who crossed the Danube River and laid waste to Rome by 500 AD, settling throughout present-day Spain, Italy, France and Germany. They were marauders, conquerors, makers of war, and have remained so for fifteen-hundred years. Father McDuffee's Irish blood goes back to the ancient Celts. Warriors no doubt, but only out of necessity in order to defend their island nation against constant attack by the sea-faring peoples of the continent.

The Romans called the Germans 'barbarians', who in turn called the Celts 'savages'. The Germanic tribes burned and looted their way across Western Europe, destroying those things both natural and man-made in an effort to unearth their enemies in order to kill and drive them from the land. Nature—the trees and fauna growing in the forests of Europe—served very little purpose for them other than to slow the pace of conquest, prompting the Germanic peoples to physically despoil what they could of it and adulterate the rest in their Teutonic mythology, leaving what remained of 'wicked' nature for the consumption of future Germanic-Christian generations.

The Celts and their later ancestors, the Irish, in contrast found not only safety and shelter in nature's glens, heathers, and shannons, but also beauty, peace, and a sense of their Celtic-self in the plush greenery of the emerald island. Nature is a part of the Irish, and the Irish are a part of nature. Even the Mosaic Law brought over by St. Patrick had to conform to this Irish 'law of nature', the two intertwined to make the new faith more accessible to the island originally catechized by druids.

Born and raised inland, near some of Ireland's most dark and mystical forests, and exposed to the complete pantheon of Celtic/Irish mythology and fairy tales as a child, the Cambodian jungle was a different place for Father McDuffee than it was for his me. I'm sure that just by watching me make my way through the thick foliage one could easily glean that I was reviled by it. I loathed the tangled vines and razor sharp leaves and grasses, their needlelike edges constantly harassing my flesh. Sometimes my hatred for the botanical world would explode in a fit of rage, hacking with my machete at a particular plant that may have unexpectedly stung me. There was very little doubt that I, made discernable from my words and actions, considered myself to be something entirely different, a separate organism from that of my jungle surroundings. It was a place I knew I did not belong, nor wanted to be.

On the other hand, Father McDuffee, initially trenchant toward it, eventually came to see God in the sublime myriad of entangled jungle vegetation. He considered it an extension of the sun and sky as well as that of the fertile ground below. Even though it was filled with enemies of his God, and he sometimes spoke metaphorically about the jungle's destruction, Father McDuffee walked in awe of its majestic splendor. And if understanding one's fate and the fate of all human beings to be intertwined with that of the natural world in reciprocal intercourse meant you were a savage, then Father McDuffee was perhaps becoming a savage.

Although the notion of the Irish priest being a savage was never really a consideration for me, I did perceive the Stieng to be savages, as did Father McDuffee for that matter. They fashioned bows and arrows from things of the jungle, tipping the arrowheads with a deadly poison made from snake venom, shooting them from high atop the trees. These primitive weapons enabled Green Tiger to kill more of the enemy than even our modern weaponry, allowing us to hit quickly and quietly without spooking other nearby North

Vietnamese. Our ammunition and fuel for the M-16s were almost gone anyway, and we had no means of attaining more.

I initially tried to get the Stieng to carry the Russian and Chinese rifles dropped by the North Vietnamese we killed, but most of them were such outdated pieces of junk that I decided to leave them for the rust to devour. The only remaining automatic weapon in Green Tiger's possession was the one I carried. Father McDuffee did not bear an implement of war. He refused to take a life. His rousing sermons were a powerful weapon in their own right, often resulting in much spilt blood and death.

Green Tiger was intoxicated, but no longer from fermented fruits as Colonel Memmington's wine and cognac had long since dried up. Even though it did not always reach up to the heavens, ours was an inebriation for a power much higher than anything that grew from a vine. For me in particular, I was drunk with the freedom afforded me to kill and take as many lives as I deemed necessary, a high left unchecked by the sobering effects of shame or contrition.

Similar to the manner in which the religious practices of the Stieng and the Americans came together and cavorted somewhere in the middle, me and the heavens seemed to do the same. Like many men who are entrusted with vast amounts of power and authority, I tried to rise above my mortal flesh, while at the same time pulling the divine realm down to my own temporal level.

Feasting on the forbidden fruits of the knowledge of good and evil, and my eyes opened, I became a god in the sense that I believed myself responsible for pressing the will of the divine upon the jungle and it inhabitants. But instead of doing so with displays of love and mercy, I was violent and ruthless, and would not terminate my inquisition of northeast Cambodia until every knee genuflected before me and my mission. Far from altruistic, my ministry was one of torment and death, no longer pushing outward the boundaries of God's kingdom, or even those of the American empire, but rather of my own nihilism and madness.

* * *

"*Shape without form, shade without color, paralyzed force, gesture without motion. Those who have crossed with direct eyes, to death's other Kingdom. Remember us—if at all—not as lost, violent souls, but only as the hollow men, the stuffed men.*"

"Oh, he's out there, Francis. He's out there," whispered Dennis Hopper to his director in reference to Marlon, who was sitting off to the side, meditating on another passage from T.S. Eliot's poem.

"I like that, Dennis."

"Like what, Francis?"

"The whole, 'he's out there', thing. I want you to use that when Willard first experiences Kurtz. I want you to say that to Willard."

"Oh yeah. Why?"

Dennis laughed.

"Just do it, Dennis" said Francis sternly. "Why can't you ever take direction from me? Yes, I want you to incorporate that into your initial dialogue with Captain Willard. Okay?"

"Okay, Francis. Don't get pissed. I'm just asking a question."

"I'm not pissed, Dennis. It's just that you don't seem to take anything I say serious."

"Oh, I take you serious, Francis. You're like some kind of wise guru. You are the...you have this third-eye, Francis, this third-eye that sees things, you know, it does more than envision all these worlds and realms. It creates them. Oh, I take you serious, Francis. More serious than you know."

Francis looked suspiciously at Dennis while Dennis laughed, seemingly proud of his little ode to his director.

"Dennis, don't try anything like that with Marlon, okay?"

"Why not? I've been working on one for him, Francis. Wanna hear it?" asked Dennis and then laughed.

"No, Dennis. I don't. Dennis, why do you always change the subject when I'm talking to you? I want you to work on some lines for when Willard first comes into contact with Kurtz, okay?"

"Okay, Francis, but you're not understanding me. That's what I'm talking about when I said I've been working on a little something for Marlon."

"So, you've been working on some lines for when Willard first sees Kurtz?"

"Yup."

"But I just told you to do so now. Until one minute ago, Dennis, you had no idea how Willard was going to meet Kurtz, or that I wanted you to prepare some lines in which your character is going to attempt to explain to Willard who Kurtz is, and what he's doing out here in the jungles of Cambodia."

Dennis laughed.

"That's where you're wrong, Francis."

"How so, Dennis?"

"You see...I'm in tune with you, Francis. Sometimes I think I know what you want before you do, Francis."

"Uh, huh. Okay, Dennis. So, what I want..."

"Wait, don't tell me. You want Willard's first experience of Colonel Kurtz to be of Marlon sitting and reading from a book out loud or perhaps philosophizing to a couple fucken monkeys, or something. Kurtz ignores or perhaps is oblivious to the fact that Willard is there. How am I doing so far, Francis?"

"You're doing pretty good, actually, Dennis. It's more than I got. Keep going."

"Okay, so Kurtz is sitting and reading, something heavy, something fucken deep, like that shit Marlon's been reading to himself over there. What the fuck is that stuff? Nietzsche or some shit like that? Hegel, Francis, is it Hegel?"

"It's T.S. Eliot, *The Hollow Men*."

"What does the T.S. stand for, Francis? Totally stoned?" Dennis giggled.

"As you were saying, Dennis..."

"As I was saying, Francis? What were we talking about?"

Dennis giggled.

"Kurtz is sitting and reading some heavy shit. Who's his audience, Dennis?"

"Whoever wants to fucken listen, man—me, the montagnards, the fucken walls. But I think he's really talking to himself, if you know what I mean, Francis. He's trying to figure all this shit out. So, he reads all this shit, all this heavy shit."

"Okay, I like it so far."

"And, so, Willard gets off the boat. He's escorted up to Colonel Kurtz."

"Escorted?"

"Yes, escorted up to where the colonel is."

"Why escorted?"

"Well, he's not going to simply sashay on over to Colonel Kurtz and shoot him, right Francis?" Dennis laughed. "I mean...you must have at least a little dramatic effect, don't you think?"

"So maybe Willard is taken captive by Kurtz's people. I can see that. As I mentioned to Marlon the other day, I want Willard's entrance into the Kurtz compound to be similar to that of the *Mutiny on the Bounty* thing. So, no big shoot-out or anything of that nature, but rather a slow, kind of quiet, tension-filled, clash of cultures, type of entrance. And soon thereafter Willard is taken captive, because they know what he's there to do. Now, back to what you were telling me, Dennis."

Dennis giggled.

"What?"

Dennis giggled again.

"Kurtz is reading or reciting something of a philosophical nature. Willard is brought or escorted in. From the way you described it a moment ago, Dennis, it almost sounds as if Kurtz is in effect receiving Captain Willard, or granting him an audience, if you will."

"Is that what I said? Because I don't remember quite putting it like that."

Dennis laughed.

"Never mind, Dennis," said Francis while briskly walking away.

"Hey Francis, where are you going? I got more for you. Francis? Francis?"

* * *

"Eyes I dare not meet in dreams. In death's dream kingdom these do not appear: There, the eyes are sunlight on a broken column. There is a tree swinging and voices are in the wind's singing, more distant and more solemn than a fading star. Let me be no nearer in death's dream kingdom. Let me also wear such deliberate disguises. Rat's coat, crowskin, crossed staves in a field. Behaving as the wind behaves. No nearer—not that final meeting in the twilight kingdom."

Marlon was not as enamored with this passage as he was with the first stanza of the T.S. Eliot poem, but it still intrigued him, nonetheless. He pondered it and attempted to draw out some meaning.

"Death's dream kingdom, Francis?"

"What? Death's what, Marlon?" Francis was unaware what Marlon was talking about. The star of his movie had caught him as he was passing by in a hurry, stopping him to inquire as to the meaning of the second stanza of Eliot's poem.

"Death's dream kingdom, Francis. What is Eliot talking about?"

Francis was not as familiar with the poem as Marlon perhaps thought he was.

"Uh, I don't know, Marlon. Read me the passage," said Francis, trying to be accommodating.

"Something about 'in death's dream kingdom'. I don't know what that means."

"Well, I'm not really sure either, Marlon." Francis scratched his head, trying to figure out what to say to Marlon. "The thing about poetry, Marlon, is that it's open to interpretation."

"Yeah, but I'm sure that T.S. Eliot had something specific in mind when he wrote these words."

"I'm sure he did, Marlon. But I don't know what that is, and I don't know anybody here who is a T.S. Eliot expert. Find your own meaning."

"How would you interpret it, Francis?"

Francis sighed.

"I really have a lot of shit to do, Marlon. I don't have time to read and analyze poems."

Marlon was taken aback my Francis' curtness. He didn't understand why Francis seemingly had all the time in the world for him on certain occasions, while other times he could not spare but a moment. Marlon felt like a child. The brief episode reminded Marlon of his father who would one moment, perhaps feeling guilty, pay attention to him, promising they would do things and go places together, and then the next minute turn into somebody else, incessantly chiding and chastising him. Marlon has always loved and respected Francis, but in that moment the director reminded him a little too much of his father. It was not just what Francis said or the tone of his voice that made Marlon think of his father, but also the dismissive look in his eyes, a pair of eyes that Marlon usually found comfort in, which made Francis' sudden indifference all the more hurtful.

But there was more going on than just Marlon feeling slighted by his director. Marlon was experiencing a surge of old, and even unpleasant memories rushing back to him. Not only were certain unhappy moments with his volatile father suddenly very vivid and clear to Marlon, but also hurtful recollections of his distant, drunken mother. The pain and isolation of living in a dysfunctional house with two alcoholic parents who could not stand one another, often taking it out on their kids, as well as the repressive Bible-belt culture of Omaha, Nebraska, was again descending hard upon Marlon, covering him with a blanket of fear and insecurity.

"That smell? What is that I smell?" asked Marlon to one of the stage-hands who was passing by. The man stopped for a moment to discern what Marlon was talking about.

"You mean the smoke? The smell of smoke?"

"Yeah, I guess so."

"It's some brush or something. Mr. Coppola wanted some smoke in order to give the compound a kind of hazy look. I'm not sure what it is they're burning, though. Everything is so green that it's not burning very well, I can tell you that much."

"It smells just like the fall leaf fires in the neighborhood where I grew up," said Marlon.

When Marlon was growing up in Nebraska, every year, on some undetermined fall evening, everyone in Marlon's neighborhood would burn the leaves they had raked. Marlon's would usually be the last house to rake their leaves, and his father would always take it out on Marlon and his sister. When all the other families would begin burning their piles of leaves, Marlon's father would make him and his sister go out and rake the yard as fast as they could while he, usually drunk, yelled at them in front of all the neighbors in an attempt to exonerate himself. Marlon's father would then be one of the last fathers in the neighborhood standing out there burning leaves. Marlon would look out his bedroom window and see his father's black silhouette against the fire light. A rake and sometimes even a pitch-fork in hand, Marlon thought his father looked like Satan standing there. Later, his father would come in the house, smelling of smoke and soot, yelling and screaming at his children one more time before going off to drink himself into a stupor.

 Marlon desperately wanted to confide in the stage-hand about the abuse he endured from his father, but decided to say nothing, fearing that any revelations he may offer up would not be held in confidence. Marlon laughed at himself, his vanity. He realized he was really more worried about his image than he was about his own mental and emotional health. This is how it has been all his life. Marlon always tried to be somebody he was not, someone who was perfect, for his parents, for wives and lovers, and for Hollywood and fans of Hollywood. He always hid the boy who had been so wounded by his father and mother, smothering the child deep inside himself with a complex and multi-layered persona. Marlon's different alter-egos—from super hunk to weirdo—served as a shield to protect him. Marlon never really identified with any of them. The real Marlon was sensitive and someone who cared for others, the poor and marginalized, and especially those who had been picked on by bullies, as he had been by his father. The neglect he received from his mother was perhaps even more painful for Marlon. At least his father would acknowledge him, unlike his mother who would simply numb herself and stare at the wall for hours at a time, not wanting to be bothered by her children.

CHAPTER 40

It would be a mistake to believe that Green Tiger was simply an army or military unit ripping its way through the jungle, killing in big bombastic fits of rage and destruction. On the contrary, much like the Serpent in the Garden, we were subtle, blending into our surroundings as if an outgrowth of the green vegetation.

In addition to the primitive weaponry, we dug holes in the ground and filled them with poison-tipped bamboo shards that killed in a slow, agonizing manner. And from high atop the trees we dropped nets made of vine onto unsuspecting Vietcong migrating southward. But unlike the North Vietnamese who were impaled on the bamboo and simply left there to die, those becoming entangled in the mesh netting would be hacked and clubbed to death with machetes as they struggled to free themselves from the green web that ensnared them.

This methodical approach gave Father McDuffee the opportunity to closely observe the Stieng as they conducted themselves in these intense conditions. He soon came to realize, evidenced by visual observations made upon investigating certain noises coming from the bush, that the Stieng were sodomizing one another. The Catholic priest was not sure if this was normal behavior for their culture, or an aberration caused by the long absence away from the female counterparts of their tribe. Either way, its continuation eventually began to affect Father McDuffee in a manner that he never expected. Initially he did not make an attempt to put a stop to this activity even though the grunts, shrills, and orgasmic cries of the copulating Stieng reverberated inside his head every night, even after the Stieng had stopped making them. Father McDuffee's faith told him this was a sin against God, but that was not what bothered the priest most about these acts taking place in the darkness.

 The object of affection for many of the Stieng was a certain strikingly beautiful young warrior. On the whole, these Stieng were a rough and grizzled lot, their faces aged and scarred by a lifetime of battling their fellow man and nature's elements. But this particular boy still basked in the springtime of his youth. Only slightly effeminate, he possessed a boyish charisma poised to burst him into manhood. His brown skin covered a thin layer of baby fat, giving his otherwise ectomorphic body a smooth appearance, while his unblemished face wore haunting big brown eyes, full burgundy lips, and a small nose that turned slightly upwards.

 The Stieng may have been at peace with their sexual desires for one other, but Father McDuffee was not. The amorous thoughts that began to fill his head as he listened to the pretty, young boy bring himself and others to climax eventually became too much for him. One night the priest charged in and demanded that they stop these "unholy acts," as he called them. The Stieng paid no heed.

Actually seeing the images that he had been fantasizing about only served to expound upon Father McDuffee's growing desire for the boy. In an attempt to cleanse his mind of these abhorrent thoughts, Father McDuffee picked up a taut branch from off the ground and walked about twenty yards away from the Stieng. There he pulled his robe down to his waist, fell to his knees and proceeded to lash himself across the back until the lustful yearnings were gone from his mind. This was only a temporary fix to his problem, however, as the increasing frequency in which he would need to perform this remedy would indicate.

Soon Father McDuffee began seeing the Stieng in an entirely different light. They were no longer God's 'primitive' children, but rather daemons put there to tempt and lure him into their bottomless pit of carnality and sick lust. His emotions would race back and forth across a broad and complex spectrum. One end was grounded in an intense loathing for the Stieng as a whole, the other in deep desire for the young Stieng warrior. Neither prayer nor self-inflicted beatings seemed to stabilize his ongoing, tumultuous ride from one end to the other. The priest resorted to masturbation, and even contemplated castration. His powerlessness to cease committing the latter act was almost as discouraging to him as was his inability to perform the former.

The beautiful young Stieng warrior initially reminded Father McDuffee of a young King David as described in the Jewish Scriptures and portrayed by Italian artists. He saw in him a certain charisma and knew he would someday be a great leader of his people. But now the Irishman could no longer see past the boy's exquisite exterior. And even though nobody understands the concept that all things of this world eventually fade away, especially beauty, more than this Catholic priest, the ravages of time were not working fast enough for Father McDuffee. He could no longer stand to look at the young boy. The comely warrior's full lips and mouth, golden brown skin, often exposed phallic, and firm backside coupled with Father McDuffee's inflamed desire for these things nearly drove him insane.

Father McDuffee agonized for weeks trying to find a solution to this problem. He was too embarrassed to confide in a fellow mortal regarding his angst, and for some reason God was not answering him as of late. So the priest waited, hoping it would pass, but it never did. Under normal circumstances, Father McDuffee probably would have requested a transfer to someplace else, away from the object of his personal torment that he was unable to overcome. But there was no way out of the jungle for him now.

In his desperation, Father McDuffee began to wrestle with the idea of actually killing the boy, finding it even harder to now stave off two urges as opposed to just one. Sure in the fact that one of them would eventually win out, the Father decided that taking the boy's life was the lesser of two evils, fearing that if he broke his vow of chastity he may end up killing the boy anyway. Better to kill the Stieng warrior now to avoid committing two mortal sins, he reasoned.

Father McDuffee waited for a night when the Stieng were engaged in one of their gluttonous ceremonies, gorging themselves with wild boar, sex, and the fermented juices from various jungle fruits that abounded everywhere. He watched to see in which direction the boy walked off to occasionally urinate. A pattern developed and the priest positioned himself accordingly. Eventually, the boy stepped away from the festivities and Father McDuffee walked out of the bush to join up with him. The young Stieng warrior had been aware of the priest's inner consternation, and assumed Father McDuffee's clumsy attempt to lure him further into the jungle to be an indication that he was giving in to his desires of the flesh. The boy went along, willing to oblige if this was indeed the case.

  As Father McDuffee led the boy down a narrow pathway he suddenly became extremely nervous and uncertain as to exactly what was going to transpire. The priest was initially very sure in what he planned to do until he saw the boy's beautiful naked body. Watching his bare buttocks as he walked in front of him, Father McDuffee began to waver at this very fateful moment. He needed more time but the boy suddenly stopped, deeming they were far enough away, turning around to face the Irishman. The boy leaned into Father McDuffee and kissed him. The priest kissed him back while firmly grabbing the young Stieng warrior's butt cheeks. These were sensations the likes he had never experienced before. For the first time in his life Father McDuffee felt like he was living and not dying, something his God was rarely able to do for him. The boy then turned around, bending over slightly, offering his backside. Father McDuffee looked up at the heavens then back down at the boy as if trying to make up his mind at this late hour. The stars looked cold and impersonal, while the boy was warm and enticing. He was right there, attainable, within his reach, while the heavens were millions of miles away, a place that deep down the priest did not really think he would ever get to anyway. As the boy looked over his left shoulder to see what was holding up his would-be sodomizer, Father McDuffee pulled a knife out from under his robe, cutting the boy's throat from left to right. He clutched tightly to his victim, helping him descend slowly until the body lay limp and lifeless on the jungle floor. The beautiful Stieng boy who may or may not have become a great king of his people was dead. Father McDuffee remained kneeling over the boy and began to weep. Not for the young Stieng warrior, but over the fact he broke the sixth commandment. Father McDuffee had killed, and at that moment it seemed to bother him more than any of his impure thoughts for the boy ever did. He cried for himself and his sin-ridden body that proved to be all too human.

As soon as the sounds of distant drumming snapped him from his inward reflection, Father McDuffee began to once again think like a cold-blooded killer rather than a repentant sinner. The priest would pray for God's forgiveness later. He was more concerned at the moment with the wrath of his fellow man. Father McDuffee picked up the body and ran with it through the moon-lit jungle until he could no longer hear the drumming. There he threw it into the brush and once again fell to his knees to cry over what he had done.

The entire next day the Stieng searched for the missing boy while Father McDuffee sat by himself, trembling, as well as praying that they did not find the body. He could not bear the thought of seeing the dead boy again. These prayers God must have answered because the young Stieng warrior would not be found. By nightfall Green Tiger was once again on the move, minus the beautiful young Stieng warrior.

Father McDuffee would become very sullen and distant, resembling more of an anchor slowing Green Tiger down rather than the sails that propelled them as he once was. The spirit of the dead boy tortured him more than his living flesh ever did. With each passing day the distraught priest added another chapter to the 'Davidic' stories about the boy that he kept logged in his head, ones that he somehow came to believe would have been the young Stieng warrior's destiny should he have lived. Father McDuffee now spent his days trying to give the boy life through his daydreams that analogized and paralleled the life of the great Hebrew king with that of the unrealized greatness of the young boy.

Day after day, inside his mind that had become remote of the world around him, Father McDuffee would recreate the Davidic scriptures of the Old Testament with the beautiful Stieng warrior playing the role of King David. His military conquests and pious love of God were exaggerated beyond the ancient Hebrew accounts, making his premature death all the more tragic. Father McDuffee would constantly weep for the warrior-king the world would never know. Maybe this was his way of justifying his earlier love for the boy, a way of making it pure—killing the boy and his own sinful avarice, then building both back up in a manner he could better understand. Whatever the reason for his continued interest in the boy, it remained for him a heavy, guilt-laden cross that Father McDuffee seemed more than willing to drag through the jungle mud, a self-imposed penance for his sins.

* * *

"This is the dead land. This is cactus land. Here the stone images are raised. Here they receive the supplication of a dead man's hand under the twinkle of a fading star. Is it like this in death's other kingdom? Waking alone at the hour when we are trembling with tenderness. Lips that would kiss form prayers to broken stone."

This passage of Eliot's poem fell on Marlon's mind, memory and imagination like a massive boulder. It encapsulated his childhood, his early days as an actor, and even his middle and later years of life. The whole thing resonated, but Marlon focused himself on the first line.

"This is the dead land. This is cactus land!"

Marlon mumbled these words to himself, drawing the attention of a few of the stage-hands who were in his general vicinity, all unaware as to what he was saying.

"Here the stone images are raised."

Even as a child Marlon felt as if American culture and American society were drab and lifeless. Life there, whether it was Nebraska, Illinois, Minnesota or California, always seemed contrived to Marlon, as if everybody is simply going through the motions. Marlon likened American culture to that of a society of actors, with everybody playing a role, pretending to be happy, pretending that there is some kind of meaning to their life. He came to consider this even more as an adult living in Los Angeles. Everybody there was fake. Nobody was who they pretended to be. Marlon has always believed he had a special kind of intuition which enabled him to see through the façade that everybody was trying to convey. He never accepted it when people pretended to be happy and self-actualized. Marlon believed he could see their loneliness, their pain, suffering and isolation. But it was during the filming of *Mutiny on the Bounty* and his experience with the Tahitian people and Tahitian culture that everything he always suspected to be true about American society was solidly confirmed to him.

"*The dead land. This is the cactus land,*" mumbled Marlon.

* * *

The Stieng's allegiance, initially split evenly between myself and the priest, had now shifted completely and wholly over to me. Father McDuffee had gone from spewing verbal fire and brimstone to talking softly of such things as repentance and atonement. Me and my urgency to kill the Vietnamese was a language they could better understand. With or without Father McDuffee's consent, however, the killing machine would continue to march, giving him no other choice but to follow. Down through the deepest, darkest reaches of the jungle we would go, searching for our elusive enemy. Green Tiger would continue to travel down a slow taper, not realizing the low altitude that we descended until finding ourselves steeped in a continuous fog, one that would only dissipate for a few hours during the afternoon, as sunlight and wind were a rare commodity down there.

As we moved deeper and deeper into the bowels of the jungle, Green Tiger began hearing what sounded to us like torturous cries and wails echoing off the thousands of fir trees standing only feet apart.

Although the air was humid and permeated with water, it still coveted the moisture that the members of Green Tiger carried inside our bodies, squeezing it from our pores then licking the salty moisture from our skin. Dehydration became more of a concern for Green Tiger than malaria or dysentery, forcing us to drink from any source of water that we could find.

With each day that passed came a lower elevation as well as less and less light. Becoming more abundant were the huge flocks of crows that flew back and forth, their loud squawks becoming almost unbearable to us when directly overhead. They also filled the trees, their presence most noticeable on the leafless, dead timber that was becoming more prominent as well. Thousands of crows would sit stoically on the lifeless limbs until something cajoled them from their roost, taking to the sky and forming an ominous black cloud with their sheer volume, screaming wildly and dropping an enormous amount of fecal matter onto the ground below.

There was so little light that I did not even notice I had been walking past a plethora of decomposed bodies, most of which had been picked clean by the crows, the remains covered in jungle vine.

Although ripe with the remnants of grotesque butchery and torture, the area had been abandoned of its occupants. I walked among the dead who were silent, yet screamed of the violent, horrible deaths they succumbed to.

"Godless savages!" I announced of whomever was responsible for the vast and varied carnage. "These must be Cambodians, huh Father? Killed by those animals right in their very own country!" I said this while waving my arm in a circular motion, giving indication as to the extent of the slaughter.

It was late morning. The sky was dark and a soft mist was filtering its way through the jungle canopy and onto this place of many heinous deeds.

"These must be Cambodians, huh, Father?" I said again, but much louder than the first time.

"I would suppose," said the priest, sounding tired.

"Well, sure they are, and it was the VC who did this,"

I said harshly in his direction, trying to get his attention.

"Look at this shit, Father McDuffee. What we need to do is parade all the God-damn war protesters and card-carrying communists living in America through this hell-hole and say, 'look what your godless heroes in Hanoi have done.' I would take each and every one of them, just like when the Germans were forced to walk through the extermination camps after World War II. Remember that Father? I would put their face down right into this fucken shit and say, look! Look at your fucken communism…"

"And another angel came out from the altar, which had power over fire; and cried with a loud cry to him that had the sharp sickle, saying, thrust in thy sharp sickle, and gather the cluster of the vine of the earth; for her grapes are finally ripe," read Father McDuffee from a book he found in a half-burned shelter. He was on his feet and boisterous, much like he used to be, catching the eyes and ears of myself and the Stieng who stopped what we were doing to watch and listen.

"And the angel thrust in his sickle into the earth, and gathered the vine of the earth, and cast it into the great winepress of the wrath of God."

He then slammed the book shut and pointed at some stone carvings that we had both seen before.

"This is Artemis!" proclaimed Father McDuffee in a manner that scolded, reminiscent of God pointing the way out of the Garden of Eden for Adam and Eve.

As it turned out, I was partly right in my initial assessment that this place was witness to a prolonged holocaust. Most of these people were in fact Cambodians, and its end-result was from some sort of insanity gone unchecked. But what I could not see from first glance was that there was actually some sort of method or purpose to this madness. Its architects were people whose fear of God was unwittingly eclipsed by their jealousy of God, a people who found their way into this dark pit of the jungle to escape the rigid constraints placed on them by both God and the civilization from whence they came. There, in the darkness, living wild and free in the wilderness, they were able to shape and form their God into something that possessed the same weaknesses and imperfections as they did. The worship of this 'god' was in reality a worshipping of our own selves, more specifically, our own primordial instincts and blood lust, spilling it out onto ourselves and everything around us.

I had been leading Strapinski, Edwards, LeBetre, Wilke, Henderson, the Jarai, Father McDuffee, and the Stieng on Western civilization's thousand-year journey to find God's lost paradise, but instead I found my own personal hell.

In light of my earlier self-righteous tirade about the perpetrators of this carnage, I did not say anything else. I instead walked around quietly, carefully observing my surroundings, taking my time before casting a second round of judgment. I studied the faces that were void of both flesh and facial expression, making them appear as if indifferent to their fate. I was certainly aware that me and Green Tiger were in fact responsible for much death and carnage in the last couple years, but it was always in our wake, something we would leave behind us, quickly moving forward to bring about more death and carnage. I had even lived alongside the sight and stench of Green Tiger's prolonged killing spree, impervious and undaunted. But I never actually walked *into* the aftermath of what we had done.

Despite the fact that I was at this moment seeing for the first time the end-result of the bodycount strategy, I, at least for now, maintained my nerve as well as my resolve as I walked around Artemis. I eventually came across a few of the Jarai who were in effect mummified by the flames that melted their flesh into an almost plastic-like coating that seemed to stave off both the crows and further decomposition. Many lay in the same fetal position they curled themselves into during their final seconds of life, their faces permanently bearing the expression of intolerable horror and pain.

I looked up at the sky, able to see the dark gray clouds through the opening where the napalm had been dropped on top of the jungle to destroy the Jarai, burning the tops of the trees, killing much of the green canopy but not all. It made me think of a giant hand reaching down from the heavens, pulling just hard enough to strip the leaves off the trees between its fingers. I listened for the sounds of artillery or machine gun fire off in the distance. I heard none, making me wonder if the war was even still going on. Green Tiger had been without a radio for almost two months. In that time our only concern was to cut a hole through the underbelly of the jungle, slaughtering its remaining vestiges of life, hoping that when we came out the other side, victory would be waiting for us. Victory was not what we found, however, if in fact this is the other side.

   Forgotten was my life back home. My home now, as it had been for almost two years, consisted of only my enemies—the jungle and the North Vietnamese communists—who became one and the same as far as I was concerned. To kill the jungle would be to kill the North Vietnamese, or so I surmised. But I have been unable to kill the jungle, managing only to kill my God, which was no great feat considering that Western civilization has done this countless of times in the last fifteen-hundred years.

CHAPTER 41

"I think the first thing Kurtz says to Willard is to ask him where he's from."

"Where he's from, Marlon? Why?"

"I think it creates a contrast."

Francis waited for Marlon to elaborate.

"A contrast?"

"Yeah. A contrast between where Willard is from, and Kurtz for that matter, compared to the place they are in now—the Cambodian jungle during the Vietnam War. Willard tells Kurtz where he's from, and then Kurtz can perhaps wax nostalgically a little bit about where he was born and raised. I just think that it would create this moment in which they both are momentarily transported back to a time and place much different than the one they are now in."

"I like that, Marlon. Let's try it and see how it works."

About an hour later Marlon's first scene as Colonel Kurtz would begin.

As Colonel Kurtz made his first appearance in the movie, Francis was just off to the side, ready to prompt his star actor, a tactic they employed during the making of *The Godfather* movie.

"Wipe the water off of your head with your hands, slowly and methodically. Slowly and methodically. Yes. Like that. Now look at Willard. Stare at him hard. You are a man of great authority. You are a colonel. You are an intimidating man. You know things that most people cannot even fathom. You can stare anybody down. You fear nobody. Wait...wait...wait...hold the stare. Now, calmly ask him."

"Where are you from, Willard?"
"I'm from Ohio, sir."
"Were you born there?"
"Yes, sir."
"Whereabouts?"
"Toledo, sir."
"How far were you from the river?"
"The Ohio River, sir? About two-hundred miles."
"I went down that river when I was a kid. There's a place in the river...I can't remember...must have been a gardenia plantation at one time. All wild and overgrown now, but about five miles you'd think that heaven just fell on the earth in the form of gardenias."
"Okay. Cut. Nice work, Marlon."

* * *

Considering that there was no real script or canned dialogue, Francis decided that it would be better to simply let Marlon and Martin Sheen ad lib their lines instead of shutting the set down yet again to develop and create dialogue. Marlon seemed to like this idea while Martin Sheen was skeptical.

"I've seen horrors...horrors that you've seen. But you have no right to call me a murderer. You have a right to kill me. You have a right to do that. But you have no right to judge me."

"Okay, nice, Marlon," said Francis softly in response to his lead actor's spontaneous line. "Now talk about horror," prompted the director.

"What?"

"Talk about horror. Give some insight into Kurtz's philosophy on war."

There was a long pause as Marlon Brando thought about what he wanted to say, what he wanted to tell the American people and the world, something that they did not yet know, something that would shock and jolt them out of their middle-class malaise. He took a deep breath and then began.

"It's impossible for words to describe what is necessary for those who do not know what horror means. Horror. Horror has a face, and you must make a friend of horror. Horror and moral terror are your friends. If they are not then they are enemies to be feared. They are truly enemies."

"Give us an example, Marlon," prodded his director from off on the side.

Again, there was a pause.

"I remember when I was with Special Forces...seems a thousand centuries ago. We went into a camp to inoculate the children. We left the camp after we had inoculated the children for polio, and this old man came running after us and he was crying. He couldn't say. We went back there and they had come and hacked off every inoculated arm. There they were in a pile...a pile of little arms. And I remember...I...I...I cried...I wept like some grandmother. I wanted to tear my teeth out. I didn't know what I wanted to do. And I want to remember it. I never want to forget it. I never want to forget. And then I realized...like I was shot...like I was shot with a diamond...a diamond bullet right through my forehead. And I thought: My God...the genius of that. The genius. The will to do that! Perfect, genuine, complete, crystalline, pure. And then I realized they were stronger than we, because they could stand that these were not monsters. These were men—trained cadres—these men who fought with their hearts, who had families, who had children, who were filled with love...but they had the strength...the strength...to do that. If I had ten divisions of those men our troubles here would be over very quickly. You have to have men who are moral...and at the same time who are able to utilize their primordial instincts to kill without feeling...without passion...without judgment...without judgment. Because it's judgment that defeats us."

When Marlon was finished he quickly broke character, seemingly satisfied with the point he had just conveyed, and was apparently done for the day as he walked off the set with the crew and some of the cast looking on in awe.

"That's why I got Marlon Brando for the part," bragged Francis to those close enough to hear him.

CHAPTER 42

"The eyes are not here. There are no eyes here in this valley of dying stars, in this hollow valley, this broken jaw of our lost kingdoms. In this last of meeting places we grope together and avoid speech. Gathered on this beach of the tumid river, sightless, unless the eyes reappear as the perpetual star multifoliate rose. Of death's twilight kingdom, the hope only of empty men."

Marlon, emboldened by his recent ad lib victory, read this passage from Eliot's poem louder than the other ones. He had a certain swagger in both his voice and body language, knowing he had given everybody a taste of The Great Marlon Brando. Marlon was at the same time thrilled and disgusted by this. On the one hand, it made him more self-confidant and even arrogant. On the other hand, this was the very thing he was trying to distance himself from. Marlon no longer wanted the fact that he was such a "good liar", as he liked to put it, to be the reason why people loved and respected him so much.

* * *

"Marlon, I like the fact that we have Marty Sheen playing the man who is sent to kill Kurtz, and kill you for that matter, and for more reasons than one." Francis was hoping his statement would seem obvious to Marlon, and that he would not have to elaborate too much.

He was wrong.

"I'm not following you, Francis."

"Marty is kind of from that younger generation of actors, along with James Dean, who were supposed to supplant you, Marlon, as Hollywood's biggest actor."

"Marty is much younger than James Dean would be."

"Well, a few years, maybe about ten. I don't know for sure. Whatever. But what is for certain is that Marty Sheen, in his younger years, was inspired by James Dean. In fact, in the movie *Badlands*, Marty is in effect playing James Dean, striking many of the same poses that James Dean made famous."

"Francis, I like Marty Sheen a lot, and respect him as an actor, but to compare him to James Dean...I'm not so sure about that."

"He's a little older now, Marlon, yes, but a few years ago he was considered very much of a James Dean-inspired actor, and perhaps was the one carrying the torch of James Dean for a few years there. I remember that in *The California Kid* movie he was even advertised as being 'James Dean-ish', or 'James Dean-like'."

"I didn't want to be compared to anybody, and I wasn't, if I remember right. And James Dean was compared to me."

"And Marty Sheen was compared to James Dean. You see, Marlon, the circle is complete."

"Well, again, I didn't want to be compared to anybody."
"You were compared to Olivier, but only in terms of who was the better actor.

You, Marlon, were the first of your kind. You were the first to do that whole rebel, leather jacket, motorcycle riding, tough guy thing."

"So, why is it fitting that Marty Sheen is the one to kill me?"

"Because he is from the line of young actors who wanted what you had. He wanted to be you."

"No, he wanted to be James Dean."

"And James Dean wanted to be you." You see, Marlon, it works with our parallel plot we are developing—this whole dying god thing. And I'm not implying that Marty Sheen is the one to replace you as Hollywood's greatest actor, but he is kind of from that generation. I know he came a little after James Dean, but he's definitely in the mold of James Dean and a young Marlon Brando."

"Yes, I can see what you're talking about, Francis. And I too am glad it's Marty who is playing this part. I don't think I could stand the idea of that fuck-head, Harvey Keitel, killing me."

Marlon and Francis looked at one another and laughed.

"Well, he's long gone, Marlon."

"Good thing, too. He's worse than Hopper."

"Really? You think so? Well, it's a good thing we cut him loose, then, because there's no way you could have handled a movie-set with both Dennis Hopper and Harvey Keitel on it."

"Nope. I would have been gone."

"Well, that's one thing I've done right out here, then."

* * *

"They were going to make me a major for this and I wasn't even in their fucking army any more. Everybody wanted me to do it, him most of all. I felt like he was up there, waiting for me to take the pain away. He just wanted to go out like a soldier, standing up. Not like some poor, wasted, rag-assed renegade. Even the jungle wanted him dead, and that's who he really took his orders from anyway."

"Excellent, Marty, excellent," said Martin Sheen's satisfied director upon the completion of the narrative that would be inserted right before Captain Willard killed Colonel Kurtz.

Later that evening Francis would play Martin Sheen's narrative back for Marlon. Francis was just as pleased with Marlon's reaction as he was with Martin Sheen's actual words and narration. Marlon really seemed to like the things said by Captain Willard, and this could not have made Francis happier.

"That's exactly how I feel, Francis. I am in effect waiting for somebody to come and take my pain away. I like what Marty says about wanting to 'go out standing up, not like some poor, wasted, rag-ass renegade', even though I do feel like one."

"Yeah, I like that too, for Marlon Brando and for Walter Kurtz. Tell me, Marlon, why is it important that Marlon Brando and Walter Kurtz go out standing up, so to speak?"

"Well, personally, I would like to end this particular portion of my career on a high note, but at the same time sending a message, or something to that effect. Maybe *statement* is a better word. Yes, *statement*. I would like to make a statement, some kind of a political, professional, and even a personal statement."

"Say more, Marlon."

"I would like this movie, this point in time, to mark a sort of transition, both in my career as an actor and in my personal life. I want this movie, and this role, to be what I wanted so desperately for many of my other movies to be. I want both—the movie and my role—to say something important, to make some kind of statement."

"But what if both—your performance and the movie—are panned by the critics and ignored by the movie-going public? Then what?"

Marlon paused.

"It won't matter."

"Yes, it will matter, Marlon. It always matters. We can say that. We can lie to ourselves and say that it doesn't matter, but the truth is that at the end of the day it does matter. If the critics hate the movie and nobody comes and sees it, then it's all a big fucken failure. You see what I'm saying?"

"Yes, but *we* will know we did something great and profound."

"But you did great and profound things with many of your other movies, things that nobody else cared about or understood. The critics hated them, and nobody came to see them. Was that good enough for you in those instances? Probably not, right?"

Marlon gave Francis an inconclusive look.

"Marlon, this movie has to be a major success..."

"Yeah, yeah, Francis, I know," interrupted Marlon. "But once it's in the can and delivered to the studio, it's out of our hands. In the meantime, all we can do, Francis, is try to make a good product. I've been involved in far too many failures to be so optimistic. You, my friend, have not tasted failure as often as I have. But nonetheless, I want this movie, and my role as Kurtz, to make a bold, profound statement, politically, and professionally for me as an actor. And let the chips fall where they may, Francis."

"Yeah, I guess you're right, Marlon. I just don't want to even think about the possibility that this movie will fail, at the box office, or in regard to the message we are trying to convey, whatever the hell that is."

"Nor do I, Francis. I want people to take away from this movie a different understanding of the history of the world, especially the history of the Western world since about 1492, and of the United States. But at the same time, I also see this as an end to the first half of my career, and a beginning of a new and different era for Marlon Brando," said Marlon in a matter-of-fact sort of way.

"You're not asking for much, are you, Marlon?"

"What I mean, or what I'm trying to say, is that I want to give a non-Western perspective of the Vietnam War, of the Cold War, even. And I would like it to be a kind of starting point or lynch-pin for a new kind of non-Western-centric understanding or viewpoint of that war, in the United States. I'm so damn tired of the fucken 1950s, American-centric world-view that people still have, and that America is the Kingdom of God, and all that bullshit."

CHAPTER 43

I looked around at what used to be Artemis. I could see the Stieng fighting over various items they were pulling from out of the rubble such as empty ammunition boxes, forks, and spoons. Father McDuffee was on his knees praying, his hands folded together just under his chin. I briefly scavenged for a radio as I watched the Stieng loot the place and each other like petty thieves. I hesitated before doing so, but eventually walked over to the priest who was still engaged in intense prayer.

"Our Father, who art in heaven, hallowed be thy name…"

"How do we get out of here," I asked the priest.

"…thy kingdom come, thy will be done on earth as it is in heaven. He who plows iniquity and sows wickedness reaps the same," said Father McDuffee, interrupting his prayer to quote from the Book of Job. "We don't," he added, answering my question. "Give us this day our daily bread, forgive us our trespasses, and deliver us from evil. For Thine is the kingdom and the power and the glory, now and forever, amen."

Father McDuffee continued reciting the Lord's Prayer, ignoring me while I stood there at his side, despite making it quite obvious I wanted to speak to him. I had to instead settle for watching him pray the same prayer over and over again. Father McDuffee acknowledged my presence only one more time, giving me a look that indicated he thought I should join him. With some trepidation I obliged the Catholic priest, sinking to my knees before the very God we both had blasphemed into a dark shade of crimson by transubstantiating the sacramental wine back into blood. Recent events have sobered both of us and our various lusts, however. Having bled our God white, me and Father McDuffee, together on bended knee, tried in vain to squeeze our dead King of one last drop of reclamation.

After ten minutes and twenty 'Our Fathers', I gave up. My God seemed as hollow and void of life as I was, and something as quiet and indirect as prayer was no longer enough to fill either of us back up. I had taken myself and my God too far. Having felt the ecstasy of godliness for myself, I could not now go back to that of a mortal man limited by such human emotions as fear and guilt, the very things pressing me into the jungle mud at that moment as if an intense gravity.

I stood off to the side as Father McDuffee dug down deep into the very pit of his soul, searching for a small spark of that once mighty flame. The Catholic priest looked pathetic to my weary eyes, clutching his crucifix, begging and pleading with nobody but himself to once again find enlightenment and saving grace in the man the ancient world first killed on a cross and then worshipped on a celestial throne. Together me and Father McDuffee carried our dead King with us everywhere we went in the Cambodian jungle, but our enemy would not bow before the divine corpse. For this was not his kingdom. We tried to revive him with pig's blood, the blood of our enemy, wine, as well as intoxicating words, but our efforts proved futile. Eventually we grew tired of dragging our dead King through the jungle, leaving the impotent God behind, becoming wild and free to chase after our own divinity, something that in the end proved to be only an apparition. Now we have returned to the side of our dead King and God, imploring his forgiveness, beseeching him to save us.

"Our father who art in heaven, hallowed be thy name. Thy kingdom come, thy will be done on earth as it is in heaven…" continued the priest.

* * *

"Here we go round the prickly pear, prickly pear, prickly pear. Here we go round the prickly pear at five o'clock in the morning. Between the idea and the reality, between the motion and the act, falls the Shadow, for Thine is the Kingdom. Between the conception and the creation. Between the emotion and the response falls the Shadow. Life is very long. Between the desire and the spasm, between the potency and the existence, between the essence and the descent, falls the Shadow. For Thine is the Kingdom. This is the way the world ends. This is the way the world ends. This is the way the world ends. Not with a bang but a whimper."

Marlon had mixed-emotions about this final passage from Eliot's poem. He liked how it talked about things beginning and ending, rising and falling, the symbolism of an encroaching 'Shadow' that blackens the created order, and a loosely defined concept referred to as 'the Kingdom'. Marlon liked the tension between permanence and impermanence, and wondered which one the ambiguous 'Shadow' or darkness—the end of all things—represented. He also wondered if Eliot's mention of 'the Kingdom' was in reference to the pre- or post-Shadow world. More specifically, Marlon wanted to know if Eliot was implying that the impermanent world of life is the Kingdom, or that the permanent world of death is the Kingdom. What Marlon did not like, however, is that the end would come, not with a bang, but a whimper. Marlon wanted this movie, his role as Kurtz, and the movie's ending, to be a bang, not a whimper. He wanted the death of Kurtz, the end of this part of his life and career, and the ending of the movie for that matter, to be a definitive bang, something that marks a distinct and conclusive end to all these things, something that will jolt people out of their complacency and make them think in an entirely different way.

CHAPTER 44

"We're thinking that Willard will kill Kurtz with a machete, Marlon. It will be a kind of primitive-style butchery. Kurtz has hearkened back to his primordial instincts, not that he has abandoned modern weaponry by any means because he and his men use and rely on machine guns and bombs and all that shit. But because much of the message here is primordial, something primitive like a machete would say more and be more telling than to have Willard come in and blow him away with a gun. What do you think of that, Marlon?"

Marlon was a bit overwhelmed and said nothing.

"It will be primal and bloody. Willard will in effect sneak up on Kurtz, kind of like he is hunting him or something, and he will proceed to quite literally hack him to death. It will be violent, bloody, and startling."

Marlon seemed to be taken aback a bit by Francis' explanation of Kurtz's impending death, perhaps because he was personalizing it with himself and the expiration of the young Marlon Brando.

"Marlon, do you think Willard should catch Kurtz by surprise, or does Kurtz see him coming? And if Kurtz sees Willard coming, does he attempt to fight him off or does he accept what's coming?"

Marlon thought for a moment.

"What's the difference?"

Marlon was getting weary of discussing and trying to formulate the plot of the movie, among other things.

"What's the difference? Are you kidding me? Marlon, it makes a lot of difference. Here's what I think. I think that Kurtz knows Willard is coming, and he sees him coming. And Willard doesn't even try to hide the fact he's coming for Kurtz, because Kurtz has been telling him, through his monologues and stories, that he wants somebody, perhaps Willard, to kill him, and Willard understands this. That's why Willard says that Kurtz is up there, 'waiting for someone to take his pain away'. Kurtz knows that at some point Willard is going to kill him. Willard, for his part, respects Kurtz to a certain extent, as a man and an officer. And because of this, he respects Kurtz' desire to die, and his desire to go out standing up, literally and metaphorically. So even though Willard stalks and hunts Kurtz, it's really a matter of Willard, being the soldier that he is, wanting to be professional about it. And so even though we will make a certain something of Willard stalking Kurtz, Willard will give Kurtz the opportunity to stand up so he can literally die on his feet."

"Okay, when you put it like that, it makes a certain amount of sense to me."

"Are you okay with that, Marlon?"

"Yes. It all sounds good to me, I guess."

"If you're apprehensive, or don't like something, Marlon, please tell me now and we can work through it. I detect a slight bit of doubt in your voice. So, if there's anything at all you would like to add, please let me know now."

Marlon thought for a few seconds.

"I'm concerned about the whole machete thing."

"The machete thing, Marlon?"

"I'm concerned about how realistic it's going to look."

"How realistic do you want it to look?"

"Realistic enough to look real."

"Don't worry about that, Marlon. We will work with camera angles and all that shit. Our editing people will make it look authentic."

"But I'm wondering just how authentic we want it to be."

"You mean realistic?"

"Well, yeah. Realistic...authentic...whatever."

"What do you mean?"

"Well, the movie could make a big splash if the killing of Kurtz is brutally real."

"Hmm, I see your point, Marlon. If it's really fucken graphic, it might be all the buzz. It will be controversial. Well, the movie already is controversial, and it's not even done yet. But to have a graphic scene of Marlon Brando being killed...yeah, it could cause a lot of buzz and make the movie even more controversial than it even is. Is that what you're referring to, Marlon?"

"Yes. Yes, I am, Francis. I'm just thinking out loud, however. I'm simply throwing it out there."

"Okay, let's talk about it. What I think, Marlon, is that if it's too graphic it could overshadow the rest of the movie, the message we're trying to convey. It can't be too graphic, if you know what I mean, Marlon?"

"Yes, I absolutely know what you mean, and I agree with you. It needs to be subtle. I've been in too many movies where we tried to make a big splash or statement with some kind of controversial scene, and they always, and I mean *always*, overshadowed the movie, reducing its overall quality because everybody focused on that one thing, and nobody could see beyond it."

"Like your sex scene in *Last Tango*?"

"Uh, yes. That most regrettable moment!"

"I see your point. I don't want everybody talking only about the brutal, bloody death scene of Colonel Kurtz, and the fact that Marlon Brando is hacked to pieces and covered in blood, and how everybody who is squeamish shouldn't come see the movie, and all that bullshit. I do, however, think it should be somewhat bloody, and somewhat brutal, but yet subtle so it's not the main topic of conversation. Plus, I don't want this thing to get an X-rating."

"An X-rating might not be all that bad, Francis."

"Yeah, I've heard that whole theory about how it would be good publicity to have the film first get an X-rating, and then modify it so it gets an R-rating. It can actually be a bragging point, the fact that it originally received an X-rating. It helps create buzz and a sense of intrigue. But I'm a firm believer that contrived publicity can sometimes backfire. I just want to make the movie, submit it to the gatekeepers of what is good and decent, and let the chips fall where they may. If it's X-rated, then I change it. If it's R-rated, I don't change a thing. But to purposely conceive the movie to get an X-rating could be detrimental. In fact, it's possible that I would have to take out more stuff than I initially would have because the movie would then be on the radar screen of the censors. You see what I mean, Marlon? You see how it could backfire?"

Marlon nodded, although not completely convinced.

"Okay, so we will do the machete scene and then edit it accordingly. I do see your point, however, Marlon. And it's a fine-line we have to walk here, between too much and not enough. I understand that."

"You know what would really get everybody's attention, what would really shock people?"

"I'm afraid to ask."

"As you should be, Francis."

"Well, I am, but tell me anyway."

Marlon paused and seemed to hesitate.

"Tell me, Marlon."

"If I we're to die, for real. If Marlon Brando died during the filming of the death scene."

"Yes, that would be big news, Marlon. But if that happened I would be arrested for murder and probably be convicted on some kind of manslaughter charge. And you, of course, would be dead. But other than that, it's a really good idea."

Francis paused and looked at Marlon.

"Why would you even say that, Marlon?" asked the perplexed director.

"I don't know. Just throwing it out there."

"Just throwing it out there? That's not something you just throw out there, Marlon. The idea of one literally dying during the scene of a movie, on purpose, is not something a person just 'throws out there', Marlon."

There was a long pause as Francis starred hard at Marlon, waiting for a response, only to have Marlon look away.

"I think I know what you're getting at, though, Marlon. I think I do."

"Do you?" said Marlon with more than a hint of both doubt and sarcasm.

Francis studied Marlon's face before speaking.

"I'm not saying, Marlon, that I know what you're talking about because I've experienced the things you have. But rather, from knowing you and following your career all these years, I think I know, or at least have some sort of an idea, what it is you're feeling."

Francis paused to determine Marlon's reaction. Deadpan. This always infuriated Francis—the fact that whenever he tried to get a reaction out the man who is arguably the greatest actor of all time, all he usually gets is deadpan. Francis knew that Marlon purposely expressed nothing in these moments, determining that it was some kind of defense mechanism he would utilize in order to reduce his vulnerability in certain circumstances.

"Never mind, Marlon."

"Okay."

Marlon then walked away, seemingly upset. Francis shook his head in disbelief of his temperamental star and walked away too.

Marlon spent the next couple days immersed among the local Ifugao people, especially the children, brought on the set by Francis to play the role of Vietnam's montagnard tribesmen. They reminded Marlon a lot of the native Tahitians in that they seemed so happy and content, unlike many of the Westerners working on the movie set who were ingesting copious amounts of drugs and alcohol in an attempt to tolerate their lives.

Marlon liked the fact that the Ifugao knew very little about him and his past. They were not impressed with the fact that Marlon was a famous Hollywood actor. In fact, none had ever even seen a Hollywood movie. Their world was one in which Marlon always wished he could escape into, and leave everything behind.

This is what attracted Marlon to Tahiti and the Tahitians. He wanted to slip away into their world and culture, somehow cutting himself off from his past. That is not how things turned out, however. Marlon's life continued to be riddled with problems, both real and perceived.

In the Philippines, on the set of *Apocalypse Now*, and amongst the Ifugao children, Marlon started to feel refreshed, a younger version of himself. In fact, Marlon was envisioning himself as the twenty-something Marlon Brando, and did not look forward to his impending return to the fifty-something Marlon Brando who would soon be needed to perform his scenes, even to the point that Francis had a hard time tracking Marlon down.

"Marlon? Where is Marlon Brando?" asked Francis Coppola through a megaphone in the direction he assumed his star actor to be. "Calling Mr. Brando. Calling Marlon Brando. Your presence is requested! Oh, hey, I think I know the problem here," said Francis playfully. "Calling Colonel Kurtz. Calling Colonel Walter E. Kurtz to the movie-set."

CHAPTER 45

I walked around Artemis, eventually going down to the river to think, just like I used to do as a child. There, crouched down next to a small bay filled with standing water, my mind was actually given the time and space to drift back, first to my family, then to the days spent by the Willow River as a child. I wondered how it was possible that my childhood haunt could be a part of the same world as the place I was in now. When I came to Cambodia I wanted to make it just like my spot down by the river. But what I ended up doing instead was introducing the peoples of northeast Cambodia to Western man's long-burning hell fires, and now there was no way for me to put them out.

I was putting up a brave front as I walked through the underworld of death I helped create. I still managed to keep my fears and doubts at bay even as the horrific sights, sounds, and smells abounded everywhere. Maybe it was because I had been immersed in it for so long now, possibly to the point of becoming numb and oblivious. It would take something much more subtle, yet complex, that would force me to see the things I was trying so desperately not to.

Still crouched down next to the river, I looked into the stagnant water at my reflection. What I saw staring back hit me as if struck by a bullet in the head. My doubts and fears came rushing in unchallenged to sack my puffed up, prideful self. A certain childhood memory had come roaring back to me, one that I had not thought about in a while now. I could see on my face the same look of despair and even shame that my father wore all those years ago after giving his sermon down by the river upon returning home from World War II. It had always been a mystery to me as to the cause or reason for my father's sudden fit of torment and anguish, but now it seemed clear to me, as clear as my reflection in the water. That late summer's day some twenty-five years ago, I heard my father tell me that the truth, no matter how deep you bury it, will always sift its way to the surface. And now there it was, on top of the water, staring back at me.
    For the first time since coming to Southeast Asia, I broke down and wept. The world I thought I knew was collapsing. A squall of anger and resentment raged in my mind, while one of thunder, wind, and a light rain commenced around me.
    In anticipation of the impending storm the animals ravenously roamed and scavenged the jungle floor, making their presence known with loud screams and shrieks. The trees and other forms of foliage swayed and bent under the force of the building winds. Like me, the jungle was aching. It was out of sync with itself, and seemingly in great pain, twisting and churning as if trying to expulse something from its intestines.
    In my own personal Gethsemane, the jungle began to descend upon me like an angry mob.

"Crucify him, crucify him," screamed the many and varied parts of the jungle, unleashing its soldiers of torment and pain to seek me out. Every plant and animal pleaded for my death. The wind seconded this motion as did the thunder and lightning. But the jungle would not be tempted.

The jungle did not need to justify or rationalize the things that it did. It needed no adulation or acceptance, and felt no pain, remorse, or regret when finished. The jungle was a great and mighty soldier.

I could not bear to look again at my reflection in the water, nor turn around and see the stark faces and mutilated bodies behind me.

A gathering of nearby Gibbon monkeys screamed and squealed in a sound that resembled laughter, chuckling at their distant cousin who was so evolved and civilized that he could no longer stand to live in his primitive body of flesh and blood.

* * *

Above the din of the impending storm I could still hear the priest praying off in the distance, his words becoming louder and more desperate.

"Our Father who art in heaven, hallowed be Thy name. Thy kingdom come, Thy will be done, on earth as it is in heaven…"

"I then walked off, deciding I would rather try and have a conversation with my Maker in this moment rather than recite, over and over again, some hollow, old, dead prayer."

"O Lord is this Thy kingdom? Is this Thy will? Is this earth or heaven, or is it hell? O Lord this place is bright yet

shadowy, hot with flame yet clammy with death. Here I am akin to a god, yet lessened to that of crawling things. O children lost of Buddha, adopted sons of Lenin. In this wilderness of pain we seek each other's blood. Where is Lenin, for whom you fight? Even his stone effigy cannot be found here, unlike those of Buddha that stare at me from around every corner. But verily, Lenin has made inroads into this place. I can feel his atheist chill blowing in from the north. It smells of death. Or is that me I smell?"

"O Lord where art Thou? Maybe you cannot hear me above the din of wild beasts and screaming demons that surround me here. I know you have not been here in at least an age, if ever, for there is too much evil in this place to be a part of your kingdom. It is bloodthirsty and gluttonous, killing and devouring all who do not fall to their knees. O Creator God, is this that surrounds me your madness or mine? If yours, then where is your kind and gentle hand to wipe away the tears? If mine, then suck the breath back out of me and put me into the ground for the worms."

"O Lord, my insides have been eaten out, hatred and guilt serving as an incompatible mixture of bile that has consumed my guts and left my exterior a dried and weathered shell. I have henceforth crumbled and fallen into the same pit as my father and his father. Like chaff we are burning together in an unquenchable fire. Even Bachus will no longer answer me. I have become too sober and would gladly welcome him even if he is full of lies, for I am empty, hollow, void. Life is like death."

I waited patiently for a response, but could only hear the priest pitifully making the same requests as me. I then turned my attention to my own father. I so desperately wished he were here in this moment. He has much yet to explain to his son, and to answer for.

"Oh father, I fear I have swilled with Bachus and feasted with Satan—-things you have warned me from doing. But father, haven't you also sat at Satan's table and suckled from the sweet vines of Bachus? I could see it, father, I could see it on your face. Was your heart blackened and your soul eaten away too? Oh father, you were as hollow as I am now. Look where your deceit has led your son, father. For I am in the mouth of hell, waiting to be devoured and will spend the rest of my days, crawling on my belly with the snakes for all eternity, right beside you, father."

CHAPTER 46

Suddenly, methodically, Marlon Brando and Colonel Kurtz emerged from amongst the Ifugao men, women, and children. Marlon looked like a giant. He was very foreboding with his physical size, bald head, and black pajamas, which hid his girth quite convincingly. Marlon very much reflected the manner in which he and Francis wanted Colonel Kurtz to look, that is, a big, gung-ho military type, but someone who had transcended the standard American military historical world-view and perspective. Marlon's Colonel Kurtz was at the same time a Zen philosopher and an unrestrained madman. He was an alpha-male who dominated with his physical presence alone, and whose stare was a burning cauldron so hot that nobody could endure it for more than a few seconds. Marlon knew that he himself possessed these traits, and did so since he was a teenager, using them to both intimidate and seduce. Marlon was aware that he was not the most articulate man, but that he could hold people's attention because of his looks, swagger, and his powerful gaze. His words alone were not much of a force, but combined with his command of the room, steeliness of his stare, and unpredictable behavior, Marlon was someone whom people listened to intently, overestimating his intelligence and the profundity of his words because they were blinded by his celebrity, as well as intimidated by his frequent passionate diatribes on various issues. He was both embarrassed and haughty over the fact that he commanded so much attention and interest, sometimes out of love and desire, sometimes out of fear and loathing—the enigma that is Marlon Brando.

Marlon strutted over to his director very much like the god-king he was supposed to be portraying. His demeanor was almost that of someone taunting all that surrounded him—man as well as the natural world—to take him down, to usurp him, to knock him off his throne. Francis, grinning, shook Marlon's hand as he approached him.

"Are you ready, Marlon?"

Marlon gave Francis a look that indicated he considered the question to be trivial and not worthy of a response.

"Maybe I should instead ask if you're clear on what we're about to do here, Marlon?"

"We're about to kill Colonel Kurtz. Yes. I understand that."

Francis waited a few seconds before responding, hoping that Marlon would offer up more of an explanation or analysis.

"It's much bigger than that, of course, Marlon."

Francis again waited for a response. None came. Francis wondered if he would have to go over everything with Marlon yet again. He seemed oblivious. Francis just wanted to throw his hands up in the air and walk away, which he knew would be a major mistake because Marlon would take it very personally.

Marlon does not like to be periodically quizzed on whether or not he gets the gist of the movie, or the character he is playing. Marlon has always considered himself to be misunderstood and underestimated in regard to how he prepares for a role. Francis knows that Marlon likes to quietly, stealthily, get himself into character, yet he still had a lot of concerns. The reason why he and other directors have had this problem with Marlon is because he always comes off so aloof, even unaware as to what is going on. Historically, Marlon's track record in these instances is somewhat of a mixed bag. There have been times when he has magnificently risen to the occasion, and still other moments in which Marlon has failed miserably in regard to the challenges posed by his character. Most of his successes came earlier in his career, while many of his recent attempts have not been so memorable, minus his role as Don Corleone in *The Godfather*. And it is Francis' belief that it was his constant prodding of Marlon that got such a great performance out of him in that movie.

"I know what's at stake here," said Marlon in a manner that did not do much in the way of convincing Francis that his lead actor's state of mind was properly focused. "Do *you*, Francis?" asked

Marlon, coming across as an accusation more than it did a question, one intended to usurp his director's authority over him. Francis smiled because Marlon's confidence made him sure again that he had chosen the right man to play the role of Colonel Walter E. Kurtz.

"Marlon, there is something I want to discuss with you."

Marlon gave Francis a disinterested look.

"No, I think this is going to be something that interests you."

"I'm listening, Francis."

"I've been talking with some of the Ifugao leaders we have here on the set, and I, well, me and my wife came up with an idea for the final scene, the climax of this whole thing, if you will, Marlon."

"Go ahead," said Marlon after Francis hesitated, doing so for the sake of dramatic effect, and the fact he was afraid of how his star actor would react to what he was about to propose.

"Well, as I said, me and my wife have been talking with some of the Ifugao leaders here on the set."

"Right."

"Damn it, Marlon. I'm trying to figure out how to best explain this to you," said an excited Francis Coppola after Marlon folded his arms as a sign of his impatience.

"I'm listening, Francis."

"Okay. So, the Ifugao, Marlon, have a certain ritual or ceremony which they celebrate or perform when someone is sick, but not necessarily sick in the sense that they have a physical ailment, but rather more in the spiritual sense, for lack of a better term."

Francis stopped to gauge Marlon's reaction thus far. Deadpan.

"The Ifugao leader said the ceremony, which includes the sacrifice of a water buffalo, is performed to appease, or invoke, the gods in order to help the individual get through whatever it is that they're suffering from. And I don't know what it is exactly that you're suffering from, Marlon, but the Ifugao would probably say you have incurred the wrath of one of the gods, or maybe you've had some kind of demon or evil spirit take over your body or spirit. Something like that."

Marlon looked at Francis, seemingly amused.

"People have been telling me for years that I'm demon-possessed," said Marlon with a big grin on his face.

"Do you believe that?"

"No. I've never believed in any of that super-natural bullshit, Christian or otherwise. And I think this is one of the reasons I've never been able to completely identify with these indigenous cultures, whether it be here, in Tahiti, or the Indians in the United States. They all see things in such a spiritualized sort of way. There's always some spiritual or supernatural explanation for everything. That's just not how I perceive things. I've tried to be spiritual, but I can't do it."

"Me neither, Marlon."

"And perhaps Christianity is to blame, I don't know, or the fact that Christianity is as responsible for the destruction of peoples and cultures as is any kind of political ideology, government or empire."

"I'm with you on all this, Marlon. I mean...we don't have to believe it. I just think it's an interesting way to end the movie."

"What is?"

"Well, I guess I haven't really told you that part yet. So, the Ifugao said that they would be willing to perform one of their healing or cleansing ceremonies, and we would be able to film it, and, we could use it in the movie."

"I thought the movie was going to end with Willard killing Kurtz with a machete?"

"It is, Marlon. Don't worry about that. But I want to add another layer to the ending, something primal, as you have been saying all along."

"Okay, Francis," said Marlon with his eyes closed in an attempt to picture what his director was talking about. "Please tell me what you have in mind."

"Well, I'm not sure exactly, Marlon. A lot is going to depend on the Ifugao. They were explaining to me what they would do, but there is a bit of a language and cultural barrier. I really don't think we fully understood one another."

"My advice to you, Francis, is to make sure you understand exactly what it is the Ifugao are going to do, because once they begin, there will be no stopping or retakes. You can't yell *cut*."

"Were there issues like this on the set of *Mutiny on the Bounty* with the local Tahitians?"

"Oh yes, Francis, of course. There were cultural issues on that set, and on *Burn* for that matter. And I can tell you that the Ifugao are far more *out there,* if you know what I mean, Francis, than were the Tahitians. The Ifugao are not going to tailor their ceremony to fit our needs, so I think we're going to have to arrange our scene to fit their ceremony."

"Okay, fair enough. We'll work all that out with them later. Here's what I want to do. This is how I see this last scene." Francis cleared his throat for dramatic effect. He was nervous to tell Marlon what he was planning to do. "So, the Ifugao will be conducting one of these ceremonies or rituals. They will be banging on their drums and gongs, and all that. They will be drinking that rice wine they drink and smoking whatever it is they smoke. There will be dancing and stuff. My wife actually witnessed one of these ceremonies."

"I've seen some smaller scale stuff here, but not a full-blown ceremony."

"Well, the one my wife witnessed and described to me sounded pretty crazy. She said it was very primal, very tense. It wasn't all that celebratory, but rather kind of moody and dark, she said."

Marlon thought for a moment while Francis allowed him the time to do so before continuing.

"So, in the movie, the reason why the Ifugao, or montagnards, are performing this ceremony is to appease the gods and to exercise Colonel Kurtz's demons, their fearless leader, because in the movie the montagnards love and even kind of worship Kurtz. They are, unwittingly of course, drawing on Frazer's 'dying and rising god' theme consistent in most indigenous cultures. They're not going to literally kill Kurtz, but rather kill a water buffalo in his stead. The effect is supposed to be the same, though. Kurtz, through a symbolic death of the water buffalo, will symbolically be reborn, refreshed and potent again."

"Will there be a special meaning in regard to Marlon Brando?"

"Thank you for asking, Marlon, because, yes, there will be a parallel meaning here. The Ifugao will in reality be performing the ceremony to exercise your demons, Marlon, to release you of whatever is ailing you or burdening you. Again, like Kurtz, the death of the water buffalo will symbolize the death of Marlon Brando. As a result of your symbolic sacrificial death, Marlon

Brando will be reborn, refreshed, reinvigorated, renewed, and more potent. Washed away will be the old Marlon Brando, all those old, stale roles, all those bad and broken relationships, all those old fears and doubts. What do you think?"

Deadpan.

CHAPTER 47

Having been made aware that the murderous devils and demons were once again in the Forbidden City by the irregular flight pattern of the crows, three Vietcong were already a half-hour into their journey to exact revenge on those responsible for destroying their villages and killing their women and children. They ran barefoot through the jungle, wearing only black silk pants and carrying Russian rifles. En route the Vietcong made their way through swamps, sharp tigergrass, and many other perils strewn about jungle. They sweated and breathed heavy in an effort to get there quickly, their brown skin clinging tightly to their bone and muscle as a lifetime of warfare has molded them into sleek hunters of men.

* * *

"I think it's gonna rain, Francis," said Dennis Hopper, and then took a long drag off his cigarette in anticipation of the director's response.

"It always looks and feels like it's going to rain here, Dennis. This place is a perpetual tropical storm."

"A 'perpetual tropical storm'. I like it, Francis. I like it," replied Dennis and then walked off giggling, puffs of smoke coming out of his mouth and nose.

The Ifugao were readying themselves for the sacrificial ceremony they negotiated with Francis. They had been waiting for the right moment, and apparently this was it. It was cloudy, very hot and humid. Dusk was approaching. It felt as if a major rain and thunder storm were about to break out. There was a lot of electricity in the air, both real and perceived. Francis and his crew were scurrying about, trying to ready themselves and the set.

"These Ifugao, Marty, I'll tell you!" said Francis to Martin Sheen. "They wait and wait and wait, and then all of a sudden they spring into action with this ceremony thing, and they think I can just get everything together for a shoot in a matter of minutes. I mean...what the fuck!"

Martin Sheen gave Francis a meager smile. He was trying to get himself into character. The filming of this movie has been the most difficult and enlightening thing he has ever done. Like Marlon, he too was using it as a means of shedding his old skin, of casting off his personal demons.

"Where's Marlon, for Christ sake?" yelled Francis to nobody in particular, yet to anyone who could offer him insight as to where his star actor might be found. "Does anybody know if Marlon has made his way to the set?" Nobody answered him. Everyone who was within ear shot was too busy running back and forth, doing what they had been hired to do in order to get the set ready.

"Marlon Brando is en route, Francis," said one of Francis Coppola's assistants in passing as she ran by.

"Who told you that?" screamed Francis in her direction as she continued on.

"What?"

"Where did you hear that?"

"Robert told me."

"Robert?"

"Yes."

"Robert who?"

"I don't know his last name."

Francis waved his hand at her in disgust.

"Robert! Where's Robert?" yelled Francis at his crew who were all moving in different directions amidst the din of a building Ifugao ceremony. The drums and tin gongs were increasing in both breadth and volume. Francis felt like he was being swallowed up as if the ceremony was taking on a life of its own. "Does anybody know where Marlon Brando is?" Francis received no response. He then threw his hands up in the air and walked off.

In the meantime, the intensity of the Ifugao celebration continued to slowly ramp up. They were all wearing the traditional Ifugao garb, which brought concern on the part of some of Francis' on-set advisors who were afraid this would compromise the authenticity of the scene.

"They are supposed to be montagnard tribesmen from Vietnam and Cambodia, not Ifugao from the Philippines, Francis," said one advisor to the movie director during a spontaneous meeting regarding the impending scene.

"How different can it be—their clothes and stuff?" asked Francis, realizing that he now needed to yell above the sound of drumming and chanting in order for people to hear him.

"Well, Francis, the differences are subtle. Only an expert in the field of indigenous garb and customs would be able to tell you that these are Ifugao and not Jarai or Stieng."

"That's not that big of a deal, then. I mean...what can we do? We can't have Jarai and Stieng garb flown in now, nor can we make them perform a Jarai or Stieng ceremony. I think we're fortunate to have what we have here. We just need to go with it."

"Okay, Mr. Coppola. I just thought I should let you know."

"Thank you for doing so. Hey, have you seen Marlon?"

* * *

Francis moved closer to the celebration. He found the rhythmic sounds of the drums and gongs to be intoxicating, as were the smells emanating from the many and varied bamboo pipes that the Ifugao were smoking. Some of the other actors were drawn to these things as well. Dennis was there, as were Sam Bottoms and Frederic Forrest, or 'Lance' and 'Chef' as they would be known in the movie.

"Have any of you guys seen Marlon?"

"Yeah."

"You have, Dennis? Where?"

"Right there, Francis," said Dennis, pointing in the direction of a very large water buffalo, which was being washed off and fed in anticipation of its ritual slaughter a littler later in the evening. All three actors burst out in laughter. Francis, however, did not find it humorous.

"Well, Kurtz is going to be killed, isn't he, Francis?" joked Dennis while still laughing.

"It's going to be a long night of shooting. You guys keep your heads clear, alright?"

Both Sam and Frederic responded in a very conciliatory way indicating that they would, while Dennis laughed as he lit a cigarette.

"I'll keep my head clear, that's for sure," he said with a cynical tone once his director was out of ear shot, bringing about renewed laughter from the other two cast members.

"Pace yourself, Dennis," yelled Francis who suddenly turned back around.

"Holy shit, man. He's got ears in the back of his head," said Dennis under his breath while giving Francis a thumbs-up.

* * *

"Thank God!" said Francis upon finally seeing Marlon, who was engaged in conversation with Martin Sheen. "I've been looking for you, Marlon. Where the hell have you been?"

"I've been looking for you, Francis. Where the hell have *you* been?"

Marlon's apparent attempt at asserting his authority over the director made Martin Sheen nervous, but did not affect Francis. He was used to this kind of thing from Marlon, and so it did not concern him. His only reservation was that Marlon did it in front of Martin Sheen.

"Can you excuse us for a minute, Marlon? I need to talk to Marty alone for a second."

Without saying anything, Marlon turned and walked off. He understood the snub to be his director's way of reprimanding him in front of another actor, and allowed him this moment, but then executed his own passive-aggressive response by again vanishing, this time into the Ifugao celebration.

Francis' first inclination was to complain to Martin Sheen about Marlon, but then refrained, realizing it would be unprofessional of him to do so.

"Have we decided on the face paint, Marty?"

"The camo?"

"Yes, the camo."

"I'm going to wear it, on my face, as well as my upper body."

"So, you'll be shirtless?"

"Uh, yeah," said Martin Sheen in a kind of matter-of-fact sort of way, but with a sense of withdrawn nervousness.

"Why no shirt, Marty?"

"Ah, well, it's kind of a statement being made on the part of Willard."

"A statement, Marty?"

Martin Sheen had a lot of nervous energy. He just wanted to shoot the final scene and get it over with. He did not want to give a lengthy explanation to his director at this juncture.

"Yeah, Francis. Uh, Willard, uh, doesn't really consider himself part of the army anymore. So, in his mind, if he's not wearing the uniform, at least the shirt, he's not in the army. He's no longer under the army's command."

"So, why is he still going to kill Kurtz?"

Marty smiled, but offered up no explanation.

"I mean...if Willard is no longer in the army...no longer under the command of those who sent him, then why is he still carrying out their orders to kill Kurtz?"

"I don't know, Francis, because that's how you want the movie to end. I don't know."

Francis could tell there was more to Marty's reasoning than that. He knew he should just let it go and not try and pursue the details from his co-star as to why Willard would still follow through and kill Kurtz, but his inquisitive mind and directorial sensibilities would not allow for it.

"Marty, that's not good enough. You know I've got to be made aware of every god-damn aspect and detail of this movie, right? I give you guys a lot of leeway. The only thing I really ask for in return is that you clarify to me why you're doing what you're doing, whatever the hell it is. You see what I'm saying, Marty?"

"Yeah, yeah, I get it, Francis," said Martin Sheen while reaching for a cigarette in his shirt pocket. "Willard is going to kill Kurtz because...oh, hell, I'd love to be able to tell you, Francis, but I just don't think I'd be able to explain it very well."

"Just give me the gist of it, Marty. I understand that we are all under a lot of duress. It's fucking loud out here, it's hot, we're all tired and just want to go home. Just give me a summary, an overview of Willard's motivation here."

"Okay. Well, I think that Willard is actually affected by Kurtz and the things he tells him. I think that Willard, well, he doesn't go over to Kurtz' side, necessarily, but Kurtz has pulled him *away* from the United States Army. He doesn't identify with Kurtz, but he no longer identifies with the United States Army, either. Does that make any sense, Francis?"

Francis thought for a moment before answering.

"Yes, it does make sense." He thought some more while Martin took a couple deep drags off his cigarette. "So why does he kill him?"

Martin chuckled. He was hoping his director's inquiry was over.

"Willard kills Kurtz because Kurtz wants him to. Willard has developed a certain amount of respect for Colonel Kurtz. He likes the fact he jumped ship, so to speak, that he decided he was no longer going to play all the games expected of him by the army. Kurtz is trying to win the war, whereas he believes the army brass, and the government for the matter, aren't. And Willard respects this. He doesn't necessarily agree with Kurtz' methods, but he respects that Kurtz is honest and truthful, a straight shooter."

"Honest and truthful about what, Marty?"

"That to win this war, any war, you have to do terrible, horrific things, and not try to gloss it over. Kurtz thinks there's too much hypocrisy in the American war effort. The soldiers were supposed to kill, but yet they had to restrain themselves. You know what I'm saying, Francis?"

"Yes, I do, Marty. Say more."

"Well, Francis, they were supposed to be violent and ruthless enough to win, but at the same time, not to tarnish America's reputation. Kurtz doesn't believe that the North Vietnamese were restricted by these kinds of limitations, and that's why they were winning the war."

"I like that, Marty. Can I add something here?"

"Sure," said Martin, feigning interest.

"Kurtz's issue, at least in part, is that on the one hand America was still trying to maintain this kind of World War II image in which American GIs were these young, wholesome 'freckle-face' boys, fighting evil. While on the other hand, they were expected to carry out such hideous and evil tactics as the bodycount, something one might associate with the Nazis, right?"

"Uh, well, yes," answered Martin Sheen, who was not prepared to engage his director at this level.

"And, so Kurtz has enlightened Willard of all this, and he has gotten him to think differently than he did before."

"Yes…right."

"Okay, good, Marty. So, in your narrative, we'll need to make some kind of reference about how Willard has been lost to the American war machine, and then possibly allude to why Willard is going to kill Kurtz anyway."

"Okay. Sounds good, Francis," said Martin who was anxious to get ready for the impending shoot.

"Now, I just need to find Marlon again."

CHAPTER 48

"I've seen horrors...horrors that you've seen. But you have no right to call me a murderer. You have a right to kill me. You have a right to do that...but you have no right to judge me. It's impossible for words to describe what is necessary to those who do not know what horror means."

"Marlon, that was fantastic!" announced Francis as he suddenly walked into Kurtz' cave-like dwelling where he found his star actor sitting there, reciting some prospective lines for the movie's final scene. Marlon had a look of both surprise and embarrassment.

"I'd like you to repeat that when we start shooting. Will you be able to remember that?"

"I wasn't finished yet, Francis. Wouldn't you like to know where I'm going with this before you waste precious time filming it?"

"Yes, I would, Marlon. But I liked what I heard so far. I didn't say I was going to put it in my movie. I simply asked if you could repeat what you just said when we do the shoot."

There was a significant amount of tension between the director and his star actor. Both men could feel it. Francis stared hard at Marlon, who looked away, but with only the slightest indication that he was annoyed. Francis knew better. He waited a moment before speaking again. Francis was not sure if Marlon really wanted him to inquire as to where he was going with the monologue he had just overheard, or not.

"Marlon, I trust your instincts. What I'd like to do is just film you dialoging for a while before Willard comes up and kills Kurtz. There's no script, Marlon. I got people filming the ceremony, and

I'll have people up here filming your dialogue, and then the Kurtz death scene. Wherever this thing goes, it goes."

"Where is Kurtz going to be killed?"

"I'm thinking right here, Marlon. Right here in Kurtz's cave or temple headquarters."

"Okay."

Marlon's response left Francis unsure as to whether or not he agreed.

"I can't see it happening outside, not with the montagnard ceremony going on. I want the sacrifice of Kurtz to be in close proximity to, but separate from, the montagnard ceremony. I don't want to mix the two together."

"No. I don't either. Here is fine. Do the montagnards know that Kurtz is being killed?"

"Yeah, that's a good question, Marlon."

"The reason why I'm asking, Francis, is because if they do know Kurtz is being killed, wouldn't they try to do something to stop it? Or, perhaps once they find out that Kurtz has been killed, wouldn't they try to avenge what Willard did? Wouldn't they ascend upon Willard and kill him?"

"Maybe," said Francis reluctantly. "That's a whole issue in and of itself. What my people—my so-called advisors—have told me is that this dead and rising god thing is something very commonplace among the montagnard tribes of Southeast Asia, so they would perhaps welcome, or at least accept, what is happening to Colonel Kurtz. They might even think that it's a direct result of their sacrificial ceremony."

"Even though he's kind of like their god?"

"Well, Marlon, they accept what's going on precisely *because* Kurtz is kind of like their god. You see what I'm saying? The ceremony is to heal the god. And most of the indigenous peoples who practice this kind of sacrificing of the god thing do so with the understanding that the divine power of the god is not the flesh and blood of the god, but rather it is something ethereal that both enters and eventually leaves the body of each succeeding king."

"Okay. I get it."

"And so, if that's true, the montagnards will simply be accepting of the time and manner in which the current god-king is lost of this divine power, only to have it supplanted into the next god-king. You see, Marlon?"

"And the next god-king, as far as they understand, will be whom?"

"Well, Marlon, this is another good issue you've raised, one that probably has not been properly addressed, simply because we haven't had time. But I suppose they would look at Captain Willard in this regard. I mean...they know he came to kill Kurtz, and they will more than likely understand that Willard is the person who has killed him."

"And Willard will then in effect have taken the place of Kurtz, because Willard is now the one possessing the power, and subsequently the one who will carry the weight and responsibility of being the god-king."

"Yes, I guess you could say that, Marlon. But we're not going to get into all that, because I envision the movie ending very soon after the death of Kurtz. The death of Kurtz will be the film's climactic moment. Well, maybe. I've got another idea up my sleeve. But either way, the movie will end soon thereafter. These other questions that you have posed, Marlon, the film will not answer. We've got too many things we need to address the way it is."

"You might want to consider offering up something, even if it's subtle, in regard to that issue, though, Francis."

"Yeah, we'll think of something. But, you're right, Marlon. We need something to indicate that the montagnards have perhaps understood the death of Kurtz to be this kind of cyclical, natural progression of things, in which divine power has passed from one person to another."

"Yes, and the burdens that go along with it."

"Right, Marlon, and the burdens that go along with being a god-king. Wait a minute, are we talking about Colonel Kurtz or Marlon Brando?" asked Francis with a big grin on his face. The two men immediately shared a laugh. "I told you this whole *Golden Bough* thing had a place in this movie, Marlon."

"We'll see."

Off in the near distance, the sound of the Ifugao celebration was becoming more and more audible.

"The natives are getting restless, Marlon. We better get on with this thing."

"Francis, follow me over here for a second, please."

Marlon walked his director over to a little corridor, which led to what was supposed to be a kind of river-view lookout for Colonel Kurtz, where he could survey his compound. The men walked through the corridor and stepped outside. From there they were elevated a considerable height above the Kurtz compound, the river, and the now in-progress Ifugao celebration. There the two Hollywood giants stood, soaking in their surroundings. The sky had now darkened. The air was thick with humidity and smoke from the Ifugao fires. Various smells filled the air. Some sweet. Some pungent. The sounds of beating drums and clanking gongs were loud and ominous. There was a certain edge or tension in the air. The energy level was high. Both Francis and Marlon were nervous. A lot was riding on this final scene for both of them. For Francis, it would define his movie. He had literally mortgaged his entire fortune, including his house, on the making of *Apocalypse Now*, and would be financially and professionally ruined if the movie did not do well. For Marlon, if the movie was a bust he would take much of the blame, mainly because of his high salary, his big name, on-going rumors that he was difficult on the set, and his many recent box-office disappointments. If he were not damaged goods already, he certainly would be if *Apocalypse Now* failed.

Francis and Marlon said nothing to one another for a couple minutes as they drank in all that surrounded them. Both were seemingly mesmerized by the surreal scene they had helped create out in the Philippine jungle. It was almost as if neither one of them wanted this moment to end, mainly because they both dreaded all that was to come—the complications of filming the final scene, the editing of the film, the publicity circuit, the response of the critics and movie-going public. Eventually, Francis put his hand on Marlon's shoulder, patting it.

"Let's go, Marlon."

Marlon Brando took a deep breath and then exhaled loudly. His death and rebirth awaited him.

* * *

"What's the time-frame, here, Francis?" asked Martin Sheen. "I don't want to put the camo on too early, otherwise it will smudge in all this humidity."

"Well, let me see," responded Francis while glancing at his watch. "The problem is, Marty, I have no idea how long this celebration is going to last. What I would really like to know is how long before the water buffalo is going to be sacrificed. I mean...is it going to be in an hour...two hours...three hours? I don't know."

"Isn't there somebody you could ask?"

"What? Ask one of these Ifugao dudes? That window has closed. They are all so spaced-out right now I don't think they know what day it is. Neither do I, for that matter. Anyway, Marty, I think we can start shooting. It really doesn't matter, to be honest with you. We don't really need the death of the water buffalo and Kurtz's death to happen simultaneously. We'll make it happen that way through the magic of editing. It would just be cool if they did coincide. Go ahead and put the paint on, Marty. I've got to go tell Marlon that the time has come for him to die."

CHAPTER 49

With the increasing intensity of the Ifugao celebration, Francis began to fear he was running out of time to get the final scenes shot, and quickly made his way back to the Kurtz cave. There he found Marlon pacing back and forth as if the Kurtz cave was in effect his prison cell, and he a death row prisoner awaiting his execution.

"The celebration is really picking up steam, Marlon."

"I know. I can hear it. It's beginning to unnerve me. I keep waiting for Marty to burst in here and hack me to death."

Francis laughed.

"How perfect, Marlon! How profound is it going to be that Colonel Kurtz, played by the great Marlon Brando, is going to be sacrificed during a montagnard or Ifugao sacrificial celebration! I love this ending, Marlon. I love it!"

After a long pause, Marlon answered his director.

"I like it too, Francis. I don't know if I love it, like you do. But I like it. I just hope the critics and the movie-going public like it."

"I don't even want to think about that right now, Marlon."

Just as Francis said this the flames from the Ifugao fires began shooting high up in the sky, casting a bright reddish-orange hue over the entire Kurtz compound.

"Whoa! Stand there, Marlon," ordered Francis, who then backed up to see Marlon's silhouette against the reddish-orange backdrop. "I like that," said the director who was having a sudden moment of inspiration. "I need to get the camera crew up here. I want this shot before the fires go out."

* * *

   The wind stopped as did the thunder and lightning, replaced by a steady downpour of rain. Even the animals fell silent. Out of the jungle and into the Forbidden City came the three onrushing Vietcong. There they found only the priest, as me and the Stieng had already abandoned him.
   With their anger and rage something more than the Russian rifles could appease, the Vietcong dropped them in favor of the machetes left behind by some of the Stieng whose arms were full of other provisions taken from what was once Artemis. With the machetes in hand, the Vietcong rushed the priest who was on his knees, praying with his eyes shut tight, and proceeded to hack him to death. With much rage and fervor, the Vietcong chopped and gashed the Catholic priest into the muddy ground, the sounds of clanking machetes filling the air until their butchery was complete. As quickly as they appeared, the Vietnamese soldiers were gone, disappearing back into the jungle to continue fighting their endless war.

CHAPTER 50

"Okay, Marlon. Kurtz is restless. Get up and walk to the overlook," said Francis with a low voice, again prompting his star actor on what to do and say while the cameras were rolling. "Maybe lean up against the wall. You're the king. You're a god. These are your people. You know things they could never fathom. And they know things that the people back in the United States could never fathom. You are wise. You are a philosopher-king. This is your kingdom. You could bring peace to the world. You could make it a paradise. But the world is not ready for someone like you. The world would rather believe all the lies."

Francis said these things, knowing full-well that Marlon believed these words and statements pertained to both him and Colonel Kurtz, and that his director could have been talking to either one of them.

"Okay, come back and sit down. You have a feeling, a sense that you are going to die very soon, probably tonight. There's more you want to say to the world. Go over to your tape recorder, turn it on and pick up the microphone."

Marlon did so, slowly, ploddingly.

"Okay, stop the cameras for a second. Marlon, I want to read to you part of what Marty is going to say—part of his narrative that will be dubbed in—just before he comes up here to kill Kurtz."

Marlon seemed annoyed at the stoppage. He was poised to begin speaking.

"I just want to set the mood a little more for you. Okay, so Willard…and remember this is from the narrative that will be overdubbed later, and not Willard's actual dialogue." Francis took out a crumbled and humidity-laden piece of paper, and put on his glasses before attempting to read from it. "Okay, so Willard says something to the effect of, 'they were going to make me a major for this and I wasn't even in their fucking army anymore'. Willard then says, and again, this is a narration that will be over-dubbed. This is not dialogue. He says, in regard to Kurtz, 'I feel as if he's up there, waiting for me to take his pain away. He just wants to go out like a soldier, standing up. Not like some wasted, ragged-ass renegade. Even the jungle wants him dead. And that's who he takes his orders from, anyway'. I love that last part, about Kurtz taking his orders from the jungle. I think it really encapsulates so much about what we're trying to say, about Colonel Kurtz and about Western civilization..."

Marlon abruptly cleared his throat, prompting Francis to realize that the camera, light and sound people, as well as his star actor were all standing there, some in awkward positions, poised to get on with the scene.

"Okay, Marlon. So that's what's going to be dubbed in as Willard approaches Kurtz's cave, with the intention of killing him. The shot will then switch to inside Kurtz's cave. Kurtz will be sitting, talking into his tape recorder. He's carrying on with his business. Kurtz thinks or suspects that Willard is going to kill him, but he doesn't know exactly when. So, Kurtz is talking, and then he sees Willard. But he's not surprised. He's been expecting this. By the way, is Marty here?" asked Francis in the direction of about four of his stage hands.

"Yes, Francis, Martin Sheen is standing by," answered one of them.

"Okay, Marlon, are you ready with your dialogue?"

"Yes, I'm ready."

"Is it the stuff we talked about earlier?"

"Yes."

"Okay, good. That was good stuff. Okay, everybody ready! In three...two...one...action!"

"They train young men to drop fire on people, but their commanders won't allow them write *fuck* on their airplanes, because it's obscene..."

At this point, Francis cued Martin Sheen into the scene.

"Give Kurtz a second to notice you, Marty," said Francis softly.

"Okay, Marlon, give Willard a non-descript look and then get to your feet. Willard is going to allow you to stand up. Marty, raise the machete, and begin hacking at Kurtz, using long, dramatic swaths."

The actors were directed to carry out the death scene slowly in order to receive intermittent direction, as well as stopping periodically for one of the make-up artists to apply more blood on Marlon. For everyone involved, it seemed at times comical, even silly, but none of that concerned them. They all knew that through editing and added layers of sound, the final product would be realistic, and very dramatic.

Colonel Kurtz offered very little in the way of resistance, and soon Willard's machete found its mark several times, quickly bloodying Kurtz, who eventually came crashing to the ground. Willard hacked a few more times before stopping, seemingly satisfied he had killed the colonel.

"Stand over him, Marty. Stare at him. Breath heavy. You've exerted yourself." Francis paused while Martin Sheen carried out his instructions. "Okay, now start making your way over to Kurtz's desk."

Marlon chose to remain lying on the floor, still playing the role of Colonel Kurtz, while Captain Willard thumbed through some of the books and writings on Kurtz's make-shift desk.

"Okay, now grab the colonel's notebooks and tape recorder. Willard is going to bring them with him."

Martin Sheen did as he was directed.

Outside, the Ifugao celebration had come to a halt, culminating with the sacrifice and quartering of the water buffalo. The drumming, the clanking, the chanting—everything stopped. The sudden silence was both deafening and dramatic. The attention of all the Ifugao extras, their bodies still bathed in firelight, was directed up at Kurtz's quarters.

"Marty, make your way to the opening. Stand there in the entrance and look out at all of Kurtz's followers. Give them a tired, weary, yet unconcerned look, then toss the machete off to the side."

Martin threw the machete onto the stone structure, making a loud sound that reverberated off the many pillars and effigies, further accentuating how quiet it had become. When it stopped, the approximately one-thousand Ifugao extras bent their knees and bowed their head to the new god-king.

Francis then turned his attention back to Marlon.

"Okay, Marlon. This is it—your last will and testament."

The camera moved in close on Marlon's bloody head, getting a side profile shot.

"Anytime you're ready, Marlon," said Francis.

There was a pause of about a minute. In that brief moment, Marlon thought about certain things—personal, professional, social—that have pained him over the years. Then suddenly, both Colonel Kurtz and Marlon Brando gave their last gasp.

"The horror!" they whispered in unison. "The horror!"

Epilogue

Morning was approaching, but the dark of night still pervaded the Kurtz compound, nestled deep in the Philippine jungle. The final scenes of *Apocalypse Now* had been shot. The cast and crew, the extras, and the Ifugao, spent the nighttime hours packing up equipment and slowly exiting the movie set, most of whom would reconvene at various later dates and locations in order to say their goodbyes, as well as tend to various post-production tasks and duties. Everybody was gone except for Francis and his pyrotechnics team, and a few camera people. There was still one more scene left to be shot. This was going to be Francis' moment, his own personal grand finale. He still was not sure if the scene would make it into the movie or not. The premise for what he and what remained of his crew were about to do was inspired by Marlon during the week the two men went out into the jungle to work out an ending, as well as deal with certain personal issues both men were having. Marlon talked about how the Western world has historically relied heavily on the cleansing effects of the flame to wash away all the things it hated and abhorred, how it was a great purifier of all things contradictory to the ideals of God, godliness, and the ascension of white Western Europeans and European culture.

Francis wanted to burn down the Kurtz compound, to destroy it and symbolically destroy all the personal pain, suffering and torment the making of *Apocalypse Now* has caused him. He did not like who and what he became during the process of making the film, and would use this occasion to destroy, wipe away, and to cleanse himself of all his sins and indiscretions. Initially, Francis had no doubt that this was going to be how he ended his epic movie, but the powerful performance of Marlon Brando and the appropriately fitting death scene of Colonel Kurtz made him think he should just stop there. Nonetheless, this is something that Francis wanted to do, and perhaps even believed he needed to do in order to appease or subdue his own personal demons. His star actor, Marlon Brando, had his opportunity. Now it was Francis' turn.

Francis was given the honor of flipping the switch that began a series of explosions which would thoroughly and completely explode and burn the Kurtz compound to the ground. Suddenly, abruptly, the quiet din and pitch-black of early morning were dramatically interrupted with an assault of deafeningly loud explosions and red and orange bursts of flames that devoured everything in its surging, rolling path. It was not long before the various stone statues of the Buddha came crumbling to the ground, as did the massively tall palm trees. Francis and the rest of the crew watched in awe and even a bit of trepidation as the ensuing inferno seemed to take on a life of its own, and for a moment they were even a little unsure if its momentum would ever yield.

"It's brilliant! Just amazing!" said Francis, although still fearful of its potential power. His mind was envisioning an ominous sounding soundtrack to what he was witnessing, something that would capture all the elements surging forth, as well as fueling the albatross before him that was still at the height of its powers. He was thinking something edgy and moody, overlaid with a blend of montagnard drumming and chanting, as well as some Jimi Hendrix style acid rock guitar soloing in order to invoke and summon the mood and feel of the American anti-war psychedelic revolution of the late 1960s.

Eventually, ever-so-slowly, the flaming monstrosity began to retreat, allowing the man responsible for breathing life into it, to start catching his own breath. And even though Francis Coppola understood that many battles lie ahead in regard to the film he created, now that the flames were subsiding, both real and metaphorical, he was finally afforded the time and space to relax, to ponder and think about what he accomplished, if anything, outin the Philippine jungle for the past several months. So many things were rushing through his mind, but one thought seemed to supersede them all in this moment.

"The horror, indeed, Mr. Conrad. The horror, indeed."

* * *

Captain Willard heard the distant sound of F-4 Phantom jets, but he did not pay them any mind. Even the ensuing explosions were not as loud as they were fantastically bright, causing him to spring up from the floor of the PBR to get a closer look, even though he had to partially look away as if trying to stare at the sun.

"What's that?" yelled Lance over the din of the distant, yet still loud sound of explosions.

"Kurtz's camp."

"What?"

"Kurtz's camp!" screamed Willard a little louder than the first time, noticeably irritated with the fact he had to repeat himself.

"They're blowing it up."

"Why?" asked Lance, moving closer to Willard, the two of them now standing side-by-side while watching the flames ascend into the night sky. "Why are they doing that?" he asked again after getting no response.

"Doing what?"

"Blowing up Kurtz's camp…why?"

"There was no camp, Lance," responded Willard about thirty seconds after Lance's inquiry.

"Well, at least we can go back to civilization now," said Lance, confused by Willard's assessment.

Captain Willard took a deep breath.

"That was civilization, Lance," said Willard with the red and orange flames still reflecting off his eyes.

"What about Kurtz?"

"What about him?"

"If that was civilization, then who was Colonel Kurtz?"

"Kurtz is dead."

Printed in Great
Britain
by Amazon